THE HONEYED TONGUE DECEIVES

MAEGWEN SALLEY-MASSIE

To those in need of an escape.

An imprint of Green Ferns Publishing House

Library of Congress Cataloging-in-Publication Data
Salley-Massie, Maegwen
The Honeyed Tongue Deceives/ Maegwen Salley-Massie
638 pages.

Summary: "After another curse being broken, Elysium sets sail for Glatania, but they face storms like never before, while the Luxen School of Magic trains students in the art of magic. Who will survive the quest and which students will uncover a lost secret?" -provided by publisher

ISBN 979-8-9870525-9-4 (paperback), ISBN 979-8-9996047-0-5 (hardback),
Subjects: High Fantasy—Fiction. Love—Fiction. Adventure—Fiction.

Printed in the United States of America

The Gelida Seas
Glatania
Golden Is...
Sacharo Lagoon
Vichinos Channel
Shu...
Havas
Pax Island
Dragon Cove
Stoltland
Ira Channel
Water Seas
The S...

The Snaer Seas
Ten Nove
Elysium
Golden Lake
Hostile Channel
Emerald Lagoon
Korpam
Southlantian Seas
The Margyger Seas

Table of Contents

Pronunciation page

Adalina (ad-ah-Leen-ah) Roedellen

Adma (Ad-ma)

Adomin (a-Doe-Min)

Aellizzabelle (Ale-Lizz-a-Bell) aka Lizz

AeLeer (Ay-Leer)

Ajorn (Ae-Jorn)

Anadelvia (an-ah-del-vee-ah)

Ashur (A-sh-ur)

Atticos (a-t-e-coe-ss)

Audayia (Aw-Day-ee-ah)

Barm (B-arm)

Bip (b-ip)

Brandle (Bran-Dill)

Brehan (Bree-Hon)

Brenna (Bren-nah)

Caelimont (Cae-li-mon-t)

Char (Ch-Ar)

Corentine (Coer-en-teen)

Corvus (Core-Vus)

Cruz (Cr-ooz)

Dag (Da-g)

Dinyelle(Din-Yell)

Doebromir (Doe-broe-meer)

Drystan (Drih-stan)

Ebbalee (Eb-bah-Lee)

Edvard (Ed-var-d)

Elladelle (Ella-Dell)

Elmond (el-mon-d)

Ezen (Ee-Zen)

Favien (Fae-Vee-in)

Finn (Fin)

Gorm (G-or-m)

Graegory (Grae-gor-ree)

Graelynd (GRAY-Lind)

Herb (H-erb)

Herbmando (H-erb-man-doe)

Hueweyn (Hui-When)

Jace (Jay-ss)

Jadelyn (Jae-d-lyn)

JaeDorn (Jay-Dor-N)

Jashun (Ja-Shoo-n) Kafur

Jdru (Droo)

Jem (Gem)

Kailani (Ka-Lan-ee)

Kaiana (Ka-ana)

Karis (Care-Ris)

Kazimir (Kaz-e-Meer)

Keawev (Key-Wev)

Laeglarie (Lay-Gla-Ree)

Laekian (Lay-Kee-An)

Laisren (LayZ-Ren)

Lezlin (Lez-Lin)

Lulana (Loo-La-nah)

Madilina (Ma-di-lee-nah)

Oslac

Maekel (May-Kel)

Malum (Mal-um)

Marin (Mar-Rin)

Mauor (Ma-oo-r)

Max (Max) Oslac
Menry (Men-Ree)
Mimby (Mim-bee)
Miola (My-O-La)
Naedon (Nay-Don)
Nanceline (Nan-see-leen)
Nawrooshall (Naw-Roo-Sholl)
Nijeel (Nie-Jeel)
Norella (Nor-ell-lah)
Novaly (Noe-va-lee)
Nyx (Nee-X)
Paetrill (Pay-Treel)
Pinx (Pin-X)
Pyry (Peer-Ree)
Quinley (Quin-Lee)
Raquel (Rah-Kell)
Rav (R-av)
Revalyn (Re-va-lyn)
Rielen (Ry-Len)
Rivers (Ri-ver-s)
Royce (Roy-SS)
Ryker (r-EYE-ker)
Ryland (rEYE-Land)
Saedeen (Say-Deen)
Saemelina (Sae-me-lee-na)
Saemeon (Say-Me-on)
Sakul (Sa-Kool)
Saven (Say-Vin)
Sealyn (SEE-LIN)
Shaenna (Shae-na)
Siany (SEE-On-EE)
Skarpin (Scar-pin)
Sorcha (Sore-Shah)
Stawyer (Staw-yer)
Stev (St-ev)

Sune (Soon)
Temm (Tem)
Tilmond (Til-mond)
Tintallina (Tin-Ta-lee-na)
Toven (Toe-Vin)
Trit (Tr-it)
Tybalt (Ti-Balt)
Tyrdon (Tear-Don) Steig (Steeg)
Vaelinthia (Vael-in-th-ia)
Wullen (Wul-Lin)
Zuri (Z-ur-ee)

Chapter 1

<u>22 Years Ago…</u>

Jace rounded the corner sharply, slipping on the wet stones of the dark alley. His chest burned, and his knee stung from an enormous scrape. He could hear them. They were gaining on him. The rain was unrelenting. His dark clothes were soaked and torn. Jace's heart pounded. He could see his breath in the night air. He had to find a place to hide.

Hearing the voices, Jace sprang forward. They were only minutes behind him. He knew the tortures that would await if they caught him. His boots splashed through puddles as he navigated the uneven stone walkways. Yellow fireflowers, which appeared sickly, cast an eerie glow down the passageway. Broken stone shops with black mildew guided his path. He looked up and saw a familiar archway. He was headed in the right direction.

Time was not on his side. Sinister laughs echoed behind him, a chilling reminder of the danger he was in. How could they have caught up to him so fast? His legs, heavy with fatigue, were giving out. The rain poured even harder, a cruel obstacle to his escape. A colony of bats flew before him; their sudden appearance caused him to trip. He fell with a bone-jarring thud to the unforgiving street.

He felt the pain in his ankle and heard it: silence. Jace quickly turned on his back and looked up. Rain pelted his face, and a harsh fog settled around him. A group of ebony eyes stared back at him. Evil grins spread across each face. A lump formed in his throat that he tried to swallow down. He didn't want to break, but he knew what awaited him: an endless night of torment.

Jace wanted to be brave and face the night with courage, but his resolve was breaking. As they dragged his tired and bruised body through the cold street, he looked through the foggy windows, hoping just one person would help him. But each time they met his silver eyes, they turned away. He cursed his eye color over and over. He hated who he was. Why did he have to be different? Jace, the silver-eyed freak; Jace, the outcast of Stoltland.

He first felt the sharp, jagged edges of the stone steps, then the ropes around his wrists. He tried to fight back, but two boys held him down, spitting in his face. Jace screamed out, feeling the shame of being born. Each arm was tied to one of the horse statues on either side of the stairs, which led to the obsidian palace of Stoltland. The group threw stones and mud at him. He felt the pain of each rock, but the cruel words of their hatred hurt worse.

The rain finally stopped, with barely a drizzle left. She flipped her cherry red hair behind her and gazed out the front palace window. The boys were at it again. She watched them afflict pain and misery on Jace, her Jace. Screams vibrated through the dark palace walls. The king would be upset if this woke him. She needed to stay on his good side, but waiting a few more minutes was crucial to her plans.

She grabbed an onyx cloak and pulled the hood over her thick, vibrant red hair, added more crimson lip coloring, and adjusted her corset. Now, it was time for her performance. She opened the palace doors and rushed down the stairs, yelling obscenities at the group surrounding Jace. The dripping-wet, black-eyed boys scampered into the dark shadows of the streets, fearing the hooded lady.

Swiftly, she cut through the ropes, then swung herself around the young, adolescent Jace, her hood falling away. Her inky black skirt cascaded down the wet steps, and she cupped Jace's cheek. "Jace, can you hear me?"

"Mother?"

"Yes, my darling boy. It's me. I'm here now," Corentine cooed. "I'll make everything better."

"Mother," Jace grunted, trying to sit up. He was covered in blood, mud, and grime. "I can't..." He landed back down, feeling the sharpness of the step jabbing into his back, and groaned.

"There, there, my sweet son. I'll help you." Corentine stood with her hand, reaching out for Jace. With a swollen eye, Jace reached his bruised and bloodied hand to his mother's, which was covered by a dark silk glove. He was centimeters from her fingers when she jerked away. He looked hurt and confused. She smiled an almost evil grin. "Now, Jace. Be honest. Who here always protects you?"

Jace moaned out, "You, Mother."

Corentine nodded. "Exactly. And who will *you* pledge yourself to because no one else cares for you?"

Jace closed his eyes, fearing he might blackout due to the pain. "You, Mother."

"And do you solemnly swear always to be faithful and duty-bound to me?"

"Yes, Mother," Jace coughed.

She held out her hand that ordered his allegiance, and Jace reluctantly grabbed it, wishing for his death with each wheezing breath. As he limped up the stairs to Stoltland's palace, he leaned on his mother and let her whisper the lies that would forever haunt his mind. He allowed her claws to sink deep into his aching heart, for he knew no one else would or could love someone like him. He would, for all eternity, be indebted to his mother's love, chained by her guilt—praying for someone to set him free.

Chapter 2

<u>Allow Me to Introduce</u>

Darting footsteps pounded behind them. They were running out of time. Their lungs burned, but their determination pushed forward. Jace crouched low between bushes and a cluster of gray and white boulders. Ashur settled in close beside Jace; a forest green cloth covered his ebony face except for his sparkling jade eyes. A twig snapped. They both tensed. The enemy was close—too close.

A deep fog crept over the riverside forest. They could hear muffled voices. Fear flooded through Jace as he watched the fog change from white to black. The dark mist was here! He tapped Ashur's muddy boots twice; they took off like bats flying from a disturbed cave. They had to make it to their checkpoint. Voices yelled out, exposing their position.

"Hurry!" Jace panted to Ashur.

Jace sped past the evergreen branches, catching minor scrapes as tokens. Ashur leaped and slid over a giant boulder, looked back, and confirmed his nightmare. Korpam warriors, or Korps as they were annoyingly known, were gaining on them. Arrows cut through the air like a hot blade on butter. Jace fell forward, feeling the arrow miss his head. He jumped up, sprinting, leaving a crimson trail from his hand.

An arrow sliced a deep cut into Ashur's leg. He tumbled to the ground and cried out. Jace skated on the dusty grass and rocks to help his comrade up.

"Push through it, Ashur. We're so close."

Ashur groaned. "Psycho, Korps."

Jace and Ashur stood and began to jog painfully. Jace draped Ashur's arm over his shoulders, hoping his strength would help, but they were just too big of a target. He felt a sharp pain dig into his shoulder blade and felt the warm sensation of blood trickling down his back. They both fell again. They weren't going to make it. The Korpam raiders were only a few feet behind them.

Soldiers dressed in auburn battle leathers with tinted orange swords surrounded Jace and Ashur. Their blazing, copper eyes showed their hatred toward the green-eyed Elysians. Onyx mist swirled behind them. Blood pooled underneath Jace and Ashur. They hadn't made it to the checkpoint. Their plan failed.

"King Jace, it gives me all the pleasure in the world to be the one to slay you," one of the soldiers growled. He lifted his blade and swung toward Jace. Elysium's king instinctively raised his arm, knowing he could do nothing against the sword. Yet, the blade bounced off a wall of swirling green, blue, and gold light. A dome formed around Jace and Ashur. They stood slowly in amazement.

The black mist hissed.

"What is the meaning of this?" The Korpam soldier yelled.

Jace wiped the sweat from his tanned brow with his bloody hand. His lip curled. He knew this forcefield meant only one thing. With all the confidence of a true king, Jace stepped closer to the wall of glistening, colorful light and grinned.

"Well, soldiers, allow me to introduce…my wife."

With a piercing screech, Dun, the giant green phoenix, flew above the Korpam warriors, and on his back, Queen Sealyn Araelien of Elysium fired her green-flamed arrows. The dark mist shuddered at Dun's screeches, and Korpam's military returned fire to the queen. With intense battle cries, the Elysian army rushed past Jace and Ashur, spilling into the Korpam force.

Elysians and Korps swung their swords with no mercy. The Korps kept invading Elysium's border along Hostile Channel, and their anger for their lost comrades was on full display today. The Elysians sliced through the flesh, bones, and limbs of the Korpam army, leaving only one man alive.

The remaining orange-eyed soldier was breathing heavily, his face and chest marked with several cuts oozing with blood.

Dun landed nearby with his massive emerald wings, creating wind gusts around him, an intimidating sight for anyone to behold. Sealyn slid down the feathers and approached the kneeling, bloody man. She grabbed the dead leader's arm and dragged his body in front of the soldier, leaving a crimson trail. Her eyes were glowing bright green, then they flashed to an icy blue, and she chopped the corpse's head off. With no remorse, she handed it to the shaking soldier, who leaked urine down his pants.

"A gift to your new queen. Tell your Korpam leaders to break the treaty with Stoltland or else. Now, go!"

The young man staggered back toward their boat, holding the head by its hair, not looking at it. Dun stomped his golden feet excitedly, breaking Sealyn's concentration on the light dome surrounding Jace and Ashur. She turned and ran to Jace. They settled into a bloody embrace, then she pushed him back and folded her arms.

"You were late."

"Forgive me, my queen, but this might have been the first time since knowing you that I've ever been late," Jace lifted his chin, giving Sealyn a teasing smile.

"True, which is why I knew you probably needed some assistance."

King Father Ryker, Sealyn's father, jumped down from his pure white horse. "Are you okay, Jace? Ashur?"

"Well, this arrow hurts, but other than that, we're good--all thanks to you and Queen Sealyn, Your Majesty," Ashur said.

Jace grasped Ryker's forearm. "I appreciate the assist. You still fight well for an old man."

Ryker chuckled and thumped the arrow still embedded in Jace's shoulder. Jace winced. "I may be old, son, but at least this old man would have been wise enough to duck."

Lord Char,

I received your concerned letter. Let me assure you 'dat Queen Sealyn can complete her mission, but your worries are valid. My t'eory is 'dat Queen Sealyn is a Co
Be warned and guar
mind.

Many prayers,
Madam Bip

Burn 'dis letter

Chapter 3

<u>Beastly Cat</u>

Sealyn pulled the tent door back as she entered her royal headquarters of the base camp at Port Saevus, the major port city of the Clarien territory of Elysium. This tent was used for war planning, filled with a long table covered in maps and figurines representing various forces. An assortment of multicolored rugs lay on the ground, and golden chairs with olive green velvet cushions were arranged around the table. Tall candles illuminated the entire room, showcasing the other tables of food and ale. She pulled off her armor and set it aside, a heavy relief. She was glad for a second of quiet, which didn't last long. A handful of people burst through her tent, all talking simultaneously. She groaned to herself.

Lord Char, Sealyn's cousin, seized the silver pitcher of ale and a goblet before plopping himself down at the head of the table. He crossed his feet on the tabletop, exhausted, and filled his goblet, nodding toward the fussy nobles. Sealyn couldn't help but smile. Char's wit always helped her get through dark times. She was glad he had decided to help with the rebellion against the curses. Char had changed. Sure, he had a full beard, and his brown hair was longer, but, more importantly, he had shifted his mentality.

Once he had seen the Shunalian king chain his entire kingdom, he vowed no one else would suffer that fate. Char was now on the same mission as Sealyn. He wanted every kingdom freed from these horrible curses. Something else was new with Char, too. He had unlocked his Transference magic. Not just any creature chose Char—a beast that had chosen solitude for thousands of years came out of hiding. The Southern Elysian tiger, thought to have been extinct, suddenly walked right into the marketplace while Char sat at one of the cafe tables at *Nijeel's Choice*. The green and gold striped tiger, who towers a shocking seven feet tall when sitting, strolled right up to Char and sat.

Everyone froze, not knowing whether they should run or scream. Char, however, felt calm and reached out to the creature, who gave him its eyes, strength, and healing capabilities. Char hasn't fully mastered healing magic yet, but he has managed to help heal scrapes and broken bones. Char chose to name the spunky tiger Shep, short for Shepherd.

His Southern Elysian tiger looked uninterested in the commotion of the tent. The gentle beast curled near Char's chair and closed his shining golden eyes for a well-earned nap after healing several wounded soldiers.

Clearing away goblets and scrolls, Prince Adomin, Queen Sealyn's uncle, unfurled another map on the table. It displayed a closer drawing of the border of Port Saevus. He began pointing out his theories to Prince Royce and King Father Ryker. Lord Jdru, cousin to Queen Sealyn and brother of Lord Char, also shared his theories. In the corner near the food, Lord Doebromir, Lord Favien, and Lord Finn stood discussing the battle that had just taken place. Sealyn massaged her temples, wishing the day were over. She was losing her patience. Voices—too many voices!

She slammed her hand, which didn't disturb the chatter. Char choked on his ale, and Shep lifted his head. He sniffed the air, and his tiger eyes dilated as he watched Sealyn. Char looked from Shep to Sealyn, then back to Shep. Sealyn's eyes flashed blue. Shep roared and stood. The room silenced. Char patted Shep's head, and the animal calmly sat, eyeing Sealyn.

Sealyn looked at the tiger, feeling like he knew her secret. Something was off about this beastly cat, but he did quiet the noise. She tilted her head in thanks. Shep bowed his head in return.

"Well, gentlemen, now that your colossal noise has stopped, has anyone heard from Commander Tilmond's unit?"

Max approached the map table, pulling off his chestnut leather gloves. "He did make his checkpoint, but that was hours ago. Would you like us to send out scouts?" Max had a sweet, handsome face and dark brown hair cut short. He was also constantly worried about his comrades.

Sealyn nodded. "Yes. They should have been back by now. Send the scouts and ready the troops."

"As you command, my queen." Max bowed and hurried out of the tent, followed by Favien and Doebromir.

Ryker folded his arms and rocked on his heels. The former reigning king's chestnut hair was thinning, and gray strands were taking over, yet he remained a fearsome warrior and leader. He tilted his head side to side, not wanting to express what his gut was telling him. "Sea, I hate to say this, but I have a bad feeling…"

Before Ryker could finish, screams echoed throughout the camp. They rushed out of the tent and saw Commander Tilmond's unit returning, covered in blood. Half the unit was being carted in on wagons with significant injuries, a clear sign they had lost others. Tilmond dismounted his sweaty, creamy white horse, wincing once his feet hit the ground. Sealyn didn't know if that was from his old injuries from Shunal or from something new. She hurried to his side.

"What happened, Tilmond?"

"We. We were ambushed." He gasped for air and grabbed his side. He figured one or two of his ribs were cracked, not to mention the searing pain climbing up his leg.

"Are you hurt?"

"I think my ankle is broken, but there are others who are worse off."

Sealyn saw Lady Dinyelle helping a soldier to the infirmary tent. "Dinyelle looks to still be in good condition. Does she have enough information to debrief me?"

Tilmond nodded. "Ugh. I may have cracked a rib, too." His tall stature faltered slightly.

Sealyn snapped her fingers. "Char, take Shep with you to the infirmary and help as many as you two can. I'm sure Lady Sorcha and Lord Prince Brandle are overloaded." Sealyn cupped her hands around her mouth and shouted, "Lady Dinyelle, come to my tent once you're done."

Sealyn walked to one of the wagons and gasped. Three dismantled soldiers lay dead with deep slashes across their chests and bellies, organs exposed. These were not from swords. They looked like claw wounds. Flies buzzed around the open gashes and entrails. Sealyn quickly turned her head before vomiting; the smell of the sun heating decaying flesh and the metallic stench of blood was overwhelming. Dinyelle patted Sealyn's back gently while Sealyn bent over, hands on her thighs, breathing heavily and spitting.

"They came from the darkness. We had no time to react," Dinyelle said.

Sealyn stretched her back and exhaled. "Not here. Let's discuss this in my tent."

The two walked in silence until they were inside Sealyn's war tent. Sealyn poured Dinyelle some ale and fixed her a plate of food. She motioned for her to sit.

"Now that we're alone. Please tell me what happened."

Dinyelle swallowed a sip of ale, not wanting to relive the horror they had just encountered. "We thought we would face another Korpam unit, which would have been no problem. Our unit is solid and well-trained, but Korpam and Stoltland sent a wave of infected tigers and wolves. Their skin had onyx scales, making it impossible to penetrate. We defended the best we could, but then came the soldiers. We took beating after beating. Commander Tilmond sounded the retreat, so we fled." Dinyelle looked down and shook her head. "My queen, I don't know why they let us go."

"What?"

"They could have killed all of us, but they let us go. Why?"

"Why indeed," Ryker said as he walked through the tent door with King Jace. Korpam letting Elysians go was not like them. Something wasn't right in Dinyelle's story. "We know Korpam better than that. This is merely an attempt to buy time for reinforcements."

Jace's wound was healing fast from Shep, but he still had it bandaged. "Sea, what do you think?"

Sealyn didn't want to think about what kind of other monsters Corentine would be sending with more Korps. She recoiled, remembering her nightmare of the bloody battle scene, bodies scattered, and the Pirate Captain's face. She cleared her throat, hoping the sound would dissipate her thoughts. Sealyn tilted her head as she took her seat. "Looks like your question is already answered."

Jace felt something was off about Sealyn's response. Why was she acting this way? Normally, she was receptive to her father's advice.

Ryker popped a cashew into his mouth and chewed, using it as a way to ponder. His daughter was struggling, and he didn't know how to help. He would lose countless nights of sleep over this. His love for his daughters was limitless. Ryker swallowed and sighed. "We should prepare the troops," he said. "We must not waver against Corentine's next round of battle."

The few members in the room nodded in agreement, but Sealyn slipped deeper into dark thoughts. She sipped her wine with no intention of letting her army fight those Korps again. She would ensure that.

Chapter 4

<u>You Can Thank Me Later</u>

The stars twinkled in the night sky above the Elysians, and a cool breeze flowed through the tents. Musicians strummed their instruments, trying to lift their comrades' spirits. Smoke drifted into the air, and the fires crackled soothing lullabies. The campfire light flickered across Sealyn's olive skin as she gazed into the flames. After Maekel had finished braiding her long, dark brown hair, Sealyn joined her army at one of their fires. She liked being among them. After all, they were risking their lives for her, for their kingdom. They were owed her respect.

Dinyelle sat beside Sealyn and scooped large pieces of potatoes and chopped beef into her wooden spoon. She took a big bite, juice running down her light brown skin. Sealyn chuckled. She couldn't believe how long it had been since Dinyelle played Feydom during Sealyn's first year as queen.

"Dinyelle, I know you like being close to your family here, but I must ask you to return to Avondelle with me."

Dinyelle's mint eyes narrowed. "You know my answer is yes, but what's happening?"

Sealyn tossed a stick in the fire, sending sparks into the sky. "I want you to be a part of my Vinurs of the Court. I need people I can trust and depend on, and more importantly, I need warriors. I believe you and your husband will make fine additions."

"And you want us?"

"Of course. I hadn't asked before because I didn't want to take you away from your family, but Herb is finding himself more and more in Avondelle, and he suggested…"

"Wait, so my father put you up to this?"

"More like he gave his blessing," Sealyn laughed.

"You two," Dinyelle said, shaking her head. "Going behind my back and planning out a better life for us? How dare you."

Dinyelle nudged Sealyn's shoulder with hers playfully. They fell into light laughter. Sealyn missed her schoolgirl days with Dinyelle. She had been so sad the day her father stationed Herb's family in Port Saevus. She cried for days, but now, she could have her close friend back. She needed allies. Dinyelle and JaeDorn would be excellent Vinurs of the Court.

"Where is your husband?"

"Oh, you know JaeDorn. He's helping repair weapons, fix tents, train younger soldiers… anything to stay busy."

"I should have known," Sealyn looked out in the darkness. "Did you hear that?"

"Hear what?"

A faint sound of commotion echoed in the distance. Sealyn slowly stood, trying not to surge panic through her camp. Others heard the sounds, too. Soldiers grabbed their weapons. Leaders called out commands. Sealyn tried to call out to Dun, but his bond was quiet for some reason. Why was his mind blocking her? Did this have something to do with her breaking Shunal's curse? Could she only channel a certain number of mythical creatures at a time?

The ground began to rumble. Horses—lots of horses—were coming. Sealyn feared what other creatures traveled amidst this army. Jace ripped his bandage off and grabbed his sword and Sealyn's. He ran next to Sealyn and handed her her sword, but Sealyn had already readied her bow. The Elysians braced themselves for the terrible beasts that were almost on top of them.

A fur-covered object dropped from the sky and splattered in the camp. Everyone froze, not wanting to guess what it was. Lord Ashur approached the hairy, smelly object. He jumped back, realizing it was the head of a large black wolf. Sealyn and Jace both looked at each other, confused. What did this mean? Why did this fall from the sky? And who killed it?

Elysians cheered as they heard the familiar screeches of their phoenixes returning. Dun landed near the entrance to their camp with an obsidian-scaled tiger in his giant beak. He snapped it in half and squawked, blood dripping from his golden jaws. Elysians cheered again. Then, the mystery of the horses became clear. Jumping from a white and brown horse, the Pirate Captain removed his tiger helmet and smiled at Sealyn.

"You know, Queen Sealyn, me saving you is really starting to add up," he jeered.

Sealyn shook her head and lowered her bow. "Pirates. Always late to battles."

"And forever cleaning up your messes."

"It's good to see you," Sealyn said, narrowing her eyes. "Can't say that I've missed you."

"I would be worried for your health if you did."

"Did you really have to bring that smell with you?"

"It's ok, Phoenix Queen, you can thank me later."

Jace stepped forward. "If you two are done antagonizing each other, I would like to offer our allies some refreshment." Jace looked at the Pirate Captain's army and motioned for them to join. "Please, everyone, rest and refresh with us. You all are welcome."

Jace walked over to greet the sons of the Pirate Captain, leaving Sealyn alone with him.

He stood beside Sealyn, both of them watching Jace. "I trust my secret is still secret."

"Which secret? The one that your name is Tyrdon Steig, the banished king of Korpam, or the one that you're Jace's father?" Sealyn turned and faced the pirate.

His orange eyes flared. "Yes, those secrets."

"Not for long…"

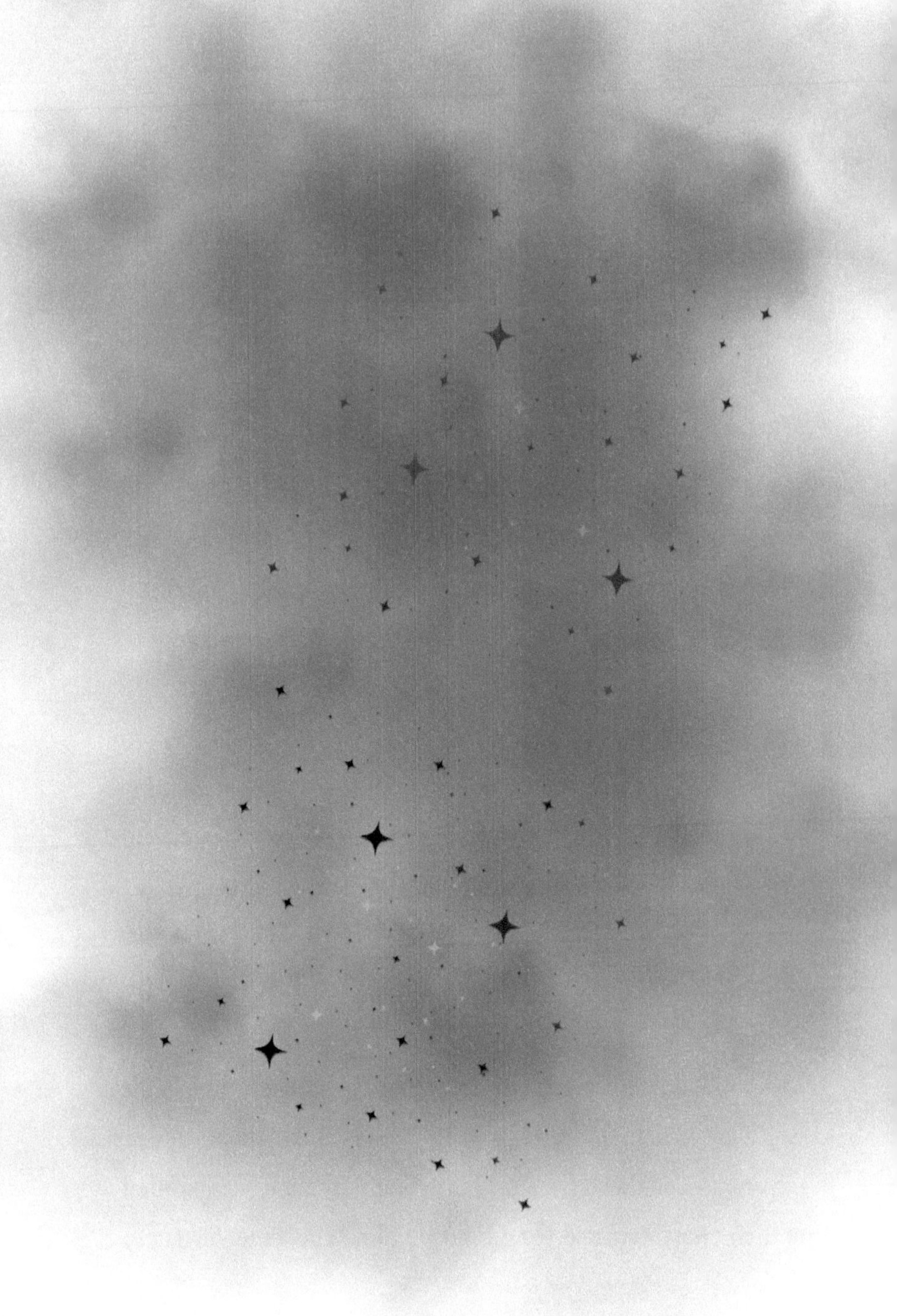

Chapter 5

<u>22 Years Ago…</u>

Jace pulled his legs closer to his body, hoping no one would see him hiding in the corner. He tugged a large vase closer, hoping it would add extra coverage. His heart pounded. Sweat slid down his brow into his silver eyes, stinging them. He blinked hard and went to wipe them, but his elbow knocked the vase over.

The bottle crashed on the black marble floor like a horn calling out. He heard footsteps stop and then begin running toward him. Crawling over the big pieces of porcelain, he cut his hands. Recovering quickly, he ran down the obsidian corridor, searching for another inconspicuous spot.

"There he is! Get the monster, or he'll eat us for dinner!"

Jace heard the group of young boys behind him. This was a game to them. It was a sport to chase him. He, however, never enjoyed these games. Once caught, the boys committed to their characters and would torture him. This time, he had to escape. He slid around another corner, knocking into a shadowy-eyed butler. The butler shoved Jace into the onyx-stoned wall.

Jace's head connected hard. Dark spots clouded his vision. He blinked and squinted. He tried running, but his feet felt like they weren't his own. Blood trickled down from his head to his neck. The boys turned the corner and lunged for him. He staggered backward, falling to the black marble. He looked at the floor and saw his scared reflection. Panic flooded his veins.

"To the dungeons!"

The boys raised their wooden swords with cheers. They tied Jace's wrists and ankles, then carried him down the long, winding staircase to the damp, dark dungeons. The air smelled of mold, urine, and sweat. Prisoners wailed and coughed. Jace felt sick. The boys tossed Jace into the last cell of the dungeon and slammed the iron bars, locking in the small silver-eyed child.

The boys ran away, filling the air with their victory songs while the dripping water and scurrying of rats filled Jace's ears. Jace curled up on the mound of damp hay. Worms and beetles crawled out of the hay as he laid down. Tears flowed from his grey eyes. He wished he had never been born. He hated his life. Where was his mother? Why didn't anyone ever stop this torture? No one cared about him.

A frail, old man shuffled close to Jace's bars. "You're just a kid. Why you in here?" he gruffly asked.

Jace sniffed and wiped his eyes. "Because they hate me. Everyone does. No one cares."

"Wait. You're that grey-eyed child, aren't you?"

Jace dropped his head and closed his eyes, wishing his eye color away, but it was no good. He was forever the silver-eyed outcast. Jace looked at the old man, who had a long white beard, a bony figure, and jade eyes. Jace's brow furrowed. "Your eyes are green."

The old man smiled, wrestling against mounds of wrinkles to show rotten teeth. "Yes. I'm an Elysian."

"Why are you here?"

"Well, I was the commander of Elysium's army, but I was kidnapped on a secret mission."

"What are they going to do to you?"

The old man huffed. "What would you do?"

"Me? I'm a nobody. I don't make important decisions."

The Elysian coughed. "Humor me. What would you do if you were in charge—better yet, if you were king?"

Jace stood and walked closer to the bars. He shoved his bloody hands into his pockets. "I would try to make peace. Seems like we're always at war, especially with green eyes, but maybe releasing you would be the first step."

"How old are you?"

"Seven, sir."

"Wow. For seven, you sure know a lot about ruling kingdoms. I can only hope that one day, the world can be governed by a king like you."

Jace smiled. Dried tears reflected the lanterns' light on his cheeks. "I'm awfully sorry you're in here. You're real nice—probably the nicest person I've ever met."

"That sounds like a great compliment. I appreciate that," the old man coughed more, blood staining his sleeve.

"Say, are all Elysians as nice as you?" Jace asked with anticipation.

The old commander chuckled. "Our kingdom isn't perfect, but our Queen Graelynd just might be raising the world's only hope."

"What does that mean?"

"Oh, just some ramblings of an old man, but I hope you get to go to Elysium one day. I've been here so long that I don't know who's in what position, but my eldest son was training to become commander. If you go, look up Lord Elmond. He'll look after you."

"Stoltlanders aren't allowed to go to Elysium."

"Ah, my boy, but you aren't really a Stoltlander. Are you?"

Jace's face crumpled into confusion. What did he mean by that? His thoughts were interrupted by boys laughing. This time, Haedon, Jace's step-brother and heir to the Stoltland throne, was with them. They each had buckets filled with jam. Jace's stomach dropped. He knew what this was for.

Jace ran to a far corner, but he was still in range. The boys scooped jam and threw the sticky globs at him.

"Jammy Jace. Jammy Jace. Why so sticky, Jammy Jace?" they all chanted.

Jace cried and pleaded for them to stop, but his begging never prevailed in their dark hearts. They were bullies, ruthless bullies.

"You kids, leave him alone!" the old man shouted.

The boys threw their remaining jam at the old man, then sprinted out of the dimly lit dungeon.

"Ha! Those boys are idiots," the commander said. He tried to overly laugh and gain Jace's attention.

Jace was covered in blackberry and strawberry jam. He wiped his eyes. "Why do you say that?"

"Because this jam tastes delicious," he licked his fingers and smacked his lips. "This is the best-tasting stuff I've had in years. Those fools don't realize they just lifted my spirits. How 'bout you try? Taste the preserves."

Jace hesitantly licked a finger and smiled. "It does taste good."

"See? You can always find something good in a bad situation. You just have to try hard enough. By the way, my name's Evan. What's yours?"

"Jace," he sighed. His head drooped, and his small shoulders slumped, defeated by what he was—what he would forever remain.

"What's wrong with that? Jace is a strong name."

"It means nothing when no one cares about you."

Evan scratched his straggly beard. Something about this child stumped him. "I can only advise you with this—find someone who loves you for just you, just Jace. You find someone like that and never let go."

Jace nodded and held onto those words. He tucked them deep into his heart, hoping one day, the old man's words would come true. They both flinched at the sound of bustling feet and clanging metal. A group of black-armored soldiers surged into the dungeon. They swarmed around Evan's cage like angry wasps. The bars creaked open, and they yanked Evan forward.

Jace yelled for them to stop hurting him.

"Well, lookie here, fellas. Looks like the grey-eyed freak got himself locked up again."

"He's definitely in a jam…"

The soldiers laughed hard, patting each other on the back for their clever jokes. Jace teared up. Anger flooded his veins. He felt a searing pain in his palms. A familiar pain he had felt all his life, but one he wasn't allowed to ask about. He grabbed the rusty bars and screamed at the soldiers.

"Jace, you best calm down, or we'll forget we saw you."

Evan stopped fighting the soldiers. "It's ok, Jace. You just take care of yourself and remember what I said."

The soldiers yanked Evan hard and pushed him toward the exit.

One soldier remained. He set a bucket of water in front of Jace's cell with a soap bar. "You best wash up before returning to the castle." He unlocked the cell and left Jace alone.

Jace grabbed the soap and immediately started scrubbing himself. Then he heard the screams—Evan's screams—followed by silence.

Chapter 6

<u>Confuto</u>

The morning light came with heavy fog, ideal for Sealyn's plans; only this time, she would be going alone. She tiptoed through her camp, avoiding sticks and dried leaves. Once out of earshot, she dashed toward the shoreline. There was only so much she could ask of her army. Today, she knew she would cross a line. Her people would likely view her differently, but she needed to put an end to the shoreline raids. They needed to return to Avondelle to finally organize their Glatania quest.

She slid down a rock bank and landed with a mild thud behind a boulder. Slowly, she peered out from her hiding place and saw Korpam's ships anchored in the water, waves gently rocking them. Korpam's kingdom was across Hostile Channel. Its riverside was full of large mountains and hidden coves.

Tonight, luck was on her side—the enemy was still asleep. With a wave of her hand, Sealyn conjured her flaming green bow and arrows, closed her eyes, and concentrated on

King Nawrooshall, king of the mammoths, a willing giver of his strength. Her eyes blazed with swirls of jade and azure, and the front of her dark brown hair developed two streaks of royal blue. She was ready. She prepared to fire, but a growl came from behind her; the growl of a tiger.

She slowly turned and stared at the face of a massive, heavy-breathing creature. Once her eyes focused, she let out a sigh of relief. "Shep, you startled me."

The beast didn't move. He looked angry. Char slid down the rock and landed next to Shep. His eyes glowed like Shep's tiger eyes.

"Char!" Sealyn whispered a hiss. "What are you doing here?"

"You didn't really think you could sneak off with Shep around, did you?"

Sealyn glared at the big cat. There might be more to this creature than Sealyn realized. She made a mental note to look into his kind once she got back to Avondelle.

"Listen, intruders, I don't have time for this. Sunrise is coming. You can't be here for this."

"Can't be here for what?"

Char peered over the boulder and spotted Korpam's ships, but he noticed that there weren't just warships; there were supply ships accompanying them. Char's stomach dropped.

"Sealyn, have you completely lost your mind?"

Shep growled.

"Back off—both of you. This is the only way to end this ridiculous fighting. You know Corentine is doing this to distract us."

"What I know is that those are supply ships. They have innocent civilians on them. Your fight isn't with them."

"Isn't it?" Sealyn pointed to the supply ships and then to the war ones. "If they don't supply, then those soldiers can't fight—the end."

Char shook his head. He couldn't believe he was having this conversation. "But at what cost? The Sealyn I knew would never risk civilian lives."

"Char, there are some things you don't understand. Get this through your thick skull." She tapped his head. "I'm running out of time, and I don't mean the sunrise; just leave this be."

"So you expect me just to sit here and what? Watch you set fire to the supply ships?"

Sealyn groaned. "If you intend on staying, then yes. And hopefully, the message will be loud and clear to all of Korpam. If you aid Korpam soldiers, then you're a part of the war."

"What about the Mer Clans? Can't they create waves to send the ships back?"

"Seriously? I don't have some magic seashell to call them. This isn't fiction, Char. This is real life. Besides, the sea kelp at the entrance would attack them, and they're not allowed to destroy it."

"Couldn't they just walk on the land around the entrance, then jump back in the water? Seems simple enough."

"Char. Ugh. I'm tired of explaining myself! There's something else in Hostile Channels' waters that the Mer Clans want nothing to do with. They have so many rules and regulations on everything that I'm surprised they're allowed to breathe without checking in with someone. They even have a rule for how they're supposed to drink their tea on land."

Char pushed his brown hair back with frustration. "C'mon, Sea. There has to be something. What powers did you inherit by breaking Shunal's curse? Did the legendary serpent give you anything?"

Sealyn paused. She wasn't ready to reveal that to anyone, not even Char. "It won't help."

"Couldn't you just make some wind and blow them away?"

"Char. I'm not the weather."

"I know that, but couldn't you make weather?"

Sealyn tilted her head. "I've never tried."

Char motioned for her to try. Sealyn wasn't quite sure where to pull sources of magic for weather. She understood she needed both heat and cool air for a storm, but that was the extent of her knowledge on the subject. She started rubbing her hands together, allowing green flames to form between them.

She said, "Vorso." The flames began to spin violently and grew larger. Char's eyes widened. Sealyn spread her arms further apart, creating even bigger spinning flames. Her brow began to sweat. She stood, facing the ships, as an intensity burned within. She feared she would lose control. After a deep inhale, she exhaled as hard as she could. The flames rolled over and over in the air, moving slowly toward the shoreline.

Fog seeped over Sealyn's boot. She bent down and swirled her fingers in the low cloud. She created a small tornado and growled the word "Praefuro." Colossal gusts of wind clashed with the flickering emerald flames, sending sparks and powerful currents of air flying in all directions. Char and Sealyn ducked behind the boulder; Shep laid across Char. Sealyn had no idea what she had just done.

They heard screams coming from the water's edge. Both of them quickly stood up and watched as a massive, stormy green cloud sent lightning bolts and gigantic waves crashing against the ships. The water rocked the boats and even overturned two warships. A supply ship caught fire from blinding, lime-green lightning. Screams echoed across the waves

"Sealyn, how do you make it stop?"

She knew the answer; she just didn't want to end it—not yet. Sealyn pulled herself atop the boulder, exposing her position to the enemy. Lightning cracked, and thunder rumbled through the angry, dark green clouds. Ships crashed against one another.

"Sealyn! Make it stop."

Shep snapped his jaws at Sealyn. She jerked her head and glared at the old tiger.

She exhaled dramatically and said, "Confuto." But nothing happened.

"Sealyn? Why isn't the storm stopping?"

"I don't know. I said stop."

Shep roared at Sealyn, his golden eyes glowing. She feared she knew his concealed secret. Great—now she had a mind-reading tiger to deal with. She let out an exasperated sigh. She grabbed her knife and sliced her right palm. Droplets of blood splattered on the boulder. Small streams of Sealyn's blood dripped onto the grass. She repeated the word "confuto." Instantly, the storm vanished, and the sunrise glittered its orange, pink, and yellow colors across the cloudless sky and still water.

The Korps and Stoltlanders appeared confused. Then they turned to the shore and saw Sealyn standing on the boulder. She shouted, "Leave. You will find no mercy on my land." The storm victims swam to driftwood and to the surviving ships. Char and Sealyn watched them retreat.

Sealyn jumped off the boulder, and Char grabbed her arm. "Why did you lie to me?"

Sealyn jerked her arm away. "I didn't."

Shep snapped.

Oh, how that mind-reading cat annoyed her. Sealyn side-eyed the emerald and gold creature. "I just didn't tell or use the whole truth."

"Since when did we start keeping things from one another?" Char was genuinely hurt. This wasn't the Sealyn he knew.

Sealyn lifted her arms, blood still dripping from her right hand. "Since Mauor and Kazimir told me that my blood now has the power of life and death. All I have to do is decide, on the spot, which I choose once my blood is spilled."

"Wait, what? That psycho two-headed serpent gave you that power?"

Sealyn leaned against the boulder. She removed a cloth from her satchel and began wrapping her hand. "Yes. Remember, the Naehass can produce life and death. A healing potion came from Mauor's fangs and venom from Kazimir's. Since life and death were evidently a part of the spell I just cast, I could use my blood to either save lives or destroy them."

"Um, Sealyn. That's a little too much power, don't you think?"

Sealyn kicked herself off the boulder and laid her non-wounded hand on Char's shoulder. "I agree. This will all one day be too much power."

Tethered-connected to plants
Transference-channel creatures
Cognition-mind manipulation

Homework: List 1 person as an example
of each type of Luxen Magic.

Tethered: Professor Gunnolf & all my
friends!

Transference: Lady Madilina
Cognition: ??

Meet Skarpin & Naedon
In the gardens
after dinner tonight

Chapter 7

<u>You Already Know the Answer</u>

Sealyn, Char, and Shep returned to a panicked camp. Sealyn felt faint and wiped her nose, blood smearing across her finger. She needed to rest; that spell had taken a lot out of her, more than she had realized. She swayed, feeling her legs turn to jelly. Jace ran to Sealyn and scooped her into his arms.

"Where were you? What happened to your hand and your nose? You're bleeding. Sealyn, what's going on?"

"I'm fine. I just need to rest, then I will answer your questions."

A crowd formed around them, eager to hear from their missing queen. Sealyn stepped around Jace to address her people.

"Comrades, today we pack up for home. We move out before noon. Rest assured, the enemy is no longer on our shorelines."

"What about that storm?" someone shouted.

Sealyn could feel irritation welling up inside her. She needed to rest. She took a deep breath.

"You are in no danger. The storm is gone. Now, I must re…return to my tent for preparations. Make haste on my orders."

A soldier moved toward Sealyn, but Lord Jem seized his arm. Lord Jem was the red-eyed warrior from Havas and a member of Sealyn's Council of Lands. He was also ridiculously handsome, tall, and muscular, with wavy blonde hair. His jawline was sharply defined, and his eyes always followed Queen Sealyn. As she walked by, Sealyn nodded her appreciation to Jem, and he smiled to himself. Looking up, he saw Sealyn's cousin, his commander, Lord Tilmond, scowling at him.

Sealyn weaved through the crowd of soldiers, overhearing their whispers. Her soldiers looked—afraid. They shared hushed conversations behind their hands, glancing sideways at their queen. Insecurities began to fester deep within Sealyn. Her ears honed in on what they were saying.

"Did she create that storm?"

"Why won't she tell us what happened?"

"Did the storm kill everyone at the shoreline?"

"What kind of magic wielder can make weather?"

She ignored them. Rumors would soon flood the newspapers. Then what would she do? Would her people turn against her? Would they demand proof of her magic? She was tired, so very tired. Shunal's curse had taken too much from her, as had the Naehass curse. The weight of such power felt nearly unbearable. She dreaded the next curse. She sank into her bed, embracing the sweet peace and quiet.

Char grabbed Jace's arm before he could catch up with Sealyn. "King Jace, I need a word with you."

Jace moved away from prying ears, feeling uneasy about what Char might want. "What's the meaning of this?"

"Your wife. Something isn't right with her." Char folded his arms and looked side to side, then leaned in. "She snuck away to set fire to the supply ships."

Jace sucked in a breath. "No. Not Sealyn. She wouldn't."

"Jace, I'm telling you. I caught her with her magic bow cocked and ready. She even admitted it to me."

Jace rubbed his hand across his face, unwilling to accept what he was hearing. "What could this mean? Is it the curses? Are they doing this to her?" He paused, glanced around, then leaned close to Char. "Could they be corrupting her mind?" Jace didn't want to consider what that could imply.

"I want that to be the reason, but if it is, what's to be done about it?" Char raised his hands, hoping Jace would have an answer, any answer.

Jace looked to the sky and shook his head. "If Stoltland hadn't invaded Havas, then none of this would be happening. She wouldn't feel like she's running out of time."

"Look, I think she feels up against a ticking clock, no matter what Stoltland does."

Jace's brow furrowed. "What do you mean by that?"

Char dropped his head and sighed. "I don't think she's telling us the whole truth. She's hiding something."

"No. Sealyn wouldn't do that."

Char glared. "No? Well, you weren't there to see everything that happened in that snake-infested kingdom. You didn't watch her have no mercy on the princes of Shunal..."

"From what I hear, they earned being eaten by the Naehass. C'mon, Char. They slaughtered their sisters each year for sport—just to gain wealth."

"Fine. I'll give you that one, but something happened between her and Cruz."

This gained Jace's attention. He knew Cruz, the rebel leader and now King of Shunal, had feelings for Sealyn. "What happened?"

"I don't know exactly, but I have a theory. I saw them conversing after the Rope snake horror of Echo Forest. Cruz stood a little too close to Sealyn. I could tell he made her uncomfortable, but their exchanged words were intense. I think he knows whatever Sealyn is hiding."

"Why would you say that?" Jace questioned through gritted teeth; jealousy loomed in his veins.

"Because in the palace, after Sealyn crowned Cruz as Shunal's new king, I overheard some of their conversation." Char hadn't shared this with anyone yet but now seemed like the right time.

Jace's jaw tightened. "Char, if you don't spit it out…"

Char raised a hand. "Easy. Easy. I only caught what Sealyn said." Char stiffened and shifted his feet, feeling uncomfortable. Throughout his life, Char had never betrayed Sealyn. He kept every secret. While he wasn't sure if he was betraying her, it certainly felt that way. He let out a sigh and crossed his arms. She said, "How about you never stop looking for another way? When you find it, get in touch with me right away.'"

Jace stood frozen, hands on his hips. "Ok, so? What does that mean?" Jace was growing tired of repeating the same question over and over.

"Well, I don't know. I hoped you would."

"How would I know?"

"Maybe because you're her husband. You know, the love of her life. The one she would tell everything to?" Char was losing his patience. Jace's lack of royal training was beginning to catch up to him. He wondered if, one day, this would become too much for Jace.

Jace surveyed the camp, where soldiers were dismantling tents, extinguishing fires with water, and loading wagons. He contemplated the words Char had disclosed

"*Another way*," Jace said to the wind. He turned and faced Char. "What would she mean by another way?"

"That's what I would like to know. Should we question her?"

"Maybe, but if we do, we should wait until Avondelle. She looked completely exhausted." Jace stepped closer to Char, shoulder to shoulder, and whispered, "Char, did she create that storm?"

Char tilted his head. "If you're asking, then you already know the answer."

Chapter 8

<u>School of Luxen Magic</u>

The hallways of Bracken Castle, now the new school of Luxen magic, buzzed with the exciting news that the king and queen would be returning any day. The children had been honing their powers, aware that the top five students could showcase their skills in front of them.

Skarpin, the adopted son of Queen Sealyn and King Jace, skipped out the side door of the castle and met his friend, Wullen, who had helped save the kingdom from the Black Phoenixes. The two had become inseparable friends after their heroic teamwork.

"Did you bring it?" Wullen asked.

Skarpin patted his pocket. "Got it right here." Skarpin's golden eyes sparkled with mischief. He hailed from the kingdom of Shunal and had curly, obsidian hair, olive skin, and a smile that could melt even a troll's heart. Wullen was the opposite. He sported bright blonde hair, freckles scattered across his ivory complexion, and striking lime-green eyes.

Wullen was also taller than Skarpin, something he enjoyed reminding his friend about often.

"We just need the others. Did you see them?" Wullen asked, looking around the grounds.

Skarpin shook his head. "No. I had to finish extra work with Professor Gunnolf. Her class is so hard." He hoped he sounded convincing.

Wullen kicked a rock. "Tell me about it. I mixed up every plant on her last pop quiz."

Skarpin didn't want to tell Wullen that his extra work resulted from surpassing his classmates, so Professor Gunnolf, or Lady Pinx as many call her, had been sneaking him higher-level tests. Professor Gunnolf suggested it might be easier for Skarpin to make friends if he agreed that the classes were challenging so other kids would feel less intimidated by his intellect. Skarpin didn't want to give anyone a reason to dislike him, so he took her advice. He sometimes found it difficult to keep up with the lies, especially regarding his age. All of his friends were eleven except for Wullen, who was ten. However, since Skarpin really didn't know his true age, the collective consensus was to tell people he was eight, even though he distinctly looked younger.

Elladelle appeared around the corner, followed by Saedeen. Elladelle was the daughter of Lord Rielen, a cousin of Queen Sealyn. She had dark brown hair and looked almost identical to Sealyn. Elladelle had her mother's sweet disposition and her father's intuition for adventure. She held out her hand. "I want to see it."

Skarpin lifted his chin in defiance. "Not until Saedeen shows the potion."

Saedeen was Lady Sorcha's niece. She had dazzling jade eyes, like Elladelle, but glowing ebony skin, like Sorcha. Her ringlet curls bounced as she plopped on the ground and crossed her legs. She dug into her brown leather satchel and pulled out a sparkling vial of silver potion.

The group gazed in awe. Their hopes and dreams were encapsulated in that small bottle of swirling, shimmering silver. Saedeen followed Lady Sorcha around her apothecary shop in the marketplace. She loved watching her aunt work, but Lady Sorcha encouraged her to stay at the school of magic and learn as much as she could. Once Madam Bip, the master of potions, took a special interest in Saedeen, her true Tethered powers began to unfold through potions.

Skarpin knelt beside Saedeen, pulling out an object hidden in his pocket. It was a small, hollow wooden ball with a hinge at the bottom and a tiny golden clasp at the top, which had a piece of twisted leather attached, forming a necklace for the smooth wooden sphere.

"Wow! It looks just like what Naedon drew," Wullen said as he knelt beside Skarpin, gathering more grass stains on his trousers.

Elladelle sat cross-legged beside Saedeen. "Speaking of my cousin, where is Naedon?"

"He said he had Roamer practice with the Red Phoenixes, but it should be over," Skarpin said.

"Ha! They better practice. Us Yellow Phoenixes are going to be even better this year." Wullen puffed out his chest, trying to impress the girls. He felt proud of their victory last year in Feydom, Elysium's famous game played during the Perdonair festival.

They heard panting, then the loud steps from Naedon. "I'm here. I'm here." He threw himself on the thick, lush grass between Wullen and Elladelle.

"Yuck. You're disgusting," Elladelle shrieked, pinching her nose for dramatic effect.

"I came straight from practice, Ells."

Saedeen shook her head as she looked at the pitiful sight of Naedon's freshly formed black eye. "Naedon, what happened?"

Naedon gently pressed the blackening, puffy eye. "Oh, ugh. I dove and hit a teammate's elbow." Naedon was skinny, dark-haired, and missing a front tooth. He was also one of the fastest boys in the school. According to Saedeen's diary, she described him as cute—very cute, in fact. He was Lord Jdru's son, or as Lord Char liked to remind everyone, his nephew.

They paused as the school bells chimed, signaling dinner.

"Okay, we don't have a lot of time. We need to do this now," Elladelle advised. She was also bright and very much enjoyed taking charge—something that maybe ran in the family.

Saedeen shook the vial; silver churned and glistened in the remaining sunlight. "We said we would test Naedon's powers first since his are the most complex."

Naedon moaned. "I don't know. I'm not really feeling up to it with this eye. Can someone else try?"

Elladelle raised her hand quickly. "I'll do it!"

Wullen rolled his eyes and glanced at Skarpin, who chuckled. Elladelle pulled petals from her satchel, which included daisies, lilies, and roses. She gently placed each one inside the ball, clicked it shut with the clasp, and handed it to Saedeen.

Saedeen concentrated, focusing on her lessons in Madam Bip's classroom. She uncorked the bottle, and a dazzling aroma of fresh rain and baked apples filled the air. As she poured the silver, swirling liquid onto the wooden ball, she carefully recited the phrase she had practiced each day: "praesidio et sigillum."

They watched in wonder as the ball glowed bright white. Then, webs of shiny silver formed around it like a fortress. Saedeen blinked. Did it work? It would now be left for the ultimate test. She handed the necklace to Elladelle.

Elladelle stood with the rest of her classmates. She scooped the necklace around her neck and took a deep breath. She closed her eyes and clasped the ball with her small hand, readying herself. But before she could perform any magic, they heard the one voice they shouldn't.

"Well, now. What do we have here?" the school's headmistress said, or as everyone else knew her, Princess Siany—sister to Queen Sealyn.

Chapter 9

<u>22 Years Ago…</u>

Screams echoed from a small peasant home in Thrallen, the village outside Stoltland's capital. Wet nurses hurried with buckets of water and clean sheets. The day had finally arrived for the blacksmith's daughter to give birth. The only issue was the big rumor circulating about her pregnancy. It was said that Laeglarie had spent several weeks with her father in Stoltland's port city of Knarr, helping to repair Korpam ships. Once they returned, she was swiftly married to a carpenter. However, many claimed that Laeglarie had intimate relations with a Korpam sailor—she wouldn't have been the first.

She was soon a pregnant newlywed—but was it too soon? Today, the village gathered to find out. For the baby's eyes would reveal whether her child was a pure-blood Stoltlander or a mixed breed—a silver-eyed outcast.

Jace had waited nine long months to see what would happen. He snuck beneath one of the military wagons and hid as the guards dispersed in front of the house. Jace pulled an ebony hood over his face, and because he was small, no one noticed him as he moved through the crowd. He heard Laeglarie cry out again.

Laeglarie had long, auburn hair styled in four braids. She had freckles across her nose and cheeks. Her lips were pink, and she always wore a sad expression on her gentle face. Jace had visited her numerous times, bringing her food and flowers when the village had shunned her. He hoped her baby wouldn't have his silver eyes for her sake.

He crept around the back of the worn, one-room house and peered through the thick vegetation hiding the cloudy window. He saw several women gathered around a small bed. Laeglarie's husband and father were in the corner, talking. Jace could only see Laeglarie's legs, nothing more. She screamed again. He winced and covered his ears.

He heard a woman yell, "Push!" More yelling and grunts were heard. Jace felt like it took an eternity, but finally, he heard a baby crying. He immediately looked through the window, nose pressed hard against the glass.

"It's a boy! Laeglarie, it's a boy," a woman said.

"Let me hold him," Laeglarie stretched out her empty arms.

Stoltland soldiers burst through the door, demanding to see the child.

"No, no, please! Let me hold him first." A guard grabbed the baby from the woman. "No! I need to hold him. Please," Laeglarie begged, tears flowing down her freckled, sweaty cheeks.

As the newborn cried, another soldier opened the baby's eyes. "Silver," he growled.

"Nooooo!" Laeglarie cried out. "Please don't! Don't! Let me hold him! He's my baby!"

The guards stomped to the rickety kitchen table, stripped the baby of the bloody linens, and raised a black sword.

Laeglarie screamed for mercy. "Stop! Please! He's my baby! He's innocent! Don't. Please, I'll do anything— anything. Stop." She kept begging.

"By Stoltland law, all babies born of silver eyes are sentenced to die. I am oath-bound to uphold the law. This monster is sentenced to death." He slammed his sword through the baby's heart. Blood dripped from under the table. Laeglarie sucked in a breath, grabbing her chest, and couldn't make a sound. Tears flowed as she painfully crawled onto the floor in her crimson-stained nightgown. She hoisted herself up, hands shaking around her child, turning ashen. Jace heard ringing in his ears.

Moans of grief, rage, and horror bellowed from deep within Laeglarie, but her silver-eyed baby remained silent as the grave. Jace couldn't bear to look any longer. He turned away and sank into the dirt, pulling his knees to his chest, crying silently.

A tiny whisper escaped his thoughts, "That was supposed to be me."

Chapter 10

<u>Secret Mission</u>

Princess Siany, clad in a pale mint dress with sheer purple sleeves, folded her arms across her chest. She hated that her nieces and nephews were involved in this matter, but she needed to distance herself from the appearance of favoritism. She stood tall over the students, waiting for their response.

"We, uh, well. We meant no, uh," Wullen stumbled over words, unable to form proper sentences. He looked to Elladelle for help.

"Um, Aunt Siany. Oops. I mean Headmistress. We were just practicing. We want to be ready for Queen Sealyn and King Jace's return."

Siany sensed something else was happening but honestly didn't have the time for this. "I'll accept that. You five must hurry to dinner, and remember, no late nights tonight. Tomorrow is a big day."

The children sprinted through the castle's side door, leaving Siany alone. She quickly walked down the courtyard path toward the school gardens. She paused before the mermaid fountain and spun when she heard his voice.

"Good evening, Princess Siany."

"Good evening, Lord Jashun." Siany placed her hands on her hips. She hated sneaking around, but this was what her life had become. "What did you find out?"

Jashun gave Siany an exasperated look, shook his finger at her, and then extended his hand. Siany exhaled loudly, and Jashun raised his eyebrows, challenging her not to comply. Siany huffed and rummaged in her skirt pocket. She pulled out a plump brown coin bag and dropped it into Jashun's hand, its contents clinking loudly. She folded her arms, rocked on her heels, and scanned the garden. She felt her nerves tighten at every sound.

"There's no records," Jashun said haphazardly, looking inside the bag.

"What?" Siany hissed. "That can't be true. There has to be."

"If there is, then they would only exist in Stoltland." Jashun hoped Siany wouldn't press the issue, but he wasn't sure what Siany was capable of anymore. Jashun's wavy raven hair had grown longer since Queen Sealyn's return from Shunal. He had cinnamon skin and a sharp jawline. He had been practicing more sword skills, which was evident in his more defined muscles. Jashun disliked the lengthy pause as

Siany considered her next moves. He was eager to return to his home. He hoped that Kailani, the mermaid princess, would return tonight; however, she had not been seen since her last meeting with Sealyn.

Siany paced back and forth; pebbles crunched under her shoes. She couldn't believe this news. "There must be a mistake. Shunal has all the records. That's why the capital has a building called the House of Records. Every kingdom is supposed to turn in its census each year."

"Yes, but since when did Stoltland follow the rules?" Jashun rolled his eyes.

"Or does it mean something deeper?" Siany looked like she was on the verge of a great discovery.

"Siany, I don't think you should look for something that isn't there." Jashun really wanted to go home. He didn't want his mermaid to return to an empty house.

"Look, Jashun. I need answers. Our entire kingdom and the whole point of Sealyn's crusade could depend on this."

"What else do you want me to do?" He raised his hands in annoyance.

"Ughhhh. This is incredibly frustrating," Siany continued, pacing. "Okay. Let's think this out. If Shunal doesn't have his records, yet all the other children born that year are accounted for, then we need to ask other questions: who else is missing? Is he the only one? If he's not, then who else are they hiding? Who else didn't they want us to know about?"

"Or perhaps the others are dead?"

Siany stopped. "What? Why would you say that?"

Jashun sat on the edge of the fountain, avoiding any splashes. "C'mon, Siany. Don't make me say it." When Siany didn't respond, Jashun sighed and said, "They were marked as monsters, outcasts, detestables…they were marked dead as soon as they were born."

"But we know that can't be true because…"

"Because *he* is alive; yes, I know." Jashun stood and closed the distance between him and the princess. "What if she faked his death? What if she made a deal for him to stay alive? Could Corentine not be the horrible monster we all think she is since…"

Siany interrupted, "Since Jace wasn't killed at birth? So, if the red-haired witch saved her silver-eyed son, why hide his birth from the world? And Stoltland killed silver-eyed babies by law, so how did she manage to keep him alive— what price did she pay?"

"Maybe she didn't pay it—maybe Jace did."

Sadeen note: Add pig grease to potion for Naedon's
Leather straps
Metal loop attachment
discard for Naedon
Wooden sphere
Tethered elements placed inside sphere then tighly closed with clasp
$V = \frac{4}{3}\pi r^3$
Naedon necklace: his wooden sphere must be painted with dragon scale paste

Chapter 11

<u>We Did It</u>

Elladelle fidgeted with her long braids while pretending to be asleep. She couldn't believe she was actually about to break school rules. If her mother found out… she shut her eyes tight. She didn't want to think about that. The necklace still dangled around her neck, but she was too scared to touch it.

Tiny taps sounded at the window near her bunk. Saedeen's head appeared from above, wrapped in a green and gold cloth. Saedeen and Elladelle chose bunk beds together on the first day of school. They were instant friends.

"You heard that, right?" Saedeen whispered.

"Yes. That has to be Skarpin's stone tapping the window."

Saedeen threw back her basil-colored quilt and hurried down the wooden ladder as quietly as possible. Her bare, ebony feet touched the cool, wooden floor. She instantly regretted her choice not to wear socks. She crouched beside Elladelle. "That's the signal. The boys are waiting for us."

The girls slipped on their fuzzy emerald robes and socks. They carried their shoes, afraid to make a sound. They tiptoed across their dormitory room, which, lucky for them, was covered in soft, cozy rugs. The door creaked slightly. They paused and looked back, making sure none of their classmates woke.

Saedeen quietly closed the door behind them and then darted down the winding stone staircase. They paused when they reached the common chamber they shared with the boys, all of whom were Tethereds. Headmistress Siany believed it was best for those with the same magical powers to live in the same quarters, which had turned out beautifully. Elladelle was tethered to plants, primarily her favorite flowers, while Saedeen was also tethered to plants; her powers favored herbs. Together, they had already created perfumes and soaps with relaxing properties for class projects. Now, they had a different project in mind.

"Pssst," a sound echoed through the dark room.

Saedeen and Elladelle jumped and turned their heads toward the large tapestry depicting a unicorn grazing in the grass.

"Pssst. Ells and Saedeen. Over here," the voice said.

The girls ran to the tapestry and lifted it. To their surprise, Naedon was hiding behind a tiny stone door.

"What took you girls so long?" Naedon huffed.

Saedeen folded her arms. "Maybe if you boys would stop hiding things, then we wouldn't need you to wait on us."

"Yeah! How long have you known about this secret passageway?" Elladelle scolded her cousin.

"It's not my fault. Wullen didn't…"

"Wullen didn't what?" Saedeen interrupted. "Didn't want us girls to know?"

Elladelle pushed the door open further. "This is not over, cousin. Blood comes first. Isn't that what your dad says?"

"I just wanted to fit in, Ells. We already have targets on our back."

Saedeen felt sorry for Elladelle and Naedon. They were directly linked to Queen Sealyn, making them like celebrities at school. Everyone scrutinized their every move. Some kids even went so far as to tease and taunt them, hoping to see them slip up. She understood Naedon's desire to blend in.

"Ok, Naedon. I forgive you, but only if you sneak us some of Baker Nicht's Chocolate Jabbles."

Naedon smiled with his missing tooth smile. "Deal. Let's hurry."

The three Elysian children crawled through the old, dirty tunnel. Glowing lenettes lit up their path. According to Naedon, the boys catch lenettes in jars and release them in the tunnel when they want to travel through it.

"Hang on," Naedon said.

"Hang on to what?" Elladelle replied.

"We have a few slides to go down. Don't be scared. It's fun!"

Naedon happily turned his body and, feet first, slid down the stone passage, bringing a sense of adventure. Elladelle and Saedeen eagerly followed Naedon, finding joy in breaking the rules just a bit. Saedeen, filled with delight, couldn't help but let out a soft giggle as she zipped down the tunnel. Bursting with wonder and excitement, the three landed with a gentle thud in a small chamber.

Elladelle frantically scanned the multiple exits. Panic began to rise. "Which one do we choose?" She asked, fearing she would be lost in the walls forever.

"Relax. We marked them. See…" Naedon pointed to the white paint above the openings. "This 'L' means lobby, but this 'S' means storage closet, which is the one we want."

"What about the rest?" Saedeen asked.

"We don't have time for that, but I promise we can come back, and I'll show you."

Saedeen and Elladelle shared a nod, trailing behind Naedon as they ventured through the shadowy opening. After a bit more crawling and another slide, the group finally arrived at the storage room door, which let out a weary groan upon being opened. They entered a dusty space brimming with brooms, buckets, shovels, mops, and rakes. Naedon positioned himself in front of the exit door, gently tapping it four times before pausing to wait.

Once they heard four more taps, Naedon opened the door to the outside grounds, where Wullen and Skarpin greeted them.

Saedeen smacked Wullen's arm. "Owww. What'd you do that for?"

"That was for not telling us about the secret tunnels."

"Oh, come off it, Saedeen. It's not like you don't have your secrets." He eyed her like he already knew. Saedeen froze. He couldn't know, could he?

Skarpin raised his tiny hand. "Easy. We're all friends. Let's hurry up before we get caught."

"Skarpin's right. Get to the greenhouse quick!" Elladelle ordered, with adrenaline pumping through her words.

The girls slipped on their shoes, and everyone sprinted across the cool, lush grass, the thrill of adventure sparking in the air. They raced excitedly around the winding pathways of the vegetable garden before bursting through the large door to the greenhouse. The greenhouse's windows, slightly tinted mildew green from neglect, hinted at the wonders that lay within. Inside, rows upon rows of foreign plants filled the room, showcasing all kinds of extraordinary vegetation from every kingdom. Fruits the children had never encountered before dangled enticingly from vibrant vines and flourishing bushes. Naedon, brimming with curiosity, reached out to pluck the dark lavender fruit speckled with quirky white spots, but Elladelle smacked his hand away just in time.

"Hey! That hurt."

"Don't eat anything in here. We don't know what's poisonous." Elladelle scolded.

"Can we hurry up? These plants are creeping me out," Wullen said, watching a shimmering gold vine slither around his feet.

"That is a Snakevine from Shunal. Harmless unless it feels threatened," Saedeen informed, wiggling her eyebrows at Wullen.

Wullen swallowed hard, sweat beads forming under his arms. He prayed the plant felt safe because death by vine was not how he wanted to go. Elladelle pulled the necklace from beneath her coat, glanced at her classmates, and let out a long breath.

"Okay, here goes nothing." Elladelle seized the wooden sphere with her left hand, lifting her right hand high. As she concentrated on the petals, she gently closed her innocent jade eyes. Electric tingles danced across her fingertips, igniting tiny, fluorescent green sparks. A gasp of pure excitement escaped Saedeen, echoing the magic unfolding around them.

"Elladelle, open your eyes!"

Elladelle's mouth dropped open at the beautiful, enchanting sight. Colorful flower petals rained from the ceiling, blanketing the dark earth. She giggled as she watched her friends leap around, trying to catch the petals. She twisted her hand in a circle, causing the sweet-scented petals to swirl. She spun her hand faster, and the magical petals whirled around them.

"We did it! We did it!" Skarpin cheered. He couldn't believe what they had invented. They had discovered a way to be mobile Tethereds. Elladelle had placed three types of petals inside the necklace, and now, all three danced around them. Tethereds would no longer be restricted to staying in one place or connecting with just one plant at a time. This was monumental.

Elladelle placed her hand on the dirt, and instantly, yellow daisies, bright white lilies, and deep red roses sprang forth. She blinked in amazement; she had never been able to grow a full plant before. She couldn't wait to tell her mom. Elladelle released the sphere and watched the petals fall. She smiled. This is what success feels like.

"Now, the next step," Wullen said. "We need to make necklaces for the rest of us. Skarpin, you're on the wooden sphere duty. Saedeen, you have to get more potion. I'll get more leather straps from my brother. Elladelle and Naedon, you two must find out when the king and queen will arrive."

Suddenly, they heard footsteps and crouched down low, their hearts racing with anticipation. They crawled to a shadowy corner where they could peer through the misty glass windows. Naedon wiped away the fogged surface, revealing a scene that made his stomach turn. He saw his Aunt Siany; technically, the princess was his first cousin, but the family, being as close as they were, regarded each other less formally. His eyes widened as he watched Siany exiting the flower gardens, her expression unreadable, followed by Lord Jashun, who was sprinting away into the darkness. What could possibly bring them together in such a secretive way at this hour?

Chapter 12

<u>Tavern Brawl</u>

The sky grew darker, and rain started to pour over Avondelle's Market, slicking the cobblestone streets with water. Char and Sakul shook off their hooded, evergreen cloaks as they entered Liquid Courage, the local tavern. Char nodded to Barm, the bartender, who prepared two cold, foaming ales and set them in front of them. The two friends sat at the bar, relieved that nothing was trying to eat them them—finally.

They clinked their silver tankards and savored the smooth, refreshing liquid. Char glanced around his establishment, still amazed that Sealyn had followed through on her deal with him. Before they set off for the second Shunalian quest, Sealyn had agreed that if Char accompanied them, she would buy Liquid Courage for him—and she certainly did. He noticed numerous people gathered at his wooden tables, drinking ales and laughing. He felt a warm sense of belonging, and everything felt just right.

Deer antler chandeliers hung from the tavern ceiling, and two large, gray stone fireplaces occupied opposite corners, crackling almost in sync with the pub's musicians. He took pride in it. This tranquil moment was exactly what he needed after their return from battling Korpam. He listened to the rain and inhaled the damp scent.

Sakul nudged Char, nodding his head to the left. Sakul was a tall, bald man with smooth, ebony skin. He had been training as a civilian warrior, and his physique appeared much fitter than usual; even his cheeks were no longer their usual round shape but had slimmed down.

Char noticed the table Sakul was worried about. To their left, enjoying themselves were Lord Brehan, Lord Ajorn, Lord Doebromir, Lord Jashun, and the one Sakul didn't want to see—Lord Sune. Sune had been part of the crew kidnapped and imprisoned by Stoltland sailors. Sakul's love, Lady Sorcha, had also been among that kidnapped crew. She and Sakul had been madly in love before their quest to break Len Nove's curse, but once she was rescued, her feelings waned, leaving her confused—all because of Lord Sune.

Sune had beautiful, thick curls of red hair and a well-groomed beard. He was a fierce warrior, having trained at the same camp as Queen Sealyn. Although several ladies had shown interest, his heart was devoted to Lady Sorcha.

Sakul took another sip of ale and grunted. "I can't believe I have to share my favorite hang-out spots with him. Can't you like banish him from your pub or something?"

Char both hated and loved drama, but today, he was simply tired and genuinely didn't have the energy to deal with it. "Just forget about him. Let's drink our ales, and then we can grab some food at Mimby's Morsels." Char wanted a quiet evening; he had earned it, and nothing was going to stand in the way of that peace.

Barm slid the *Elysian News* parchment in front of Char. He tapped the front page. Char looked down and read:

Who will win Lady Sorcha's Heart?

Too Sune to tell

Greetings, my fellow Elysians.

Your Lina here, ready to spill all the blushing details of Lady Sorcha's heart.

Sakul laid his head on his arms and let out a loud sound of frustration. Char downed his drink and pointed for more. Barm filled it up, patting Sakul's bald head. Char sighed, "Okay, so maybe having your personal life splattered across the front page is bad."

Sakul lifted his head. "Bad? You think that's bad?" He grabbed the paper and shook it. "This is horrific!"

Barm made a face at Char before quickly moving on to attend to others. Char nodded his head and looked to another table, hoping someone else could help. He spotted Commander Tilmond, Lord Max, and Lord Finn sitting together and felt a wave of relief. If nothing else, the commander could diffuse any potential fights.

In strode a drenched Lord Jem, along with Lord Favien and Lord Graegory, ushering in the demise of Char's tranquility. Commander Tilmond rose, and the atmosphere in the room froze. It felt as if the very air of the tavern had been inhaled, leaving a suffocating silence. Char shifted his gaze between Tilmond and Jem, his mind racing with confusion. What was unfolding?

Jem bowed his head in greeting. "Commander Tilmond, good to see you."

Tilmond snarled. "Look at my cousin, our queen. *That* way again, and I'll…"

Jem raised his chin. "And you'll what? Kill me for admiring?"

Tilmond slammed his silver tankard down, splashing its contents onto the wooden table. Char winced as he calculated in his head how much a tankard cost. Wow, being an owner had definitely changed his thought process.

Tilmond pointed his finger at Jem. "I'm ordering you to keep your red fox eyes off Queen Sealyn."

"Forgive me, Commander, but there's no law against looking," Jem smirked, showing off his dimples.

Commander Tilmond, towering a full foot above everyone in the room, strode purposefully toward Jem. Max and Finn stood firm, their hands pressing against Tilmond's chest, bracing him back as tension filled the air. Char chugged his ale and pointed for more again, brimming with irritation. He glanced to his left and noticed the other lords, including Sune, also standing. Sune and Sakul locked eyes in an intense standoff. With a groan, Char dropped his head back and looked at the ceiling.

"Ah well, this isn't good," Char said to no one in particular.

Finn pushed Tilmond backward. "Commander, he's not worth it."

This angered Favien. He recalled how his comrades had abandoned him, Sakul, and Herbmando in the maze during the Shunalian quest. He felt as though his life was over, and no one returned for them. Favien stepped in front of Jem and asked, "What about my life, Finn? Is my life worth it?"

"What in all Creation are you talking about, Favien?" Finn was honestly confused.

"I'm talking about you and everyone else on that mission, leaving me for dead."

Max chimed in, "How was that our fault? If you want to blame someone, blame that psycho king who put us in there."

Graegory huffed. "Of course, a dragon lover would say that." He folded his arms, his almond-shaped eyes narrowed.

"What did you call me?" Max demanded.

Char pulled his tankard from Barm before he could finish filling it and drained the contents.

"You're a dragon lover, just like your wife!" Graegory yelled, pointing his finger.

Max threw his chair back in frustration. "That's it!" He leaped over an empty chair and swung at Graegory, landing a punch on his cheek. Chaos erupted almost immediately. Graegory yelled and charged at Max, tackling him to the stone floor and fiercely pummeling his face.

Favien hurled his drenched cloak at Finn, then landed a punch on his nose. Jem flipped the table, scattering plates and drinks across the ground. He pinned Tilmond against the wall as both retaliated, shoving against one another.

"Hey! Stop! Break this up at once," Char yelled. "Those plates are expensive!"

No one heard him. They kept punching, kicking, and throwing each other against walls and tables. The other lords in the corner rushed to help break up the fights, but Sune bumped into Sakul's back, and that was all it took. Sakul turned and jumped on top of Sune, and both fell to the ground. Sakul unleashed punch after punch; then, he felt a hard kick to his side from Ajorn. Sakul skidded across the floor, gasping from the pain. Ajorn and Sune loomed over Sakul, ready for round two.

"What do we do, Char?" Barm panicked.

"Port."

"What?"

"Port. We switch to port. I'll take that bottle over there."

Barm, in his innocence, thought Char would use this as a distraction weapon, having witnessed countless fights involving broken bottles swinging overhead. However, embodying all of Char's essence, he popped the cork and downed its contents instead. So much for his quiet night.

Suddenly, the door burst open, carrying gusts of wind and the sweet scent of the sea. Jashun gasped. The mermaid princess stood confidently in a skin-tight, silver-scaled dress that showcased her luscious curves. Her eyes blazed pink, and in her hands, she held spheres of water. She shot streams of rainwater at each warrior, encircling their necks like deadly tentacles. Barm watched in horror as the mermaid choked the warriors

"Enough!" the mermaid princess commanded, her wet pink hair clinging tightly to her neck and cheeks. She released their watery chains, sending splashes onto the stone floor. Everyone gasped for breath air.

Char clapped and wobbled. "Well done, Princess Kailani! Would you and your friends care to join me for a drink?"

"Uh, Char," Kailani tilted her head; water dripped from her nose. "It's just me."

"Oh. Ha! Well, I've had too much port then," Char turned to the bloodied and bruised warriors. "You rats owe me for all the damages-es-es that you caused." Char slurred his words.

Kailani giggled, having missed Char's wit. Her shoes splashed over her puddles of water and grabbed Jashun's shirt. "And as for you, you have some explaining to do."

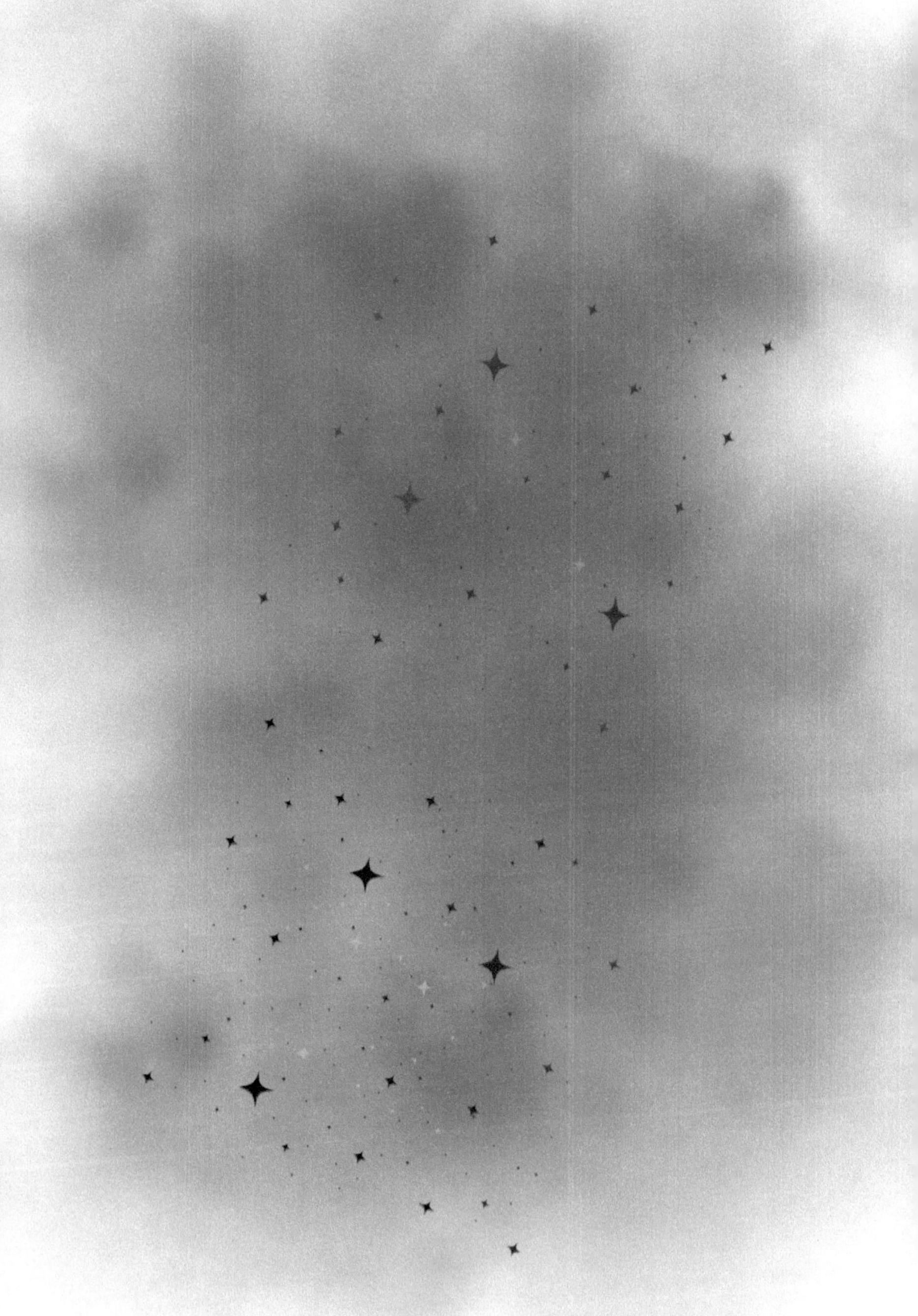

Chapter 13

<u>22 Years Ago...</u>

All the Stoltland royals had bed chambers in the upper eastern rooms of the castle, but Jace's bedroom was situated above the kitchens on the western side. He didn't mind this except on days when the cook burned something, which happened more often than not. His room was a pitiful affair, consisting only of the bare essentials: a thin bed, a rickety table and chair, and a crooked shelf he had built himself out of scrap wood.

As he lay patiently on his hay mattress, he read another page of *The Pirate and the Sea Monster*, wishing for a more adventurous life beyond these walls. It was one of his favorite books. The pirate in the story is a banished Stoltlander who is wrongfully accused. He sets sail to prove his worth by defeating the sea monster that continues to destroy all the port cities. Jace often dreamed of being a pirate's shipmate and going on the wildest adventures he could imagine.

Finally, he heard footsteps. He hurriedly lifted the blanket and stuffed the book into the hay, desperate to keep its presence a secret from everyone who entered his room.

Without warning, the door swung open, and Lady Corentine stepped in, her flaming red hair billowing from the gust of wind. "Good morning, my son. Doctor Olkin is here to see you."

Jace tried not to groan as the skinny figure appeared. Doctor Olkin resembled a skeleton draped in black attire. He wore spectacles that accentuated his piercing, inky eyes. His skin was so pale that it almost appeared blue. Jace always had to make sure he didn't inhale around Olkin because his breath stunk of old coffee, and his clothes carried the scent of mildew and urine.

Olkin dragged Jace's only chair to the bed, scraping its legs against the stone floor. Jace heard Olkin's joints crack as he sat down. The doctor rummaged through his black leather bag, pulling out a needle and a small, empty glass vial. He took hold of Jace's hand and pricked his finger; blood began to ooze out.

Jace sniffed and glanced at his mother. She shook her head. He turned back to watch his blood drip into the vial that Olkin held under his finger. Deep red blood with silver flakes slid down the sides of the bottle. Olkin stood and shuffled to the table, setting the vial down and pulling out more bottles from his bag. Jace peered curiously around his mother's majestic ebony-scaled dress. His eyes widened as he watched the doctor carefully pour shiny, deep plum droplets into his blood vial. The blood hissed mysteriously, and enchanting swirls of purple smoke danced above the bottle. Jace couldn't help but wonder if he smelled a hint of sweet sugar in the air.

Olkin glanced back at Jace and squinted before refocusing on a golden liquid potion. He tilted the bottle, letting a single droplet fall into the darkened blood. As the brilliant golden drop joined the shadowy liquid, a puff of dark smoke burst from the bottle, transforming the liquid in the small vial into a vibrant orange and making it whirl in mesmerizing circles.

The doctor shot a side-eye at Corentine. She glared back, challenging him to say anything. Olkin coughed and pulled out one last bottle filled with a shimmering white, milky liquid. He poured the orange blood into the white mixture. Bright sparks flew from the bottle. Olkin dropped it, and it crashed to the floor, exposing Stoltland's fear: the liquid had thickened and transformed into silver blood.

Corentine and Olkin jerked their heads toward Jace. Jace's heart sped. He didn't know what this meant.

"It must be today. You can wait no more," Olkin's raspy voice whispered into Corentine's ear.

"I know what must be done," Corentine pulled away from Olkin. She walked to Jace and stretched out her hand. Jace hesitantly took it. "Jace, you're sick. Doctor Olkin will fix you, but we must go to his…um…headquarters."

Olkin snickered. Jace glared. What was happening? When someone was sick, no one said to fix it. People said they would make you better. What was being fixed? Were they able to change his eyes? His heart raced with excitement. Jace jumped off the bed, ready to go on an adventure. He would be as brave as the pirate in his book and might even be cured of his silver-eyed plague.

After a long wagon ride into the dark woods, the three of them came upon a cave that seemed to whisper warnings. Fear crawled over Jace's skin like ants, each minute more daunting than the last. He hesitated, unwilling to step inside, but his mother's grip was firm as she gently urged him forward. Olkin struck a match, and the wick of a lantern sputtered to life, casting flickering shadows down the dark tunnel of the cave. The air was thick with anticipation. Finally, Olkin stomped his feet, and suddenly, fireflowers erupted in brilliant hues, illuminating the vast cavern before them. Shelves lined the walls like sentinels of forgotten tales, filled with bottles of potions, strange cooking tools, ancient books, and even bones that seemed to hold evil secrets of the past.

A stone table jutted out in the middle of the cavern. Olkin patted it for Jace to sit on. The frail doctor handed Jace a vial of black liquid. Jace didn't want to drink it, but his mother forced him to swallow every drop. Almost immediately, Jace felt a wave of fatigue wash over him. His eyelids fluttered, and then he passed out.

Jace didn't know how long he had been passed out. His hearing came back first, but he couldn't move, couldn't feel anything, and couldn't make a sound. Fear bubbled within him as he tried not to panic, focusing instead on the muffled voices around him.

"When will we know if it worked? Corentine asked.

"A month. We must wait a month. We do the same potion testing I've been doing since he was a baby. All we need is just one more test—that's it."

"Just the purple, gold, and white potions—the ones right here on the shelf?" Corentine pointed to his colorful potion display.

"Correct. This will be enough time for the chains to block all the power."

"Power? You act like he could potentially wield magic now."

Olkin sighed. "Lady Corentine, I simply do *not* have all the answers. Normally, grey eyes cannot wield magic because they are not permitted to live, but in theory, if curses are broken, then they can unleash magic as we've never seen. We also must face the scary unknown: what if they can wield magic without curses being broken? Regardless, they will be the monsters from the storybooks, monsters from our nightmares."

"Don't call my son a monster!"

"Forgive me, my lady. We just don't have a history of silver ones. The Second Chance hid so many of our history books and scrolls. All the knowledge we need cannot be seen—only the one who fulfills the prophecy can reveal what was lost."

Corentine scoffed. "The prophecy. I'm sick of prophecies. I think I can decide my own fate."

"What are you saying?"

"One day, I will conquer the seven kingdoms, and then, I will unleash my son upon the world."

Olkin gasped, "You. You used me!"

"And now, I'm done with you."

Jace heard a blade slice through the air, followed by a slash of flesh. He heard Olkin choking, then a thud. His mother's heels clicked against the stone floor. He heard bottles being dropped into what he assumed was a satchel. Corentine's footsteps returned next to Jace. His eyes remained shut. He still couldn't feel anything, nor did he want to wake and witness the horror his mother had unleashed on the doctor.

"Come, my sweet boy. I'll take you home, away from this filth."

After hours of listening to the forest birds and the banging of wagon wheels on the uneven roads, Jace heard the bustle of the palace kitchen and knew he was back in his bedroom. He desired peace, but the excruciating pain in his wrists made it impossible. He attempted to move, but the restraints pinned him down. He yelled out in agony.

Guards and servants were in his room, attempting to calm him, with no pity evident in their cold expressions. He opened his silver eyes, tears streaming down his face. Glancing at his wrists, he saw they were swollen and red, with stitches encircling them. What happened to him? What had Olkin done to him?

His mother sat beside him, laying a hand on his sweaty chest. "Jace, listen carefully. We had to insert magic into your wrists to fix you. Don't worry; with time, you'll barely feel the magic bands. They're very thin. You'll have scars, but that's it, my darling." She kissed his feverish brow and whispered harshly, "Who here always protects you?"

Jace whimpered, "You, Mother."

The evil red-head grinned. "Who will *you* pledge yourself to because no one else cares for you?"

"You, Mother."

"Do you solemnly swear always to be faithful and duty-bound to me?"

"Yes, Mother. Always." Jace felt his throat sting.

Corentine stood, satisfied. "Now, sleep and stop screaming."

Elladelle Araelien

Tethered Magic

Luxens can only tether to nature (minus creatures) if they accept the magic. Some will never open their magical abilities  because of fear.

Each Tethered has a unique ability given by nature's choice.

So far, the scariest Tethered is Naedon. He's tethered to fire. Extremely hard to control.

Remember to ask Saedeen about Naedon's potion. Don't forget Wuller has Feydom practice before the Red Phoenixes.

Chapter 14

<u>The Demonstration</u>

Sealyn rubbed her temples, nursing another headache. She tried to listen to her father reprimanding those involved in the tavern brawl, but her head throbbed. She knew her father would say everything right, as he always did. Oddly, Sealyn found she didn't care much about the brawl. She was increasingly indifferent to her people's daily issues. Still, she pondered the recurring nightmare, wondering if that dream would ever end. Why did she see the Pirate Captain's face on a hill surrounded by bloody corpses? She was losing the battle of her mind; this wasn't good.

"This is embarrassing!" King Father Ryker yelled again. He hated it when his military acted shamefully. He believed this reflected poorly on his family's leadership, which weighed heavily on his heart. Where had he gone wrong? What more could he do?

In the throne room, all the soldiers' heads hung low as they knelt before King Father Ryker, King Jace, and Queen

Sealyn. Their faces were bruised, swollen, and bloody, reflecting the disunity of their force. How were they supposed to fight side by side with comrades they held such disdain for?

"Those horse stalls better be shining by daybreak!" Ryker said, pointing his finger.

Sealyn stood, irritated. "Okay, so are we done?"

Jace looked confused at Sealyn. Ryker's brow furrowed at her rude question. "We can be done." He nodded to his daughter. This was a tone he had not experienced with Sealyn before.

Sealyn clapped her hands together. "Excellent. Now that you fools are finished airing your insecurities, we have work to do. I need the Glatania quest to go flawlessly. The Glatanians are full of trickery. This won't be easy."

The soldiers agreed and nodded their heads. They were in no position to question anything right now.

"Good. Right now, we need to attend a school ceremony, so while we're there, you all will be mucking out the stalls. We will have a grand dinner tonight to discuss the quest. If any of you show up smelling like horse manure, then I will have you decapitated."

The room gasped.

"Sealyn!" Ryker hissed.

"Just kidding." She smiled a little too wide, then dropped her positive expression and narrowed her eyes. "But seriously, don't come smelly." Sealyn walked down the throne steps and exited without glancing back.

Jace and Ryker looked at one another.

"Is she okay?" Ryker asked in a hushed voice.

"Part of me wants to say that's Sealyn still being Sealyn, but the other part is saying that sounded like she was pretending to be herself, and she really messed it up.

"I agree with your second theory." Ryker scratched his thinning hair. "Let's deal with that after the ceremony. We're late." Ryker turned to the soldiers, still kneeling. "What are you all still doing here? Get to those stalls!"

The soldiers jumped up and ran out of the throne room.

Jace chuckled. "You know we hadn't dismissed them; that's why they were still kneeling."

Ryker smiled. "I know. Sometimes, you must have a little fun, son."

In the spacious dining hall of Bracken Castle, the Luxen magic school, the teachers had cleared away the tables and arranged the room with rows upon rows of chairs for the students. At the far end, on a raised platform, sat the royal family and the teachers. Skarpin waved to Sealyn, and she couldn't help but wave back. Skarpin certainly had her heart.

They were very impressed with the students. So far, they had witnessed a young girl channel a lenette, sprouting vibrant orange wings while her entire body glowed with ethereal light. Another Transference showcased his talents by channeling a chameleon, effortlessly blending into the floor as if he were part of it. Two teenagers who were Tethereds conjured ice, creating a whimsical snowstorm and forming a shimmering ice bridge that sparkled in the light. The final performance featured a young boy named Taelson, who enchanted everyone with his control over a coffee bean. He crafted Sealyn the most delectable cup of coffee she had ever savored, leaving Madam Bip utterly baffled by his skill. They made a note to have Sir Nijeel mentor Taelson, anticipating great things to come.

Headmistress Siany began her speech with thanks and congratulations, but Skarpin's crew couldn't pay attention. He leaned forward, signaling to his friends. They were going to perform their magic without anyone noticing it was them.

Skarpin and Wullen went first. They collaborated, constructing a gazebo right in front of the royals. Skarpin had stones and a piece of marble in his sphere, while Wullen had sand and dirt. Gasps and whispers reverberated throughout the large room, filled with confusion. As the boys shaped stones and built the platform, columns, and benches, Saedeen held everything together with her sticky, glue-like potion. Inside her sphere was a substance that helped bond the stones together.

"What is the meaning of this?" Princess Siany asked loudly. She hated being in the dark about what was happening. As the one in charge of the school, this situation reflected poorly on her. She needed to regain control before the students revolted.

The children worked quietly from their seats, engrossed in their tasks, striving to prevent their fears from overshadowing their concentration. Skarpin conjured a stone firepit in front of the pavilion for Naedon. Once the structure was complete, Wullen sprinkled dirt around the base. At the same time, Elladelle adorned the soil with a vibrant tapestry of red, white, and yellow flowers, transforming the area into a scene of enchanting beauty.

"Who's responsible for this?" Siany asked even louder than before. Her palms started to sweat as her eyes flicked from student to student.

The grand finale of their enchanting project was Naedon. He had burned through countless necklaces in his practice. However, Saedeen had finally mastered a mesmerizing new potion for his sphere. Naedon clutched this special necklace tightly, and suddenly, brilliant flames danced within the firepit. A chorus of gasps and squeals filled the air, echoing through the room. Elladelle, unable to resist the call of magic, unleashed her powers again. She conjured a cascade of brightly colored petals that rained gracefully over everyone present, soothing their anxiousness. Students eagerly extended their hands, delighting in the fragrant petals as they floated down like gentle whispers of magic.

Sealyn stood up and walked to the front of the structure, stepping on flower petals as she went. She applauded the performance, and the others seated there followed.

"Now, will the ones responsible for such a feat come forward?" She asked with an even tone.

Slowly, Wullen, Saedeen, Elladelle, Naedon, and Skarpin stood up. Sealyn tilted her head, realizing her adopted son was part of something so incredible. She tried to suppress a smile, feeling proud. The five stepped in front of the gazebo and bowed.

"I'm impressed, and it takes a lot to impress me."

The children smiled broadly. Saedeen grasped her necklace, catching Sealyn's attention. Sealyn looked over all five and noticed the similarities. Her emerald eyes twitched.

"Headmistress, I would like to request a private audience with these five. We can use your office. Madam Bip, will you please escort these children to the headmistress office?"

"Right away, Majesty." The children followed Madam Bip out of the side exit of the great hall, leaving the rest of the students in awe.

Skarpin dangled his feet back and forth from the oversized chair in Princess Siany's office. He felt nervous but sensed that Sealyn wasn't mad at him. Madam Bip stood outside the room, letting the children chat freely.

Elladelle leaned to Naedon and whispered, "Do you think we're in trouble?"

Naedon shrugged. "I don't know. I hope not."

"Did you see Queen Sealyn?" Wullen asked. "She looked super happy."

"Yeah, I think we're going to be fine," Saedeen said.

The door swung open, and a furious Headmistress Siany strode in. "How dare you interrupt our ceremony!" She stomped behind her desk, cluttered with papers and books.

The children straightened, their eyes widening in surprise. This was unexpected. Queen Sealyn, King Jace, King

Father Ryker, Queen Mother Graelynd, and Madam Bip entered the room and closed the door behind them.

Siany continued, "That was incredibly rude and selfish. I'm guessing you five even snuck out after hours to practice." She lifted an eyebrow. "Well... did you?"

The kids looked at each other. Skarpin hung his head low and nodded.

"Ugh. I knew it. Sealyn, we can't praise this kind of behavior," Siany said.

Sealyn folded her arms and leaned against the wall. This was typical Siany, always the rule follower. Sealyn, however, liked to challenge the rules. She needed to tread lightly, though. She had given Siany full charge of this school, so if she undermined her authority, it could encourage bad behavior.

"How about we let these students explain themselves?" Sealyn proposed.

Madam Bip walked up to Saedeen and held the necklace in her hand. She examined every part of the sphere and sensed the magic pulsing around it. "Yes, I, for one, want ta know exactly what 'dis is."

"It was Skarpin's idea," Elladelle blurted.

"Ells!" Skarpin squeaked.

"I mean, it's not all Skarpin. Naedon drew it," Elladelle said, ignoring Naedon lifting his hands, feeling betrayed.

"Saedeen came up with the sealing potions. Wullen provided the leather." The two looked at each other in shock as their friend revealed their contributions. "I helped discuss the theories with Skarpin and organized everything, so I guess it was a team effort," Elladelle spoke quickly; her heart pounded. She decided it was better to confront the truth than to keep up with lies.

"But an effort for what? Are you sayin' 'dese necklaces helped you channel magic?" Madam Bip asked. Her lime green eyes sparkled with excitement.

"Yes," Elladelle said.

"So these are not just friendship trinkets?" Headmistress Araelien asked.

"Yuck! No way. I would never have a friendship trinket with girls," Wullen said, scrunching his face.

Jace laughed. "Someday, you might actually want to, Wullen. I did." He raised his hand, showcasing his wedding band, and wiggled his eyebrows at Sealyn. Sealyn smiled and glanced at his finger, but her eyes drifted to his wrists. Jace refused to discuss his scars. She didn't like that he had such a big secret. Why did he feel he couldn't confide in her?

Ryker placed his hands on his hips. "Skarpin, can you tell us about these necklaces?"

Skarpin's yellow eyes brimmed with tears. He was constantly haunted by the anxiety of failing and being sent back to Shunal, despite Sealyn's reassuring promise that she would never do that. Still, that fear clung to him, an innocent hope amidst uncertainty.

Jace noticed his tears and felt a tug at his heart. He stepped forward and knelt in front of him. "Easy there, little man. Remember, you're safe here. We just want to hear about this spectacular idea you had."

Skarpin smiled. He loved Jace so much; he was the best father he could ever hope for. "Well, I had overheard a story about Queen Sealyn's training. The one about her challenging the sword master to a treetop duel."

Sealyn laughed and interrupted, "Ah, yes, that was pretty funny."

"I'm not familiar with 'dis story," Madam said, cutting a mischievous smirk at Sealyn.

"Ryker, why don't you tell it?" Graelynd cooed. "You're so good at telling stories."

Ryker beamed. He felt like he grew five inches every time his wife complimented him. He cleared his throat, ready to entertain. "So as the story goes, Sealyn, princess at the time, was off at Fort Kippen. I had received word that Sealyn had staged a protest against sword fighting."

Madam Bip whirled around to face Sealyn. "You? Against sword fighting?"

"It's not what it seems," Sealyn chuckled and waved a hand in the air.

"I gathered several palace guards, and we made our way to Fort Kippen. Little did I realize that Sealyn had become exceptionally skilled with a blade, just not with the Swordmaster. When I arrived, I told the Swordmaster that I had received his letter about the protest; the only problem was—he hadn't sent the letter."

"Nooo. It was Sealyn, wasn't it?" Bip said, very locked into the story.

"It was her," Ryker continued. "She wanted me there to demonstrate her theory. With all military eyes focused on us, she challenged the Swordmaster. She began dueling flawlessly but finally chose to show us what we were missing. A large tree loomed over the training area, so she climbed up and walked out onto its thick branch. She called for the duel to continue on the branch. I was shocked he went up there, but he ultimately lost his sword, his balance, and his pride."

Sealyn pushed forward from the wall. "The theory was that in real-life battles, you don't always have perfect landscapes during combat, so why should we train only in those conditions? We need to practice in the toughest environments because we never know what challenges we will encounter."

"Brilliant, my queen," Madam Bip said, clapping rapidly.

"Thank you, but let's get back to Skarpin. Keep going, darling. Tell us how that story inspired you."

Skarpin's cheeks blushed. "It's the same with using magic, especially for Tethereds. We need to hold onto that plant or herb, but if we're on the run from a bad guy, how can we defend ourselves?"

Sealyn's heart ached. She hated that Skarpin would ever feel he had to defend himself against something evil. Growing up on the streets of Shunal, he had witnessed his fair share of horrors. The thought made Sealyn lose her concentration. Her left palm burned. She looked at it and watched the dark ebony veins moving like snakes. She felt the urge to return to Shunal and kill anyone who had wronged Skarpin. Fortunately, Skarpin's voice brought her back to reality.

"I thought, if we could have an object like a box and put what we channel into it, then maybe we could continue wielding magic on the move."

"Are you saying your necklace has stones in it?" Siany asked, taking notes as he spoke.

Skarpin nodded. "And a piece of marble. I just found out that I can tether to marble, too."

"But how is that possible with Naedon's powers?" Graelynd asked. She moved to stand behind him and placed her delicate hands on his small shoulders.

Saedeen sat a little taller. "That's where I came in. We needed a potion that could seal the sphere without harming it because he roasted quite a few wooden versions." She side-glanced at Naedon, dark curls bouncing, and giggled. "Ours were pretty simple, but since Naedon is tethered to fire, his was way more complicated. We tried tricking his ability with coals and ashes, but none of those worked."

Naedon folded his arms. "Yeah, my power only works with live fire." He grabbed his necklace and snapped his other fingers. Bright orange and yellow flames flickered in the palm of his hand. He smiled, then let go, and the fire vanished.

Leaning over her desk, Siany twirled her green-feathered quill in her hands, willing Naedon to finish his story. "Yes, we're well aware of your Tethered powers, but you can't be saying there's live fire inside that ball around your neck—can you?"

The air grew heavy with urgency. Unspoken plans filled the room, nearly suffocating the royals' minds. If this were true, they would have to act swiftly to conceal it.

"Well, yes. That's the only way I can wield fire. Saedeen created a special potion, just for me, for my sphere." He nudged Saedeen's arm and watched her look down as she fidgeted with her hands. Was she being shy? She smiled, and he thought he saw something in her eyes, but who was he kidding? That couldn't be right.

Jace turned his attention back to Skarpin. "And what could possibly keep fire alive in an enclosed space?" He knew his brilliant son had the answer.

Skarpin grinned. "Dragons," he said with a scary voice.

"Dragons!" Siany screeched. She looked at Sealyn, who glared. "Forgive me, Skarpin. I didn't mean to raise my voice. Please tell me you kids did not disturb our dragons?"

Skarpin shook his head, full of bouncing onyx curls. "That would have caused Nightlight and Gorm pain for what we needed."

"Which was…" Siany drug out the word. She was losing patience. She hated long conversations, and this one was dragging on particularly long.

"Dragon powder," Saedeen piped in. "Skarpin's theory was that the dragon scales must provide the perfect protection to keep fire alive. So, we figured that if we ground up dragon scales, I could use that powder in my potion. It didn't turn out quite like I thought. It made more of a paste than a liquid, so we painted it inside for Naedon's sphere, but in case the fire needed encouragement to stay alive, I mixed a potion with a dash of pig grease, which for some reason formed spiky vines around the outside of the sphere."

"And that's when I lit a small stick on fire and dropped it inside. I can produce fire whenever I want now."

Siany looked at her father. She could tell he was already plotting military strategies with this kind of advancement in magical technology. A power like Naedon's could serve as a formidable weapon and become a major enemy target. He was just a boy. She had to protect him and the rest of her students.

"We must keep this a secret," Siany said hastily. She dropped her quill, ink slightly splattering on her parchment, and folded her arms. She was determined to keep military influence out of her school.

"How are we 'ta keep 'dis from 'de other students? 'De already saw 'dem perform the magic," Madam Bip said.

Sealyn smirked and raised her hands. "If you can't hide it, embrace it. Can we take a moment to recognize that the first magic-enhancing instrument has now been invented? And by children. Again, I'm impressed."

The children beamed. They hadn't thought about anything bigger than wanting to perform in front of the king and queen. What the adults were saying was starting to sound like they were on the way to fame.

Sealyn clasped her hands behind her back. "First order of business: I want every Luxen in my military fitted for one of those necklaces."

Chapter 15

<u>Declare War Now</u>

The next day brought dazzling sunshine and a cool breeze, signaling that summer was almost over. With a growl, King Jace slammed the *Elysian News* parchment onto the table in his sitting room. Anger boiled within him. He didn't know how much longer Elysium could delay declaring war against Stoltland, his mother's kingdom. She had formed an alliance with Korpam, Elysium's neighboring enemy, and had violently invaded the Havas kingdom; now, she was making threats toward Glatania. The *Elysian News* was calling for a stance—a stance against Stoltland. He didn't blame Lady Adalina, the author of the *Elysian News*, for making this request. Part of him wanted that, too.

However, another part of him recalled his vow to his mother. Those words still haunted him, reverberating through his nightmares. Her essence lingered ominously in the shadows. Jace stood and walked to one of the floor-to-ceiling windows, gazing across the lush, beautiful Avondelle. He watched the Yuppathites glide gracefully through the air. Their white wings reminded him of a round stingray swimming. Yuppathites had silky wings, four legs, necks like a swan's, short trunk-noses, and tails resembling that of a phoenix. "Magnificent creatures," Jace thought.

Jace repeated the article's words, "Declare war now or forever be known as a Stoltland sympathizer."

He was startled at the sound of the knock on his dark wooden door. Everything about his sitting room was dark: dark green walls, mahogany furniture, and dark chocolate couches. Jace hoped that his choice of décor wasn't a reflection of something sinister within himself. The word monster echoed in his mind.

"Enter," he called out to the unknown visitor.

In walked the one person he could truly be himself around, the one person who could always find delight in the darkest times: Lord Char, cousin to Queen Sealyn.

"Good morning, King Jace."

"Good morning to you, Char. What brings you by?"

Char strolled across the room and held up his copy of the *Elysian News*. He smiled impishly. "Guess we read the same garbage this morning."

Jace huffed.

"I heard last night's quest planning went long," Char said.

Jace walked back to his desk and sat, motioning for Char to sit, too. Jace leaned back in his chair and folded his hands behind his head. "Let's not do this dance. What are you really here for?"

Char laughed while taking a seat in one of the chairs in front of Jace's desk. "Okay, you caught me. The necklaces. I'm intrigued. I'm also worried about my nephew, Naedon. This advancement puts a target on him. If Stoltland were to find out…"

"They won't!"

"Jace, I like to think we can talk freely, so I'll speak without sugar. Stoltland has spies everywhere. There's no telling who's on their payroll. We must protect our secrets at all costs, but we must prepare for the worst-case scenarios."

Jace sighed and leaned on the table. "You're right. You're right."

"Let's put that in print."

"Ha! I'll never admit it."

Char stood and walked to the window, watching the odd flying creatures. "Jace, this quest will steal away Avondelle's best fighters, leaving our children and civilians vulnerable. You know Corentine's tactic will be to come for the Heart of Elysium."

"We don't have any reports of that."

"Jace, I'm not trying to tell you how to do your job, but one thing Pax Island taught me was to read what isn't in those reports."

Jace's brow furrowed. He squinted at the maps on his table. His mother's movements looked like they were targeting kingdoms away from Elysium. What if that was her strategy? What if she wanted them to leave Elysium so they could invade?

"You think she's coming here next, don't you?"

Char saluted Jace. "Now you're thinking like a Stoltlander."

"How dare you!"

"Whoa, Jace. Easy. I meant that as a good thing." Char walked next to Jace and placed his hand on his shoulder. "A good king can get into the mind of his enemy to know their plans before they make them."

Jace tried to escape the burden of his home kingdom. He didn't want to be a Stoltlander; he longed to be an Elysian, but his eyes would always stand in the way.

"Have you discussed this with Sealyn?"

Char folded his arms and shifted his stance. He chewed on the side of his cheek, then finally spoke, "So that's the thing and also part of why I came here. She's, well, she's missing…"

Chapter 16

<u>Eklaezia</u>

Sealyn knew she shouldn't have sneaked away, but she really needed peace. Too many people used her natatorium for reading and hanging out, so she couldn't go there. Her secret passageways were no longer concealed, so she fled to the one place no one would find her. It was her forever childhood secret haven. She didn't come often because she was afraid someone would follow her.

She was willing to take the risk today, though. She could feel herself drifting away. She wanted to ground herself and reconnect her heart to Elysium and its people, and her clandestine hideaway would provide her with that. As a child, she had slipped over a smooth rock hill near one of the oldest estates in Avondelle, not far from the marketplace. Sealyn fell into a small pool of water that pulled her under; panic coursed through her body.

The pool created a current that pulled her through underwater tunnels until she resurfaced, gasping for air in the most breathtaking scene she had ever seen. Today, Sealyn ventured down this same path and embraced the familiar currents, now welcoming to her. She inhaled the sweet, fresh air as she rose from the cool aqua water.

In her enchanting sanctuary, a delicate waterfall tumbled into a shimmering blue pool, where lily pads floated like dreams, adorned with mesmerizing white and silver blossoms. Stone walls embraced the pool, draped in a tapestry of lush, green vines. The ground sparkled with stepping stones, leading through soft, velvety grass that felt like a caress beneath her feet. Over the years, Sealyn had cunningly smuggled in tools, crafting her own paradise. Nestled beneath a majestic stone archway was a charming table and chair, where fireflowers hung elegantly, their vibrant yellow and white colors cascading around her sanctuary, infusing the air with a sense of rich, sweet floral scent that tickled the imagination.

It was a pristine jungle soaked in tranquility. Sealyn sat on the bank, her legs savoring the water. She inhaled the fragrance of jasmine and felt her tension dissolve. She realized this was her first time down here since before her coronation. What a silly young girl she had been. She wished she could return to that time before she felt the world's weight on her shoulders.

A glimmer caught her eye among the thick ferns. She lifted herself from the pool, leaving behind wet footprints.

Kneeling, she pulled back the ferns and discovered a tarnished gold chest. She felt confused. This hadn't been here before. Had someone found this place? That couldn't be. Everything was the same, except for this chest.

She carried the heavy chest to her table, setting it down with a loud clang. The emerald queen grabbed a rock and smashed the rusted old lock—it shattered. The hinge creaked as she opened it. Sealyn instinctively looked around, ensuring no one was watching, even though she was alone. She peered into the musky box and saw ancient scrolls, emeralds the size of fists, and golden cuffs. The cuffs resembled the ones Mauor gave her after she won the battle against Mauor and Kazimir in Shunal, but she also recalled they looked similar to the cuffs that Shunal's king forced all his citizens to wear to suppress their magic.

This chest must have revealed itself after Elysium's curse was broken, part of the consequences of the Second Chance. Carefully, she unrolled one of the oldest-looking scrolls. It was a map of all seven kingdoms; however, it was an early edition. Pax Island hadn't been included yet. She examined all the labeled kingdoms, but there at the top of the parchment was a name she had never heard before. A name that dated back to before the Second Chance. The name that had united all seven kingdoms: Eklaezia.

Sealyn whispered the name, "Eklaezia." The leaves in the cavern trembled, and the water rippled. She scanned her surroundings, listening to the plants sing. What was occurring? What kind of magic was this? How could uttering this one word evoke joy and awe even in the plants and water? She read aloud the faded words at the bottom of the map:

"Assemble the seven. Unite as one. All hail Eklaezia."

This was why she had come down here. She needed to rediscover her motivation, and she had. Reviving Eklaezia was her mission, her sole mission. Her blood held the key to breaking the curses that began thousands of years ago. It was time to sacrifice her life so that others could live in a free and peaceful Eklaezia. Her death would liberate the world.

Chapter 17

<u>22 Years Ago…</u>

Blood splattered across the dirt floor as the tip of the blade grazed Jace's cheek. He stifled a yell and glanced back at his opponent. He could feel his strength faltering. His wrists ached and throbbed. Against the doctor's orders, Jace chose to persist with his private sword training. He would need to think of a clever excuse for the gash on his cheek, but wounds weren't uncommon for him.

An old veteran from Stoltland's army took pity on him and told Jace he would train him in the stables if he kept it a secret. Naturally, Jace agreed.

"Focus, Jace," the old man ordered.

"Sorry, Lord Paetrill."

Lord Paetrill was a tall, aged warrior with a thick, white beard he groomed into a long braid down the front. His face bore several battle tattoos and scars, along with deep wrinkles. Wisdom and pain lingered in the dark abyss of Paetrill's eyes. They held secrets—secrets he never wished to reveal.

Jace lifted his sword and felt the searing pain in his wrists. Even though the wounds had healed, his wrists were still far from ready to fight. Lord Paetrill disarmed Jace with two swift moves, causing Jace to drop his head in disappointment.

Lord Paetrill drove his sword into the dirt with a crunching sound and leaned on the hilt. "Jace, something's bothering you. What's going on?"

Jace didn't trust many people; the number of betrayals against Jace had taught him that. However, Paetrill had proven himself over the years.

"My wrists," Jace stuttered.

"What about them?"

"I don't really know."

"What do you mean?"

"They're just really sore from surgery."

Paetrill's brow creased, and he squinted. "What surgery?"

Jace swallowed, fearing what his mother would do if she discovered he told someone outside the palace about what had happened. "Um. I. Well, you see," Jace faltered, hoping to find courage in his words. He huffed and decided to let it all out. "My mother made Doctor Olkin operate on my wrists. He implanted magical bands of metal around them. She said it was to fix me, but I'm not sure what that means. I can feel the metal against my bones. Apparently, they will grow as I do." Jace tried to hold back his tears, but a lump formed in his throat. "Lord Paetrill, I don't understand why they did this to me." A tear slipped from his innocent, silver eye.

Paetrill inhaled deeply. He didn't want to be the one to tell Jace, but someone had to. "Jace, I don't like being the one to share difficult news, but it's a miracle you're even alive. You're a grey-eyed—meaning, by law, you're considered an abomination. I don't know what kind of deal your mother made to keep you alive, but here we are." He sighed and brushed back his white hair. "Kid, your life is going to be really tough, and most likely, you'll end up with more questions than answers. I know what it's like to be cast aside and treated like an outcast, which is why I'm helping you. I don't think you should go through life without knowing how to defend yourself. We're going to keep practicing, and maybe one day, you'll earn a spot in the military."

Jace wiped his nose. "Thank you, Lord Paetrill. I won't forget your kindness."

Paetrill cleared his throat, an action to defy showing emotion. "Alright, well, that's enough for today. You run on back to the palace and try to find something cold to put on those wrists—maybe Cook will give you some ice."

Jace nodded. He concealed his sword behind the broken slats of the barn and then sprinted up the hill toward the palace. His heart sank as he heard the horns blow. These weren't just any horns; they were warnings—dragons were coming. Jace was overwhelmed with panic. He didn't know what to do or where to go.

He darted toward the first house he saw and banged on the door. A middle-aged man with bright blonde hair and evil, beady eyes opened it. Jace begged for shelter, but the man slammed the door, yelling obscenities at Jace. He ran to the next house, knocking frantically. An older lady opened the door, but once she recognized him, she screamed, "Get away, you filthy beast! Maybe that dragon will finally get rid of you." She shut her door with a thud.

Tears of anger, fear, and loneliness filled Jace's silver eyes. He thought that returning to the stables and hiding there might be safer and quicker than running to the palace. The dragons hunted for quick meals during this season, so they typically stole sheep or cattle and were gone within minutes. He felt nauseous, knowing he had to run through a sheep field to get to the stables.

He sprinted quickly. The wind battered against his face, and his tiny legs burned. He passed all the houses that had rejected him and was darting into the black-tipped, grassy field when he heard a door creak open. He paused, thinking someone might actually let him in, but when he turned around, he saw the same blonde-haired man glaring at him—only this time, he had a bow and arrow aimed at him.

Jace's heart raced as he sprinted away, his eyes wide with terror. The chilling sound of an arrow slicing through the air sent adrenaline coursing through him. A jolt of searing pain exploded in his leg, causing him to crash to the ground. He rolled frantically through the dense, dark grass, desperation igniting his cries of agony. Peering toward the village, he desperately sought help, but silence met his pleas. The attacker had already vanished behind closed doors, leaving no trace of the assault or the pain that now consumed Jace.

A thunderous roar erupted from the dragon, sending shockwaves through the ground. It was drawing nearer. Jace let out a desperate yelp as he struggled to his feet. He made a brave attempt to step forward but stumbled and fell once more. Time was running out; the dragon was about to emerge from the mountain range any second now. He looked at his bleeding leg, and a cold sweat trickled down his spine. Dragons could smell blood from miles away. He would be its target.

With all his might, young Jace picked himself up and began limping across the field, every step a struggle. Fluffy black sheep darted chaotically in every direction, further impeding Jace's progress, matching the agony in his wounded leg. At last, he found himself heading downhill, which gave him a burst of momentum. However, as he glanced up, dread washed over him; a gleaming obsidian dragon was hurtling toward him with terrifying speed. Knowing he couldn't escape, Jace pushed himself to quicken his pace, but fate was against him. He lost his balance and tumbled down the hill, limbs flailing in a desperate attempt to regain control. A sharp pain shot through him as he felt his finger crack, and with a sickening snap, the arrow embedded in his leg broke free. Jace screamed for help, his voice echoing across the fields, as fear consumed him.

The dragon swooped down, closing the distance with a fierce speed as it snatched a black sheep in its large, razor-sharp claws. Jace finally stopped rolling. He attempted to rise, but a wave of pain shot through him. He glanced towards the menacing figure of the dragon advancing toward him. This was it—he was facing his doom. His end was to be met by a dragon, a terrifying dragon.

"Jace!" Lord Paetrill yelled from the barn.

Jace lifted his head and saw his only friend standing at the open door, waving him forward. Paetrill's encouragement gave Jace the strength to rise. He hobbled toward the barn, but his pace was weak—no match for a dragon's speed.

Paetrill saw the arrow wound and the blood dripping from Jace's ripped clothes. He jerked his head toward the dragon. Jace wasn't going to make it. This child, who hadn't known a moment's peace and who hadn't even had his eighth birthday, was about to die. Paetrill finally understood—all lives mattered. Pride didn't mean anything. Jace was innocent. He deserved to live. Paetrill had taken his fair share of innocent lives; it was time for him to stand up and do what was right.

"Come, Jace! Run!" Paetrill pulled out his sword and ran toward Jace. "On my orders, Jace, you don't stop running! Get to the barn and go to the underground. Don't stop running—no matter what!" Paetrill yelled every word.

They could feel the dragon's heat. It was only feet away, filling their entire vision. Jace could barely run; his lungs burned, and every part of him ached. He saw the dragon's red eyes as it opened its mouth. Jace looked ahead, trying to run faster. Paetrill was so close to him, moving with swift sprints.

Paetrill raced past Jace, his sword raised high as he dashed forward. Suddenly, Jace noticed a dark shadow looming above him. He continued running and glanced upward. The dragon darted away but quickly started to circle back, readying for another attack.

"Keep running, Jace!"

Jace obeyed. He felt immense relief when he reached the barn door, gasping and wheezing. Bracing himself against the doorframe, he turned around, expecting to see Paetrill right behind him. Instead, he found Paetrill with his sword drawn and the sinister obsidian dragon charging straight at him. Jace shouted for Paetrill to run, but the old warrior held his ground. This time, the dragon unleashed its orange flames, engulfing Lord Paetrill, only friend to the grey-eyed child.

Chapter 18

<u>A Spy</u>

Sealyn burst through the war room doors, startling everyone inside. She walked quickly to her seat, ready to hand out orders. It was time to sail for Glatania.

"Sealyn! Where have you been?" Jace asked as he ran to her. He grabbed her shoulders, scanning for any injuries.

"Not lost if that's what story has been spun." Jace dropped his hold on his wife, stepping back in confusion. Sealyn smiled reassuringly. "I promise all is well; I just needed some alone time."

Jace looked at Char. Char lifted his hands and shook his head.

Ryker leaned in close to his daughter and whispered, "The next time you need some alone time, make sure to tell someone so we don't waste time with a search party."

"Understood, Father." She flinched at her father's quiet scolding, feeling like a child. This didn't go over well with her.

Sealyn signaled for everyone to sit down. She filled a goblet with the bright, shimmering purple drink famously known as PurFizz. She was going to need Madam Bip's renowned energy drink to endure this meeting.

"Elysians, it's time to sail for Glatania."

Prince Adomin chuckled. "Yes, majesty. That's what we've been planning since your return from Shunal. We should be ready in three months minimum."

Sealyn, still standing, said, "No. We leave in two days." Gasps resounded. "This is no joke. We can't waste any more time."

Prince Royce raised his hand. "Uh, Queen Sealyn. You know I'm in support of this quest, but we need more time to prepare. Besides, Lady Adma hasn't even given us anything useful to use against the crowned family."

Lady Adma hailed from Glatania and was a member of Queen Sealyn's Council of Lands. She was reserved, often feeling more like a wallflower than a socialite. She wore dark purple spectacles that complemented her shy violet eyes and typically styled her auburn hair into a thick bun. Adma had wide hips, a large bust, thick arms and legs, and an adorably round face.

Part of being on the Council of Lands was providing intel about your home kingdom, and so far, Adma had not lived up to expectations. Sealyn gripped the stone table. She was tired of hiring people for certain jobs and not receiving their work.

Sealyn peered up at the rafters and saw Maekel sitting with Trit. She loved witnessing her favorite Nichts enjoying their married life. She almost hated to interrupt them, but she needed their help. "Maekel. Trit." The two Nichts swooped down, hovering in mid-air by their sparkling wings before Sealyn, their pointed ears attentive to her requests. "Please bring Lady Adma to me, Maekel. Trit, ask Lord Jdru to bring me those two luggage trunks I ordered. Quickly, please."

The two Nichts sped off, their wings shimmering in the candlelight. Char had no idea why Sealyn wanted those trunks along with Lady Adma, but he was eager to discover the reason. He always admired how Sealyn anticipated people's movements. She was skilled at organizing strategies, but when hurried, those plans often ended in utter failure.

Sealyn turned her attention to her mother. "Queen Mother Graelynd, you were charged with the organization and production of the magical necklaces. How is the process for my soldiers?"

Graelynd's lips parted, unsure of how to proceed. Her daughter was showing a different side—one she was not familiar with. She proceeded with caution. "Considering we were supposed to have three months to prepare, not very far. Queen Sealyn, each person possesses a special gift, so if the theories are correct, each sphere will need its own potion brewed for that power. This process takes time."

Sealyn shook her head and raised her voice. "I don't have time, Mother."

"Sealyn…" Ryker said in his most father-like voice. "That is enough."

Sealyn slowly looked at her father. "I'm not interested in an argument today. I'm only interested in ideas that propel this quest forward." She turned her gaze back to Graelynd. "I'm sorry, Mother. I didn't mean to sound harsh, so here's what we'll do: let's focus only on those who are going on the quest."

"And what, leave the rest defenseless—like you did before?" Favien snarked, not realizing the anger he would invoke.

Sealyn hurled her goblet across the room with her mammoth strength, smashing it against the stone wall as purple liquid pooled around the broken fragments. Everyone froze. They had never seen this behavior from Sealyn before. Her eyes flamed blue; ebony spider veins appeared in her palm. She observed the itchy skin—onyx blood slithered in her veins. It wanted her to kill Favien. She could feel the enticement. She stretched her neck from side to side, attempting to ward off the darkness that was creeping into her thoughts.

Jace stood and draped his arm around Sealyn's shoulder. "Favien, remember, Avondelle is not defenseless without these necklaces. Our military has never had this before, so do you think King Ryker left Avondelle defenseless when he fought against Korpam? What about King Saevon when he battled at Calinburg? No? So why are you reluctant to show Queen Sealyn the same grace? Besides, you should have more faith in your fellow warriors. The forces not going on the quest are not any less skilled. These are also the ones who fought and triumphed against the Black Phoenixes. I fear for anyone who chooses to confront any Elysian warrior!"

"Here. Here." The council banged their goblets and fists on the table. King Father Ryker beamed with pride for his son-in-law. His lips curled, happy to have such an outstanding man married to his daughter.

Sealyn still glared at Favien. "Don't worry, Lord Favien. Avondelle will be in good hands because you're not going on this quest."

"What?! Queen Sealyn, I didn't mean harm. I'm sorry."

"After what happened in Shunal, you're lucky to still be a part of the Groundlers. You froze in action again because of Pinx! It almost cost my life and the Pirate Captain's, too too."

"I'm sorry. That room made it seem like she was trapped. I know now that it was all a trick, but please, Queen Sealyn, please give me another chance."

Sealyn folded her arms. "On the battlefield or on a quest, you can only hear one voice—your leader, your queen, your shepherd. I can't trust you."

Favien laid his head in his hands, trying not to sob in front of his comrades. Although he was shorter than most soldiers, he was one of the toughest warriors in the queen's military. He had short, thick, chestnut hair, a full beard, and shaved sides. Favien was the jokester of the group and one of the most loyal companions a person could ask for, so Sealyn's words of distrust pierced his heart. He was crushed.

Char felt sorry for him. That torture chamber had messed them up horribly. They all had to undergo countless hours of counseling with Faith Commissioner Herb. Some would probably always suffer from that awful memory.

"Earn back my trust by captaining the palace guards here in our absence."

Favien lifted his head. "You want me in charge of Avondelle while you're gone?"

"Is that an issue, soldier?"

Favien's heart leaped. He realized Sealyn couldn't have lost all confidence in him if she was appointing him in charge of her capital. He would make sure Avondelle remained safe, no matter what. "No, my queen. It's not. I won't let you down."

Sealyn eyed Dun, the giant green phoenix, in the corner. He tilted his head, scolding her. She had to remember these were still her friends. She closed her eyes and thought of Eklaezia. The onyx veins and blue eyes disappeared. She looked at Favien and smiled. "Consider it my gift to you and Lady Pinx since your firstborn is soon to arrive."

Favien grinned. He was so happy to be a new father. Pinx, who was two months along, was just as eager as he was, and now, he would be home for the birth—not away on a quest.

Lady Adma arrived, looking frightened at the large group in the war room. She wore a glittering violet ball gown with an oversized skirt, decorated with dark purple roses on the heart-shaped bodice. She appeared regal, yet shy.

Sealyn walked to Adma with no mercy in her eyes. "Lady Adma, you are hereby commissioned to reveal all secrets you know about your kingdom right now."

"But, Your Majesty, I've told the princes all I know. There's just not much to disclose about our kingdom. It's sweet and full of the most delicious foods you'll ever taste."

Lord Jdru, Char's brother, kicked open the door, balancing two large trunks. He let them slip to the stone floor; loud bangs resounded in the chamber. "Sorry for that. I brought the trunks you wanted." He pulled a handkerchief from his pocket and dabbed his sweating bald head.

"Thank you, Lord Jdru. That will be all. I'll come find you later."

Jdru scrunched his face and scratched his reddish-blonde beard. His eyes narrowed as Sealyn turned her head and winked at him. He shrugged and walked away without another word.

Sealyn whirled on Adma. "Here's the deal, Adma. I'm out of time and out of patience, so either you tell me those details now, or I'm shipping you home. I've already had your belongings packed, as you can see."

"What? No, please," Adma squeaked. Genuine fear was displayed across her round, freckled face.

Sealyn's plan clicked in Char's mind—she was bluffing. Sealyn was taking a significant risk, but what other choice did she have? Adma had been hired to advise on her kingdom, but so far, she had delivered nothing.

A knock sounded at the war room door.

"Enter," Sealyn called.

The palace butler entered. "Majesty, you asked to see me earlier?"

"Your timing is perfect, as always. Please prepare a carriage for Lady Adma. She apparently is leaving us presently."

Adma frantically tugged at her skirt, wiping her hands on her sparkly dress, her plum eyes darting from side to side. What was she about to do? Would she really return home to a cursed kingdom, or would she finally give in and reveal her kingdom's secrets? No, she couldn't return with a failed mission; her life depended on it. Lady Adma adjusted her round spectacles and stepped forward, her heels clicking on the stone floor, the sound of defeat.

Adma cleared her throat and lifted her chin. "That won't be necessary." Sweat broke out over her brow, and her cheeks flushed. "May I make one request?" Her voice caught in her throat.

Sealyn dropped her head back and stared at the ceiling. She sighed deeply, then looked at Adma, who was shaking. "Make it one I won't regret."

"Yes, Majesty. May I speak to you in private? I. I have a hard time speaking in front of crowds." She bit her lip, fidgeting with the purple roses on her bodice.

Sealyn suddenly understood the circumstances. Adma couldn't handle public speaking. Maybe it wasn't the details she feared, but spilling them in front of multiple people.

"Choose one to remain with me, and the rest will dismiss themselves."

Adma peeked up slightly and surveyed the room. Her breathing sped up, and she felt dizzy. She blinked, trying to focus her blurred vision. Then, she spotted the friendliest face she knew and blurted, "Lord Char, please."

Lord Char stood, delighted with himself. He bowed dramatically. "You heard the lady. Scram! Why wouldn't a fair maiden want to reveal her secrets to me and not the rest of your smelly swine?"

Once the room had emptied and only the three remained, Adma felt a wave of relief. She sat at the legendary war table, studying the maps and notes. Her Glatanian eyes settled on their capital, Milska.

Char saw Adma's eye twinkle. What was she thinking? Could they trust her? Was her curse still controlling her?

Sealyn drummed her fingers on the stone table. "Today, Adma," she said flatly.

"Oh, right. Yes, Majesty." Adma shifted in her chair, petting her lilac skirt full of dazzling crystals. "Well, we are a lovely people just subjected to a curse that looks to trick you."

Char's jade eyes darted to Sealyn and then back to Adma. "Looks to trick? Explain."

Adma chewed on her bottom lip. "Um, I, um." Adma stood up, knocking her chair back. "I can't! I can't explain further. They'll kill me."

Char felt pity for the lady. It was obvious she feared someone or something. He only wished to help, but he noticed

Sealyn's eyes were yellowing. They almost looked like snake eyes.

Sealyn slammed her hand, shaking her head. "Fine. If you don't want to save your kingdom, you'll get a front-row seat to watch those you fear bow."

Char blinked. Had Sealyn lost her mind? Why was she acting this way? "Sealyn, what's going on?"

"Shut it, Char. Adma, you're coming with us on this quest. You can be a guest or a prisoner. I care not." Sealyn stood to leave.

Adma ran to Sealyn, gripping her arm. "Majesty, please don't. Please don't make me."

Sealyn yanked her arm from Adma's grasp, giving her a look of disgust. "How dare you grab me like that! Who do you think you are? Adma, I offered you the world with only one stipulation: tell me the details of your kingdom, including the secrets. You have refused. I have no use for you, except maybe for ransom. Maybe your rebels will be willing to take you back in exchange for helping us defeat the curse."

Sealyn began walking toward the door, but Adma screamed out, "I'm not a rebel." She gasped and covered her mouth with her hand.

Sealyn winced at the betrayal, still facing the door. Char stood quickly. He understood that lies and betrayal were the two things capable of pushing Sealyn over the edge. Would he have to confront Sealyn to protect Adma?

Sealyn growled, "What did you say?"

A sinister voice filled Sealyn's head. *"End her. She will only lead to more deceit."*

Adma looked at Char, begging for help with her tear-filled eyes. "I'm not a rebel, Majesty."

Sealyn slowly turned, her eyes blazing, and green flames formed around her hands. "You said you were part of the rebellion in your kingdom, and now, you say you're not. Then who in all Creation are you?"

Char made his way to stand next to Adma, observing her closely. It was clear she had lied to gain this position in Elysium, but why? How had she managed to pull this off? Adma's letter claimed she was from one of the lesser houses and had heard from one of the great ladies about Queen Sealyn's Council of Lands offer. She had joined the rebellion as a spy, writing a plea to be part of such an honor, stating her willingness to do whatever it took to break Glatania's curse. Elysium had believed her, especially Sealyn.

Adma sniffed and spoke, her lip quivering. Revealing this final secret was all she had left, but fear still prevented her from speaking the entire sickening truth about her lineage. If she disclosed the deadly truth about her father, Sealyn would undoubtedly kill her without hesitation. "I'm Princess

Admadaeva Stelio, daughter of King Pullex Stelio and Queen Amaera Stelio, the youngest of their line of succession."

Sealyn's jaw tightened. "And let me add another title…Glatanian spy."

Chapter 19

<u>A Rusty Hero</u>

The Market of Avondelle buzzed with shoppers and diners at the beautifully colored stone shops. Today was especially busy because a band from Hill Chimes was performing in the square. They called themselves the Magical Musicians, and their melodies enchanted everyone's ears. Enhancing the cheerful atmosphere, freshly brewed coffee wafted from *Nijeel's Choice*, the market's favorite café. Max, Finn, and Ashur sat outside *Nijeel's Choice*, sipping their much-needed caffeinated drinks.

Finn's blue eyes narrowed at a figure moving through the crowd. Despite being from Len Nove, he never felt like an outsider. His friends all regarded him as part of their Elysian family. He was a trusted ally, especially to King Jace, which was why they were on a special mission. Finn stroked his freshly shaved ivory jaw and nudged Ashur, who was sitting in the middle of the trio. He nodded towards the figure, gliding pompously.

Ashur bobbed his head to both Finn and Max. This overly dressed Elysian stood out. Something was wrong with him. Wearing his usual coffee-stained apron, Sir Nijeel walked to the table to refill the soldier's cups.

Nijeel noticed the intensity of the table and looked around. "Everything okay, gentlemen?" He kept filling each cup, being careful not to spill. He despised wasting anything, especially his expertly brewed coffee. He spent years perfecting his magical blend—no one even knew his secret ingredients, yet everyone returned for more.

Max turned to Nijeel as if awakening from a trance. "Hey, Nijeel. You know just about everyone in Avondelle. What can you tell us about that lad over there?" Max pointed toward the well-dressed individual.

Nijeel pushed up his spectacles and squinted. He tugged at his reddish-brown beard and said, "Hmm. That's odd."

All three of their ears perked at the word "odd." Max quickly asked, "Why do you say that?"

"Because that's ol' Rusty."

"Rusty?" Ashur questioned. "I guess that is an odd name."

Nijeel leaned closer. "No, that's not why it's odd. People call him Rusty because all his farming equipment is basically rust. His family is poorer than a Needlebob's toe."

Finn snorted at the joke.

Max's brow creased. "Then how is he wearing what looks to be the most expensive clothing from Sir Clive's shop?"

"That's why it's odd. His family can't afford new farming equipment, much less fancy clothes like that." Nijeel watched the silent exchanges between his three customers. Something was at play, and he wanted in. "What's going on?"

The soldiers looked at one another. Max whispered, "Ah, c'mon. It's Nijeel. We can trust him."

Ashur slightly shook his head. He was a rule follower and didn't want to jeopardize this mission. Finn shrugged, then nodded. Max beamed and grabbed Nijeel's collar, pulling him close.

"This is top secret, Nijeel, but we think your pal, Rusty…"

Nijeel held his hand up. "He's not my pal…" Nijeel huffed dramatically, recalling how Rusty had the audacity to insult his latest masterpiece: *Shep's Roar*, the perfect invigorating concoction. Seriously, how could anyone turn their nose up at such culinary genius? If there were a way to concoct some revenge on this brew-basher who dared tarnish his velvety brown elixir's reputation, Nijeel was all in— perhaps a prank involving dunking a gallon of his special blend over his head? No. No. What a waste …

Max snapped and shushed him. "No matter. No matter. Listen, we think he's a spy for Stoltland; from the looks of it, he's been paid nicely. He's just too stupid not to show off."

Nijeel's jaw hit the floor. A spy! A spy had dined at his café! The scandal! How could he have let such a sneaky fiend enjoy his legendary coffee? This culinary criminal had to face the consequences! "What are you lot planning to do?" Nijeel whispered.

Ashur smirked. "What we do best—capture bad guys."

Like stealthy cheetahs, Finn and Max jumped from Nijeel's tabletop to the rooftop of his café. Nijeel blinked in disbelief. They had moved so fast that he almost missed it. He looked at Ashur, who covered his raven hair with a dark green hood and grinned. He leaned close and whispered, "You're our backup, Nijeel." Then, he disappeared into the crowd.

Nijeel stood there dumbfounded, still clutching his fancy porcelain coffee pot. He yelled out, "Backup, how? Hey! How?" he yelled into the void, but all he got in return was the sound of his own confusion echoing back. After a moment of realizing he was talking to himself, he begrudgingly wiped off the gross boot prints those two had left on his table, muttering about the state of humanity. His gaze then landed on Rusty, who was casually ambling past Baker Nicht's bakery, twirling a shiny gold necklace and whistling as if he had just discovered his own musical genius. What an idiot.

Finn drew back his bow and arrow while standing on the roof of the market library, which was next to the bakery. Max was on top of Baker Nicht's bakery, trying to ignore the tempting aromas of chocolate and cinnamon. Ashur shouted to the traitor, "Hey, Rusty! You're wanted for questioning by the crown."

Rusty froze with a scowl plastered across his bearded face. "Oh, yeah? For what? What they want with me?" His farming accent was thick, nothing noble about it.

"You're accused of spying and taking bribes from Queen Corentine of Stoltland."

"I have not! Them's lies is what them's are," Rusty said gruffly.

"We have you surrounded, Rusty," Max yelled out. "Come peacefully, and no one gets hurt."

Ashur stepped closer to Rusty. The crowd formed a circle, observing the drama unfold. Rusty's milky green eyes looked wild. He tensed as he squinted at Finn and Max, who had arrows aimed at him. He jerked his head toward Ashur, who was slowly drawing his sword.

As if on cue in the distance, the Magical Musicians fired up a fast, upbeat song, and Rusty began his revolt. He lunged and swung his gold necklace across Ashur's smooth, ebony cheek. It slashed his skin, spraying droplets of blood on the cobblestones. Rusty pushed Ashur aside and sprinted past. Max and Finn missed their chance as the crowd closed in.

Ashur regained his footing and sprinted after Rusty, darting through the swarm of onlookers. Rusty hurled people, chairs, and even caged birds as he dashed away. Meanwhile, Finn and Max vaulted over the shingles, gaining ground. Suddenly, Ashur stumbled over a barrel Rusty had intentionally shoved in his path, tumbling to the ground in frustration.

Rusty laughed, believing he had escaped, but to his utter shock, blistering hot, perfectly brewed coffee splattered across his face. He fell to his knees, grabbing his face and wailing as brown liquid dripped from his mangled beard. Max and Finn slid down the café's roof, landing powerfully on their feet as if they had done it a thousand times together. They pointed their arrows at Rusty, ready for backlash. Limping, Ashur approached the weeping criminal and gently patted Sir Nijeel on the shoulder.

"Well done, backup," Ashur said, wincing slightly at his ankle.

Nijeel beamed with triumphant glee, feeling like a kid who had just discovered coffee for the first time. This was the most excitement he'd had since accidentally turning his first brewing stove into a miniature volcano. "All in a day's work!" he declared, trying to sound nonchalant, but his over-the-top grin gave him away. Sleep? Ha! Not a chance! Instead, he devised a plan to create an even wilder blend, dedicating it to today's adventure. He would call it… A Rusty Hero.

Ashur pulled Rusty's hands behind his back and roped them together. He helped him to his feet and forced him to walk toward the palace.

Max shook Nijeel's hand. "Nijeel, thanks for the assist. Know that this is just one of many. Keep your eyes peeled for more spies. They're everywhere."

Chapter 20

Flaming Orange Eyes

The market was filled with everyone from Avondelle for a grand feast and celebration in honor of the Glatanian quest that was set to begin the next day. The aromas of savory meats and sugary treats twirled in the air while children danced to the sounds of strings. Stage performers had the crowd roaring with laughter, yet a certain group was absent from the festivities. Sealyn remembered Lady Pyry's poisoning all too well before their Len Novian quest, so she set a curfew for her team members. She knew they wouldn't want to end their celebrations early, so she organized a private party for them in the palace's banquet hall.

Little did she know how many secrets were about to spill …

Each wall featured a table brimming with scrumptious foods and bubbling drinks. Round tables were spread throughout the hall, allowing everyone to move freely while still having a spot to place their drinks when needed. Even Char's tiger, Shep, wandered the room, waiting for scraps. Young Naedon and his friends dashed around the room, disregarding the reprimands from palace elders. Char wrapped his arms around Naedon before he could dash past him, tickling him until Naedon burst into laughter.

"Okay. Okay. I give. I give. Uncle Char!"

Char released him, smiling. "Are we going to slow down now? You five could really cause some damage in here." The five stood in front of Char with slumped shoulders and nodded.

Naedon exhaled loudly. "We'll be careful." Naedon froze as he watched Lord Jashun walk by. He remembered the secret meeting they had witnessed several nights ago in the gardens. Naedon also knew about Jashun's betrayal of King Jace when Jashun revealed details to the Pirate Captain before the pirate became an ally. Living at the castle had its perks, which Naedon took full advantage of; because he overheard these particulars, he didn't trust Jashun. Jashun had a tendency to waver in his loyalty to Elysium, leading Naedon to personally consider him slimy and untrustworthy. He stiffened and narrowed his eyes as he watched Jashun start conversing with Lord Favien.

Char couldn't shake the feeling of something unsettling in Naedon's demeanor. What could provoke such a reaction? Jashun had always shown him nothing but kindness. As Char felt Shep lean against him, he was suddenly struck by the eerie sound of a child's voice, even though none of the children in front of him seemed to be speaking.

"*I can't believe he was sneaking around with Aunt Siany*," the voice said.

Char blinked and stepped back. "What did you say?"

Naedon's eyes bulged. He forced a look of confusion. "I didn't say anything." Naedon looked at Skarpin, then back to Char.

Char heard the voice again, "*What could be wrong with Uncle Char? He can't hear my thoughts. Maybe he had too much ale. Yeah, that's probably it. Hmm. I wonder if I can sneak a bottle of ale without getting caught.*"

Char shook his head. "You will not!"

Skarpin looked around in confusion. "Uh, Lord Char, no one said anything."

Char's mouth opened and closed like a fish's as he tried to comprehend the situation. "Will you four excuse me and Naedon? I need to speak with him privately." The four scurried away, relieved they weren't in trouble. Char knelt in front of his nephew. "Naedon, what do you know about Jashun and Siany?"

Naedon's face went pale. "How did you know that?"

"So you *do* know something! You must tell me."

Naedon dropped his head. "I saw Aunt Siany leaving the gardens at night, and then Jashun followed soon after. They looked like they were having a secret meeting or something. Uncle Char, you can't say anything. I don't want to get in trouble."

"You won't. Why not go catch up with your friends and maybe take them to the music room?" Naedon scurried away, catching up with his friends.

Char turned and narrowed his eyes at Shep. "Did you do that?"

"Do what, silly human?"

"Ah, so you can speak to me through our minds and read them. Is that what just happened?"

"Be wise with this gift." Shep turned, swishing his long, striped tail, and walked over to the beef table, where he sat begging for food.

Char stood dumbfounded. What was he supposed to do with this gift? Fortunately, he could only use this power while channeling Shep, but still, this was huge! Also huge was the secret meeting between Jashun and Siany. Why would those two meet?

Char felt a sting on his back from Sakul's smacking him. Sakul swayed and smiled. He lifted his drink and bowed.

"Char, my dear friend, you want to know what I love about tonight?"

"Do I really want to know?" Char asked with true concern, seeing the state Sakul was in.

Sakul wrapped his arm around Char's shoulders and pointed across the room to where Lady Sorcha was giggling with Lord Sune. "That. How could I not enjoy seeing the love of my life enjoying herself with another man?"

"I think we should get you home. Our journey starts early tomorrow."

Sakul jerked his arm away, spilling ale on his green and gold tunic. "No. You know what? No! Tonight, I want the truuuuuth," Sakul yelled, startling the entire room.

Sakul stepped to the center with unstable movements. He spun around, capturing everyone's attention. "Tonight, let us speak openly and truthfully. I will start. Sorcha…"

Sorcha took a step forward with her arm outstretched. "Sakul, please don't do this."

"I can't wait any longer. I've been patient. Sorcha, me or him."

The room gasped at the ultimatum. Sorcha looked angry and scared. Before Sealyn could stop the madness, Jashun opened his forever large mouth.

"Oh, come off it, Sakul. That's no way to treat Lady Sorcha."

Sakul pointed to Jashun. "Stay out of this."

"No, I won't. Why do this now? That's no way to treat a lady, especially Sorcha."

Something inside Char snapped. "Really, Jashun. Since when do you know how to treat a lady? You're the one who has secret night meetings and not with Princess Kailani." A cold chill went down Char's spine. What had he just done? Sure, he might be getting Jashun in trouble, but he was also outing Siany, his cousin.

Kailani smacked Jashun's cheek. "You dare cheat on me! How could you? Who is it?"

Jashun rubbed his cheek. "I didn't. I wouldn't. I swear."

"Liar!" Char yelled, laced with bitterness. "You were seen leaving the school gardens with another." Char eyed Siany, whose face turned pink behind her freckles.

Jashun didn't know what to do. Telling the truth was the only way to avoid losing Kailani, but it would also reveal Siany's secret mission, which would put him right back at betraying a royal—again. He let out a frustrated moan. "We were talking about Sakul, not me. I believe Sune and Sorcha have earned the opportunity to explore what they have. You took ages to announce your feelings for Sorcha, so yeah, you do owe her time."

Sakul's mouth dropped. He felt hurt that his friend would choose another's side. Tears spilled down his ebony cheeks as he shook his head.

Char tried to redirect him to help save his best friend. "Don't deflect, Jashun. Admit it. You were having a secret meeting at night in the garden—weren't you?"

As soon as Char finished his accusation, he looked down to see his nephew standing there with eyes full of betrayal. Char felt a lurch in his stomach. The one kid he never wanted to disappoint, and he just did.

Naedon's face drooped into sadness, and tears formed. "You said you wouldn't say anything. Now, Aunt Siany will hate me!" Naedon ran out of the room with his mother trailing after him.

This piqued Sealyn's interest. "Siany? What does my sister have to do with a secret meeting with Jashun?"

Kailani's pink hair glowed, and her eyes turned like those of a wild beast. She squared off with Siany. "Are you sneaking around with my Jashun?"

Lady Adalina couldn't write these juicy details fast enough. She scribbled everything she witnessed, imagining how many newspapers she would sell.

Siany folded her arms in embarrassment. "What? No. Of course not." She was caught. She had to come clean. How would Sealyn react? Worse, how would Jace react?

Jashun slightly shook his head. This would be bad. It didn't matter that Siany was behind his mission; he accepted the job. They would see him as a traitor—again.

"I hired Jashun for a special job. Night was the only time I could meet, and I didn't want any questions surrounding the job."

Jace immediately felt something was off. Siany nor Jashun would look at him. What was this special job? Why was it so important that they needed to keep it secret, even from Sealyn?

Kailani flung her sparkling rose hair. "I want details. This must be an impressive secret mission to convince me of your innocence, Jashun."

Jashun placed his hands on his hips, and his head fell back. He was in deep trouble. He wished this night had never happened.

Siany rung her hands nervously. "Well, I, um." She looked at Jace with concern. "I felt like we needed more information about King Jace."

"Me?"

"What?" Sealyn snapped, feeling her rage start to boil.

Siany cowered. "I'm not trying to upset you. I only wanted to help. We don't have a lot of history about Jace nor grey eyes, for that matter."

"Why would you need that?" Sealyn questioned, glaring at her sister.

"So many are unlocking their powers, but there are no records on what a silver-eyed's powers are or if they even have any."

Jace swallowed. He felt like he was back in Stoltland with everyone judging him based on his eye color again. He wanted to disappear.

Sealyn was about to speak, but a manly voice spoke behind the crowd, "I think Princess Siany's commission was brave and worth it." The crowd parted, and there stood Lord Jem, red-eyed and muscles bulging.

"How dare you speak about our king!" Commander Tilmond growled. Clearly, these two had not buried the hatchet.

"Here we go…" Char said to no one in particular.

Jem balled his hand into a fist. "No, I will. It's time the people know who he is or what he is."

"That is enough!" snarled Sealyn. "You will show my husband, the king, the respect the position is owed."

"That's just it, majesty. You don't even know him; none of us do. Can he tell us what power he possesses? Or if he will ever gain powers? If he can't, then why—what does that mean?"

Sealyn looked at Jace, who was rubbing his wrists. Her heart ached. She saw the sadness in his eyes that he had when he first came to Elysium years ago. She snapped her head back to Jem. "You will speak no more."

"Sealyn, please," Siany interjected. "We should speak privately."

"I, for one, would like to know what Siany discovered about King Jace," Kailani said.

"Back off, fish," Sealyn bit.

Siany threw her hands up. "I wanted to know how Corentine was able to keep Jace alive. Jashun looked for records of his birth, but no records exist. It's like his birth was meant to be secret."

Jace's brow furrowed. "There's really no record of my birth? Wait—you were looking to find out who my father was, too, weren't you?"

Siany sighed. "Yes, that would be helpful for potential allies in this never-ending war."

"Why? We have plenty of allies," Jace remarked.

"Well, so far, the Mer Clans are proving unreliable," Siany said.

Kailani threw her goblet. It shattered against the wall. "How dare you!"

Sealyn positioned herself protectively in front of her sister, her gaze urgent and challenging, as if she were silently pleading with Kailani to take a swing at her. "I may not endorse my sister's methods, but her claims regarding the Mer Clans are undeniably true, and deep down, you know it."

"It's not our fault that you're requesting magic that doesn't exist, nor ever has."

Sealyn twisted her neck back and forth, trying to ignore the voices in her head, yet she couldn't help but listen.

"*These people are weak. Be done with them and go alone. You don't need them,*" the familiar sinister voice said.

"*Sealyn, remember, the longer you take to break the curses, the sooner your mind will not be your own,*" a wise voice whispered.

Sealyn closed her eyes, wishing the voices of Kazimir and Mauor would fade away. She despised that the serpent's riddle was correct. Her mind was speeding away from her. The curses would continue to torment her and take from her; she couldn't afford to waste time and slip into madness before breaking all seven curses. Shep's ears piqued, and he lifted his emerald and gold-striped head. He quickly channeled Char.

Char felt dizzy and heard countless voices, but he heard an unfamiliar snaky voice. Who was that? Where was it coming from? His eyes stopped on Sealyn, who was struggling. Then he heard the voices again.

"These humans are trivial. Distance yourself," Kazimir sneered.

"Remember, your sacrifice will save them, but you can't waste time like this," Mauor advised.

Char's mouth dropped. What did this mean? Those snakes were advising Sealyn, but what did it mean by sacrifice? Sealyn wouldn't sacrifice herself? There's no need for that, is there?

Sealyn felt herself losing control. She couldn't process her thoughts fast enough. Too many voices. Too much pressure. Her mouth spoke before she could check herself, "It does exist. That rickety shack in Emerald Lagoon is proof and has something to do with Abyss magic. Your people need to fess up and be better allies since Jace's father's kingdom won't be of any help."

The room froze. Sealyn winced, realizing what she had just said. She didn't want to look at Jace. She couldn't. She closed her eyes tightly, wishing this moment away. Instead of facing Jace, she stared at the far corner, where the Pirate Captain was shaking his head.

Jace's head tilted. "Sea, what does that mean? You said that like you already know which kingdom my father belongs to."

"I. I didn't mean…" She looked to Tyron, begging him to do the right thing. She didn't want to lie to her husband.

Tyron rolled his flaming orange eyes and stomped forward. His boots echoed in the banquet hall as the crowd parted for the fearsome pirate. He cleared his throat and directed his fiery gaze at Jace. "It means that I'm your father, King Jace."

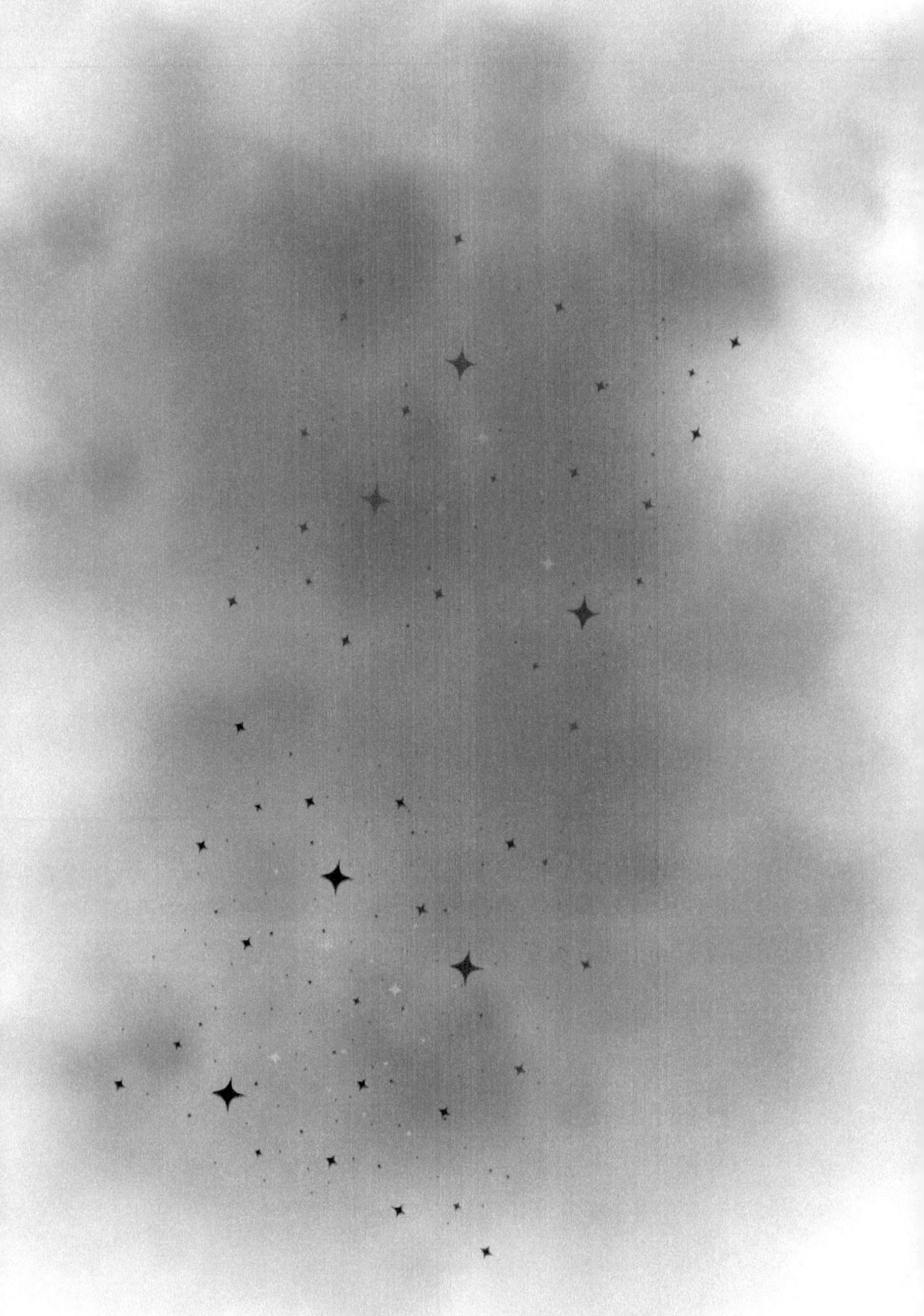

MAEGWEN SALLEY-MASSIE • THE HONEYED TONGUE DECEIVES

Chapter 21

<u>22 Years Ago…</u>

The fire crackled and popped, almost angry that people were hustling around so early. The morning had an odd chill in the air, signaling to Stoltland that summer was over. Jace shivered as the nurse pulled back his blanket to inspect his wound.

Weeks had passed since Jace had watched his only friend, Lord Paetrill, sacrifice himself to the dragon, and with each day, he felt the loss more and more. The infection had finally subsided, and his leg had returned to its normal size and color. The elixir she used was helping heal the injury at a faster rate. The nurse unwrapped the wound and performed her usual cleaning without saying a word. Jace had had enough of the silent treatment.

"So, how much longer?" he asked.

No response. She dabbed the wound dry and wrapped a clean cloth around his leg. Without making eye contact, she pulled the dark wool blanket over Jace.

"Why won't you speak to me?"

"Because no one in this entire kingdom is allowed to," Corentine said sternly as she entered Jace's cold bedroom. She snapped her fingers and pointed at the door. The nurse jumped at the command and left, not looking back.

Jace's eyes narrowed. "What do you mean no one is allowed to speak to me?"

As she walked around the pitiful excuse for a room, Corentine spoke, "Your actions cost a warrior's life, so Queen Phyre issued a decree of shunning."

Jace repeated those words in his head. He had so many emotions swirling around. They had exiled Paetrill to the stables. Jace would never have met him if they hadn't done that. If Stoltland hadn't treated Jace like an outcast, he wouldn't have had to train in secret. If someone in that village had opened their homes instead of shunning him, Paetrill wouldn't have found himself in a position where he needed to sacrifice himself.

Why are they not being held accountable? Why is he the only one at fault?

"That's not fair," Jace grumbled.

"Fair?" Corentine yelled. "You dare speak to me about fair, you ungrateful child."

Jace's silver eyes burned and filled with tears. Was he ungrateful? Should he be content with injustice being done to him? The alternative was death. His shoulders slumped.

"I'm sorry, Mother. I'm grateful to you." He rubbed his wrists, remembering the man she killed.

Corentine exhaled and looked at the ceiling. "Who do you pledge yourself to because no one else cares for you?"

Jace felt a tear escape his silver eyes. "You, Mother."

Corentine's head snapped toward the window as she heard a loud commotion. "And do you solemnly swear always to be faithful and duty-bound to me?" She asked with rushed words.

"Yes, Mother," Jace said, holding back the lump in his throat.

Corentine turned from the window and raced out of the room, red hair flowing.

"Mother, what's wrong?"

When she didn't answer back, he threw the covers off and grimaced as he attempted to stand. He forced himself to hobble to the window, feeling the burning pressure of his injury. The cold against his bare feet sent chills racing through his body. Grabbing the windowsill for support, he gasped at the sight of all the orange eyes he saw.

A crowd of Korps marched toward Stoltland's palace. They looked enraged, but why? He thought Korpam was the one kingdom Stoltland wasn't on bad terms with. He recalled hearing that the alliance with Korpam was hanging by a thread, so what could this mean?

He suddenly feared for his mother. Staggering out the door, Jace descended the winding stairs, grabbing the walls for support. He wasn't sure what he could do. But he was determined no one would harm his mother—ever. He surprised himself by how fast he could run with his semi-healed injury and made a mental note to thank the silent nurse.

Jace knew all the secret entrances to the throne room and remained quiet as he rounded the dark corner. He slipped behind one of the tapestries, which depicted a dragon battling a unicorn. Jace had hidden here many times, so he knew no one would notice the lump. A large black-scaled dragon tree stood in front of the tapestry, providing excellent coverage, too.

Dragon trees are the only trees that can withstand dragon fire. They grow from the shells of dragon eggs and always have shiny, obsidian scales, regardless of the type of dragon egg. The tree's scales are used in potions, but for the past one hundred years, the scales have been ground into a powder and mixed with juice from the Glatan berry, Glatania's famous and favorite wild berry. When consumed, this dangerous combination creates mystical illusions that might allow you to communicate with past loved ones, catch a glimpse of your future, or even kill you. Stoltlanders became addicted to the thrill of which event would happen.

Jace peered between the holes of the tapestry and the dark branches to see the Stoltland royals gather around Queen Phyre. He focused his youthful ears on the heated conversation.

"I want this declaration signed now," Corentine barked.

Queen Phyre narrowed her obsidian eyes, her dark hair beginning to gray. "You, Lady Corentine, are in no position to make such demands." She threw her hands up, agitated at Corentine's voice. "Why is that even a concern right now?"

"Because you're speaking of treason." Corentine pointed at the closed silver door. "Those Korps want your backing to Korpam's throne; a coup is treason, is it not?"

Queen Phyre laughed, as did her eldest and youngest sons. "No, you stupid girl. Go read a dictionary before you embarrass yourself more."

Corentine's husband placed his hand on her shoulder. "Darling, we must consider Commander Ginnarr's proposal."

Corentine looked from face to face, then pulled her husband away from his family and, lucky for Jace, near his tapestry.

"Making this move weakens my power." Corentine placed her hands on her hips, disturbing her furry skirt made from a black bear.

"How? Corentine, you're my wife now; that trumps everything."

"Our deal with the Steigs was supposed to secure our path to the throne. If you back this coup, then what?"

"Then we're no worse off than we are now. Corentine, we have wealth, position, and respect. What more could you want?"

Corentine's dark eyes twitched. "Power and fear. And let's get something straight: you have the wealth, position, and respect. I'm still labeled 'Lady,' not a princess."

"You made that deal!" He pointed his finger, tapping it just below Corentine's neck.

"Don't turn this around on me. I had our throne secured because of Jace." Corentine's eyes widened, fearing she might have just revealed one of her many secrets.

Jace's ears heated. "Me?" he whispered to the threads. He couldn't understand why he would matter to a throne.

"I'm glad you're finally admitting it. I knew there was something more than a family connection between your father and the Steigs."

Corentine's nostrils flared. "I'm admitting to nothing. If I were queen..."

"But you're not, and most likely never will be because we're backing the commander. Korpam's reigning king will die, and Tyrdon Steig will be banished."

Corentine's husband walked away. She stood defiantly and whispered to herself, "One day. You wait. One day, I will be queen—queen of all seven kingdoms, and then Jace will be unleashed."

Chapter 22

<u>The Send Off</u>

The morning of the quest arrived, bringing crisp air with it. Birds sang their whimsical cadences, but no melody could ease the tension surrounding the send-off site. Everyone had gathered at the shore of the giant, crystal-clear lake, which felt odd because most had expected to take ships to Glatania, but this lake offered no access point to the sea.

Jace bent down near the sandy shoreline, his battle leathers creaking with the movement. As he watched the ripples tickle the surface, he felt the harmonious connection he always experienced when he was near water. He scooped up a handful of sand and stared at it, hoping that somewhere among the granules lied the answer to all his problems. The silver-eyed king let the sand pour from one hand to the other, providing the calmness he needed to face the send-off.

Jace felt memories from his past tugging at the back of his mind. To survive, he had trained himself to forget—forget the torture he had endured—but certain sounds, certain smells, even certain experiences triggered memories. His brain felt like it was on fire, repeating the words of him swearing loyalty to Corentine. He felt torn. Guilt weighed on his shoulders like yolks on oxen. Today, he was plagued not just with his past, but also his present.

The outcast king walked closer to a boulder, boots crunching on sand and pebbles. Gentle waves polished the stone with sunlight, reflecting a whisper of hope. Jace fought against the memory of his and Sealyn's silent night. He didn't know how to speak to her. The sounds of her tears pained his chest as if a mammoth was standing on him. How were they to move past something like this? He opened his calloused hand and let the sand slip through his tan-skinned fingers, allowing the wind to guide away pieces of the shore and part of Jace's confidence in his wife.

He turned when he heard footsteps and saw the fiery ginger eyes of the man claiming to be his father.

The Pirate Captain cleared his throat. "Uh, Jace or King Jace, if you will, could I have a word?"

Jace paused, watching this man who was notorious for games and deceit. How could he know without any doubt that this pirate was indeed his father? He tried to ignore his gut feeling, but he couldn't. He knew. He knew this man without a home was part of him. Jace shook his head, brushing past, and said through gritted teeth, "No. Now is not the time."

Standing beside Char, he joined the crowd, listening to Sealyn's send-off speech. He observed Sealyn's distant stares and the lack of emotion in her words; she wasn't the same carefree spirit as when they first met. His heart ached for her to open up to him, but her focus was more on breaking curses than sharing what was plaguing her mind.

Finally, the moment of surprise had arrived. Sealyn would unveil a hidden project she had commissioned her cousin, Will, to create. A smile tugged at the corner of Jace's lips as he anticipated the looks of wonder that would fill each person's face.

A light breeze ruffled the loose strands of Sealyn's hair as she turned to face the glistening water. She nodded—at nothing. People exchanged glances, wondering why their queen had just gestured to empty air. Rumors were already circulating that Sealyn was losing her mind. Was this it? Had their queen completely lost her sanity?

Suddenly, the opacity of three colossally enthralling ships came into view, as if they had been floating on the lake all this time. Jace had seen these boats several times, but their stunning grandeur took his breath away each time. These ships were unlike anything the seven kingdoms had ever witnessed. Sunlight bounced off the freshly applied linseed oil on the railings, and the wind frothed the Caledonian-feathered sails, but it was the gargantuan green phoenix wings attached to each side of the ships that caught everyone's attention.

The crowd murmured questions. How was this possible? Wings couldn't just appear on the side of boats. What kind of magic was this?

Sealyn lifted her toned arm toward the ships. "As you can see, we've been working on a spectacular project. My cousin, Lord Prince Will Araelien, had several prototypes that would have taken longer to succeed, but …" She dropped her arm and signaled to Skarpin and his friends to join her. They eagerly ran to Sealyn, hugging her legs and torso. "These brilliant young minds discovered a missing link to what we wanted to accomplish, but it would take more than spells and tools to create what you see before you. We needed the strength of green phoenix wings, and this would require a powerful Luxen. However, as you know, phoenixes aren't willing to channel just anyone. We had to find one pure of heart." Sealyn grinned with pride as she heard footsteps on the ship's deck behind her. "It should come as no surprise that Dun's mate, Angan, chose Queen Mother Graelynd to channel. I give you… my mother." The words tumbled from her lips with a quiver.

She was immensely proud of her mother. Tears pricked at her emerald eyes amid the sounds of cheers and clapping as her mother waved from the middle ship, dressed in battle leathers. Sealyn felt a pang in her chest. She would hurt her parents with the conclusion of her mission, and there was nothing she could do to prevent it. She glanced at Jace and knew she would shatter his heart once he discovered her secret.

Sealyn's chosen army bid farewell to their families and friends. Tears of sadness and fear glistened on several cheeks. Glatania was a kingdom with little recorded history, and Elysium hadn't set foot on Glatanian soil in over five hundred years. Those left behind had every reason to worry about their loved ones.

The team climbed into small landing boats that glided toward the floating marvels. Jace let his fingers skim the water's surface; cool liquid spilled through, reassuring him. He felt a sense of peace and home, but he also sensed an odd sting against his wrists.

Once the crew gathered on the middle ship, Commander Tilmond took charge with instructions. "Rest assured, comrades, our Elysium is in good hands with King Father Ryker and Captain Favien. Now, let's focus on our task at hand. Upon boarding, each of you received a scroll with a specific ribbon color. Those with the same color will be on the same ship. Blue, gather over here. Green, group together over there, and yellow, stand right here." Soldiers moved to their assigned positions, bumping into each other. "Here's the reality: no one has ever sailed the skies, so we don't know exactly what to expect. Luckily for us, Madam Bip has reconfigured the protection spell to help with the 'breathing at high altitudes' issue. Madam Bip and Professor Draemamoor, or Lady Novaly as most here know her, created a concoction for invisibility that includes the use of Mirron hair. I'm not skilled in potions, so I won't try to elaborate on the matter, but just know we will be invisible to those below us. Any questions so far?"

Lord Max was the first to raise his hand. The group chuckled, well aware of Max's reputation as the one who always had a thousand questions. "Commander, what should we do with the scrolls?"

"Excellent question, one I was just about to address, so," Tilmond clapped his hands together and rubbed them excitedly. "Those scrolls represent your assigned chores on the ship." He laughed, only to be met with groans. "Now, now. Cheer up. It's not all chores all day; we need to be in top shape, and that includes our vessels."

Max's hand shot up again. "How will the ships not collide if we're invisible?"

Head nods signaled that more than one soldier was thinking the same thing.

"Full of great questions, aren't you, Max?" The soldiers snickered and patted Max on the shoulders. "Only the bottom and sides of the ships will have invisibility. We will still be able to see the decks, flags, masts, and sails."

Sealyn caught Jace's eye and signaled for him to step aside for a private conversation. Jace's shoulders sagged. He didn't want to talk. His emotions felt confusing to him. He needed time to process.

Out of earshot from the team, Sealyn folded her arms and whispered, "Jace, I'm so sorry. I wanted to tell you …"

"But you didn't," Jace snapped. He felt anger boiling within him. Why did a mistake made by a loved one sting so much more?

Sealyn fought against Kazimir's rude advice, bubbling in her head and focused on the man she loved. "Please, Jace. He begged me not to tell."

"From what it sounded like, it seemed to be a bargaining chip for the pirates to assist you in breaking a curse."

Sealyn shifted her stance and placed her hands on her hips. "Okay, maybe it started that way, but I couldn't be the one to tell you. It needed to come from him." They both looked at the Pirate Captain, who was whispering to his other two sons.

Jace shook his head, and his jaw tightened. "Sea, I expect full transparency from you. That's what this marriage is—no secrets."

Sealyn knew she was in the wrong but couldn't help what slipped out, "Kind of like those scars on your wrists, huh?"

Jace's eyes flared a quick orange before settling back to their sparkling silver. He began to see red as anger overtook him. He didn't want to say something he would regret. Space. He wanted space. Jace held up his scroll tied with a green velvet ribbon and shook his head before stomping away into the crowd of dispersing soldiers. Char was next in line to slide down the rope to a landing boat when Jace grabbed his arm. He spun Char around, swapped his scroll with Char's, and leaped over the railing with the rope in hand.

Char understood Jace's intentions. "No, Jace. You really don't want to do that." But his words fell on deaf ears as Jace landed in the boat, swaying on the unstable waters.

Sealyn stood next to Char, her eyes clouded with rage and tears. She peered down at her king, who glared back at her. Jace jerked his head away and started rowing toward the blue ship with his new crew.

"Why did you let him leave, Sea?" Char asked pleadingly for reconsideration.

Sealyn wiped her tears from her olive-skinned cheeks, and her lip curled before facing her cousin. "Because he thinks he's running away, but what he doesn't realize is that he's about to face his troubles head-on."

Jace's raft was the last crew to board the blue ship. He welcomed the fresh air as he climbed the swinging rope ladder, but his entire world came crashing down the moment he jumped over the polished wooden banister. Now, he found himself trapped and face-to-face with Tyrdon Steig, his father.

Chapter 23

<u>A Felistilio</u>

Midafternoon light streamed through Lady Norella's classroom window, adding a sense of wonder to the ancient texts the class was studying. Her heels clicked on the stone floor as she wove through the rows of wooden desks. She stopped at the green chalkboard and wrote the words "Second Chance" in white, gritty lettering. Setting down the piece of chalk, she rubbed her hands together, brushing the white powder off her fingers. Professor Norella Vidya turned to face her classroom and gave her students a cheeky grin.

"Who would like to read for us today?" she asked in her most exuberantly vivacious voice. No one raised their hand. She lifted her arms in defeat. "Elladelle, why don't you continue where we left off yesterday? Third paragraph on page seventy-two, please."

Elladelle's face flushed. She sometimes stuttered while reading aloud. Her mouth felt dry, and she swallowed hard, praying she wouldn't mess up. "The Second Chance can be summed up in its very name—a second chance for humanity."

"Good," Professor Vidya interrupted. "Let's pause here. Can everyone tell me what this means before we read more?"

Wullen raised his hand, blonde eyebrows bouncing excitedly. "It's because people messed up and were given a second chance."

Norella clapped her hands, her teeth sparkling in a wide smile. "Great response, Wullen. Let's continue reading to find out more, shall we? Pinny, would you start where Elladelle left off?"

"In the year 1900, all seven kingdoms were at war. Massive casualties caused economic and psychological breakdowns in each region. The bloodlust of those in power could not be stopped; therefore, Creator took it upon Himself to erase the bloodshed and remove the bloodthirsty leaders from existence.

According to multiple accounts, an ethereal pearl light so bright that people fell to their knees, shielding their eyes, enveloped all kingdoms. When the..." She paused, sounding out the next syllables in her head. Luckily, their vocabulary words correlated with their history lessons, so she was prepared, just nervous. She started the sentence again, "When the luminescence dissipated, the leaders were nowhere to be found, and all bodies had been buried with glowing markers. Even every droplet of blood had disappeared as if battles had never occurred. On each throne rested a luminous white scroll, detailing Creator's message to the world."

"And stop right there, please, Pinny. Excellent job reading. I'll make a note to write to your parents and let them know how much you've improved." Norella walked to the chalkboard and wrote the word "scroll," dust particles drifting in the air. She turned to face the class, still holding the chalk. "Who can tell me in their own words what the instructions were for each kingdom?"

Skarpin raised his hand, but before he could say anything, a loud, piercing screech sent shockwaves through the classroom. The children jumped, panic flooding their eyes. Professor Vidya rushed past the desks and flung open her heavy wooden door. She quickly jerked her head back just in time to avoid being clipped by a runaway herd of Felistilios. Norella tried to close her door, but one managed to escape inside her classroom.

Children squealed and took cover under their desks as the creature soared above them with its bat-like, shimmering, blush wings. The Felistilio hails from Glatania. It has the body of a scaled cat and a long, dragon-like tail. Its hues range from pink to purple, with hints of blue near its belly.

Books lay scattered on the stone floor, disturbed by the intrusive tail of the cat-bat creature. A breathless Professor Rendell leaned against the doorframe, swallowing gulps of air. Sweat dripped from his dark brown hair onto his rosy cheeks and nose. He clutched the wooden sphere of his necklace and reached out his hand, purple and pink sparks swirling around his fingertips. The dazzling creature paused in mid-air, its indigo slit eyes glaring at Professor Rendell.

Hueweyn Rendell was the professor responsible for teaching *Magical Creature Studies* and *Transference Applications*. He was exceptionally brilliant, but sometimes the creatures would grow bored, and off they would go on their own. He understood that bringing in an entire colony of Felistilios was a risk. Still, he wanted to conduct a comprehensive study on these specific beasts since Queen Sealyn's crew would most likely encounter them.

With majestic elegance, the creature glided through the air and perched on Professor Rendell's shoulder, wrapping its twinkling magenta tail around Hueweyn's chest. The children cautiously emerged from their hiding spots, and Norella marched toward Hueweyn like an angry moose. She placed her hands on her hips and glowered.

"Professor Rendell, what is the meaning of this?" She tapped her foot impatiently as some of her class giggled.

Professor Rendell fumbled through his words. He wasn't skilled at speaking during confrontations. "I, um, well…I thought it would be best for each Transference student to have some one-on-one time with a Felistilio." He continued to sweat, and his mouth felt dry.

Professor Vidya folded her arms and huffed. "And look how well that turned out. That blasted tail could have poked a child's eye out."

The Felistilio hissed, then nuzzled Hueweyn's disheveled head.

Professor Hueweyn lowered his jade eyes. "My apologies, children, and to you, Professor Vidya. I'm simply investigating these misunderstood creatures. Not much is known about them in our part of the world, and Queen Sealyn's team will need all the information they can gather for a successful mission. I just want to do my part."

Upon hearing about his adopted mother, Skarpin jumped up, golden eyes wide, and said, "If there's a way to help my mother, then I want in. Do you have any other ideas, Professor?"

Knowledge sparkled deep in Professor Hueweyn's eyes, and a relieved smile etched in his sweat-stained face. "Why, Skarpin, I thought you'd never ask."

Chapter 24

<u>Shunalian Checkpoint</u>

The cool, fresh air whipped past Jace's face as he stood at the bow of the flying wooden ship. Strands of dark chestnut hair slipped free from their ties, blowing wildly in the wind. His knuckles turned white as he clutched the railing. His tanned jaw flexed at the thought of his argument with Sealyn. He shook his head, preparing to walk away to his quarters, when Lord Finn patted his shoulder before he could turn.

"Hi, King Jace. I hope I'm not disturbing you."

"Not at all. I actually could use a distraction from my thoughts." Jace gazed out at the horizon of light blue sky and fluffy white clouds.

Finn leaned on the railing, scared to ask his questions. "So, I wanted to check in and see how you were doing, you know, after that big reveal the other night."

Jace let out an exasperated sigh. "I'm not sure what to do with that information. Can you believe it? I mean, Finn, that pirate is my father—*my* father."

Finn always had a calm and relaxed presence, not letting much bother him, but even he had to agree with Jace's shock. "Have you thought about what to do?"

"I don't know," Jace shook his head. "What does anyone do in this situation? I thought my father came from the Steigs of Korpam, but maybe that was wishful thinking. Childish."

Finn's face crumpled. "Steigs? Who are they?"

Jace flipped around, watching the ship's crew dally about their chores. He leaned his elbows on the railing. "They were the royals of Korpam before the commander's coup."

"So, why would you think one of them was your father?" Finn took an apple from his pack and bit into the sweet fruit, juice running down his lips.

Jace didn't want to recall the Steigs' demise. Pools of dark, sticky blood flashed in his memory. He blinked, pushing the memory away. "It was just something that had occurred during the overthrow, but I'm obviously wrong."

Finn swallowed the apple. "But why would you want to be a son of a Steig? That would put an even bigger target on your back, right?"

Jace chuckled. "Yeah, I have a pretty big one of those, don't I?" He pushed away from the banister and stepped closer to Finn. He had always trusted him. "Because that would mean I had royal blood." Jace threw his hands up quickly. "I know I still have gray eyes, but royal blood could show that…" He dropped his head and folded his arms, embarrassed to express what he thought. He felt Finn place his hand on his shoulder, giving him the courage to share feelings he had kept secret since the day he met Sealyn. Jace looked into Finn's ice-blue eyes, a friend's eyes. "It would mean that I was truly worthy of Sealyn—worthy of her love, her value, her everything. Ha! Even this kingdom that I'm king of. I could finally be seen as more than just a charity case."

Finn nodded, unaware that Jace had been bottling up so much for so long. It made sense, though. He couldn't imagine all that Jace had endured, yet he still turned out to be an incredible human — that speaks volumes about what's in a person's heart. "Listen, Jace, I haven't known Queen Sealyn long, but from what I can tell, she looks beyond what the world sees and looks straight at a person's heart. She recognized something in you all those years ago. I wouldn't doubt or question it anymore. You're King Jace of Elysium, with or without royal blood."

Jace swallowed a lump in his throat. "Thank you, my friend."

They heard someone running behind them. When they turned, they saw Laisren yelling and pointing, "Look down. Look down. It's Shunal!"

Everyone clung to the railing and peered down at the newly freed kingdom as the giant wings adjusted themselves to the crew's movements. Several people onboard shivered, remembering the kingdom filled with snakes and trickery. Flying had made their journey quicker than they had expected, so as the sun began its stunning display of oranges, pinks, and yellows, the three ships approached their checkpoint in the northeastern region of Shunal.

Sealyn stood beside her mother as Graelynd guided the ships with graceful landings into a vast lake, its bottom covered in gold coins. King Cruz had specific docks built for this mission and stood at the edge, watching the three massive ships sail into position. His long, honey cape billowed in the calm night wind, and his golden crown glimmered in the light from the torches along the docks.

Sealyn turned to her mother, grabbing her hands. "Mother, you've done a fantastic job. I can see that this has already taken much of your strength. You need to rest and recover for the next part. Please enjoy your dinner in our chambers, and I'll check on you before turning in for the night."

Graelynd cupped Sealyn's cheek with her delicate hand. "My darling, be cautious with King Cruz. Power changes people." She squeezed her daughter's cheek and smiled, then made her way to the royal chambers, accompanied by Lady Madilina.

Her mother's words weighed heavily on her mind. Surely, Cruz was the right choice to lead Shunal? Or were her mother's words about her? Could her mother sense her struggles? Sealyn shook off the nagging questions and descended the rope ladder. King Cruz immediately embraced her tightly. His royal golden clothes smelled of spices and pine.

He pulled back, mischief dancing in his golden eyes. Cruz still had his luscious, curly locks of licorice hair and a smile that spelled trouble. He bowed his head and took Sealyn's hand in his. He raised his other hand, waving it across the landscape. "Welcome, Queen Sealyn. Welcome to Vaelinthia." His eyes watched hers.

A gasp escaped Sealyn's mouth. Her emerald eyes welled with tears that threatened to fall. Sealyn's mind flashed back to when she first met Vaelinthia among the golden cattails along Shunal's shoreline. She was the brave barmaid who helped rescue Elysium's captives from the Stoltlanders. Sealyn remembered running through the streets in golden hooded capes with Vael. Nightmares tormented Sealyn, with visions of Vaelinthia comforting Ashur while snakes piled in the cave, Vaelinthia struggling out of the garden maze, and Vaelinthia striking the rock in an attempt to collect gems. Sealyn didn't want to remember the next part. The part that haunted her dreams. Sealyn saw Kazimir's black head coming for his killing blow; then, her face felt the hot droplets of blood from Vaelinthia's sacrifice. The rebel who saved her life. Almost every night, Sealyn saw Vaelinthia's limp body in Kazimir's jaws

"Sealyn?" Cruz whispered.

Sealyn's mind snapped back to reality. "Ww-what?"

"I thought renaming the city in honor of Vaelinthia fitting, no?"

Sealyn wiped away a rogue tear and nodded. "Yes. Yes. Of course. It feels like she's still here helping our mission."

"Exactly." Cruz looked around, then tilted his head. "Where is King Jace?"

Still in a daze, Sealyn said, "He's on the other ship. Over there."

A rakish smile split Cruz's face. "Trouble in paradise?"

Sealyn rolled her eyes. "Not enough for you to be happy about it." She looked past him, seeing his crowd of advisers, guards, and none other than the massive Naehass.

Coiled on the canary yellow sandbank was the legendary serpent with its two giant heads: Mauor and Kazimir. They both waited anxiously; Sealyn wished she could just curl up in her bed with Jace stroking her hair, but alas, duty called.

"I need to speak to Mauor and Kazimir alone," Sealyn said.

Cruz's jaw stiffened. "Sealyn, I really must protest…"

A loud hiss echoed across the darkness.

Sealyn raised her eyebrow. "I wouldn't finish that sentence if I were you, King Cruz. As you know, Kazimir is not your greatest fan." She brushed past him. Cruz may be the king of Shunal, but the source of Shunal's magic was Sealyn's possession: the gold cuffs.

Before entering the enormous canvas tent, Sealyn looked back and smiled, seeing her people welcomed by their allies. Friends reunited like Char and Herbmando. Even Lady Jadelyn was giving out hugs as the Elysians gathered around the warm fires, drinking fresh ale. Sealyn's eyes narrowed at the sight of Cruz shaking hands with Jace. Perhaps those two could bury the past, but an icy feeling crept over her. Someone was watching. Her eyes darted from side to side, ears pricked for any movement, but she saw no one and heard no one.

She heard a low growl. In the darkness, away from the festivities, she saw Shep's glinting, distrustful eyes. The tiger glared, almost as if telling Sealyn he knew her secrets. This cat was starting to work on every nerve she had. She jerked her head away and stomped inside the tent.

Kazimir's beady, dark eyes twinkled with mischief when Sealyn walked in. "Ah, my queen, did you miss me?"

"About as much as I miss being stung by a wasp."

Mauor laughed. "Welcome, Queen Sealyn. We know you need your rest, so we won't take much time. Are they with you?"

Sealyn sighed. "The 'they' you're referring to are Nawrooshall, king of the mammoths, and Dun, our Green Phoenix?"

"Yes, majesty," Mauor answered, lantern light bouncing off his golden scales.

"Well, not physically."

Kazimir rolled his eyes. "Obviously," he dragged out the word.

"You're always full of sugar and honey, aren't you?" Sealyn pulled out a chair from the wooden table and flopped into the seat. She leaned her elbows on the table and propped her chin on her hands. She locked eyes with the Naehass. "Yes, the communication line is open; they're here in my mind with me, so talk."

Sealyn closed her eyes and visualized the tent now filled with the giant, shaggy-haired mammoth king and her close ally, Dun. Weary from her travels, she focused because she desperately needed this time to communicate with them all.

Outside of the tent's activities, Char had felt Shep's calling, so he brought Herbmando to meet his tiger. However, when he saw how intense Shep looked near the royal tent, he kept quiet. Char grabbed his necklace and instantly heard Herbmando's thoughts: "What an awesome tiger! I wish I were a Transference. I mean, just look at Shep. He's got green and gold stripes; how cool is that?"

"Shhhh, Herbmando."

"I didn't say anything," he whispered.

Char swatted the air. "I meant your thoughts."

"You want me to quiet my thoughts? What?" Herbmando chuckled. "Be honest. How drunk are you?" Char waved Herbmando's jokes away.

Shep nodded to the tent. Char quickly snuck to the back and pressed his ear against the fabric. He heard voices. Herbmando did the same but heard nothing.

"Char, I don't hear anything. What are we doing?"

"Shhh. I need to concentrate. I'll tell you in just a minute."

Char focused, and to his surprise, he heard all the legendary creatures speaking. He couldn't believe it. No one but Sealyn had heard their voices, so how was he able to? He was completely lost on how they were all here. His head pounded and begged him to stop, but he wanted answers.

"We cannot ignore the Cognition powers any longer," Nawrooshall said.

"And just what are you proposing?" Kazimir snarled.

Mauor nudged his neighboring head. "Easy, brother. This burden is becoming more than Sealyn can handle. It would have been easier for her to have been born a Transference rather than a Cognition."

"Well, she's not," Dun snapped. "She's stronger than you know." Dun eyed Sealyn and gave a slight nod.

"But she's married to her weakness. Jace could be her downfall." The mammoth huffed and stomped his leg, fur shaking.

"I'm hungry. Shall I dispose of him?"

Sealyn glared at Kazimir. "Touch him and die, lizard."

Kazimir chuckled

"This is going nowhere. We all know that Cognitions usually go mad after the first few years of their powers unleashing, so where does that leave Sealyn?" asked Mauor.

Tears streamed down Sealyn's olive-skinned cheeks, each drop a testament to her agony. She felt tired, lonely, and angry—always angry.

"She needs something to ground her, something that can stall the inevitable long enough," Nawrooshall said.

Dun looked at Sealyn. "Jace will be her anchor."

Kazimir hissed. "You mean distraction. He hasn't proven his worth yet. He's only made things worse."

Blood dripped from Sealyn's nose onto the table, seeping into the cracks.

"He can do this. He can be her lighthouse in the storm," Dun argued.

Sealyn slammed her fist on the table. Char and Herbmando jumped at the loud noise. Sealyn's bloodshot eyes scanned the table, meeting the gazes of the creatures before her. "So that's your brilliant plan? Use Jace's love for me? Then what? We all know how this ends. Am I supposed to depend on him, never revealing my fate? Then, once I've completed the mission, his heart will be shattered—devastated." Sealyn sobbed loudly into her hands. "It's not fair to do this to him."

"Sealyn, the sacrifice of the third-generation bloodline was written long ago," Dun said softly, his yellow eyes filled with sadness. "You can choose to walk away, but everyone who has died so far will have died in vain—not to mention all the other lives Corentine will kill."

Sealyn wrapped her arms around herself, rocking slightly. "I didn't ask for this. If I had known…" her words trailed off. "I never would…" she gasped for air. "Jace. Oh, Creator, why me? Don't do this to Jace!"

Blood pooled from her ears and nose, mixing with tears. Char could stand no more. He didn't like what he was hearing. He got up and ran to the front of the tent, Herbmando and Shep trailing after him. Char burst through the tent flap. "Sealyn!"

The Naehass snapped and hissed. Sealyn's eyes flew open, her face soaked in blood and tears.

"What the…Sealyn! What happened?" Char lifted his head angrily at the Naehass. "What did you do, you stupid snake?!"

The shock of Char made Sealyn's head spin. Shadowy spots clouded her vision, and her cousin caught her before she could fall to the floor. Char cradled his cousin, praying she would wake up. Herbmando raced out of the tent, shouting for help. Char couldn't organize his thoughts; he was in shock. He could only focus on the phrase "the sacrifice of the third-generation bloodline." What did that mean?

What he truly understood was that the legendary beings proclaimed Sealyn required an anchor—a beacon of hope amidst the darkness. Lighthouses not only provided guiding light, which Jace was destined to provide, but they also stood resilient against raging waves. Char was prepared to embody that steadfastness. He would endure the relentless storms for his queen and his family. She would never face the torments alone.

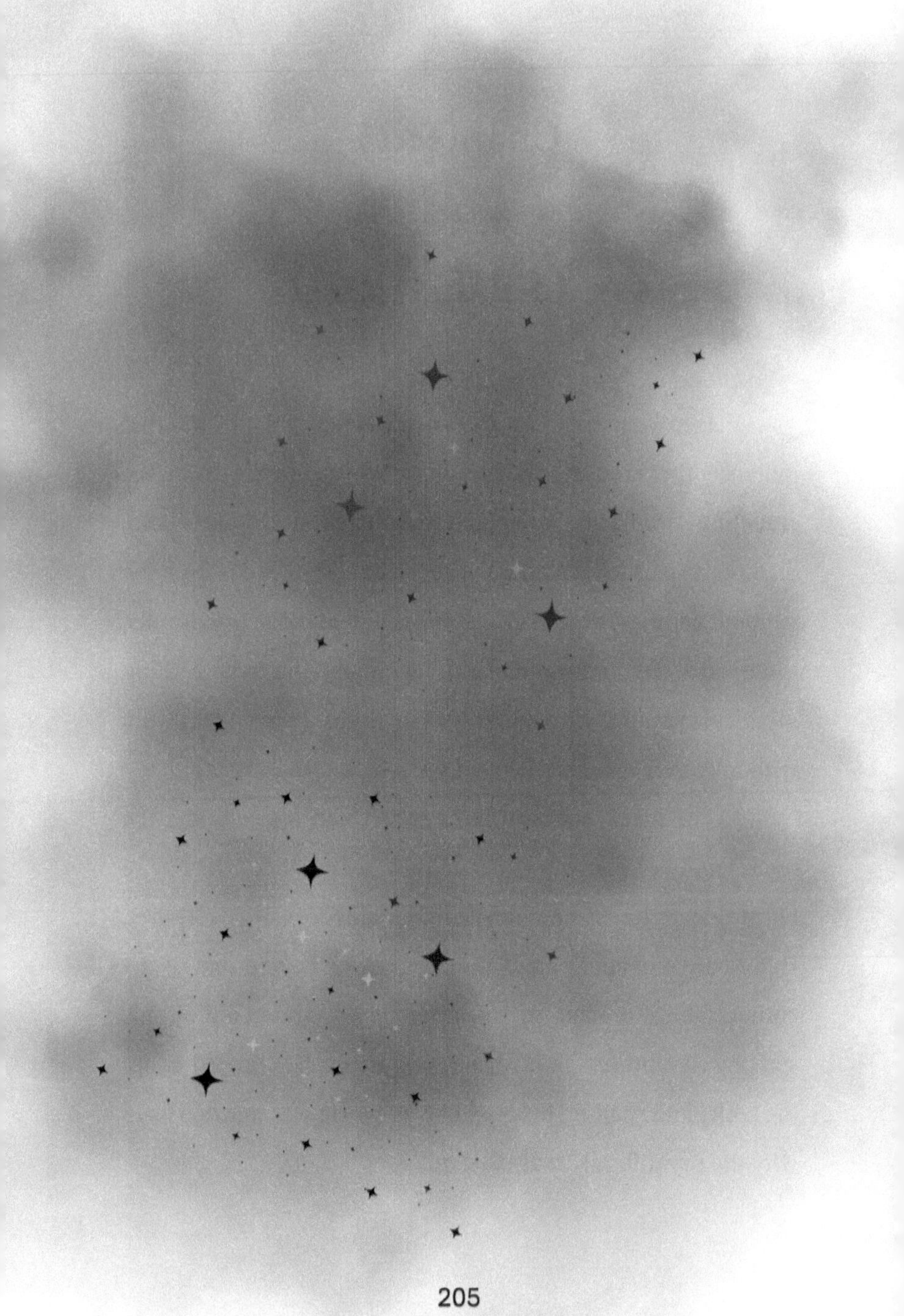

Chapter 25

<u>22 Years Ago…</u>

Jace marveled at the royal banquet hall. Infernal radiance flickered across the black marble floors from the crackling fireplaces. Chandeliers lathered in gaudy ebony diamonds sparkled with their shadow-bound splendor from the vaulted ceilings above. Jace marveled at colorful murals, illuminated by the candlelight, depicting dragons battling mythical creatures from all seven kingdoms. Pure silver chairs with inky velvet cushions lined the long rectangular table.

The black doors to the banquet hall opened, and the royal family of Korpam strode in with heavy steps. They wore burnt orange tunics embellished with amber-gemmed sashes. Before anyone could catch him, Jace dove behind one of the corner tables draped in thick midnight fabric, aiding his stealthy adventure. On his hands and knees, he crawled under the tablecloth, willing his breath to slow. He was puzzled as to why the royal family was present.

Just weeks earlier, he had overheard Corentine's husband mention that Stoltland would support a coup with Korpam's commander. Was Stoltland planning to betray the commander? Jace lay on his stomach and lifted the tablecloth just enough to see feet passing by.

Servants positioned themselves behind the guests, ready to serve dinner. The doors swung open once more, and the Stoltland royal family glided to their seats. Jace inhaled the delicious aromas of roasted potatoes and pheasant. He wished that one day, he could sit at the royal table and truly be a part of the family. Until then, he would settle for leftovers and observe the conversations.

Queen Phyre, queen of Stoltland, wore a lacy onyx gown festooned with obsidian peacock feathers around her neck. She clapped, and the servants immediately began serving plates of food. The dark queen cleared her throat, "Welcome, old friends. We hope your journey will be worthwhile once you enjoy our scrumptious pheasant."

The Korps chuckled, aware that the bird would be nothing short of dry and overcooked. Stoltland was not known for its savory foods. They ate merely out of necessity, not for pleasure.

King Tashton raised his silver goblet. "As you said, Queen Phyre, we are old friends, and we hope to continue our relationship and understanding *as friends*."

Jace wished he could see everyone's faces. He attempted to shift his small body for a better view but suddenly felt a cramp forming in his leg. He couldn't create a scene. His heart raced. Trouble was the last thing he needed right now. He bit down hard on his finger, trying to distract himself from the cramp.

"Is there an accusation behind that statement?" Queen Phyre asked. She sipped her red wine, relishing the slight burn as the liquid washed down her potatoes. She watched the Korpam king like a spider eyeing a fly in its web.

Korpam's queen fired back, "If we were accusing, you would know it." Her orange eyes blazed.

Stoltland's youngest prince huffed. He swallowed his ale. "Such rudeness. After we greeted you all with a warm welcome." He huffed again, trying to be dramatic.

The servants removed the plates and replaced them with bowls of cold tomato soup. Several Korps cast sidelong glances at each other. Nobody wanted to eat the cold, mushy food.

Jace thought he heard several scuffles outside the banquet hall. He wondered if the Korpam guards were just fooling around or if perhaps someone had fallen.

One of the Korps high council members slammed his goblet, splashing red wine. "As warm as you welcomed our commander—I'm sure," he said through gritted teeth.

The room fell silent. Jace couldn't understand why the atmosphere had changed, but his heart sank when he noticed the crimson liquid oozing under the door. Blood. Why was there blood? He began to panic.

Servants stood behind each guest, waiting for their next instructions.

Queen Phyre laughed a husky laugh. "Your commander was only securing our alliance. Unless you're not interested in that anymore."

Jace scooted farther away from the sticky liquid creeping toward him. The cramp intensified. He needed to escape, but he was trapped.

"Queen Phyre, we traveled all this way to protect our *invested* interest," King Tashton of Korpam said. He pulled at his salt-and-pepper beard.

There was a long pause. Jace's heart pounded. He tried to massage his calf, but instead, he felt blood. He flinched, knocking the table. Jace sucked in a breath, praying no one heard.

"If that's your only reason for aligning with us, then I'm afraid it's time for dessert," Queen Phyre spat.

Tashton looked confused and began to speak, "Dessert …"

The knife slicing King Tashton's throat prevented him from finishing his sentence. The servants had stepped forward and slit each Korp's throat, all except one—their queen.

Korpam's queen screamed. She attempted to run, but a servant held her in her chair, a knife pressed to her throat. She glared at Queen Phyre, afraid to move against the blade. Jace watched in horror as blood spilled from the table onto the black marble floor. He wanted to scream with the fear building inside him.

Through gasps of air, the fire-eyed queen whimpered, "Why? Why would you do this?"

Queen Phyre stood, her chair scraping against the floor. She leaned on her skeleton-like fingers. "That is not for you to know. Your only purpose now is to return with these corpses and the message that there is a new king now for Korpam."

The dethroned queen sucked in a breath and let the words spill out like a waterfall, "Spare my sons, please. Tyrdon and Taevon. They're innocent."

A cruel grin was plastered across Phyre's face. "Taevon, your youngest, will be sent to the mines at the new king's pleasure."

"And Tyrdon?" the desperate mother squeaked.

Phyre looked at Corentine with distaste, then back at Korpam's remaining guest. "He will have a fate worse than death: banishment."

"No, please. Please let him stay with me."

"He will always feel the sting of wanting what he can't have." Phyre chuckled. "But all of this depends on the new king's choices. I'm sure he won't break his word and will spare your children—the only threats to his throne." Phyre grabbed her goblet and turned away from the table. "Let's go. The stench of blood has ruined my appetite. Clean this up."

The Stoltlanders departed as guards dragged Korpam's former queen. She kicked and clawed, desperately trying to hold her husband one last time, but she was no match for the soldiers. Other guards carried the limp, bloody bodies out of the room, leaving a scared young boy behind.

Jace's body trembled. Blood pooled around him from the door and the table. He was afraid to move, afraid to open his eyes. He didn't want to see the cruelty displayed on the chairs and floor. The crimson liquid brushed against his cheek and hair, mingling with his innocent tears. He despised his life and loathed his family. Why did they do this? They had murdered so many in a matter of seconds. He wanted to run away and escape their evilness. With his jaw clenched, he sat up, blood staining the entirety of his left side. He would leave.

Anywhere was better than here. His mind was made up. It was time for him to vanish and never come back.

Chapter 26

<u>How Dare You?</u>

Sealyn heard muffled whispers and the sound of scampering feet. Her head throbbed. She wanted to sit up but couldn't. She felt weak and so, *so* tired. Her eyes slowly opened, sunlight burning her corneas. Figures began to come into focus. She saw Jace in the corner talking with Cruz and Char. Her mother was asleep on a chaise next to her bed. What had happened? What was the last thing she remembered? Everything was fuzzy.

Jace looked over at Sealyn and saw her eyes open. "Sealyn?" He rushed to her side, wrapping his hand around hers. He kissed her cheek, then her hand. "Sealyn, how do you feel?"

Sealyn squinted, surveying the room. She wasn't sure what to say. "I, um, I'm a little tired, I suppose."

Queen Mother Graelynd shifted to the edge of her chaise and took Sealyn's other hand in hers. "You had us worried, my dear girl. I'll have some food sent for you." She stood, eyeing Jace, and took Cruz's arm, motioning for him to leave with her.

"Uh, Jace," Char said. "Could you give Sealyn and me a moment alone, please?"

Jace flinched. This was unusual. Char wasn't one for secrets with him, but he trusted him. "Sure. I'll see if Laisren can make more coffee. For some reason, his coffee is the best I've ever tasted, but don't tell Sir Nijeel I said that." He smiled awkwardly. Jace leaned in, kissed Sealyn's cheek, and whispered, "I don't want to fight, my love, but we still need to talk. I love you."

Once Jace left, Char pounced. "Sealyn! How dare you?!"

Sealyn grabbed her head. "Uh, Char. Not so loud, you thick-headed mongoose. What's wrong with you?"

"With me? With *me*? You! You're the…I can't even… Sealyn, how could…"

"Char, I swear. If you don't learn how to finish your sentences in the next five seconds, I'll feed you to Kazimir." She heard the snake hiss-giggle in her head.

Char took a deep breath. "Okay, okay. So, here's the thing. Shep. You know Shep—my really awesome tiger buddy." Sealyn glared. "Yes, to the point. So, Sheppy Boy can read minds, and he's decided to give that power to me." Sealyn recoiled. "And I just so happened to channel him when you were having your creepy, 'not-speaking-to-one-another' creature meeting."

Sealyn tilted her throbbing head. "Exactly what are you saying?"

"That I basically heard everything that those psycho creatures were saying in your head."

Sealyn closed her eyes and sighed deeply. This was not good. Char was the last person she wanted to know her secret. He was too unpredictable. "Char …"

"No, Sealyn. Don't. Just don't." He paced with his hands on his hips. "You are not sacrificing yourself for us— that's number one, and two, you're not alone. Let's get that straight right now."

Her heart ached. She loved her cousin just like a brother. She smiled and weakly pushed herself up, propping herself against the wooden headboard and fluffy pillows. "I appreciate your words more than you know, but Char …"

"No. No. No. There is no 'but,' Sea. Not happening. Nope."

"Let me finish. I'm serious, Char. I've searched and searched for another solution, and if you have one, then please, by all means, let me hear it, but there is no other answer to fit the prophecy. The third-generation bloodline must …" Sealyn dropped her head and fidgeted with her hands on the blankets.

"Die. Die, Sealyn? Really? No, there has to be another way. That can't be the solution. How does that make sense? After you miraculously break all seven curses, Creator just wants you dead? Does He just kill you? Do you poof, cease to exist? What?" His voice cracked, and tears spilled from the sides of his jade eyes.

"Aw, sweet Char." Sealyn bit her lip, pushing down her tears, and tried to give Char what he needed. "We don't have to stop looking for an alternative, but these curses have lasted too long. The world needs this. I can give everyone freedom; it just costs…"

"Your life," Char said so lightly that Sealyn wasn't sure she heard it. "Listen, Sea. I'm going to be here for you. I know these curses are taking their toll on you, and apparently, you're on schedule to go mad from those insane Cognition powers of yours, so I'll be here to pull you back from whatever darkness you will face."

Sealyn shook her head, stifling a laugh. "How can you always find a way to make me laugh even when facing death?"

Char smiled. "It's a gift. Now, when are you telling Jace about this?"

Sealyn's expression soured. Her chest felt like a horse had stepped on it. "I can't, Char. Maybe if we break more curses, but Char, there are still four more kingdoms to claim. We're not even close to being finished. Why burden him with this when it might not even happen? Give him the gift of ignorance, please."

Char didn't like it. He didn't want to keep such heavy secrets from Jace, but it was Sealyn's choice, not his, to disclose. She was right about how unsure the mission was. They had a long way to go before completing the exploits. War was everywhere, making the conquest of kingdoms even harder. They had no idea what they were stepping into with Glatania.

Rumors circulated about what awaited them. He recalled how Shunal's curse reacted once it recognized Sealyn's intentions. Would the same thing occur when they arrived in Glatania? Sealyn was already struggling, so how would she resist this next challenge? If she gave in, what would happen to all of Elysium? Would they be trapped in Glatania?

Char pushed aside all his questions. They didn't matter. He would stand by Sealyn, no matter the cost—even if it cost him his life.

Chapter 27

<u>Feydom Rivals</u>

Crisp autumn air finally blew through the school grounds, tickling the trees into changing their greens to reds, yellows, and oranges. The students had pleaded with Headmistress Araelien for practice Feydom scrimmages. She finally relented but decided that only two teams would compete against each other in the scrimmages; this way, the layout was smaller, and the players received more practice time.

The school was humming with excitement, for today was the first scrimmage. The Blue Phoenixes were facing off against the Purple Phoenixes. Sparkling blue and purple flags flowed gracefully from the hallway ceilings. Students painted their cheeks with vibrant colors of the phoenix team they were supporting, embodying the spirit of the game. Even the chefs conjured up bewitching foods to celebrate the Feydom teams, from whimsical cupcakes topped with swirling blue icing to steaming purple mashed potatoes.

Skarpin dropped his books at the end of the long dining hall table. He sat next to Elladelle and grabbed a few blueberries, chicken legs, and purple mashed potatoes before joining the lively conversation.

Wullen pointed with his chicken leg to Naedon. "There's no doubt. The Blue Phoenixes will blow the Purple Phoenixes away. Did you see their Roamers?"

Naedon let loose his contagious laugh. "Yeah, I can run circles around them. Most of their Roamers should be Tacklers."

"That's so mean, Naedon," Elladelle scolded.

Wullen rolled his eyes and brushed back his bright blonde, shaggy hair. "It's true, though. Oh, I forgot to tell you everything. I heard that Draekin is making a betting chart."

"A what?" Saedeen asked innocently.

The boys snickered.

Wullen folded his arms, freckles displayed across his nose and cheeks. "We're making our own tournament, and then everyone places bets on who they think will win."

"That's not against school rules?" Elladelle asked.

"Well, since this is all new, I don't think they've had a chance to make it against school rules," Wullen laughed.

Skarpin bit into one of the swirled blue icing cupcakes; sugar and vanilla exploded on his tongue. "These are delicious," he said with a mouthful, icing on his top lip.

"So, who do you think will win Feydom this year?" Naedon asked.

"C'mon. You can't be serious? You know we Yellow Phoenixes are going to win again." Wullen beat on his chest.

Naedon shook his head. "No way. We Red Phoenixes have been practicing every day, and we've recruited some amazing players. There's no way you break past our Tacklers."

Skarpin glanced between his two friends, concerned that their rivalry could harm their friendship. He secretly hoped the Green Phoenixes would win, as green had become his favorite color—the color of freedom.

Saedeen leaned in close to her friends. "How do you feel about wearing the, you know, bracelets?"

Wullen chewed on his cheek. "I talked with my mum about it, and she thinks it's safer this way, but my aunt was steaming mad. She said it was a slippery slope."

"Slippery slope to what?" Elladelle asked.

Wullen shrugged. "Something about the past. Not sure what that means."

Bursting through the dining hall doors, the Blue Phoenix team entered with chants and clapping. Naedon, Wullen, and Skarpin, along with several others, stood cheering them on. Saedeen and Elladelle looked at each other and rolled their eyes; they secretly wanted the Purple Phoenixes to win.

Once the Blue team left, the Purple Phoenixes came next with their chants. The girls rose excitedly, cheering on the dreamy boys who passed by them.

"Ah, c'mon, girls. Seriously?" Wullen asked, deflated by their reasoning for cheering on the enemy team.

They giggled. Elladelle looked at the clock. "There's not much time left. Let's hurry to the field so we can get good seats."

The group of friends slung their leather book satchels over their shoulders, grabbed one more cupcake each, and darted out of the dining hall. Students crowded around the entry, bouncing on their toes and waving blue and purple flags. The palace donated moveable amphitheater seats from the main Perdonair Feydom stadium. These were constructed with ten-foot-high raised platforms and several rows of wooden stadium seats above. The seating encircled the carefully designed Feydom enclosure. Dazzling team banners hung below the raised seating.

Finally, the gate opened, hinges creaking. Students pushed past one another and ran to find the best seats. Saedeen gasped for air as her friends hurried up the forever-high staircases. She was relieved when they managed to find decent seats—not front row, but "good enough," as Wullen deemed them. She marveled at the verdant euphoria below. Lucious trees were scattered all over the enclosure, along with several glittering silver boulders ranging in size.

Wullen rubbed his hands together. "Oh man, this is going to be so good. I can already see several excellent hiding spots. Look!!" Wullen pointed to a far corner with a purple flag violently flapping in the wind. "Right behind that boulder is a perfect spot for a Tackler."

While Wullen continued coaching from the stands, Skarpin looked for his adopted family. He hoped King Ryker would come. Skarpin talked for hours with him about how excited he was for this game.

"Hi, Skarpin," a small girl wearing two blonde pigtails said as she passed by. She waved and blushed. Her friends giggled when Skarpin waved back.

Elladelle nudged Skarpin. "Eeekk. Looks like you have a crush."

"A what?" Skarpin asked, genuinely confused.

"Alistin obviously has a crush on you."

Skarpin's mouth fell open. "On me? You're joking."

Saedeen and Elladelle jointed elbows and chuckled. "I'm serious. It's apparently all the girls are talking about."

"But why would she like me?"

Saedeen cocked an eyebrow. "Skarpin, you're cute. I mean, you're too young for me, but for Alistin's age, you're perfect. That's what all the younger girls in our dormitory are saying."

Elladelle draped her arm across Skarpin's shoulders. "And it does help that you're Elysium's prince."

Skarpin's heart nearly stopped. With all the information about the adoption, he hadn't taken the time to realize that being the son of Queen Sealyn and King Jace meant he would now be known as—a prince! His yellow eyes blinked. He had gone from starving on the streets of Shunal to living in the palace as a prince. How was he this lucky?

Trumpets blared their tunes as royals entered the vicinity. King Father Ryker, along with other royals and the professors, walked to their golden seats. Ryker waved and smiled at all the students. He lifted his hand, silencing the audience's cheers.

"Thank you for that warm welcome. I'm excited to be here for Elysium's first Feydom scrimmage. I think I can agree with my grandson, Skarpin, that these games should continue." Skarpin's stomach fluttered. He blushed when he saw so many green eyes staring at him. Ryker continued, "Let us now bring in the teams. Make as much noise as you can for the Purple Phoenixes!"

As the purple team entered the arena, students clapped and cheered, waving their violet flags adorned with painted gold phoenixes.

"And now, let's hear it for the Blue Phoenixes!" Ryker roared, very entertained by the students.

The Blue Phoenixes entered to massive amounts of cheers, clapping, and stomping.

"Your pretty boys are going down today, ladies," Wullen jeered to Saedeen and Elladelle.

Naedon clapped loudly and cupped his hands around his mouth. "Let's go, Blue! Make us proud!"

"Well done, Father," Princess Siany whispered to Ryker.

"All in a day's work of being king." Ryker sat and nodded, signaling it was time to start the game.

Shimmering cerulean and purple fireworks exploded above the arena. Everyone stood to their feet, cheering for their team. The nervous competitors sprinted to their positions, eager to be the first team to win a Feydom scrimmage.

Siany wasn't sure if it was the day's jitters or a sickness, but something felt off. She tried to steady herself and enjoy the game. Smoothing her seafoam satin dress, she focused on a purple Roamer dodging a dive from a blue Tackler, but she thought she felt something—a vibration. No, that couldn't be right. She pressed her hands to the wooden seat and felt it again. Tremors, faint tremors—not from the cheering, either. The ground was shaking.

Chapter 28

<u>You're Our Brother</u>

Jace was glad to be back on the ship, flying toward Glatania, but his anger had returned. He couldn't believe Sealyn didn't want him on the same ship as her. He ripped open another scroll, reports from Elysium that Cruz had received from his Shunalian spies. He tried to focus on the inked words, but his emotions fogged his brain. His head jerked up when he heard a light knock at his door.

"Come in," Jace said.

Laisren and Taeg popped their heads around the cracked door. They gave awkward smiles and nods.

"Uh, hi, King Jace," Laisren stumbled over his greeting.

Jace leaned back in his wooden chair, hands folded behind his head. "What can I help you men with?"

The two brothers looked at one another, arguing with twitches and gestures. A small smile tugged at the corner of Jace's lips. These two were definitely brothers.

"Well, we wondered if we could discuss a delicate matter with you," Taeg offered.

Jace snorted. "Delicate matter. And which delicate matter might that be?"

Laisren stepped forward. He was small-framed with shaggy, dirty-blonde hair and zesty coral eyes, possessing a quick wit and a lively personality. He cleared his throat, tapping his finger to his lips. "Seeing as how our father is your father, then that makes us brothers."

Jace froze, not knowing where they were going with this. The hairs on his neck stood. Did they want money? Were they going to use this newfound information as leverage?

Taeg, who shared the same body frame as Laisren, had light brown hair and a somewhat sparse beard. His eyes sparkled with a flaming copper hue, radiating wisdom and kindness. His head was more rectangular than his brother's, but there was no doubt that Taeg and Laisren were related. Taeg shoved his hands into his pockets.

"Yes, so we thought maybe you would like to join us for a game of cards, maybe even an ale?"

Jace was taken aback. Was this a trick? He dropped his hands and stood up "Why?"

Laisren laughed. "Why? Why not, silly? We like playing games, so if you have the same blood as us, we figured you might like to play games, too."

"You're serious?"

Taeg looked at Laisren, then back at Jace. "Yes, of course. We're not messing with you, Jace. You're our brother, and contrary to what you may believe, we'd like to get to know you."

Jace dropped his head. "And my eyes don't bother you?"

"Your eyes?" Laisren expelled. "Your eyes? Why would silver eyes bother us? We're pirates, remember?"

Taeg stepped in front of Laisren. "Matter of fact, your eyes are fascinating. I even did some research and found ..."

Laisren smacked Taeg's arm. "Not now, Taeg."

Jace's head snapped up, and he glared, feeling the sting of betrayal and embarrassment all over again. "You researched me?"

"Well, no—not you, per se. You don't really exist in the records..."

"So, I keep hearing. What did you uncover then?" Jace asked, curious if his brilliant brother could do better than Princess Siany's scheme.

"Uh, well. It's more about the silver-eyed history. I found an incredibly ancient chest hidden in my father's or our father's private study. It was barricaded behind the wall planks."

Jace had to admit he was intrigued. No one ever discussed the history of the silver eyes, and he had done his fair share of research, so perhaps this was finally his chance to get some answers—and from his brothers, oddly enough.

"May I?" Taeg gestured to the leather pouch hanging across his chest. Jace nodded. Taeg dug inside and pulled out a large book. He set it on Jace's desk with a loud thud, rattling the candle holders and goblets. He slid the aged parchment from the middle of the book and pointed to the faded, dark letters. All three huddled around the mysterious writing.

Taeg read aloud,

"Beware, my kindred ones, for fear does not lie in the darkest parts of the forests. Fear should only reside in the eyes of silver, for those eyes command unending storms and unstoppable herds of galloping death.

What hope can we have against such power? Only in chains of dragon scales and scorpion's wrath will you find your salvation.

Master the monster before the monster becomes our master."

All three exchanged confused and worried glances. Jace stepped back, stumbling over his chair. He braced himself against the wall and reached his hand out toward his brothers. "What ... What does that mean?"

Taeg shook his head. "Past scribes wrote in riddles, so it's not always as it seems."

"So, I'm not a monster?"

"On the contrary," Taeg responded. "See, look at how he phrases his words. He used the word 'Master.'"

Laisren scrunched his face and scratched his blonde hair. "And?"

Taeg rolled his eyes, irritated at the lack of knowledge standing in the room. "Master can signify numerous titles, but I believe this time, the writer is referencing a negative connotation rather than something toward a teacher, more like a power-hungry tyrant."

Jace folded his arms, brow furrowing. "You're saying that monster could imply something positive because 'it' would go against the tyrant?"

Taeg smacked the wooden desk and pointed at Jace. "Exactly! Brilliant, Jace. That's my theory. I think everyone has it wrong. I don't believe *you* are a monster. I think you are the *obstacle* to the master's plan."

Laisren grabbed Jace's goblet and turned it upright in his mouth, bracing for cool liquid, but it was empty. He turned it upside down, shaking it in frustration. With a grunt, he set it back on the desk and sighed. "The question is—who's the master? And ... what's the master's plan?"

Taeg shook his head and walked around the room to where he stood between his brothers. "Wrong. The first question we should ask is why Jace can't access his powers?"

Jace immediately grabbed his wrists, which didn't go unnoticed. Laisren looked from Jace's scarred wrists to his silver eyes and realized the torture his brother had endured all his life. He shouldn't have faced that alone; he should have had his brothers there to defend him. Laisren's expression softened. "We don't have to. I know what's blocking them, and I know how we will unleash them."

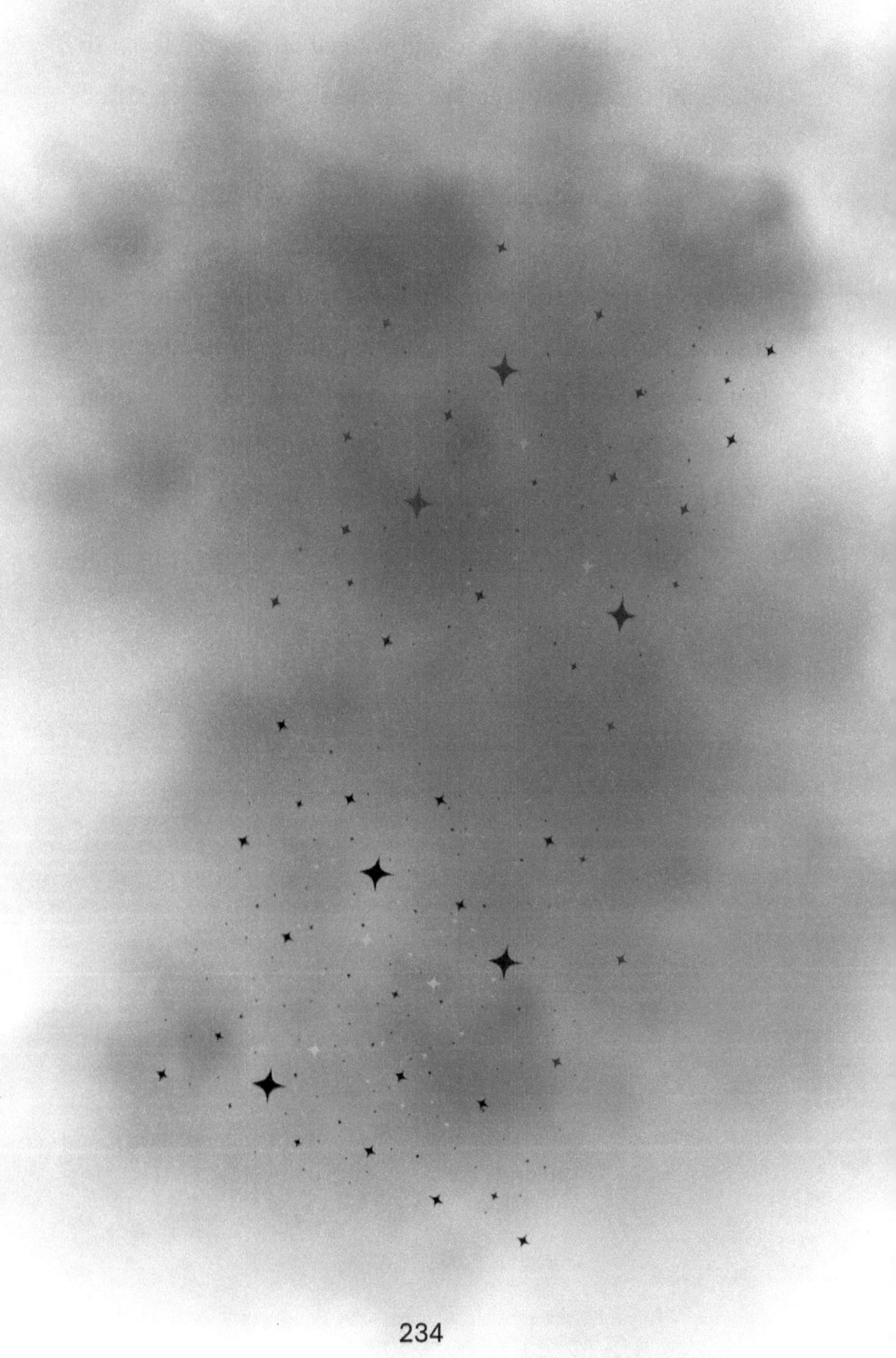

Chapter 29

<u>22 Years Ago...</u>

Three weeks had passed since the bloody meal with the Korps. Jace still heard the slicing of necks in his dreams, the sound of dripping blood. He shuddered at the thought. He stuffed his favorite book, *The Pirate and the Sea Monster*, into his pack. The moonlight cast an eerie glow over his tiny room. He wouldn't miss this place.

He watched the last fire light, signaling that all the night watch were stationed at their posts. It was time. He was leaving Stoltland forever, or at least, the capital. Jace had heard rumors of a place where Stoltlanders didn't dare to go. He wasn't sure what could be intimidating enough to keep Stoltlanders away, but he didn't care—that was his path to everlasting freedom.

With a deep breath, Jace slid his tiny fingers around the splintered wooden door handle and pulled it open, stepping into his first adventure toward a new life. The hinges made no sound. Jace ensured he had stolen sheep grease to coat them, preventing any noise-awakening echoes. He had planned and practiced his escape route daily. The sheep grease had been his last task to accomplish.

He crept past the kitchen table overflowing with woven baskets of fruits, vegetables, and stale breads. Dried herbs and an array of kitchen tools dangled above him, almost as if bidding him farewell. He inched towards the door that led to the small herb garden, yearning for the grate concealed just behind that entrance. Suddenly, the echo of approaching footsteps sent adrenaline racing through Jace's veins. Heart pounding, he quickly crawled back into the kitchen and hid under the table, concealed among the burlap bags of flour.

His ears peaked. Kissing and moans were coming from the hallway.

"Hey! What are you two doing down here?" a guard yelled.

"Uh, we were … Uh, sorry, sir," the guilty male answered.

"Get back to your post! And you, you filthy harlot—get back to the streets where you belong!"

Jace heard the footsteps fade away. He exhaled, thanking Creator that he hadn't been caught. Slowly and cautiously, he climbed out of his hiding place and sneaked into the hallway. He found the garden door again; black ivy was painted on the wooden surface. His heart raced when he spotted the grate, his tunnel to peace. He jumped down the dark chasm, an old friend welcoming him home. Even in the total darkness, Jace knew these tunnels like sheep know their shepherd's voice.

He sloshed through the shallow water, careful not to get his pack wet. After what felt like hours of walking, Jace reached his destination: the rusty iron ladder that would take him to the banished stables—the very place where the dragon had devoured his only friend and training mentor. The palace still housed horses, but it only had one tender, who always left each night, and tonight was no exception.

Jace grasped the first rung and stepped onto the iron with his wet boot but slipped, his shin hitting the metal. He stifled a yell, clenching his eyes so tightly that he saw spots in the darkness. He had to remain calm. Rushing through his quest would only lead to more mistakes, and he couldn't afford any more. He steadied himself and took his time climbing the wet, algae-covered ladder.

Moving like a sloth, he slid the grate from its resting place, trying to make as little noise as possible. It was heavy for a boy his size, but his determination made him stronger. Before leaving the hole, he scanned the darkness; moonlight illuminated the black sheep's pasture. He saw and heard only the fluffy cloud animals and their annoying calls. Jace smiled to himself, feeling like he was on a pirate adventure, just like in his favorite book.

He hoisted himself out of the grate and quietly replaced the cover. The wind whipped against his face as he sprinted as fast as his legs would carry him toward the barn. He remembered the last time he had run this much in this same field. He tried to push aside memories of the dragon, the arrow, and the loss of his friend. With trembling hands, Jace unlatched the door and slipped inside, undetected. He froze, listening for any sounds, but all he could hear was his own heartbeat thudding in his ears.

Horses stirred as he walked through the barn. He welcomed the scent of hay and musk; it reminded him of Lord Paetrill. His chest ached, and a tear escaped down his cheek. He stood in front of the empty stall where Lord Paetrill would sleep. A thick layer of hay remained from his bed, but it was also Jace's hiding place. For the past three weeks, Jace had practiced the route, but he had also been storing everything he would need to survive a long journey to the west.

Jace didn't waste any time. He respectfully bridled his favorite ebony horse, then secured the animal with a saddle that fit him well. He made sure to check every strap, just as Lord Paetrill had taught him. The musty saddle was old and worn, discarded like he was, but it would carry him to Stoltland's western coast. According to the rumors, a legendary creature lived there, possessing magic that created a barrier that prevented anyone from entering its territory. His plan wasn't to get inside, only to make a small home for himself on the creature's border. Surely no Stoltlander would risk coming to fetch him so close to what they feared.

Pulling back the hay from Lord Paetrill's stall, Jace revealed all the supplies he had gathered over the past weeks. He secured his packs of hatchets, a bow and arrows, food, blankets, and other items he had seen soldiers carrying. The silver-eyed boy tugged on the reins, leading the horse outside the barn beneath the starry sky. Again, he listened for any trouble, but all he heard were crickets, sheep, and the occasional owl hooting in displeasure over the lack of mice.

After traveling for three nights and four days, Jace completely ran out of food. Hunger clouded his judgment, leading him to make his first mistake. Rather than using stealth tactics, Jace rushed into a field of potatoes and grabbed as many as he could from a loaded cart. The farmer and his workers reacted quickly, chasing Jace through the field and catching him just before he could mount his horse.

"Look what we have here, boys. This grey-eyed creature is quite old. Never seen one live past a squawking babe's age," the farmer said in a raspy voice. Deep wrinkles marred his tanned face, and a scar blinded his left eye.

Jace pulled and thrashed against the henchmen's grip, but it was futile. These men were strong; there would be no escape.

"Say, Grey Eyes, where you off to?" the farmer asked, curious to know where a condemned child would try to go.

Jace didn't want to answer, but perhaps if they knew he would be no trouble to them—that he only wanted to live away from everyone, then maybe, just maybe, they would show him mercy. "Forgive me, sir. I only wanted to live near the Western Wall, as some call it."

The helpers snickered.

The farmer tilted his head. "The Western Wall? Well, that's only a few miles from here. We're the last humans you would see. No one ever comes out here."

"Tttthen, let me be on my way," Jace stuttered. "I mean no harm."

The farmer huffed and folded his arms over his tattered shirt. "A monster to live with the monsters. Ha! You think we'd let you live after you stole from me?"

Jace's heart sank. He felt dizzy. Was this man about to kill him? He was so close. Panic set in as he looked around the woods, but there was no one to help. No one would hear his cries.

The farmer grabbed a rope from Jace's horse and threw it over a thick tree branch. "We hang thieves 'round these parts."

"What?! No! Please, sir. Please! I can work for you. I'll do anything. Please!"

Jace's horse pawed at the ground. The farmer tied the noose fast, too fast for Jace to think of a plan. Before he knew it, the scratchy rope was around his neck. The farmer tightened it, almost choking him right there. Jace tried to reach for the rope, but the helpers still restrained his arms.

"Alright, string him up. We've got potatoes to cook. We can feed his body to the pigs."

Jace felt the release of his arms. He instantly tugged at the choking rope, gasping for air, but his feet were lifting off the ground with no help in sight. Jace attempted to scream, but his voice burned as the rope cut off any words pleading for his life. He heard the horse neigh loudly, and then his vision began to fade to darkness, except for a distant glowing white object in the distance.

The bright light expanded, and Jace felt a sense of peace. He surrendered to death's sweet embrace as his small body hung suspended in the air, swinging gently back and forth. It was the nudging that roused him, causing him to gasp for air, coughing and crying. He tugged at the rope still wrapped around his bruised and tender neck, loosening it. The warm air made him feel dizzy. He froze, sensing the metallic tinge of blood. Rising from the dirt and grass, Jace sat up and stroked the nose of his loyal horse; then he noticed the bloody, mangled bodies.

The farmer's face was smashed to mush. He didn't want to look at the other two. His nightmares were already full of disturbing images, and that farmer's nonexistent face was sure to make the list. He stood with the help of his horse and gasped at the size of the imprint in the dirt.

"What could have made this?" Jace asked the horse.

Jace traced the outline of the massive hoof indentation. He looked at his horse's hoof, which was ten times smaller than the impression before him. Gazing toward the Western Wall, he saw the bloody tracks leading in that direction. He swallowed and coughed. Should he follow the same path? Had this creature spared him, or did it merely think he was dead, so it didn't kill him? Wolves howled, having caught the scent of blood. He had to escape the crimson scene before the pack attacked. He mounted his horse with all the strength he had left. Perhaps the farmer's house was vacant. He would stay there for the night and then make his final decision: to join the monster or return home.

Chapter 30

<u>The Berserker Badger</u>

Another twinkling, powdery cobalt pipscot burst over the arena, coating the stands and trees. The crowd cheered for the Blue Phoenixes as they scored another point. They were now ahead by four flags and feeling incredibly confident. Absentmindedly clapping, Siany wished she could enjoy the sport, but her mind lingered on the vibrations she had felt earlier. She promised herself that she would leave and investigate if they occurred again. With that decision made, she began to relax, only for a moment.

Lady Novaly leaned into Siany, having to raise her voice over the crowd. "Did you receive any more backlash from the parents about the bracelets?"

"A few more 'concerned' letters came this morning. No doubt the *Elysian News* inspired those. Did you read what Lady Adalina wrote?"

Novaly rolled her pistachio eyes. She adjusted her blue and violet flower crown, determined to stay neutral throughout the competition. "Of course I did. Didn't surprise me in the least bit. You remember how she dragged my name through the mud with that professor poll she did before the school opened?" Siany nodded. "I don't trust anything she has to say."

Siany stiffened and placed her hands quickly on the bench. "Did you feel that?"

"Feel what?"

"Put your hands on the bench. There. Did you feel it?"

Novaly's eyes widened. "I guess I could feel something, but it's probably from the clapping and stomping…right?" Her raised, red-orange eyebrows begged Siany to tell her everything was fine.

Siany gazed over the crowded seats full of innocent children. She would never forgive herself if she didn't check. "Father. Father," Siany repeated, raising her voice over the cheers.

Ryker cupped his ear. "What? It's hard to hear."

"Lady Novaly and I are going to check on something. We'll be right back."

Ryker, being the overconcerned father he was, said, "Take two of my guards with you. These are troubling times, Siany, so if you know something, don't keep it to yourself."

Sparkles of deep blue powder rained down on them once again. Siany and Novaly coughed through the dust and hurried down the winding staircase, their heels clicking rapidly. Once outside the gate, Siany knelt on one knee, her mint-green skirt fanned out around her. She placed her hand on the grass and felt its vibrations. Something was definitely wrong, but what?

The same blue-feathered bird that had channeled Siany on her first day of becoming a Transference flew before her. The princess clutched her necklace tightly, and immediately, her vision soared into the air, as the bird transferred its sight once again to her.

This allowed her to see what was ahead. The bird soared high, enabling her to gaze over the vast landscapes of the ethereal verdure. Trees had just begun to change to autumn colors, and she noticed the plump, shining apple orchards ready for picking. However, there were no armies, no mass of anything rushing toward them that would cause vibrations. Was this an earthquake? Throughout history, no one had ever recorded an earthquake in Elysium.

Hearing Madam Bip's voice, Siany released her necklace and regained her normal sight. "Uh, sorry, Madam Bip, can you repeat yourself?"

"All I said, Majesty, was, 'how can I help?'" Madam Bip had shiny, ebony skin, salt-and-pepper curly hair, and a deep woodland accent. She wore a blue and purple day dress, trimmed in green, that fit snugly around her large chest and wide hips. Bip was one of the wisest individuals in the kingdom, so Siany hoped she could provide guidance.

"I keep feeling these vibrations, but they don't seem like quakes. I've already channeled my sweet bird, and I see nothing. No large mass of anything coming toward us. What could be causing this?"

Madam Bip balanced her excessively large potion book on her hip, pondering Siany's question. Why would the ground shake? She, herself, ensured each morning that the protective enchanted barrier spell was secured, so they were safe—weren't they? A cold shiver went down her spine, and her head slowly looked at the ground like a snake would pop out and eat her.

Lady Novaly clutched Siany's arm. "Uh, Madam Bip, I don't like that face. What's wrong?"

"I hate ta say 'dis, but 'de protection spell stops at 'de ground," her voice quivered.

"Okay, so what does that mean?" Siany said insistently.

Madam Bip looked into Siany's jade eyes, wishing she didn't have to be the one to tell her. "Majesty, we're under attack, and the enemy is coming from underground."

"What?!" Novaly shrieked.

Two more dazzling sapphire pipscots exploded in the sky, caking everyone even more with the Blue Phoenixes' victories. Siany could barely hear the crowd roaring over her heartbeat. *How do they do this?* They didn't even know where the enemy was. *Where would 'it' attack first? What was even coming? Humans or creatures through tunnels? How did she manage to avoid causing a panic with these children?* Her breath quickened, and she felt dizzy. She had to think fast without passing out.

"Madam Bip, you take Novaly with you. Start working on lengthening the protection spell into the ground. I need to warn the king."

"Siany—the children with the bracelets..." Novaly squeaked.

Siany shook her head, now angry that she had agreed to make the athletes wear the magic-blocking bracelets. "I know. They will be tended to first." She turned and ran back inside, with guards following closely behind. A purple glistening pipscot rained down on the students and players. She hated that she would ruin everyone's fun, but their safety was more important.

With her thighs burning and breathing heavy, Siany grabbed Ryker's shoulder. "Father, we must evacuate now."

"Siany, what's wrong?"

"Something's coming. There's an organized attack happening from under the ground."

"What?! That makes no sense."

"I know, Father, but trust me—whatever is coming is almost here. We must protect the children."

King Father Ryker sprang into action, commanding his guards like the fierce king he was. "Send the Nichts to warn the palace and prepare our army. I want the archers positioned in as many trees as possible. Professors, gather your students and ensure they're all accounted for; they must stay in their dormitories. Before I announce the end of Feydom, I want a professor at each exit, guiding them to safety. Go!"

Pinx, Norella, Hueweyn, and several others raced down the stairs, anxious for the children. Once everyone was in position, the trumpets sounded, and a strange silence fell. Ryker shouted his commands, hoping every child would follow his orders. "By my command, the game is over." Loud moans reverberated across the students. "Everyone will now exit the arena in an orderly manner. The professor at the bottom of the stairs will provide instructions. Make your way back to your dormitories immediately. If you disobey this order, you will be thrown into the dungeons." Ryker glanced at his guards, who chuckled and shook their heads. "What? I needed to instill a little fear in them."

Students covered in indigo and mauve powder rushed down the stairs, bumping into each other and whispering about what might be happening. Elladelle felt her chest tighten, and nausea rose in the back of her throat. She took a few deep breaths, hoping it would help ease the panic threatening to spill out in vomit. When her friends reached the bottom of the stairs, she saw King Father Ryker in the distance.

She cupped her hand around Skarpin's ear and whispered, "Why don't you find out what's going on?"

"Me?" Skarpin said with genuine surprise and confusion. "Why me?"

"Because! If there's anyone who can get secrets out of the king, it's you."

"But. But…"

Elladelle pushed Skarpin aside. "Now, go. Hurry!"

Skarpin didn't like being coerced into deceiving his new family, but he had to admit—he was scared too and wanted to know what was happening just as much as Elladelle. Luckily, Skarpin excelled at slipping in and out of places he shouldn't be in. Growing up on the streets of Shunal taught him how to be invisible, so sneaking close to the king amid all the chaos posed no challenge. He made himself small among the bushes beside the walls of the Feydom stadium and listened.

"Alright, think, soldiers. Think! What are the chances that any of our enemies could have dug tunnels without our knowledge?"

Favien huffed. "Zero, my king. It would take years, and honestly, I don't know what Korp or Stoltlander has that kind of patience."

Graegory shifted side to side, making his battle leathers crack. His almond-shaped, evergreen eyes narrowed. He was a small-framed man with a kind face, raven hair, and just as bright as his sister, Lady Pinx. He scratched at his clean-shaven face. "I agree with Favien. These must be creatures, so I believe we need to think outside the box and ask ourselves what beasts can move underground at rapid speeds."

Favien lifted his hand. "Hey, wait. I bet Professor Hueweyn Rendell would know. He's in charge of teaching *Channeling Creatures: First Term* and *Magical Creatures Studies*."

Graegory squinted through the crowds of children, heart thumping. "There he is." He pointed. Graegory cupped his hands around his desirable pink lips and yelled, "Hey! Professor Hueweyn. We need you over here." He motioned for the professor to join their group.

Skarpin wished he could take Professor Rendell's classes, but he wasn't allowed to since he wasn't a Transference. His classmates told him such amazing stories that he sometimes felt jealous of their special powers, yet he held onto the day when he and Wullen saved everyone from the Black Phoenixes using their Tethered powers. Filling the bubbling gash in the earth with Wullen's sand and his rocks made them heroes. He rubbed the spiderweb-looking scar on his forearm, where he once tried to carve a pebble into his flesh, hoping to be seen as valuable. Shunal's curse played tricks on his people's minds, forcing them to cut sections of flesh and place jewels inside the wounds. He was astounded by how much Queen Sealyn changed his life that day; now, instead of the pebble symbolizing enslavement to worthlessness, it represented his memory of being a hero.

Kicking up dust as he stopped and panting from the sprint, Professor Hueweyn gasped for air. "Your majesty." He inhaled deeply. "How can I be of service to you?" Hueweyn tried to catch his breath, but he was much out of shape, especially since joining the teaching staff, and those breakfast cinnamon apple tartlets seemed to be his downfall.

King Father Ryker folded his arms and leaned in closer to the circled group. "Professor, we need to know all the creatures capable of digging their way to us."

Hueweyn's mouth fell open. Well, this was not what he had expected—maybe another dragon, but this? His mind spun, trying to remember all the pages he had studied about the beasts from other kingdoms.

He propped his stance on one hip, then started counting creatures on his fingers. "Let's see. There's the mole, the ant, the gopher…"

"No. No. Sorry, I should have been more specific. Animals that could attack, perhaps form an army of some sort?" Ryker interrupted.

"Ah, okay. That limits things a bit." Hueweyn rested his fingers on the side of his cheek, tapping as if that would unlock the answers to the king's questions. "The Fennec Fox, perhaps, but those are native to Havas' deserts. They wouldn't form tunnels like you're referring to. Shunal does have an aggressive type of mongoose. Oh, what's the name of that thing?" He snapped his fingers several times. "Ah, ha! The Gullinn mongoose. It's shimmering gold with almost scale-like fur that protects it from snake bites."

Skarpin scrunched his nose. Gullinn mongooses weren't aggressive toward humans. Shunalians treated them like pets, even allowing them to sleep in baby cribs because their only desire, more than anything else, was to kill snakes—certain types of snakes, that is. He remembered watching his first Gullinn mongoose fight a rattlesnake. It was over in five minutes, and the mongoose walked away, shaking the rattle of the snake's tail like a child with a toy. He could hardly believe it.

"So, we're about to be attacked by a horde of mongooses?" Favien asked incredulously.

"Well, mongooses don't travel in hordes, Lord Favien. They are called packs or troops, but no, I don't think they would be your attackers. From all my studies, they appear quite calm with humans."

Favien grunted. "Then, why did you mention them?" He threw his hands up in frustration.

"Process of elimination?" Hueweyn's voice quivered. He didn't like this type of pressure. He needed peace and quiet to process, but he would persevere for his kingdom. Suddenly, a dreadful thought popped into his head. "There is one creature, but it couldn't be ..."

Losing patience, Graegory folded his arms and glared. "And why not?"

"It was banned. Most kingdoms sought to eradicate this breed in hopes of its extinction. After Shunal prohibited the sale of this breed in their markets, all kingdoms decided to eliminate them, but of course, one kingdom kept a few hidden. We only know this from sporadic reports of villages being attacked by these creatures, or occasionally, one might appear for sale on the black market in Shunal."

A chilling dread coursed through Skarpin's spine. He recognized all too well the creature the professor was alluding to. If this was indeed the creature, Avondelle was on the brink of facing unimaginably dark and terrifying days ahead.

"Don't dance around, Hueweyn. Just spit it out!" Favien said loudly. Favien liked Hueweyn, but sometimes the professor tested his patience.

Hueweyn stumbled over his words, not wanting to speak the creature's name, fearing the beast might appear if he uttered it aloud. "The Berserker Badger."

The color drained from their faces; Graegory turned mint green. Berserker Badgers are the size of mountain lions. They have grey fur with a deep burnt orange stripe running down their back and face, plus long, razor-sharp claws and teeth. What makes these creatures so terrifying is that after two years, they go psycho. They become completely disconnected from life and go on killing sprees, not even pausing to consume their kills.

Ryker placed his hands on his hips and sighed. "Korpam. Those …" He stopped himself and looked up, praying for answers. "My guess is that Korpam kept those abominations for an opportunity like this. They probably let them loose on one of our beaches, and now a clan of Berserker Badgers is heading this way."

"And has anyone here fought a clan of these badgers before?" Favien asked, already knowing the answer.

Skarpin heard his opportunity. He popped out of the bush and ran to King Father Ryker.

"Skarpin!" Ryker yelped.

"I'm sorry, but I've heard how to deal with those badgers. One got loose in Shunal, and it was all the pubs could talk about for months afterward." He swallowed, hoping no one would scold him. Once he noticed their interest, he continued, "You must penetrate its brain either with a sword or arrow, or even a knife. I'm sure smashing its brains would work, too. What the professor didn't tell you is that beneath the fur is a layer of hardened leather, or at least that's how the soldiers described it. The only soft spot is its head."

Ryker once again thanked Creator for bringing little Skarpin into their lives. He pulled the child close. "Professor, thank you for the information. Please take Skarpin back to the school and inform all professors to bar the doors; no one is to be left on floors one and two." He turned to Skarpin and placed his hands on the child's tiny shoulders. "Thank you for the information. You might have just saved us again. Hurry back." He watched the professor and his adopted grandson run back to the school; then, anger burned inside him. Once again, his people faced the threat of evil. "Men, prepare yourselves. We are about to fight a clan of bloodthirsty badgers."

Chapter 31

<u>The Storm</u>

"It's not too late. It's not too late. It's not too late." Sealyn repeated the phrase over and over in her head. She had found the hidden note inside her satchel, written in Cruz's handwriting. He didn't want her to sacrifice herself, but it was too late for that. She picked at her now-cold eggs, only hearing muffled voices from her mother and Lady Madilina. Sealyn found it strange—the closer they got to Glatania, the more bland their food tasted. Maybe it was anxiety, or maybe she was losing her mind.

"Sealyn, darling, did you hear me?" Graelynd placed her hand on her daughter's, worried about how distant she had become.

Sealyn snapped her head up. "What? No. Sorry, Mother. Can you repeat that?"

"I said, I'm going to make the extension potion."

"Already?"

"Sealyn," Graelynd chuckled, masking her worry. "It's been two days. I need to do this now. We can't risk any longer."

Sealyn felt as if she were waking from a dream. "Oh, yes. Of course. My apologies. I guess being at sea has made me forgetful."

Madilina's brows knitted together. "At sea? But, Queen Sealyn, we're flying."

Sealyn slapped her forehead playfully. "Silly me. That's what I meant. Flying—the high altitude."

Graelynd and Madilina looked at one another.

"My darling, why don't you take a rest while I complete the potion? Lady Madilina can assist me."

Madilina sat up straighter. "Oh, yes. Madam Bip taught me before we left. I think she was marvelous for inventing it on such short notice. How did she discover that using a person's blood can extend their powers?"

Graelynd tilted her head back and forth with a cheeky smile. "It was an honest mistake. She was chopping willow bark for some tea and accidentally cut herself. Later that same day, she practiced with her new necklace, which was tethered to tomato and sunflower seeds. She grew a few sprouts of each, but to her surprise, the spell didn't break when she let go of the necklace. The sprouts grew larger, and more sprouts popped up. She couldn't figure out what was happening.

Hours later, after a greenhouse overflowing with tomato plants and sunflowers, she noticed her cut was slightly bleeding and then looked at her necklace. There was the crimson culprit. Bip washed the necklace quickly, and when she turned back to the overgrown greenhouse, she found that everything had stopped. Thus, the invention of the extension potion was born."

"Wow. I love that story!" Madilina gushed. She pushed back her long, blonde hair and stood. "Let's prepare the potion before anything bad happens." Madilina was thrilled to be on this quest. Her husband, Max, had been against her joining the Len Novian quest, but her Transference powers had helped save many lives. Sealyn wanted her to go on the Shunalian quest, yet Madilina chose to stay in Avondelle to help launch the magical creatures program for the new school. She adored the students and the animals, but this quest was simply too enchanting to pass up.

"Yes, let's finish this potion," Graelynd nodded. "Sealyn, please eat something first, then take that rest."

Sealyn sighed as she ate the cold eggs and toast. She watched her mother close the door, then took a bite of a juicy, sweet apple. The sweet flavor filled her with energy and increased her hunger. She grabbed a biscuit, cut it in half, stuffed it with sausage, cheese, and honey, and enjoyed the tasty breakfast sandwich, feeling the dizziness fade away. She could handle this mission—as long as she had savory food to sustain her.

Aboard the blue ship, breakfast had just begun. They had chosen to sleep in today. Dinyelle set her plate down gently and sat beside her husband, JaeDorn. This was their first quest beyond Elysium's borders, and so far, it was not disappointing. They would be the first to use magical necklaces and fly on ships to a new kingdom. Their names would be recorded in history books. She couldn't wrap her mind around it.

Dinyelle had freckled, pecan skin, was tall with defined muscles, and possessed an exceptionally sharp mind. She was loyal to a fault, making her the perfect addition to the Vinurs of the Court for Queen Sealyn. Her dark, curly ringlet hair was twisted back with green and gold feathers woven into the strands, and she was dressed in her battle leathers with the addition of gray furs. Glatania's weather was colder than Elysium's, and the high altitude didn't help. She watched Jace, Laisren, and Taeg huddled in a corner, whispering. An odd feeling stirred within her stomach.

"JaeDorn," she lowered her voice. "Look over there. What do you suppose those three are talking about?"

JaeDorn turned his shiny bald head and saw what intrigued his wife. "Well, my guess would be their family history." He turned back and sipped his coffee. JaeDorn wasn't one for gossip; he much preferred action, as his hands needed to be busy. With ivory skin and a sweet, welcoming face adorned with a dark goatee, he was slightly taller than his wife and built like an ox. He was a strong warrior and gifted strategist.

"I feel bad for King Jace," Dinyelle said, chewing on a mouthful of eggs.

JaeDorn laughed. "Why? He's literally the king of Elysium—married to Sealyn of all women. I don't think his life is in shambles." JaeDorn shook his head and began spreading a thick layer of strawberry jam on his fluffy, hot biscuit.

"But think about everything he's had to go through. I'm sure we don't know half of it, and now finding out you've had brothers…" She sucked her teeth several times. "I can't imagine the psychological damage that does to a person."

JaeDorn leaned back in his chair and tilted his head dramatically. "I came from a rocky family, and look at how well I turned out." He wiggled his brown eyebrows and smiled with jam on his lips.

Dinyelle couldn't help but laugh. She loved her husband and his positive outlook. "Of course, you turned out fantastic." She watched the three brothers rise together and scurry off toward the stairs leading below. She shrugged and glanced out the small window on the first level. Strange. It seemed darker than before. Dinyelle blinked her radiant malachite eyes and took another look. Her heart sank, and she felt the weight of her breakfast churning in her stomach. "Uh, darling, look outside."

JaeDorn snapped his head to the right when he heard the tone of his wife's voice. His lime eyes froze and widened. Dark, stormy clouds were moving at an unnatural pace toward them. "We must sound the alarm. To the upper deck, now!"

As they stood up, their chairs tilted backward, nearly tripping them. They took the stairs two at a time, dashed to the storm bell, and yanked the rope. The bell's chimes resonated across the deck, instilling fear in every heart. This was the one day when the crew should not have overslept.

Within minutes, the entire crew stood at the bow, staring into the swirling dark gray clouds charging angrily toward them.

The Pirate Captain pushed toward the front. "Aren't we supposed to be near our landing site by now?" He glanced at his navigator, who appeared unwell.

"Yes, Captain, but with the clouds under us, I can't see where to land. We must fly lower."

"We could hit trees!" a soldier yelled.

"Or mountains…" another pirate chimed in.

"So, what do you suggest?" The Pirate Captain snapped at the navigator.

"I'm not sure, Captain. Flying is completely different from sailing on the seas," he whimpered. His face turned a pale shade of green.

Lightning flashed in front of them, and thunder boomed, the sound lasting torturously too long. Heavy, thick raindrops began pelting the deck as if they were under attack. However, it was the wind that proved to be the soulless force. Massive gusts blew the sails and wings with such intensity that it felt like giants were shaking their ship.

Jace's heart panicked, and he sprinted to the stern. He needed to spot Sealyn's ship. He slipped and stumbled over the soaked deck along with overturned crates and barrels, but when he finally grasped the stern's railing, his worst fear was painted across the gray sky. Her ship was gone, or at least, he couldn't see it or the other vessel. The dark, thick, swirling clouds filled the sky. He shouted for Sealyn but was met only with the growls of thunder and the howling winds.

Rain hammered against his face, drenching his clothes. What were they supposed to do? How was he going to find

Sealyn? How were they supposed to land safely? Too many questions and no answers.

His brothers appeared beside him, grasping his arm and shoulders. "Jace, what should we do?" Taeg asked, having to yell over the monstrous storm.

Jace's mind sifted through possibilities. "We should get below deck, and maybe the storm will pass before it kills us."

It wasn't much of a plan, but it was the only one he could think of. They made their way back slowly, only to find that the crew had the same idea. Everyone was scrambling to get below safely. Once the last person was under the deck, they sealed the hatch and were left with the eerie sounds of the storm pounding against their ship.

Dinyelle stared out the window, shivering. A droplet fell from her nose and splashed on her wet leather boot. The vessel moaned, pleading for relief. But none came. The ship suddenly dipped, making it feel like they were in freefall. She craned her neck, straining to see the green-feathered wings, but they had vanished. Vanished! What did this mean?

"The wings are gone!" Dinyelle screamed.

Everyone froze. Jace ran to Dinyelle and confirmed what she saw.

"What does that mean?" asked Laisren.

Jace didn't have the words.

Dinyelle stepped back. "Don't. Don't say it. Our queen…" She shook her head violently. "No. Please, King Jace. Our beloved queen mother can't be dead!"

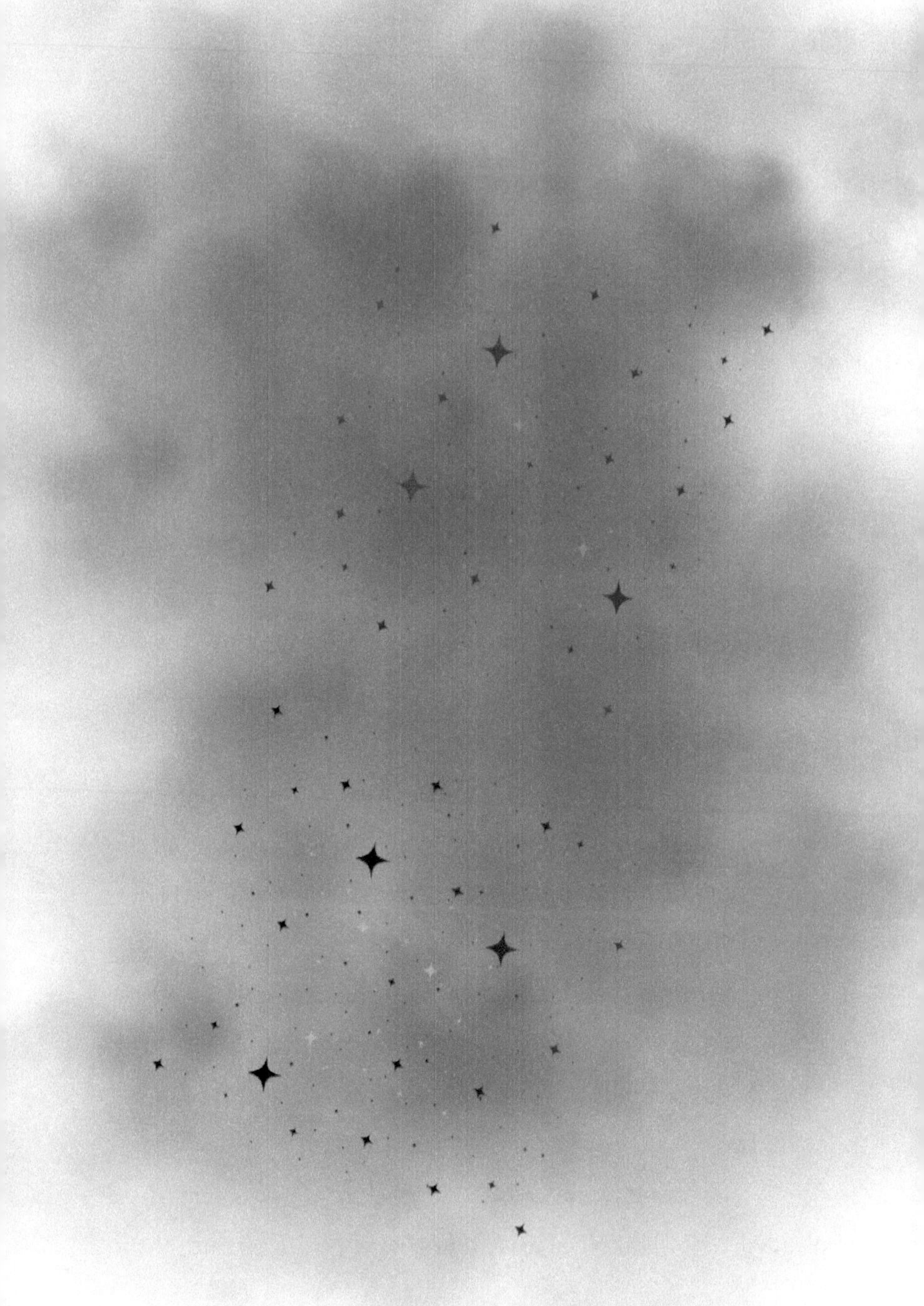

Chapter 32

<u>22 Years Ago…</u>

Jace discovered that he enjoyed living on a farm. Two weeks had passed, and no one had visited the deceased farmer's property. The bruises around his neck from the hanging attempt had finally healed, leaving only a faint yellowish-purple spot just under his chin. He hadn't mustered the courage to follow the giant hoof prints; instead, he created a new home on the farm.

He got up when the rooster crowed. He milked the cows, gathered chicken eggs, and tended to the gardens. Jace finally felt like he had a purpose and maybe even a home. He cleaned up after playing with the new piglets and started making his usual breakfast when he heard a rumbling. Was that a storm? He left his eggs frying in the iron skillet and peered out the window; clear blue skies stretched as far as he could see.

His paranoid, silver eyes caught sight of movement. He pleaded, "No. No. No. Please don't let it be." He ran to the door and opened it, the fear nearly crippling him. With dust rising behind their weary horses, a large group of black-armored soldiers charged toward the farm. If they caught him, he couldn't fathom the torture they would inflict. He rushed to the stove and grabbed the iron skillet, but it was scalding hot and burned his hand. He yelled out, dropping the pan; the sound drew the riders' attention

"Halt! You three search the barn. You two search the field. You three, in the back, search the forest. The rest with me to search the house."

Jace's body trembled with panic as he heard the orders. Pain pulsed through his hand, and tears flowed down his tanned, dirt-streaked cheeks. He was desperate not to go back. He had left for a reason: those people were murderers. Jace's heart raced as he grabbed a rag and sprinted to the cellar. He frantically wrapped his hand before flinging open the door. Stepping inside, he hurriedly latched it shut behind him, a frantic hope that this would be enough to conceal himself.

The room was as dark as the night sky. Jace could see nothing, paralyzed by a bone-deep fear that any movement might betray him. The sound of approaching footsteps combined with muffled voices made him dizzy. He sucked in a breath, convinced they could hear every inhale of his terrified gasps.

A loud voice echoed above the hatch. "I found the cellar, Commander." Jace squeezed his eyes shut as the soldier attempted to open the door. "It seems to be locked."

Another voice, "From the inside?"

"Yes, Commander."

"Then someone's down there."

Jace felt sick. He recognized his mistake: he should have kept the door unlocked and concealed himself behind some shelves.

"Grab an ax. I want to know who's in there."

Jace flinched at the first crack of the ax. Another chop. Jace started to sob. He stepped back, wishing it all away. He could see the blood pooling around him in that banquet hall. Another smash. He felt the sticky jam coating his skin and clothes from his stepbrother's bullying. Another chop; this time, a small crack appeared above him, allowing a thin stream of light to filter in. He watched the dragon devour Lord Paetrill and felt the arrow piercing his leg. Another swing broke a hole large enough for a soldier to reach through and unlock the door.

This was it. The hatch flew open. The light felt like a betrayal, and it showed the soldiers who they had been searching for all these weeks. Jace sat on the ground, pulled his knees to his chest, wrapped his arms tightly around them, and cried out for them to leave him there. The soldiers laughed and cheered.

"Well, boy. We've been hunting you for quite a while now. Your mother wants you home—at all costs." Two soldiers stomped down the dusty wooden steps and grabbed Jace by his arms. They hoisted him up and dragged him through the house to the front. They tossed him in front of the Stoltland Commander.

"Finally, we can go home now." With his graying dark hair and full beard, the commander grinned chillingly. He stood tall and muscular, a formidable presence. "Let's not leave empty-handed. Yarwren mentioned he found the bodies of three men in the forest. They looked pretty mangled, their flesh eaten by worms, so I'm guessing that was the farmer and his helpers." He bent down, resting his hands on his knees, his nose just a foot from Jace. "Isn't that right, you little killer?"

"I didn't kill them! They tried to kill me!"

"Shut up. Either way, soldiers, pack the dead farmer's wagon with food and supplies. Also, take his animal cage carts and load the pigs, goats, and sheep. Tie the cows and horses to the wagons. Then, set fire to the house and barn. Leave a sign not to harbor fugitives." He looked at Jace with disgust. "And you…you filthy rat…you will walk back with us as our prisoner." He noticed Jace coddling his wrapped hand. "Aw, did we hurt ourselves?"

With tears in his eyes, Jace looked at the commander and nodded, silently pleading for him to provide medical treatment, but to Jace's horror, the commander grabbed his wrist violently. He tore the bandage off and thrust Jace's burned hand into a fire ant mound. Jace screamed. "Stop! Stop! Stop!" He kept screaming as he felt the stinging, burning bites from the ants. The commander pulled his hand out and plunged it into a water trough; ants floated around Jace's arm.

Laughing, the commander released Jace and signaled his men to tie Jace's hands. Jace pulled his hand out of the water, gasping for air, and noticed the countless ant bites in and around the burn. His hand throbbed and stung. He leaned over the splintery wooden fence and vomited. How was he supposed to survive the journey back to the palace? These men were ruthless.

A soldier wrapped a rope around Jace's wrists and fastened it to the horn of his saddle. Jace already dreaded the blisters he knew he would inevitably collect. He wished he had never left, for he would never have known happiness and peace. His life here would continue to haunt his dreams—forever.

After hours of packing wagons and securing all the livestock, the group began their long journey home. Jace winced at the first tug of the rope, praying his boots would hold up against the distance. He managed to avoid the piles of horse dung left along the way, but his legs were growing tired. Asking for a rest or even for water would not go over well for him.

Daylight was beginning to fade, and Jace felt his eyelids growing bitterly heavy. He must have dozed off for just a moment because he stumbled and fell, but he didn't hit the ground. Instead, his head experienced a terrible whip effect, and the rope yanked at his shoulders, stretching his body as his boots dragged through the dirt. He couldn't help but cry out. The rope cut into his wrists, and his shoulders felt as if they were being pulled out of their sockets. He tried to regain his footing, but the momentum was too swift for his weary legs.

The soldier pulled on the reins, stopping his horse. "Uh, Commander. We have a situation."

The commander rolled his eyes. "We might as well camp here. It will be dark soon. Make sure to feed and water the animals. Be on guard for wolves, especially now."

Jace hoped for wolves. He hoped they would attack during the night and kill them all, including himself. This world was cruel and wasn't worth living in—at least for him.

"Feed the little monster, then tie him to this here tree." The commander patted a large pine tree, whose bark was cracked and rugged.

Jace scarfed down his food and drank as much water as he could. The soldier took Jace's canteen and pulled his rope toward the tree. "Wait. Wait. Please don't tie me to the tree."

"Commander's orders."

"Can I at least go to the bathroom first?"

"Listen, kid. I'm already missing mealtime, and I'm ticked that I'm the one stuck babysitting you. If it were up to me, I'd slice your neck here and now—and be done with you and your kind. So don't look to me for pity. You can pee and fill your pants for all I care."

Jace felt shame and embarrassment wash over him. He longed for the sunshine of the farm and the warmth of the fireplace. Rather than risk incurring this soldier's wrath, Jace closed his mouth and pressed his back against the tree.

The soldier laughed. "Turn around, boy."

"What?"

"Face the tree, dummy."

"…but"

"Commander didn't say I had to tie you with your back to the tree. Now, face it. Nose to bark."

Jace felt the tears slip from his silver eyes once more. He pressed his nose against the bark, and the abrasive surface scraped his skin. With his hands still bound in front of him, Jace counted how many times the soldier coiled the rope around him and the tree. Ten. Ten wraps secured him in the most uncomfortable position he would attempt to sleep in. He heard the soldier walk away laughing. Then, Jace relaxed and let the tears fall. He prayed that one day, this life he was cursed with would be worth living—one day. One day.

Chapter 33

<u>Panic in the Tethered Common Room</u>

After sprinting up all the stairs, Skarpin gasped for air as he entered the enchanting Tethered common room. The common room was grand, filled with giant floor-to-ceiling arched windows that offered a view of the gardens. Sunlight illuminated the cozy space, enhancing the lush greenery ornamented with tiny yellow flowers climbing the walls and cascading from the ceiling. On the multitude of rugs, yellow and green chairs and couches were scattered throughout the room, which were said to be so comfortable they felt like warm embraces.

Golden candlelit chandeliers glowed above, casting their light on the hundreds of books lining the library's shelves. Heat wafted from the massive round stone fireplace, which was embellished with jarred plants and dried herbs hanging from a string. Various types of potted plants filled the room, from vegetables to flowers, adding vibrant red, blue, and purple hues.

The room's centerpiece was also the favorite accent; above the library stood a vibrant, magnanimous tree with branches spread wide and tall, reaching the ceiling and providing a canopy over the colorful books. Its twisting trunk was as tall as King Jace, or so Skarpin believed, and its limbs were full of dark green leaves and tiny shimmering purple blossoms. Next to the library, a golden spiral staircase led to a second level behind the majestic tree. The banister of this level matched the staircase, and the floor was covered in thick, short-tipped grass, inviting students to escape their classes inside.

Skarpin surveyed the room and noticed his friends huddled on a yellow couch beneath one of the detailed tapestries depicting an old woman brewing a red potion. He sprinted toward them.

"Oh, Skarpin! I was worried," Elladelle squealed. "Did you find out anything?"

Beads of sweat formed across his brow. He took a deep breath and began his story. "I overheard King Father Ryker speaking with Lord Favien and Lord Graegory; then they called Professor Rendell because they needed his help with creature questions."

"Creature questions? Like what?" Wullen asked, snacking on a Puffin Pie. These were quickly becoming his favorite treat.

"Like what creatures could make tunnels underground and attack us—those types of questions."

Elladelle gasped. "Nothing, right? Surely, an animal like that doesn't exist."

Skarpin didn't want to scare them, but they were his friends. They needed to know. He sighed. "If I tell you, you must promise not to cause a scene." They all nodded. Skarpin glared at Elladelle. "I mean it, Elladelle."

"Uh, Skarpin. Why'd you single me out?" She folded her blue-powered arms across her chest. Clearly, the students hadn't had time to shower.

The boys rolled their eyes. Naedon nudged his cousin. "C'mon, Elladelle. You know you always overreact."

She narrowed her eyes. "Do not!"

"Do too!" Naedon argued.

Saedeen rubbed her ebony temples. She hated it when the cousins fought, which was often. She held up her hand. "Okay, enough. Can you two please let Skarpin finish his story?"

"Fine," Elladelle and Naedon said together.

Skarpin hesitated. "Well, Professor Rendell offered several theories, but the final conclusion was that a clan of

Berserker Badgers is making its way underground to attack us."

"A ber-what?" Wullen asked, not convinced he should be worried yet. He licked his fingers, enjoying the last bit of icing.

"Berserker Badger. Those badgers are the literal worst! After two years, they just go nuts and start killing anything and everything. A Korp let one loose in Shunal once. It killed almost an entire village before someone put an arrow through its head."

"Cool," Wullen hiccupped.

"No, not cool," Elladelle scolded. "This is bad—like, really, really bad. If there's an army of psychotic badgers coming for us, then what are we supposed to do?"

Saedeen pointed toward the door as Professor Gunnolf walked through. "I'm guessing she's here to explain."

Pinx motioned for the students to come closer to her. "Students. Shhhh. Everyone. Please gather around. I have some announcements." The room became silent except for the crackling fireplace. "Thank you. First, you will be having your meals in this common room until further notice. Second, you will continue your studies." Moans ricocheted. "Silence. The studies will merely consist of you reading chapters and then writing down questions from what you didn't understand. Third," Pinx paused and placed her hands on her pink skirt.

Her pregnancy was barely starting to show. "The latest intelligence from the palace is that we are presuming an attack from a clan of evil creatures."

Screams of panic set off a chain reaction. Some students ran to the windows, shouting, "Where? Where?" Others fell to their knees, crying and begging to go home. Those who chose to remain calm had thousands of questions for their professor.

"Professor Gunnolf, can we fight them?"

"What kind of creatures?"

"Where will they attack first?"

"Could the Transferences control them?"

"This was Stoltland, wasn't it?"

Pinx felt dizzy. Anxiety churned in her stomach. "Children, please. I can't answer all of these questions. I'm sharing everything I know. Have faith that your king is doing everything he can to protect you and everyone else in our great kingdom. Right now, I want each of you to go to your rooms to shower and change. School Nichts and other staff will set up food tables, so you'll have your dinner here once you're finished. Now, hurry off."

She watched her students race up the winding stairs, but then an unusual movement caught her eye in the window. She almost brushed it off, yet an unsettling chill raced down her spine. Pinx approached the window cautiously and peered out. What she saw sent ice through her veins. Was that a monstrous badger scaling the protective barrier?

Chapter 34

<u>Welcome to Glatania</u>

They were falling at rapid speeds. The storm sounded distant; then they felt the first impact. It didn't sound like trees or mountains but rather a thud, softer in nature. Jace was confused. How could an impact from their failing heights sound soft? Another thud, and the sweet smell of sugar wafted through the air. What was happening?

The ship surged through the air, bouncing wildly from one obstacle to another. Crew members were tossed about like rag dolls, each one struggling to maintain their footing. Jace felt the impact as he crashed into a chair, his eyes wide as he watched his brothers slam against the wall. Pain shot through him, but it was a trivial ache compared to the trials he had faced before. A swirling, violet haze crept into their failing vessel, and with a thunderous crash of splintering boards and shattering glass, the once-noble ship stilled.

Jace felt a sting on his forehead and gently touched the spot. He pulled his hand down and saw sticky red blood. He dreaded the headache that awaited him. He heard moans and grunts from his crew as they moved and tried to stand.

Jace pushed himself up, astonished by the devastation of their dining area. "Everyone, before you start moving around, you need to assess any damage to your own bodies first. Those with minimal issues, please stand up." He felt relief seeing Laisren and Taeg rise without difficulty. JaeDorn followed next with a slight limp, helping his wife, Dinyelle, to her feet. She was bleeding from her elbow and had a cut across her cheek.

He searched for Finn and Ashur, who were already assisting others. Ashur was wrapping a soldier's leg while Finn was applying pressure to another soldier's abdomen, where what appeared to be a lodged object was protruding. That looked serious. Jace hurried to Finn's side.

"How is he?" Jace asked.

Finn shook his head. "There's a broken table leg stuck in his side. He's already passed out from the pain, and I don't know how to help a wound like this. He's lost too much blood." Finn choked over his last words. Realizing this was the same soldier he and Ashur had just become friends with last night, Lord Corin. Finn heard a long breath escape Corin's lips. He quickly felt for a heartbeat, but there was nothing. His new friend had passed in seconds.

Jace put his hands on his hips and shook his head. "Crew, I hate to say this, but we need to treat this like we're at war."

"What are you saying?" asked Ashur.

"We need to secure the perimeter, then evaluate the ship. Those too injured to walk, remain inside and try to help other injured."

"And the dead?" Finn asked.

"We can do nothing for the dead. Leave them and continue the mission."

"But ..."

A loud fist pounded the wall. "You dare question your king. He said to consider this war. We've crashed into unknown territory. Your job is to protect the king—no matter what," the Pirate Captain yelled. At that outburst, every able-bodied person hustled to assess damages.

He and Jace exchanged a glance, slightly surprised, but they nodded. Jace cautiously approached the crumpled stairs and sighed.

"Allow me, majesty." Finn balanced himself on Ashur's shoulders and opened the hatch, then pulled himself up and over. "Oh, holy roasted unicorns, what is this place?" Finn marveled.

"Finn, what do you see?" Jace yelled.

"My king, you must come see this!"

The Pirate Captain stood under the hatch and patted his shoulders. Jace flinched. He hated how much he admired his father, but right now, he wanted to see what Finn was gawking at. He shimmied up on his father's shoulders and pulled himself over the edge. One by one, those physically able saw the enchanting, spellbinding land of Glatania. They couldn't believe what they were seeing.

With expansive, dome-shaped caps, giant fly agaric mushrooms as tall as pine trees formed their own forest, decked with plum tops, each shimmering with white spots like stars in a twilight sky. Their long, slender stumps sparkled against the backdrop of purple, hazy sunlight. The air was sweet, reminiscent of fresh chocolate and frosting, evoking a sense of joy. Laisren gazed at the ground, marveling at the grass, which bloomed in a gentle violet, softening the landscape with its pastel charm.

He tilted his head at the crash site. They had brought down several of these strange, mysterious mushroom trees, but they didn't appear broken; they looked like a dropped cake. He couldn't help himself. He took off toward the splattered mushrooms, leaping over broken debris and ignoring the shouts for him to stop. Laisren froze next to a ruined tree—was it even a tree? He knelt beside the white, fluffy substance and inhaled an intoxicating caramelized aroma.

He reached out and touched it—oh, how it felt like the softest, spongiest cake he could imagine! Should he investigate further? Why, of course! He plucked a piece and popped it into his mouth, where a jubilant explosion of sugar, butter, vanilla, and cream danced upon his taste buds. Surely, this must be a slice of heaven itself! With another bite, he was once again swept away by those same delightful ingredients, which made his knees quiver with joy. How could it possibly taste even better the second time? Surely he must be dreaming!

He saw a shattered fragment of a plum-hued topper and felt a whimsical urge to explore it further. He broke off a portion that sparkled with a large, dazzling white spot. Bringing it to his nose, he detected hints of blueberry and blackberry mingled with a sprinkle of sugar. He took a bite, followed by a delighted "wow!" that escaped his lips. Bursting with the flavors of the succulent and luscious berries, its texture resembled a fluffy macaroon, while that glistening spot was nothing less than a treasure trove of pure sugar crystals. In that magical moment, he wished never to awaken from this enchanting dream.

The crew had finally caught up with Laisren. His mouth was full of crumbling purple dessert. "You guys have to try this," he mumbled through it.

Before they could indulge in the sugary delights, a rustle in the mushroom forest caught Jace's attention.

Instantly, he whistled a sharp bird call, signaling trouble, and gestured urgently to his left. Finn felt a wave of regret wash over him for not having grabbed his bow and arrows. The sound of approaching footsteps grew louder, and with a surge of adrenaline, Jace drew his sword, steeling himself for the unknown threat that lay ahead.

Tyrdon grabbed his necklace, channeling his tiger's night vision. "I see bodies. There looks to be three humans walking toward us. One female and two males." Tyrdon drew his sword, along with others, releasing his necklace.

"We know you're there. State your business. We have come in peace and mean you no harm," Jace spoke loudly.

A dark purple, hooded figure emerged from the forest. His leather tunic matched his hood, and he wore a pure white rabbit pelt around his neck. A bow was strapped across his chest, and knives decorated his belt. He pulled back his hood, revealing shaved sides of his head marked with swirling mauve tattoos and thick inky hair pulled into a long ponytail. His pale-skinned jawline looked sharp enough to cut glass, and his eyes were so dark purple they almost appeared black.

"Destroying half a forest is peaceful?" the dark figure questioned. His voice sounded smooth and too inviting, like melted honey over whiskey.

"That wasn't our intention. We merely crashed." Jace tried to sound as sincere as possible.

"Ah, I can see that your sea-faring ship smashed into our nowhere-near-the-sea Ploema Mushroom Forest, so yes, I would call that, as you said, a mere crash."

"Look, friend," Jace started. "We're not looking for trouble."

A giggle erupted from behind them, catching them off guard. A coffee-skinned, undeniably gorgeous woman stepped into view. Ashur's jaw dropped in astonishment. Her eyes glimmered with a mesmerizing shade of orchid purple, and her athletic build showcased an hourglass figure. Her frizzy ebony hair was parted in the center and styled into multiple twists and braids.

"I think trouble is precisely what you came for." Her voice was confident and flirtatious. Her face was adorned with white and purple tattoos, but Ashur couldn't help but focus on her unusually thick, dark plum lips.

Jace held up his hands in surrender, feeling like he was losing. "I know what this may look like, but right now, we have injured passengers, and we need to find our other two ships."

The male huffed. "You won't be able to reach them."

"Why?" Jace growled.

"They're in cursed territory. You're close, but not close enough." He stepped forward, closing the gap between him and the crew. He squinted, his eyes widening as he scanned the crew members. "Ha! Wait... you are Elysians, which means this silver-eyed person is the infamous King Jace." He clapped his hands together in his leather gloves. "This is my lucky day."

From behind them sprang the other man, who tackled Laisren. He straddled him while Laisren fought back, mushroom cake smeared across his face, but the mysterious figure was too large. He landed a punch on Laisren, knocking him out cold, blood trailing from his nose. The Pirate Captain raised his sword, ready for it to taste death once more.

The mystery man turned and faced the crew. "I just saved his life!"

Dinyelle glanced at one of the other female warriors standing beside her, Ovaena. Ovaena mouthed, "Wow. He's hot." Dinyelle laughed silently, not wanting to draw attention to them. The new arrival wore no shirt, just leather straps that held two swords on his back and crisscrossed over his bulging pectorals. White rabbit fur draped over his broad shoulders, and his abs were so defined they resembled six freshly baked dinner rolls. He had piercing periwinkle eyes and a chiseled jaw that could melt the heart of almost any woman.

"Explain," the Pirate Captain snarled, the sword pointed directly at the violet-haired man.

"He ate of the Ploema mushroom. It's cursed to all, not just Glatanians. Eating it means you're enslaved to its taste. If his body allowed, he would eat every mushroom here. Many have eaten themselves to death in this forest. We try to save as many poor souls as we can from here. Now, we can waste no time. He must come with us. My sister has a tonic that can heal his addiction."

"No!" yelled their female companion. "Leave them to their own fate. They chose to invade. Let them figure it out."

"We're not invading," Jace pleaded. He was becoming weary of having to persuade them of their innocence.

The black-haired man cleared his throat. "Then, why are you here? Tell us the reason, and if it's good enough, we'll bring you peacefully back to our camp and heal your companion. If it's in no interest to us, then we go our separate ways."

Jace didn't like gambling, but what choice did he have? "Fair enough." Jace cleared his throat, praying he wasn't making a mistake. "We flew three ships here with our Queen Sealyn to overthrow Glatania's throne and break your kingdom's curse."

All three looked at one another.

"Lies. No kingdom would risk both monarchies on such a mission," the female snapped.

"Well, we're kind of a 'you go, I go' couple, but also, there are three Elysian monarchs here. Queen Mother Graelynd is on Queen Sealyn's ship," Jace said.

"You're all mad," she barked back.

The violet-haired man stepped forward. "What my comrades mean to say, yet have remarkably failed to express, is that your agenda aligns with ours. Let's begin with introductions. The dark, sinister one over there is Corvus of House Silv, our mission's second-in-command, and the beautiful yet sharp-tongued one is Nyx of House Unknown. I'm Laekian of House Leis, leader of the Glatanian resistance."

Chapter 35

<u>You Sure Showed Me</u>

Sealyn jolted awake from the screams around her. Her head throbbed, and a faint ringing filled her ears. "Jace?" she thought, panic creeping in. Smoke filled the air. What was burning? She scanned her surroundings as her vision began to clear. Confusion engulfed her, but she quickly sat upright, heart racing. Their ship was ablaze, yet somehow she found herself outside of it. How had this happened? It didn't matter; she needed to get everyone to safety.

She tried to stand, but her knees buckled, and vertigo pushed her down.

"Whoa, easy, Queen Sealyn," a deep voice said.

She looked up and saw Lord Doebromir standing over her, bald head bleeding. "Doebromir?"

"Yes, Majesty. You're safe. We retrieved everyone from the ship except two, but they were already dead: Villery and Umpatar. They were excellent soldiers. Before we could get their bodies, the ship exploded." Doebromir took a deep breath and exhaled. "But I have to say, this view isn't what I expected."

Sealyn didn't care about views or even that their way home was in flames. "Where's my mother?"

Doebromir pointed to a group huddled around a small makeshift fire, warming themselves. She saw Princess Adma, Lady Madilina, and her mother. Relief filled her heart. But where was Jace? She scanned the area but didn't see anyone from the blue ship. Doebromir extended his hand, and Sealyn took it, grunting as she stood. She noticed Lord Sakul lying beside her, blood dripping from a bandage wrapped around his head. She looked at Doebromir, pleading for answers.

"He's another who was unconscious when we were unloading the ship. We laid everyone in that condition over here so we could keep an eye on them all at once. He's the last one who hasn't woken up, but my queen, have no fear; his breathing is normal, and his heartbeat is steady. He will wake up. I believe Lady Madilina has been brewing some broth if you'd like me to escort you there."

Quick footsteps were heard. "No need for that, Lord Doebromir. I can handle my dear cousin." Lord Char took Sealyn's arm and linked it with his. He gently pulled her away and started walking. "Here's the short version: we crashed because the rain washed the blood from your mother's necklace. The yellow ship is about fifty yards behind that massive rock thing over there. All of their crew is accounted for, but some have serious injuries, like broken legs and arms. We don't know where Jace's ship is, but it can't be too far. We have no idea where we are because—surprise, surprise—Lady Adma isn't talking, but this is definitely not the landscape we prepared for."

"Why do people keep saying that?"

"I'm guessing you hit your head harder than we thought. Here, take this seat." Lady Madilina handed a bowl to Char. He took it and gently set it in Sealyn's hands. "Drink this. It may help settle your mind." Char eyed his aunt, then joined Lord Max and Lord Jashun with a few others. Graelynd wrapped her arm around Sealyn, thankful her daughter had woken.

Sealyn kept her eyes closed as she sipped the salty, warm broth. She feared for Jace. Anger boiled inside. She didn't hesitate. "So, you're refusing to help again?"

"Sealyn ..." her mother scolded.

"It's okay, Queen Mother Graelynd. I'm growing accustomed to your daughter's outbursts," Adma snapped. She pushed her cracked glasses up her nose and folded her arms.

Sealyn slowly lifted her head and glared at Adma. "Watch your tongue, spy."

"Why? You're in my territory now."

"Are we? Your silence suggests you might be out of your element. Perhaps the dainty princess doesn't know her kingdom as well as her elite indoor education would imply."

Graelynd exhaled. "Sealyn, that is …"

Adma stood, spilling her broth. "How dare you! I know this kingdom better than any of my siblings." She pointed behind Sealyn. "You see that oddly shaped forest? Well, that's Ploema Mushroom Forest, deadly to those who eat from it, but if you somehow make it through, you'll run smack into what's being called The Resistance. Such fools." She looked to her left and gestured to the sparkling white-tipped mountains. "Those are the Frosting Ridge Mountains, and beyond them lie the Sult Plains, where people go to starve themselves." She rolled her eyes and shook her head, unable to fathom why people would do that. "The trees you see to my right are where most of our military bases are located, and behind me, past that boulder and your other ship, leads straight to our beautiful capital city, Milska. Yes, the only city with a river of chocolate."

Sealyn propped her elbows on her thighs and cradled her chin in her hands. She wished Jace were here to see this exchange. "My, my, impressive. You sure showed me," Sealyn said, smiling slyly before leaning back.

Adma froze. Had Sealyn tricked her? Should she not have revealed all the details about her kingdom?

"Lord Doebromir, Lord Max, Lord Jashun, and Lord Char, please join me." The men hurried to their queen, obeying her request. "We need to venture through Ploema Mushroom Forest. Through it will be The Resistance, but no one is permitted to eat anything from that forest—anything."

"But ..." Adma began.

Sealyn jerked her head toward the wide-mouthed princess. "What? Did you really think you were smarter than all of us?"

Graelynd stood. "Sealyn, a word." She stomped away from the others. Sealyn reluctantly followed.

"Yes, Mother?"

"You need to stop with this ill treatment toward Adma."

"But she ..."

"I don't care what she's done. You must be the light. If she's done something wrong, then you show her the way. You don't stoop to any level. Remember, no one is beneath you—no one. You treat people how you would want to be treated. You can attract more flies with honey than vinegar."

"You can also do that with manure."

"Sealyn!"

Sealyn threw her hands up. "Alright, alright. You've made your point. I know you're right."

"Come again?" Graelynd smiled a teasing grin.

Sealyn chuckled. "You're right. You're always right." She sighed. "Fine. I'll talk with the little prick—I mean, princess."

"Much better."

They heard numerous loud footsteps running. Looking toward the boulder, they saw the crew of the yellow ship sprinting toward them. Sealyn's heart sank.

"Mother, grab your pack and make Char carry mine. You must stay safe—do I make myself clear?" Graelynd nodded.

Commander Tilmond yelled out before they made it to the green ship crew. "Soldiers. Soldiers are coming!"

"Grab only what you can carry while running and make for the Ploema Mushroom Forest!" Sealyn ordered.

Her crew raced to stuff their packs and satchels. Just as fortune would have it, Sakul had recently woken up; with his arm slung around Doebromir's neck, they staggered toward the mesmerizing forest. Sealyn yanked Tilmond's tunic, bringing their faces inches apart in a tense confrontation.

"Protect my mother, cousin. I trust only you with this task. Hear my words, Glatania cannot have more than one of our monarchs in their procession."

"No, you're not saying what I think you are."

"Yes, Tilmond. I must go with the soldiers. It's obvious those are our ships. Yours didn't burn. It will look like we're spying, which will be treated as an act of war. Me showing myself will show something different."

"You can't go by yourself."

"She won't." Char put his hand on her shoulder. "I'll be going with her."

"No, Char …"

"Listen, it's already a big enough rumor that wherever there's an adventure with you—I'm right there beside you, so it would look worse if I didn't go."

"Let us go too. You will need a lady with you to look the part," Lady Madilina said as Max wrapped his arm around her shoulder.

Red eyes blazing, Jem stepped up to the group. "You will need a sword wielder, too. I will fight to protect you."

Char nodded. "No more than this. Keep it small enough to warrant no suspicions."

Sealyn shook her head. "This doesn't feel right. Everything about this feels off."

"Please, Queen Sealyn, let us do this with you. We don't have much time." Madilina squeezed Sealyn's arm.

"Tilmond, go! You can't be seen, or all this is ruined," Char ordered.

Tilmond nodded and started to run, but Sealyn grabbed his arm. "Find Jace, and when you do, tell …" Her voice cracked. "Tell him I love him."

"I will." He nodded.

"And don't let that little witch, Adma, out of your sight."

Char couldn't help but laugh softly as they watched their crew sprint into the dark, mysterious mushroom forest. They could hear the soldiers. It wouldn't be long until they were captives—again.

Chapter 36

<u>22 Years Ago…</u>

Jace tasted the metallic tang of blood from yet another crack in his chapped lips. They had been traveling for days, perhaps even longer. He had lost track of time. He felt the agony of blisters and blood in his boots and around his wrists, the itching of ant bites and the burn on his hand, the aches and pains in his muscles and joints, the intense hunger for proper nourishment, and more than anything, the embarrassment of his saggy, smelly, feces-filled pants.

His silver eyes were red-rimmed, bloodshot, and oh, so very tired. He felt himself drifting in and out of consciousness, contemplating escape and whether he needed to cook his eggs. He kept dreaming about his days on the farm, only to wake to the nightmare that was his reality. He replayed where he should have hidden each day, hating himself more and more.

They finally arrived at a village that Jace thought he recognized, but he passed out again before he could assess his surroundings. He woke up to cold water being poured over his head while lying in a scuffed, white porcelain bathtub. He looked around and encountered a pair of obsidian eyes staring back at him. This was the same woman he watched have her baby murdered because it had eyes like his: Laeglarie.

She gave a half-smile and continued scrubbing. "The soldiers dunked you in the river a few times before bringing you to me. I burned your clothes, so don't worry about them. Another village woman lost her son to the sickness months ago. He was about your size, maybe a little bigger. She donated some clothes and boots."

His wounds stung, but he was too exhausted to care. He embraced the pain, as it helped him stay awake to spend time with this sweet woman.

"Do." Jace's voice scratched his throat, and he coughed. "Do you remember me?"

Laeglarie smiled a sad smile. "Do I remember the most famous silver-eyed child in history?" She chuckled. "Of course, I do."

Jace placed his small, wet, soapy hand on hers, wincing as the air sizzled the burns on his wrists. "I'm sorry about your son. Thank you for helping me."

Her soft face fell, and for a fleeting moment, Laeglarie seemed to age ten years. Then, it disappeared. She smiled again. "It's okay. He lives on through you."

"Me? How so?"

"Silver eyes are special." She poured another bucket of water over his head, rinsing the soapy white bubbles away. "Now, let's stand up, get you dry, then I'll tend to your wounds." Laeglarie wrapped him snugly in a thick cotton towel, gently helping him out of the tub. She allowed him, still wrapped in the towel, to sit in a chair while she dabbed a special, foul-smelling ointment on his wrists and feet. The ointment burned, yet soon provided instant relief. Next, she applied a green paste to his burned hand and over the bites, then wrapped it with an off-white bandage.

His dripping wet hair hung in his face as he slouched. She tossed a few strands and laughed as they fell right back over his eyes. He smiled in response.

"How about I give you a proper haircut while I tell you a story? Would you like that?" Jace nodded, feeling the soreness in his neck. "Alright, you just sit back and listen." She gently glided the wooden comb through his long brown hair. The gesture was soothing to Jace, and he felt himself relaxing. "Now, have you heard of the silver-eyed person who is more famous than you?"

Jace didn't realize he had closed his eyes, but they sprang open. "What? No! Who?"

"Ah, good. Just relax and listen, then. Long ago, in a distant kingdom before the Second Chance, there lived a man with silver eyes." She snipped away his long hair, trimming it into short layers. Chunks of hair fell silently to the floor. "It was said that his mother hid him among the perilous rocks of a shattered seashore. The only issue was that she was fleeing from her kingdom."

"Why?" Jace asked, fighting to stay awake.

"She had stolen a highly valuable artifact from her kingdom's palace. She took refuge with a man from another kingdom, who took advantage of her during the night, prompting her to flee—never looking back. After months of traveling to this desolate seashore, it became clear that she was pregnant. She negotiated with the lighthouse keeper to allow her to stay in the vacant, old, shabby hut among the rocks. After he agreed, she gave birth to a beautiful silver-eyed boy, just like you."

"No one killed the baby?"

"She told the lighthouse keeper that the baby was sickly, so no visitors were allowed. He took pity on her and ultimately found himself falling in love with her. After three years of keeping the boy away from the lighthouse man, she finally revealed her secret just before the boy's fourth birthday." Laeglarie took a razor and began shaving the side of Jace's head, careful not to nick him. "As the woman feared, her new husband sided with the world. Instead of killing the child, he offered to at least chain him with magic-blocking shackles."

Jace glanced at his wrists and swore he saw a glint of metal peeking through part of the wound—or was it a dragon scale? "Did she agree?" he asked with a yawn.

"She did, but several years later, the lighthouse man took to drinking, which led to him beating his wife and the chained child." Laeglarie finished shaving the left side, then began shaving the right, wishing Jace were her child, not the red-haired witch's. "The mother made an exchange deal with an enchantress: the artifact for a powerful protection spell. She had had enough of the beatings, so when the child had grown into a healthy young man, she freed him from his chains." Laeglarie saw Jace's eyes open and close, sleep calling his name. "When the husband returned home intoxicated, prepared for another night of abusing his wife and the silver-eyed, the son protected his mother—and the lighthouse man was never found."

"Wha-What happened to him?" Jace asked in a trance-like state.

Laeglarie dried and wiped the sides of Jace's clean-shaven head while his freshly dried locks fell perfectly into place. "Well, some say the husband was so terrified of the silver-eyed that he fled and fell to his death. Others say the silver-eyed killed him; either way, mother and son were safe, but the son feared for their lives from the villagers. So instead of his mother, who was too weak to do so at this point, the son cast the most powerful protection spell our world has ever known—one that still exists today. Because you see, dear one, silver eyes can manipulate …"

"Baaaaaaaahhhhh!" echoed in Jace's ear, waking him up. The loud sheep cry wasn't the only surprising thing; he was in one of the sheep carts, bouncing along the uneven road. At least he was riding instead of walking. Of course, those cowards would do something like this. If his mother knew they tortured him, she would behead them all.

He saw his feet, wrists, and hand wrapped in bandages and felt the fresh, new clothes on his body. With his uninjured hand, he rummaged through his pockets, finding the treats sweet Laeglarie had left for him. He munched on a biscuit and stuffed the rest back for safekeeping. Then he remembered he didn't know how her story ended. He had fought sleep the entire time to find out what happened, but now he would never know.

Jace vowed to return and ask Laeglarie to finish her story, and perhaps he could sneak into the library to search for books about this mysterious, powerful man. Jace peered through the bars and observed the soldiers pouring water over themselves and their horses. What were they doing? It was cold outside, and they were only minutes from the palace.

"Onward! No stopping! Full speed ahead," the commander yelled.

Jace heard the whips crack and the horses neigh, then he felt the wagon jerk. His head slammed against the wooden panels. Tears welled in his eyes. He was so ready to be done with these soldiers.

"Bring us Lady Corentine! Bring us Lady Corentine!" the commander shouted through the streets and up the palace steps. The people of the capital chased after the caravan, unaware of what was happening. The first thing Jace noticed was her flaming red hair; the second was her scowl.

Lady Corentine glided down the dark stone steps without any rush. She wore a strapless, form-fitting onyx-scaled dress that revealed a bit too much cleavage. Her lips were as red as cherries, matching her hair, and her eyelids were painted with thick charcoal. A group of palace guards followed her closely, almost in reverence.

She stopped in front of the commander's horse. He dismounted and gave a slight bow. "My lady, you look more ravishing than any woman I've ever seen. Allow me to show you what we've brought for you." He kissed her hand and escorted her to the sheep wagon.

Jace locked eyes with his mother. He wrapped his good hand around the bar and slipped his bandaged one through the spacing, waving. "Mother ..."

"He's injured," she said, her tone carrying both a question and an accusation.

"Yes, my lady. We found him in a rather poor state. A farmer had captured him. We did our best to patch him up, then rode as fast as we could."

She narrowed her skeptical raven eyes at Jace. Jace didn't want the soldiers to escape the consequences of what they had done to him. He shook his head slightly.

Corentine relaxed her face and pulled back her shoulders, pushing her chest out more. "Farmer, you say?"

The commander stumbled over his words. "Ye-yes, my lady. A farmer and two helpers."

Corentine stepped closer to the commander, blocking her view of Jace. "And what did you do with these farmers?" she asked in a sweet tone, biting her plump bottom lip seductively. "Did you kill them for me?"

"Uh. Uh, yes, my lady. For you, yes. Always anything for you."

She slid her lip away from her teeth and grinned wickedly. "Excellent," she purred. "And you hurried my son back to me…" She left the statement hanging in the air for him to complete.

"Yes, my lady. You can see we're covered in sweat— our horses as well."

Jace huffed at his lie.

Corentine twirled her delicate fingers in the commander's salt-and-pepper hair, allowing water droplets to slide down her pale-skinned arm. "Ah, I can see you're wet." Corentine seized the commander's front armor, drawing his face closer to hers. From Jace's perspective, it appeared she was kissing him. As she slid her hands down his armor, Corentine slowly licked the commander's cheeks and then his mouth before pushing him back, concealing the dagger she had taken from him behind her. The commander stood speechless. "Well, Commander, your sweat doesn't taste like salt, which makes you a liar."

"No, my lady. No! I'm telling you the truth. I beg of you. Please, believe me."

She spun around, tossing her long, strawberry-red hair behind her, and faced the other soldiers. "You all will die with the commander unless one of you tells me the truth. My offer expires in five seconds. Five."

"No, please, my lady. I beg you!" the commander pleaded.

"Silence. Four..." she counted.

"My lady, please ..."

Corentine moved so quickly that the crowd nearly missed what had occurred. She slashed the commander's neck with the stolen silver dagger. A waterfall of crimson flowed from the gash, and he plummeted to his knees, choking and gurgling, then falling face down to the ground. A pool of blood flowed from beneath his lifeless body.

"Three," she continued without showing any emotion.

"We found him hiding in a cellar of a farmer's house!" a soldier cried.

"And?"

"And the bodies of the farmer and his helpers had been severely smashed. Their remains were in the woods. It looked like Jace had been living there for a week or two."

"Explain his injuries."

The soldier stumbled over his words. "Um, well, we, uh. H-he burned his hand on a pan; then the commander shoved that hand into a fire ant bed, and um, he ordered his wrists to be tied and to walk the entire way back. It wasn't until the last village that he finally received a bath and medical treatment."

Corentine nodded thoughtfully. She closed her eyes and tilted her head back. Taking a deep breath, she began to issue her orders. "You who spoke the truth, go retrieve my son and bring him to me. The rest of you, dismount and kneel before me."

Every soldier did this with trembling knees and shoulders. Corentine looked at her loyal palace guards and nodded. They lobbed off each head with clean, forceful strikes. Corentine kicked one head away that had rolled too close for her liking. The honest soldier held Jace in his arms but stopped in shock when he saw his comrades' heads scattered across the obsidian stone street. He began to shake, and urine streamed down his pants, creating a puddle beneath his boots.

"Guards, take him to the dungeons. It's a crime to betray your comrades, isn't it?"

"Yes, my lady."

Jace smiled at his mother. She was avenging him! This was what he had wanted all along. He knew she loved him; deep down, he had always believed it.

Corentine stepped closer to her imprisoned child, and whispered, "Who always protects you?"

Jace was more than eager to say, "You, Mother."

Corentine nodded. "That's right, and you still pledge yourself to me?"

Jace nodded excitedly. "Yes, Mother."

"Swear it! Swear that you are always faithful and duty-bound to me," she growled.

Confusion grew on Jace's young face. "I—I swear it. I'm sworn to you, Mother."

Corentine jerked her head to the guard. "Take Jace, too. It's also a crime to run away from the palace, especially for an ungrateful silver-eyed."

She turned and walked back up the unwelcoming, obsidian steps, her heels clicking with each stride. No, what was she doing? Surely this wasn't right, yet she never looked back. Jace's heart crumbled into pieces, and he felt more alone than ever. As soon as the iron bars of the mildew-smelling dungeon closed, Jace cried himself to sleep, praying for someone to take him away from this murderous, uncaring kingdom.

Chapter 37

<u>The Badger Attack</u>

Pinx collapsed into Madam Bip's arms, gasping for air after running through the castle. She needed to tell the group about the badgers, mouthing the words as she sucked in another stream of air.

"Badger," Pinx inhaled. "Climbing the barrier." She gasped.

Bip patted her back. "It's okay, child. We already know."

Pinx let out a sigh of relief and frustration. She saw that Bip's ears had dried blood stains, and she reached to touch one, but Bip pulled away, cupping Pinx's hand in hers.

"But Bip…"

"All is well, my dear. All is well. I was able ta' lengthen 'de protection barrier. It should go close ta' a mile below."

Pinx blinked in surprise. "A mile? Bip, that's extremely far. No wonder the magic took such a toll on you. Please sit down. Let me fetch you some cheese and crackers."

The bench creaked as Bip sat down, squeezing her body to fit at the student's table. "I won't ever say no ta some cheese and crackers, but don't go makin' a fuss over ol' Bip. I'm okay."

Pinx sent several of the Nichts to grab plates for all the professors. She glanced at her worried friends. "What's happening, and how is that badger climbing?"

"According to my findings," Professor Novaly began. "The protection barrier consists of a material and actions, meaning that it functions like gelatin and reacts as a result when an object impacts water from a significant distance."

Pinx furrowed her brow and glanced at Lady Norella, whose face was turning red from suppressing a laugh. "That sounds fascinating, Novaly, but what does it mean?"

"Oh, yes. Of course." Novaly lightly tapped her head, disturbing her mangled flower crown. "How silly of me. So, the spell has its commands, courtesy of Madam Bip—it shields from attacks, which is the part I described with water. You know that objects shatter when dropped from a great height above water, right? I mean, theoretically, if you added enough soap to the area where said object would land, then technically, that object or even a person would simply splash straight through the water with no injuries."

Pinx shook her head. "Novaly, focus. I don't need the lecture version. Give me the version you would explain to a soldier."

Novaly frowned. She didn't understand. Everything she said was straightforward. Novaly shrugged and pressed on. "Since the badgers don't seem to be attacking us, the barrier is in a gelatinous state, allowing the creatures to use their claws to climb more easily. See—it makes perfect sense, right?"

"Sure," Pinx replied. "Any plan on how we exterminate these wild beasts?"

Siany stopped pacing the room. "All we know is that the only way to kill them is by stabbing their brains."

"Gross!" Pinx said. "There must be another way. Is there something we haven't considered? Remember the last time this school was attacked by the Black Phoenixes? Why not utilize Nightlight and Gorm?"

"Uh, in this case, I don't think little Gorm will be useful. His bubbles would have to target such a small area that he'd most likely get killed, but Nightlight's blue flames could inflict some serious damage. Maybe we could have fried badger for dinner?" Hueweyn chuckled at his joke; the silence made him sweat.

"Odd jokes aside," Siany said. "You both make valid points. We may not have Lady Madilina and Lord Jashun, but we still have Princess Kailani and Nightlight. A Noxhorn dragon and mermaid facing off against Berserker Badgers sounds like the perfect matchup."

"But where is Kailani?" Norella asked.

Bip shrugged. "Last I heard, she still has a few more gallons left ta' fill of that lake she drained during 'de Black Phoenix battle. King Ryker wasn't letting her return home 'til she finished."

"That's right. I've seen her there, but she mainly looks like she's just swimming around, not working," Pinx added.

"Sounds like her," Siany sighed. The Nichts fluttered into the room, carrying plates full of cheese, crackers, and grapes, along with goblets of cider. Siany munched on a cracker topped with goat cheese, savoring its sweet, tangy flavor. "Here's what we need to do …"

The door swung open, and in walked the stunningly beautiful, dripping wet, pink-haired mermaid. She was in human form, wearing her iconic shiny, iridescent silver gown that showcased every curve of her body—and there were *a lot* of those. Her pink eyes sparkled with excitement. "Um, did you all know a clan of badgers is climbing the barrier?"

The professors looked at one another and burst into a fit of laughter.

Kailani folded her sculpted, ivory arms that still glistened with a hint of blue. "What's so funny? Shouldn't you professors be casting spells or something?"

"It's not that simple," Norella snapped. Norella wasn't a fan of Kailani or any members of the Mer Clan. She didn't trust their historical background. Even after Kailani helped save the school—she still didn't trust her. "Spells are much more complicated than you understand."

Kailani huffed. "Magic is only complicated if you make it so." She wrung out her hair and walked forward, leaving a trail of water droplets behind her. "Let's make this easy. Nothing can survive being boiled alive, so Bippy, why don't you create a tear in the barrier? I'll create a large water bowl to catch the hairy creatures; then good ol' Nightlight can do her thing by spitting her blue flames onto my water bowl and boiling them." She wiped her hands together and then stretched them out wide. "See. Nothing to it."

The professors looked horrified. How did she come up with boiling badgers so quickly? Apparently, mermaids had a dark side that most weren't aware of. Norella moaned, not wanting to admit that the fish had a good plan.

Kailani snapped her fingers. "Now, hop to it. I have more pressing matters to attend to than constantly having to save this school." She turned and walked out of the room.

Princess Siany's mouth was still open when she went to speak. "I can't believe she just said that. Ugh, either way, let's follow her plan and deal with these badgers. I don't want anything to disrupt these students' progress. Hueweyn and Novaly, retrieve Nightlight and bring her to the lake. Madam Bip, you and Pinx should work on creating that tear under the badgers. The rest of you, please return to the students' common rooms, assist them with their studies, and keep them calm. More importantly, don't let them look out the windows."

The group split up, prepared to defend their school once again. This time, they had a solid plan. Hueweyn pushed open the stone barn door, welcoming the scent of hay and old leather. He heard Nightlight snoring. They moved quietly, careful not to wake the sleeping dragon nestled in its bed of large pebbles. They soon saw that it was the tiny white bubble dragon doing the snoring. Gorm was curled up next to his big sister, standing out against her shimmering, electric cerulean scales.

Hueweyn swallowed, always fearful of waking Nightlight. She was moody as it was, but when first waking up, she was downright mean. He decided on a different approach. He tapped Gorm's foot, full of white claws. The dragon laughed like a baby human, then returned to snoring.

"Are you tickling him?" Novaly asked with a whisper.

"I didn't mean to." Hueweyn leaned closer and smacked Gorm's foot harder.

The tiny dragon's lime green tongue slithered from its mouth like a snake tasting the air. Hueweyn kicked his foot again, frustrated. Gorm's yellow eyes shot open and released hundreds of bubbles, letting out a squeak.

"Shhhh. Shhh." Hueweyn tried to calm the little dragon, but it was no use. Nightlight's glowing blue eyes were fixed on Hueweyn. She huffed steam from her nostrils. Hueweyn let out a nervous laugh. "Uh, hi there, Nightlight. Um, so we really could use your help. We have a badger problem." He swallowed, his mouth dry. He was relieved Nightlight hadn't eaten him yet, so he continued, "They're climbing the protection barrier. Madam Bip is going to create a tear to drop the badgers through it, but Princess Kailani— you know, the mermaid you fought alongside—well, she's going to form a water bowl to catch them." Hueweyn wiped his sweating brow and took one last breath. "We need you to boil those terrible beasts with your mighty blue flames."

Gorm sat up excitedly. He clapped his little white paws, his claws clicking. He spat more bubbles and pointed at them.

Hueweyn shook his head. "Not this time, Gorm. Your bubbles won't help today."

Gorm's yellow eyes brimmed with tears. He turned and clung to his prominently bigger-than-him sister, wailing. Nightlight glared once more and growled at Hueweyn.

Waving his finger back and forth frantically, Hueweyn said, "No. No. No. I didn't mean that Gorm isn't important or valuable; he just wouldn't be the best opponent against Berserker Badgers."

Nightlight's eyes dilated, and her nostrils flared. She sat up, towering over Hueweyn, and seized Gorm. She stuffed him into an oversized satchel and threw it at Novaly, who surprisingly caught it without dropping the poor dragon, bubbles spewing from the openings. Nightlight galloped out the doors and soared into the air, stretching her glistening sapphire wings wide. She glided effortlessly and landed beside the lake where Kailani was in her scaly, blue mermaid form, commanding the water.

Bip and Pinx stood nearby. "Are you ready?" Bip yelled.

Nightlight roared, and Kailani shouted, "Yes!"

Pinx held her necklace and grasped Bip's hand. Bip clutched her necklace, focusing on the area right beneath the hundreds of snarling badgers. She felt Pinx's powers flowing through her. With a friend's help, she could do this. Drawing on all her strength and willpower, she commanded the barrier to open. A bright light erupted from beneath the badgers, prompting them to scratch at its glow. Kailani swept her arms wide, releasing water from the crystal-clear lake into the air. She hurriedly made a circular motion with her arms, and the water formed into a swirling bowl. It appeared as though the mermaid was pushing the air, guiding the bowl to float under the emerging crack in the barrier.

"Now, Bip! Now!" Kailani yelled.

Both Bip and Pinx tried to pull the barrier apart, but it resisted them, trying to protect the students. Bip felt another hand grasp her wrist. It was Lady Norella. She and Novaly held their necklaces and helped channel their powers through each other to Bip. With the combined strength of four Tethered Luxens, Bip shattered the spell, and badgers tumbled into the swirling bowl of water.

More and more kept piling in, and some were starting to figure out how to swim to the sides.

"Can't you enclose them?" Novaly shouted to Kailani.

"Not until all have fallen in!"

One badger fell to the ground, dripping wet and mad. He sprinted toward Bip, but Princess Siany let loose her arrow, slicing through its head. Down it went. Bip nodded at Siany. Siany smiled. She had to admit—she missed this kind of adrenaline.

After the last badger fell into the water, Kailani clapped her hands together, engulfing the badgers in a spherical water chamber, just like she had done with the Black Phoenixes. Two other badgers escaped the water, and before they hit the ground, arrows were lodged into each brain.

Gasping for air, Hueweyn said, "Go, Nightlight. It's your turn now." Hueweyn held Gorm in the satchel, his little white head poking out, watching his vibrant sister.

Nightlight flew with unnatural speeds, blue flames escaping her mouth.

"Not too much too fast, Nightlight! You'll evaporate the water!"

Nightlight growled and retracted some of her flames. She watched with a broad smile as the boiling bubbles formed in the sphere. Her wings flapped gently, keeping her in place. She was focused on her kill. There would be dead badger to feast upon tonight. She watched as, one by one, badgers sank to the bottom, motionless, bubbles rising from their lips.

Once the last badger sank, Nightlight unleashed a blast of blinding blue flames. The water turned to steam, and dead badgers plopped to the ground, steam rising from their wet bodies. Nightlight landed beside them and released more flames, setting the pile of Berserker Badgers on fire.

"Gah, why does that smell so good?" Hueweyn asked out loud. Gorm gave him a funny look, then wiggled out of the bag and flew to his sister.

Kailani crawled to Hueweyn in human form, draped in her silver gown. Then, she rolled onto her back, her wet pink hair strewn across the yellowing green grass.

"Excellent job, Kailani," Hueweyn praised.

She moaned. "What is the saltiest food in that pitiful excuse of a cafeteria you have?"

"Hmm. I know we have a fantastic batch of olives and pickles."

"That sounds perfect. A meal fit for those who boiled Berserker Badgers!"

Chapter 38

<u>A Squifflewig</u>

The Pirate Captain paced back and forth in front of the treehouse where Laekian's sister tried to heal Laisren. He winced every time his son screamed out. Almost every scream was followed by violent vomiting. Jace and Taeg sat at a table on the deck in front of the house, watching their father pace. They had no idea what was happening to their brother. Could they really trust these Glatanians? It sounded more like they were torturing him than anything else.

Laekian walked across the netted treetop bridge with two handmade bowls filled with chopped purple potatoes and beef stew. Jace and Taeg's stomachs growled at the delicious aroma. He handed the bowls to the visitors and sat down with them, chuckling as they devoured the stew.

"I know those sounds from your comrade …"

"He's my brother," Taeg snapped, stew dripping down his chin. "I mean, our brother. He's our brother." He waved the spoon back and forth between himself and Jace, letting stew drip onto the table.

Laekian raised his hands in surrender, biceps flexing. "My apologies. Those sounds from your *brother* may sound bad, but this is completely normal. He's lucky we got to him so quickly. He should be on his feet in the next day or two. I've seen much worse." His periwinkle eyes twitched, with dark memories swirling behind them.

"Well, I'm grateful," Jace said, wiping his mouth with the back of his hand. "Lucky for us, it was your lot we ran into first. Do you have any news of our other two ships? We need to rescue them."

Laekian leaned back in his wooden chair and chewed the inside of his cheek, analyzing Jace. "Ready to see your queen?" Jace gave a nod. Laekian leaned forward, propping his elbows on the table. "I must admit. I'm quite curious to see this queen of yours. Her beauty has a reputation."

"I would advise you not to utter any more words like that," Jace said through clenched jaws.

"Easy, tiger. It's a simple curiosity."

The treehouse door opened, and Laekian's sister walked out, wiping her hands with a rag. She had the same violet hair as her brother, and she wore a thick braid to one side with loose wisps framing her face. Some strands of her hair looked so light they appeared white, matching her face tattoos. She had ivory skin with rosy cheeks and plump, light pink lips. She was short and had a petite frame. She unhooked the white rabbit fur draped around her shoulders and laid it on the back of the empty chair at the table.

Jace and Laekian laughed at Taeg's open mouth.

"Hi, I'm AeLeer. I'm guessing you know I'm this guy's sister."

Jace and Taeg nodded in unison. The Pirate Captain, who was standing beside her, touched her shoulder. "Please, can you tell me how my son is?"

She stared too long. "Forgive me. We don't see many orange eyes here and definitely not green ones, so this is all hard to process. Your son will make a full recovery. You can see him, but I wouldn't go in there right now. The smell of vomit is horrendous—that's why I left the door open. Give it a few minutes. If you want to go get some more water from the water hut, which is three houses down, then that should be plenty of time."

Tyrdon hurried onto the netted rope bridge, legs wobbling. Taeg laughed. "Yeah, that's going to take him a while."

AeLeer sat in the chair, unable to take her eyes off Jace. Jace tilted his head and stared back at her. She jumped. "Oh, my. Oh. I'm so sorry. I didn't mean to …"

"It's okay. Staring at my silver eyes is nothing; hitting on my wife is another."

Laekian lifted his hand. "Okay, I did not hit on your wife. I haven't even met her."

AeLeer smacked her brother's arm. "Laekian! You know better. We're not like the Havasians. Forgive my brother; he's been infatuated with the tales of the blinding beauty and fearlessness of this emerald queen for years—ever since he was a teenager, really."

Laekian exhaled. "All right, thanks for that embarrassing story. Speaking of your other ships, we should be hearing back from our scouts any moment. Honestly, they should have returned over an hour and a half ago." He looked at the sundial in the center of the table and stood. "I should go. Something must be wrong."

AeLeer grabbed her brother's hand. "Can't you send Corvus?"

"I'll be fine, little sister."

They heard loud commotion coming from the base of the tall, giant trees. Purple fireflowers illuminated the faces of the resistance's scouts and the other Elysian crew members. Jace leaned over the banister and saw the good news.

"Sealyn?! Char!" he yelled out. "Sealyn! Sealyn!" He scanned the crowd, unable to find her. Panic coursed through his veins like ice water. Then he noticed Queen Mother

Graelynd. She placed a hand on her heart as if to communicate a message. What did that mean? Where was Sealyn?

"Come with me. We'll bring them to the eating lodge and debrief."

Jace hesitated at Laekian's proposal. Shouldn't he speak with his people privately first? "Um, listen, Laekian, before …"

Laekian raised his hand. "No offense, King Jace, but if you're about to say that we shouldn't be privy to certain information, let me stop you because from the looks of your face, your precious queen isn't among them, which can only mean one thing …"

"What's that?"

"She's captured, and you're going to need a team for a prison break."

With wide eyes, Jashun gazed at the magnificent elevator system the resistance had built, sparing the Elysians from the labor of ascending countless stairs. Towering for miles, the thick amethyst-leafed trees cradled the wooden homes of the resistance, creating a magical landscape. He marveled at the intricate network of rope bridges that strategically interconnected each enchanting tree. Cascading down from the roped railing of every bridge were clusters of purple and yellow fireflowers, their glow illuminating the paths. At that moment, he longed for Kailani's presence to share in the wonder of it all.

Doebromir shifted uncomfortably inside the wooden box. Small, enclosed spaces had made him queasy since his captivity. Jashun noticed the change in Doebromir's breathing and placed his hand on his shoulder. "Remember, my friend, we're free. We're not prisoners. This is not a cage."

Another box carrying Sune and others was being pulled beside them. Sune looked over at Doebromir, who was still struggling. "Hey, Doebromir. Over here. Look at me. We're safe."

Tears threatened to spill from Doebromir's eyes. These two had stood by him through those horrible days, and he appreciated them immensely. He took deep breaths, calming his nerves. "Gents, I think I've found my sea legs. You can call off the Rana frogs," Doebromir said. Sune and Jashun laughed at the painful memories, but they had made it, and they were on another historic quest—together. This was something to celebrate.

When they halted at a platform, their eyes widened in wonder at the exquisite craftsmanship of the wooden decks and the playful creatures artfully carved into the trees. Ajorn was utterly enchanted by the glowing, sparkly, plump beings bouncing about with wings that seemed far too small for their purple, furry bodies. Each of these adorable creatures sported only a round head and a chubby torso, along with tiny legs that appeared completely useless. Curiosity got the better of him, and he bent down to poke one. It let out an embarrassed and irritated squeak. The fierce warrior jumped back in surprise, stumbling over Brehan, who erupted into laughter.

Ajorn looked at his finger; touching that little creature felt like poking jelly. He watched it hop away, appearing highly offended; its two leaf-like antennae were waving violently.

Their guide placed his hand on Ajorn's shoulder. "Phew, you really annoyed her. She used some terrible language that I won't repeat in front of these ladies." His deep purple eyes sparkled with mischief.

Ajorn held up his hands. He didn't want to offend anyone; moreover, he was always the one defending his friends and family. He enjoyed being the peacemaker. "I'm so sorry, sir. Is there something I should do?"

The guide let out a deep belly laugh. "Creation, no. Squifflewigs are always offended. They may be among the cutest creatures in our kingdom, but don't let their chubby faces fool you. They constantly curse, are always rude, and the only one they like around here is Nyx, but that's probably because they share the same insulting personalities."

Ajorn blinked. He tried to pronounce the foreign name, "Squifa-what? And you said they talk?"

"Squifflewigs. Yes, they use their version of sign language with their leafy antennas." He gestured for them to keep walking across another netted rope bridge. "Don't worry. There's a lot to learn here. By the way, I'm Vinzil of House Leis. Our leader is my cousin. He's a good man."

"I'm Ajorn, and this is Brehan. Back there is Sune. We grew up training together."

"Is it true you three were with your Queen Sealyn when she broke Len Nove and Shunal's curses?"

Ajorn rolled back his large shoulders and stood a little taller. A large, toothy grin spread across his ebony face. "Yes. Those were quite the adventures. I almost died on the Shunal quest. Took a poisoned arrow to the shoulder. It still hurts from time to time."

"Wow," Vinzil marveled. "To make such a difference as that. I hope one day I can do something as grand as you all."

"Well …"

Brehan smacked his hand on Ajorn's shoulder and shook his head.

"Am I missing something?" Vinzil questioned. "Perhaps this has something to do with how you all ended up here?"

Ajorn fumbled through his words. "Well, it's best for us to let our king tell you himself."

Vinzil smiled. "I like you. You're loyal. Fear not; we're almost there."

The crew entered the wood-plank dining lodge, where purple fireflowers cascaded over the rounded, large doorframe. The lodge was wrapped around a massive tree, offering a 360-degree view of their village through several carved windows. Worn wooden tables and chairs were scattered, with several Glatanians already dining and chatting. The wood-plank walls were swirling with symbols and designs, matching several face tattoos, painted with various shades of purple and white. The air was infused with the scent of fresh forest mixed with roasted beef and potatoes. Ajorn's stomach growled.

"So, our custom is to start with these tables positioned to your left and right. These are your main meal, then opposite of us—you can't see because of the tree trunk—is the finisher table."

Of course, this being about food, Doebromir stepped forward from the crowd. "Uh, what do you mean finisher table?"

Vinzil scrunched his face. "You know … finishers. Your after-meal elements."

Doebromir crossed his arms and shook his head. "Nope. Never heard of this. I don't think any of us have."

Vinzil scratched his violet curly hair. His right side was shaved with deep purple tattooed symbols. "Hmm. Okay. So, the finisher table has herbal spiced teas, elixirs, leafy greens, powders like ginger and turmeric, and certain seeds, especially fennel seeds, to help aid with digestion. It also has other potions to help heal if you're experiencing any illnesses."

"Wow, I wasn't expecting…" Doebromir paused. He didn't want to offend Vinzil, but they had just walked through a forest of edible cake-like mushrooms, and apparently, their capital had a chocolate river, so why would these people choose to eat nuts and seeds compared to that?

"It's okay. I know our ways might seem strange to you, but this lifestyle helps us resist the curse." He gestured toward the tables. "Please take a plate. Your comrades are waiting for you."

Their crew, numbering seventy-eight in total, filled up the circular lodge. Jace hugged Queen Mother Graelynd tight.

He pulled back with tears in his eyes. "Tell me," he choked. "Please, tell me what happened. Is she alive?"

Graelynd tried to form the words to tell Jace, but she couldn't. She hated leaving her daughter. Tilmond stepped up beside Graelynd and took charge. "I think we should address the room, King Jace. There will be no hiding this." Jace nodded, eyeing Laekian, who looked too eager.

"Can you hurry this along?" Nyx sighed, swinging a small blade around with her hand. "I've got things to do." Squifflewigs squeaked with giggles. To everyone's surprise, Peri Pixies were scattered throughout the room in large numbers. They had encountered one on their Shunalian quest, but they believed these tiny creatures to be shy. The ones present here were quite sociable with each table and the Squifflewigs.

Peri Pixies began as deformations of the original Nichts. Most perished, but enough survived to form a new species. They have tiny bald heads with silver skin, standing at the height of a person's pinky finger. Their wings are green-tinted, and their ears resemble another set of wings. They possess slightly wider-than-normal noses and have child-like faces with eyes spaced farther apart than human eyes.

Tilmond cleared his throat, feeling calm since Peri Pixies only appeared when they sensed no danger. "Once we had cleared our ship and attended to our injured, we prepared to secure the perimeter when we saw a group of Glatanian soldiers marching toward us. We packed what we could and ran to the other ship to warn the queen." He cleared his throat again.

"Do you need some hot tea or something?" Nyx barked.

"Hush, Nyx!" Laekian ordered.

Tilmond sighed. "Queen Sealyn made the judgment call. She ordered us to leave her behind."

Jace slammed his fist on the table and stood. "What? Why?"

Tilmond placed his hands on his hips, frustrated. "She said that if she didn't show herself, then our ships would appear as an act of war. So, Char, Max, Madilina, and Jem all volunteered to stay with her to help reduce suspicions. I'm sorry, my king, but it was either that or declare war."

"I would rather declare war than have my wife—your queen—in the hands of a corrupt monarchy! Don't you remember what happened last time? The Shunalian king put her and the others in a torture game, hoping to kill them all. What do you think is going to happen this time?"

Tilmond slumped. "I understand, Majesty, but you know Queen Sealyn. Once her mind is made up, there's no changing it. She's strong. She can still do this."

Jace wiped his face with his hand. "You don't understand! She's ... she's ..." He stopped and looked at Laekian, then back at Tilmond. "Never mind."

"No, please do tell us. She's what?" Laekian asked.

"She's none of your business!" Jace snapped.

Laekian huffed. "Sounds to me like she's every bit our business, and if you want her back, then you'll have to learn how to trust us."

"We have an army here. Look around. We don't need you."

Nyx laughed and jumped down from the branch where she had been lounging. "This is a broken army, if you can even call it that. Half of you can't even walk. One is still puking in his sister's house. You green-eyed folks wouldn't last a day without us." She leaned closer to Laekian. "I say you make him beg. Make the silver-eyed king remember his place in this world."

At those words, the entire Elysian crew stood up and moved forward, drawing their swords. Peri Pixies vanished, blending into their surroundings. The army's sudden movements took Jace by surprise. Ashur stepped in front of Jace, recalling Queen Sealyn shooting an arrow through a Stoltlander's neck in the Shunalian pub after insulting Jace. "By orders of Queen Sealyn Araelien of Elysium, the third-generation bloodline, breaker of curses. She has declared any insult against silver eyes to be an international offense and crime. You are allowed only one warning; the next will result in your life."

Jace's eyes widened. When did Sealyn sign this code? He had no clue, and clearly, she wanted to keep this from him—he loved her all the more for it. "Who is this queen to declare laws for all kingdoms?" Nyx snapped.

The petite Queen Mother Graelynd linked her arm through Jace's and narrowed her eyes at Nyx, then Laekian. "*She* is your only saving grace. *She* will break your curse. The question is—are you with her or against her?"

Chapter 39

<u>Glatanian Hospitality</u>

Shep's tiger ears perked up at the sound of the Glatanian force approaching. He let out a low growl. Char looked at Shep with worry shining in his jade eyes. He couldn't let them capture his tiger, too.

"Shep, hide quickly. Stay close, though, and follow us. You mustn't be seen." The ancient emerald and gold tiger nodded before sprinting toward a cluster of large, glistening lilac-leafed bushes, with several glowing purple and pink butterflies dancing above them. Char inhaled as he watched the soldiers closing in on them. The air smelled sweet, laced with a hint of campfire smoke. His heart pounded. Could Glatanians be trusted? Would they turn out just like they had in Shunal?

"Let me do the talking when they approach," Sealyn said.

A plump soldier wearing boysenberry-tinted metal armor spoke first. "Greetings, travelers. State your business."

Sealyn rose and pulled back her green velvet hood, which was which wa lined with gray rabbit fur. "I am Queen Sealyn Araelien of Elysium. I landed here to discuss alliance negotiations with your king. We would greatly appreciate your kind escort."

Char stiffened, hoping the leader would recognize the truth in her words. He replayed them repeatedly, memorizing them just in case they were all questioned separately. He glanced at Max, who was clearly doing the same, his lips moving slightly.

"Queen Sealyn?" His mouth opened and closed like a fish out of water. Char forgot how much he enjoyed watching people's reactions to seeing Sealyn for the first time; Jem, however, glared at the Glatanian. "I wasn't aware of such a meeting," the Glatanian said.

Sealyn tilted her head. "Why would you be?"

His eyes flashed anger. "Because I'm the commander of my king's army. That's why! Any special meetings are always discussed with me."

"Good to know."

He grunted at her lack of interest and short response. "Clearly, you didn't have a meeting scheduled with our king, and you came here uninvited."

Sealyn smirked. "I never said the meeting was scheduled. Did I? I'm sure you're familiar with the game of war, so you could understand why I would come unannounced to a kingdom neighboring Havas, which Stoltland has overrun."

Char noticed the frustration etched on the commander's face. He hoped Sealyn wasn't pushing too hard, but she needed to maintain her composure like a monarch.

"Regardless, we will take you and your companions to the castle. Is this all you brought? Seems small for two massive ships."

Sealyn's eyes twitched, and she forced her voice to crack. "We … we are the only ones left. A massive storm hit us. The rest are with the sea or burned in the fire. May we start this journey now? Your air is cold, and we are in need of food."

Max watched as an evil grin spread across the commander's round cheeks. He stepped closer to Madilina, feeling distrustful of these barbarians. The last thing he wanted was for any of them to touch his wife.

"Certainly. Follow us."

As they drew closer to their capital city, Milska, the air became increasingly cloyingly sweet, infused with a sense of dangerous mystery. They passed through a village filled with houses and shops crafted from gingerbread, chocolate, and hardened candy, featuring windows made of delicate sugar glass. Instead of bushes, fluffy clouds of cotton candy in vibrant shades of purple, pink, and blue grew in abundance.

Growing! How could one actually grow cotton candy? Max's mouth watered at the thought, filled with a magical desire to taste the fluffy, sweet swirls of joy. Cotton candy had been his favorite treat at all the Elysian festivals since he was a small boy, a childhood delight that sparked nostalgia in his heart.

"We're stopping for a coffee up here," the commander pointed.

All six mouths dropped at the sight before them. Above the house, whose walls looked and smelled suspiciously like cinnamon tea cake, was a sign that read, *Coffee Fix Café*. However, what was most peculiar about this café was the giant teapot floating in mid-air beside it. There were no ropes, no stand; simply put, a magically enchanted porcelain pot floated weightlessly, creating a sight that was not easily forgotten. The teapot was painted with luscious green vines adorned with sparkling purple blossoms, yet it was the size of three grown men.

The commander walked inside, then returned, signaling for them to sit at the round, plum wooden tables near the enormous teapot. The chairs were painted violet with small yellow flowers, welcoming them to enjoy the patio. The outdoor seating was filled with the mouthwateringly indulgent scents of cinnamon and sugar, but above all, the velvety, spiced aroma of coffee permeated the air. Fresh, steaming brown liquid flowed from the giant teapot, spilling into layers of teacups stacked atop one another and forming a delightful coffee fountain.

The commander chuckled at the Elysian reactions. "I thought it was time to show you some Glatanian hospitality. This café is renowned for its perfect brew. You can pick up a teacup from that table over there and fill it from the fountain. I ordered enough for several cups for all of us, and they'll also be bringing out cinnamon cakes."

"Wow. Thank you, Commander," Max said with great enthusiasm. He rushed to a table filled with hundreds of mismatched teacups and saucers. He handed one with unicorns painted on it to Madilina and kissed her cheek. "For your love of unicorns, my darling."

Madilina blushed and smiled. "Thank you. I'm glad we're experiencing this together." She clinked her cup with his and skipped to the teacup fountain, filling her cup happily.

Max looked in his teacup, painted with a bear's face, and eyed Char.

Char laughed. "Still checking your cups, I see."

"Thanks to you and that frog you placed in my goblet."

"C'mon, you must admit, once you spit it down Adalina's dress, it was the funniest thing you've seen."

Max chuckled. "All right, I'll give you that one. I've never seen her jump so high."

They each filled their decorative porcelain teacups with warm, rich coffee, adding cubes of glistening white sugar and fresh creamy milk. The crew felt relaxed, soaking in the captivating Glatanian atmosphere. Sealyn made a mental note to tell Sir Nijeel all about this magical café. Suddenly, she missed home and longed for her family—and Jace. Gah, she needed Jace. She missed his touch, his arms around her, and his lips—those addictive lips. More than anything, she missed his presence and his words as her anchor. He was her pulse.

"Here come your cakes," a raspy voice said, snapping Sealyn out of her trance. A large, round lady with white hair and deep wrinkles on her face balanced an oversized round tray on her hip and waddled to their tables. She served plates of cinnamon tea cakes and blackberry macaroons that matched the color of her lilac eyes.

Before Max sank his teeth into the treats, he held the plate close to his nose and took a dramatic, savoring breath, filling his nostrils with the intoxicating, sugary aroma. Once he took his first bite, bursts of sugar, butter, cinnamon, and a hint of salt danced across all his taste buds, leaving him eager for more.

"Holy roasted unicorns! Have you ever tasted something so rich ... so grand ... so perfect?" Max asked, crumbs falling from his lips.

Madilina giggled, wiping her husband's mouth. "Easy, love. You almost sound like you never want to leave."

"Would it be so bad to stay?" He leaned in closer to her ear. "Think about it. We break Glatania's curse, then buy a house right here, in this very village. We could make such a magical life together, don't you agree?"

Madilina realized he was being serious and set down her blueberry macaroon. "But Max, you're the leader of Elysium's archery unit. How can you think of abandoning your post?"

He waved her question away like batting a gnat. "Oh, I'm sure Sealyn would understand."

Madilina sat uncomfortably, unsure how to respond to her husband's proposal. Elysium was her life, and all her friends and family were there, but starting a new, enchanting life here also sounded exhilarating. She loved their home in Avondelle, but was it so wrong to want something more? She smiled and sipped her coffee, dreaming of the kind of cake their house would be made of. "Yes, my love. If Queen Sealyn approves, then let's build a house made of chocolate with a pool of coffee." She giggled and covered her mouth with her hand. Max leaned over, resting his head on hers, soaking in their love for each other and pondering their future together.

Jem scooted his chair closer to Sealyn and whispered, "I don't trust them, Majesty. They're being too nice."

"Should we be cautious of kindness?" she asked, taunting him.

His strawberry-red eyes flared. "I don't believe they bought your story. Glatanians are tricksters, full of honeyed tongues."

Sealyn tried to avoid engaging with Jem. She wanted to savor her mind-numbingly scrumptious cake; her tongue almost missed the sugary delight as she swallowed. Her eyes drifted toward the café's shop. She wondered if its walls tasted as good as what she had just eaten.

"Queen Sealyn," Jem hissed. "Did you hear me?"

His voice snapped her back to the conversation. She sighed dramatically, not wanting to have this talk. "Okay, and what do you suppose we do?"

Jem grumbled. "I don't know. Just be cautious."

"Noted, Jem. Noted. I'll forever be cautious." She slurped her coffee, hoping to annoy him.

Jem scooted his chair back and slouched. He ran his large, callused hands through his light blonde hair, his short locks falling perfectly back into place. Jem's strong jawline stiffened. He wanted the queen to trust him, to understand him, and maybe even love him? No, he couldn't wish for that—or maybe he could. After all, he was here, not her monster of a husband.

The commander stood up, downed the last drops of his coffee, and licked his fingers. "We must go. We aren't far from the palace. That bridge over there conceals it, but you'll see our mighty castle once we start hiking."

As they walked over the shiny sugilite stones, they noticed creatures they hadn't seen before. Madilina kept shaking Max's arm and pointing.

One of the soldiers chuckled and began educating them about the visible beasts. He pointed to a sleeping cat with bat wings. "That multi-colored creature is a Felistilio. Most around here are nice if you give them sugar cubes." He strummed his chin with his leather gloves. "Let's see. Ah, look at the little bouncing creatures on the bridge railing. Those things are called Squifflewigs. Cute but incredibly rude."

Madilina laughed. She wanted to take one of each home. She wondered if she could channel them but didn't dare show her magic or her necklace. Sealyn made them hide those.

A tall purple cotton candy tree stood on either side of the bridge. One tree featured three small, fuzzy grape bears with shiny white horns protruding from their heads, curled under the sugary tree. Each bear was licking honeycombs in its paws and appeared ever so happy.

The soldier stopped and scratched one of the bears' tummies. "These little guys are called Quam-Quam Bears. Most Glatanians have them as pets. We let them roam free during the day, but they always return to their owners' homes at night."

They heard and smelled it before they saw it: the Chocolate River. "Is that the Chocolate River I hear?" Max asked.

"Yes, if you walk a little further and look over the railing, you'll have a nice view," the commander said.

Max ran up the bridge and peered over, his eyes wide with shock. A massively wide, gushing, creamy chocolate river flowed as naturally as the rivers of Elysium. He breathed in the rich, decadent scent and imagined himself diving in. How was all this possible? This land was full of wondrous magic beyond anything Elysium had ever seen or heard of. Were they sure this kingdom was cursed? What if there was another third-generation bloodline person here who had already broken Glatania's curse? No one had considered this possibility.

Sealyn peered over and felt a familiar tug. She had experienced the same tug while sailing the Golden Lake on the Shunalian quest. Soaking in the warm, chocolatey goodness below felt right. She needed to immerse herself in the creamy liquid.

Jem accidentally nudged her arm as he folded his arms across his chest, shattering Sealyn's chocolatey fantasy.

"Well, Commander, I'm no expert in chocolate, but don't you need to heat the chocolate to a specific temperature to turn it into liquid?" Jem said mockingly.

The commander glared at Jem. "Correct, Havasian."

Jem nodded with a coy smile. "And what, do tell, could be the source of all this great heat? I see no volcanoes or dragon nests nearby."

Sealyn noticed the silent, intense exchanges between the commander and Jem. Something felt off. Glatania and Havas had a rocky history, but she believed they were on good enough terms to maintain a free trade agreement; in fact, she recalled that the agreement had been signed almost seventy years ago. So what could be causing tension between these two?

"We should keep moving." The commander turned and walked away, followed by the soldiers.

Jem smiled, feeling pleased with himself. Havasians were aware of the dark secrets hidden beneath this magical city, and every bit of it contradicted Elysian law and morals. At times, the elements in this world that seem enchanting and magical are simply illusions, masking the decrepit secrets humanity is willing to embrace for selfish desires.

Finally, the group arrived at the enchanting, gem-studded steps of the chocolate-coated castle. With its many whimsical levels and soaring towers, they found it challenging to decide where to focus their attention. Each window and door frame glimmered with sparkling white sugar borders while vibrant purple fireflower vines playfully climbed up the walls.

The silver and white candied doors swung open, revealing the entire royal family as they marched down the gemmed steps in a powerful, intimidating formation. The king, dressed in royal purple and silver robes, sported a large belly, round cheeks, and a thick salt-and-pepper beard that matched his hair. All their joyful feelings vanished at the sight of the king's scowl.

"What is the meaning of this intrusion to my dinner?" he yelled, neck hidden behind his chin.

The commander bowed. "Your Majesty, I bring you Queen Sealyn Araelien of Elysium and her comrades. She says they have traveled here to discuss an alliance."

The king's eyes narrowed at Sealyn. "I wasn't aware that our two kingdoms weren't on good enough terms to *not* be called an alliance, young queen."

"Forgive me, Your Excellence," Sealyn stepped forward. "We merely want to discuss the future of all kingdoms since the invasion of Havas from Stoltland."

"Sure you do," he said, looking her over as if she were one of his delicious snacks. He licked his sugar-dusted lips. "I want to be clear. Glatania is neutral in this war between you and that crazy red-haired witch. I want no part in it. There! You had your discussion."

"Please, Your Grace. From one powerful monarch to another …"

"Powerful? Let me show you how much power you have here, little girl." With a movement that was far too fast for a man of his size, he drew his dagger and sliced Madilina's throat, and before Max could catch his dying bride, the king stabbed Max swiftly in the heart three times.

Sealyn screamed and fell to her knees, blood pooling around her. Char shouted, "What have you done?" Jem began to draw his sword, but soldiers seized him, pinning him to the ground.

Sealyn wailed for her friends and yelled, "Why? Why do this?" Tears fell from the emerald queen's eyes. The king smiled and snapped his sausage-sized fingers. Within seconds, guards clasped magical blocking shackles around their wrists and dragged them toward the palace's dungeons despite their protests and resistance. Sealyn felt the blow to her head from the soldier's fist, and blood trickled down her face. Hope began to fade into a distant memory.

Sealyn forced herself to look once more at the murderous scene and saw Max reaching his bloodied hand toward his lifeless wife; then, he lay still. Gone too soon, deprived of their dreamy future—the devoted and brave Lord Max and Lady Madilina.

MAEGWEN SALLEY-MASSIE • THE HONEYED TONGUE DECEIVES

Chapter 40

<u>22 Years Ago...</u>

According to the markings on the wall, Jace had been in the dungeons for sixty-one days, and the oppressive atmosphere weighed on him like a long, bitter winter. Icicles clung to the sides of his cage, and he could see his breath swirl in the damp, cold air. During winter, Stoltland provided a small iron bowl for each occupied prison cell, a meager offering. Each day, well-behaved inmates were allowed only two hours outside, a brief reprieve to chop wood for themselves. Jace, burdened by his circumstances, had another daily task assigned by Corentine: he had to fill three pages with the phrase, "I must not disobey my mother." This repetitive chore felt like chains binding him to his despair, a stark reminder of his shame.

Once he finished writing and chopping for the day, he huddled around the small crackling fire that exhaled clouds of gray smoke. He wondered when his mother would finally allow him to go outside. Would this be his new home? Should he attempt to escape the next time they chopped wood? He couldn't take that risk. If he got caught, he wouldn't have any wood for his cell; then he would freeze to death.

The final task of Jace's day was always the guard stationed in front of the iron bars, asking him to recount his runaway adventure, including the journey back home. He told the same story every time and couldn't understand why. The guard looked sad for him last night, but it could have just been his eyes playing wishful tricks.

He heard the guard's footsteps and smelled the paste and burnt bread they served each night; only this time, when the guard handed him the burnt bread, he held onto it longer than usual and looked down at the pitiful excuse of food before he finally released it. Jace didn't understand until he examined the bread. A slither of torn parchment was stuffed inside. Jace looked up, and the guard gave the slightest head shake, barely noticeable.

Jace curled himself around the fire, his back to the bars, not wanting anyone to see the note. He unfolded it, thinking his mother had written to him, but it was anything but. He read, "Change your story. Speak ill of the village woman. Only love Corentine. Burn this." Jace dropped the parchment into the fire, afraid that if he stared at it too long, his mother would hear him reading those words. His breathing quickened. Any minute, the guard would return for the story.

If this guard was telling Jace to change his story, why couldn't the soldier twist it for him? Why did the guard need him to say it? Soldiers could write or say whatever they wanted, but then a strange, paranoid thought crept in: what if Jace's mother had secretly been listening? What if she was already here? Jace's chest tightened as he recalled the rolling heads on the obsidian stone streets. He fought back tears; he just wanted a normal life, free of these endless worries.

He heard the footsteps again and the clunk of the wooden stool. It creaked as he sat. "All right, Jace. You know the drill. Tell me your little adventure story. Leave nothing out. If you remember something new, then make sure to expound on that."

Jace slowly slid around on the dirty, moldy stones. He tried to read the expression on the guard's face, wishing for one more note, one more question answered, but there was nothing. The guard maintained the same emotionless expression he always wore. Jace began his tale with the usual stories but paused when he reached the part about the village woman.

"Why'd you stop, Jace?"

"Um, well, I really thought long and hard about that lady, and I know I said she would have made a great mother, but the truth is, there's no one greater than mine." He noticed the slight smile on the guard's lips, which spurred Jace to say more. "I would much rather spend all my time with my mother than anyone else." He felt pleased with himself and hoped that if his mother was listening, she would finally free him.

"Interesting. Now, yesterday, you said that you would like to see that lady again, is this still true?"

Jace hesitated. He really wanted to see Laeglarie again. In fact, he had planned for her house to be the first place he visited after being freed. He couldn't let his mother know that, though. "Yuck, no way. That place was dirty and boring. My mother lives in the palace. I could care less if I ever see that lady again."

Jace thought he heard someone clear her throat, but the dungeon always made weird sounds. The guard sighed. "And if she were to, let's say, die—would that make you sad?"

Why would he ask such a question? Was this a test? Perhaps he was meant to demonstrate that if Laeglarie wasn't part of his future, it wouldn't affect him. He hoped his acting was convincing enough. He shrugged it off and replied, "No, why should it?"

The guard stood and picked up his stool. He glanced at Jace before walking into the darkness. The next face Jace saw was his mother. She wore an onyx velvet hooded cloak trimmed with black bear fur, yet her hair remained as fiery and apple-red as ever.

"Mother!" Jace squealed and latched his small hands around the bars; coldness penetrated his raggedy gloves.

"Good evening, my sweet, sweet boy. I knew you missed me. Who is always your protector?"

"You, Mother! Always you."

Corentine grabbed the icy bar. "Do I still have your allegiance?"

"Of course, Mother."

"Forever bound to me?"

Jace smiled softly, not wanting to displease her. "Yes, Mother. Forever."

Corentine smiled. "Good. Tonight, you will sleep in your own bed."

Jace's heart leaped for joy. It was finally over. His captivity had come to an end. She unlocked his door and took his hand. He held on tightly to hers as they walked through the dark corridor. At the entrance to the staircase leading out of the dungeons, the guard with whom Jace had spoken each night and who had provided the note sat at his post. He stood up when he saw Corentine and bowed. Jace noticed he was younger than his mother and had a pleasant face. Jace wanted to thank him but thought better of sharing his gratitude.

Corentine released Jace's hand and nudged him toward the stairs. "Jace, why don't you wait for me at the top? I have some business I need to discuss with this young man." Jace swallowed hard; fear trickled through his veins. The prospect of venturing alone was daunting, yet he began the ascent of the twisting stairs. Once beyond his mother's gaze, he paused, yearning to decipher the meaning behind her cryptic word: "business." Carefully, he crept back down a few steps, staying hidden, but he could hear their conversation. As he leaned closer, his heart raced, and he peered around the carved stone staircase and watched.

Corentine playfully snatched back the iron key from the guard as he reached to take it. "Not so fast, soldier. I believe you owe me an update."

The guard's expression suddenly turned cold and cunning. "Am I of such little worth to you?"

Corentine smiled and licked her cherry-red lips. She pulled the guard closer, and their bodies collided. She gasped softly as the guard ran his dark leather glove down her velvet cloak, which covered her from her neck to the floor, closing with dragon claw clasps down the middle. She gently stroked his cheek while wearing long, ebony satin gloves. Jace winced. What was she doing?

"Why is this absurd cloak between us?" he asked, fiddling with one of the lower clasps.

"It's there to keep me warm, you evil man."

"I'll make a deal with you," he said. "One clasp for every detail."

She giggled. "You and your games. Fine. Tell me. The remains?"

He lifted his chin. "Smashed to unrecognizable conditions."

Corentine bit her lip and undid her lowest clasp. "And the indentations?"

He shook his head, long dark locks waving like ink in water. "I'm afraid too much time has passed to be completely sure. I can do another search if you would like."

"No, that kept you away from me for too long. And …" her voice gasped again as he kissed her neck. Her breaths were shallow as if she were drowning. "The woman," she gasped. "What is her status?"

He ran his kisses up her chin to her ear. He growled, "The price is that last clasp."

She inhaled. "You don't play fair."

"It's the only way you know how to play." He wrapped his arms tighter around her.

She shoved him back, inches from the stone wall. She pulled her hood back and undid her last clasp, allowing the velvet cloak to melt to the floor. She stood in a thin, black, floor-length silk gown with a slit all the way up to her hip. It was strapless and had a plunging neckline to her navel.

He whistled and sucked his teeth. "You, my lady, should not have worn that dress tonight."

"No more games, Larson. The woman. Where is she?"

He chuckled. "She's all wrapped up. Safe and secure, ready for you."

Corentine lunged forward, pressing Larson against the wall. He wrapped his arms around her waist. She held his face and kissed him passionately. Lifting his chin, she pulled back, gasping for air. "I knew I could trust you."

"Of course, Corentine. Anything for you." He kissed her again, savoring her lips as if he would never have the chance to do so again.

She moaned against his touch. "Oh, Larson, I need to have more of you. I can't stand my husband touching me. It's you I want, all day—every day."

Larson kissed her neck and nipped at her ear, then whispered, "I dream about you each night, about every moment we've shared. But before you leave, I'll give you all of me right now." He pushed away from the wall, guiding Corentine backward against the other wall, out of Jace's view.

Jace was sick of what he saw and heard. He winced at the moans coming from them and never wanted to hear that again. He raced up the stairs and sat at the top, trying to forget everything.

Jace woke up the following day in his bed, a smile spreading across his face as he basked in a feeling of happiness and warmth. His heart was light, and his first thought was that he might be able to sneak away to thank Laeglarie today. He stretched with joy, bounced out of bed, and heard the clangs of ringing bells. He quickly threw on a fresh pair of socks, jumped into his pants, slipped on his coat, and stood by the window, feeling a sense of excitement. Outside, he noticed people gathering around a wooden post in the center square. Their lively chatter aided Jace's curiosity.

He looked closer and saw his mother waving at him, signaling for him to join. She wanted him to participate in a Stoltland gathering? Jace was overwhelmed with exhilaration and acceptance. He chose to overlook the terrible act his mother had taken part in the previous night because today, she was including him. He wrapped a midnight knit scarf around his neck and secured a worn stocking cap on his head, then rushed out the door and down the stairs.

He hurried to catch up to his mother, weaving in and out of the crowds. He felt a wave of nausea at the sight of her in the same onyx cloak, but he took her outstretched hand and walked with her to the newly built pyre. Jace felt uneasy. He didn't want his first public acceptance with his mother to be at an execution, but he had no choice.

Corentine stepped onto the pyre, holding Jace by her side. The crowd booed as Larson brought out a hooded woman. She wore thin, dark cotton nightsleeps with her arms bound in front. She struggled against his grip but was no match for his size and strength.

Corentine yelled, "Silence!" The crowd fell quiet. "I want it known and understood that aiding and harboring a fugitive is a crime under any circumstances." She pointed to the woman being tied to the wooden pole. "This woman here aided a palace fugitive."

The crowd booed and stomped. Larson yanked the hood from the woman's head; the morning sun blinded her eyes. She cried and pleaded for mercy, and Jace gasped. It was the same kind woman who had helped him, who had watched soldiers murder her newborn on her kitchen table: Laeglarie. She didn't deserve this.

"She gave refuge to my son when he was a fugitive, but he has served his punishment and even during his imprisonment admitted that I am the greatest mother he could ask for." She jerked her head toward the crying woman. "Not this traitor. He even said that he could care less if you died."

Laeglarie stopped crying. She looked defeated, as if that phrase was the final blow to the tiny spirit she had left. Lowering her gaze from Jace, she let her head hang. She was ready to be done with this cruel, cruel world.

"But …" Jace said.

Corentine shot him a harsh glare, causing Jace to close his mouth. Tears welled up in his angry, silver eyes. He wasn't free; he had been moved to another cage. Corentine stepped down from the pyre and grabbed a flaming torch.

"The penalty for such a crime is death by fire."

The crowd cheered and clapped. Corentine and Larson threw their torches onto the pyre and watched as the flames spread. Laeglarie tried to suppress her scream, but she couldn't help it. The flames scorched her feet first, prompting her to cry out. Tears stained Jace's cheeks. He could smell her burning flesh. He coughed, fighting the urge to vomit. He hated his mother. How could she do this? How was she so willing to kill innocent people?

Corentine grabbed Jace's shoulders and spun him until he was nose to nose with her. "You made me do this. Her ashes are on your hands. The blood of those soldiers is on your hands. The blood of the farmers is on your hands. Lord Paetrill's death is your fault. You are the problem, not me. Do you see how much destruction you cause when you don't obey your mother? When you don't love me?"

Jace didn't know what to say or do, so he just nodded, scared to think or move.

"Good, because if you ever love someone more than you love me, I'll burn this whole world to ashes, along with everyone you care about."

Chapter 41

<u>Coven's Gang</u>

The clock's pendulum swung back and forth, reminding Elladelle that she had only minutes to finish her Enchanted Potions quiz. She eyed Saedeen's empty seat, noting that Saedeen had already submitted her quiz. Thumping her glimmering green feathered quill against her cheek, she hoped the phoenix feather would magically provide her with the answers. In front of her, Wullen scratched his head frantically, as he typically did when he was nearly in full panic mode.

"Ten more minutes," Professor Draemamoor sang out. Wullen grunted and let out a loud huff.

Elladelle forced her eyes to her parchment and stared at the quiz. She could do this. She only had two more questions to answer. She hated that she struggled in this class. She excelled in both Phytocology and Phytotherapy, but potions ... she sighed. She promised herself that after this quiz, she would swallow her pride and ask Saedeen for tutoring.

The clock ticked loudly. Alright, focus. It was now or never to finish this quiz. She squinted at the test and started rereading question number nine.

9.) Define what the Stormcaller's Vial can do.

When _________ and swallowed, the drinker can summon a personal ___________.

9.a) What are the ingredients of the Stormcaller's Vial?

A. Dragon mucus, toad wart, elderberry flower, and spongy moss

B. Raindrops, unicorn breath, ogsweed, and a pig's tail

C. Raindrops, ogsweed, dahlia pollen, and ice crystals

D. Raindrops, ice crystals, dragon's breath, and hellebore pollen

She figured talking to herself in her head might help.

"Okay, Elladelle, we know the last blank is raincloud, so at least write that." She filled in the blank with the word raincloud. "Now, if you look at the multiple-choice questions, three of them have raindrops, so the answer must have raindrops in the recipe." She drew a line through option A.

"Here comes the tricky part. B and C have ogsweed, but I can't remember if that weed is part of this recipe. I

373

thought ogsweed grew in the swamps, so why would that help with storm clouds? Good thinking. Both C and D have ice crystals and pollen, but which pollen? If I do the process of elimination and don't go with ogsweed, then that just leaves D! Yes, I'll go with D." She circled option D.

"But what does the first blank instruct? Shake? No, that's for Glowprint Elixir. Uhh. Maybe swirl? Yes. It has to be swirled. That's what storms do, right? Okay, that's my final answer." She quickly scribbled the word swirled just as Professor Draemamoor said, "Five minutes." Wullen moaned again.

Elladelle's palms were sweating. She wiped them on her skirt and readied herself for the last and final question. Of course, it would be the hardest one.

10.) Memory Mirror potion: What does this potion do, and how would it best be used?

"Think. Think. Think. It clearly relates to memories. Mirror. Mirror. What does this darn mirror ... No. No. I won't think negatively. A mirror reflects, so the potion must reflect something—a memory. The potion reflects a memory. Wait! I remember this. Wullen found this potion amusing for some reason. The potion reveals a memory of the person you touch—that's it! Once you drink this potion, you can touch someone and see their memories. Okay, let me write that down first."

She dipped her quill and swiftly wrote her description on the parchment, smudging a few letters.

"Now, what would I do with this potion? I'd get Skarpin and Naedon to tell me all the secret passages they found in the castle. Ugh, focus. Hmmm. If I were Queen Sealyn, then I would drink the potion and touch Glatania's king to find out where their source of power is and break their curse. Yes, I'll write that!"

Swirling her letters together, she completed the quiz, and even before the professor said, "Quills down."

After everyone had left the classroom, she handed her parchment to Professor Draemamoor, who was wearing a green and silver flower crown today.

"Thank you, Elladelle. You had me worried for a second, but I knew you could do it," Novaly smiled wide at her student.

"Thank you, professor. Um, Professor Draemamoor, could you look at my answer for the last question, please?"

Novaly tilted her head. "Aw, Elladelle, you know I'm not supposed to do that." Her heart sank as she saw the innocent eyes before her turn sad. "But as long as you don't say a word ..." Novaly pressed her finger to her lips.

"Of course, professor. I won't. I swear."

Novaly scanned the parchment to the last page and read quietly. "Wow. Great job, Elladelle. You answered the definition correctly, and I love your creative response. Next time Queen Sealyn goes on a quest, I'll be sure to pack her that potion since you suggested it."

Elladelle beamed with excitement. She couldn't wait to share the news with her friends. She rushed out of the classroom, down the winding staircase to the second-floor platform, raced across the marble corridor, and burst through the large wooden double doors. After taking a shortcut through the garden sunroom lounge, she hurried down another staircase to the first floor, then zipped through the dining hall doors to join her friends, who were already seated at their table. Ultimately, she was out of breath.

"Easy, Elladelle. Did you run all the way here?" Saedeen asked, and she sipped her lemonade. Saedeen adored lemonade. She would drink buckets of it if they would let her.

Elladelle gasped for air. "I got the last question right. I'm not sure about the others, but that one, I have no doubts about." She guzzled a goblet of lemonade.

Wullen swallowed a piece of cheese. "Oh yeah? What'd you put then?"

"It's about revealing another person's memories. You must touch them once you drink it. I hope she doesn't take points off for me not writing down the timeline. I don't remember what that is."

"The potion only works for three hours. After that, poof—it's all gone," Saedeen said with dramatic hand gestures. She loved potions, so she enjoyed adding a bit of flair when discussing them.

Naedon shook his head, smacking on chicken wings. "You're wild, Saedeen." He chuckled to himself and bit into another juicy, spiced leg.

Arguing could be heard at the entrance to the dining hall. The tables quieted to see who it was. "Stop smacking, Naedon," Elladelle scolded. "We're trying to hear. Hey, wait. Isn't that Skarpin's voice?"

Skarpin pushed the door open, followed by a group of teens much larger than him, all dressed in their Yellow Phoenix uniforms. "I don't know. I don't know. I don't know! How many times do I have to say it?" Skarpin shouted.

Coven Wilchard, the captain of the Yellow Phoenixes, shoved Skarpin. "You must know. You just don't want to tell us because you really want the Red Phoenixes to win, don't you?"

Skarpin raised his hands. "No. I'm telling the truth. I don't know if the Feydom scrimmages will continue."

"C'mon. The badger problem is over, and the king hasn't said a word to you? Nor your new auntie?" Coven snickered.

Skarpin fought back tears. He was telling the truth, and these bullies wouldn't stop. Without hesitation, Naedon, Wullen, Elladelle, and Saedeen ran to the scene and stood behind Skarpin.

"What's your deal, Coven?" Wullen asked. "Skarpin would've told me if he knew something, and he hasn't, so leave him alone. He's telling the truth."

"And if I don't? What exactly is your little band of misfits going to do? Is Miss Elladelle going to flower petal me to death? Or maybe Saedeen can whip up a potion, but uh oh, she doesn't have a cauldron in front of her. How about you and Skarpin? Are you two going to team up again with some dirt and rocks?"

The friends seethed with anger and embarrassment. They were furious that the school had confiscated their necklaces during regular school hours, and they loathed how Coven's words hurt. But Naedon…Naedon slipped his necklace from his pocket around his neck and held it tightly.

"Game on, you piece of …" His hand caught fire, and Coven screamed and ran for the door with the rest of his pack running after him. He released his necklace and laughed.

The dining hall erupted in cheers. Everyone patted Naedon on the back, except for Professor Vidya. Norella crossed her arms and narrowed her eyes at Naedon. "Naedon! You know better. March yourself to the headmistress's office this instant, and that goes for your friends as well."

They moaned and dropped their heads. None of them wanted to face Princess Siany—again. After slowly walking all the numerous steps, Naedon knocked on Headmistress Siany's door somberly.

"Who is it?"

"It's me, Naedon, Headmistress, and the rest of my friends. Elladelle and Skarpin are here too."

"Come in."

They walked into the office, stunned to see that Siany wasn't alone. Lady Quinley, Lady Revalyn, and Princess Kailani were apparently all in a meeting.

"What can I help you with, Naedon?" Headmistress Siany asked.

Naedon sighed dramatically. Siany tried not to laugh. "Well, Coven and his stupid Yellow Phoenixes ..."

"Hey!" Wullen smacked Naedon.

"Not you—Coven's gang. Yeah, so Coven's gang was bullying Skarpin, so we stood up for him, but Coven kept making fun of us and wouldn't stop, so I ... uh ... I slipped on my necklace and created fire in my hands—and Coven and his rats ran away like scared little girls."

Kailani and Quinley erupted in laughter. Siany turned her head toward them. "This is something you can't laugh at if you want to be a professor here."

Kailani folded her arms. "Seriously, Siany or professor or whatever you are? Naedon should have roasted that kid's …"

"I beg you not to finish that sentence," Siany said, standing. "Listen, Naedon. Standing up for those in trouble or being bullied is the right thing to do, but school policies state that necklaces should only be worn under professor supervision during the appropriate times."

"But we invented them …"

Quinley snorted, and Revalyn snickered. Quinley raised her goblet. "The man's got a point, Headmistress."

Siany side glared at the other women in the room. How were they ever going to be educators? How could she control them? Was she crazy for even considering them? No, Kailani would be perfect for teaching *Marine Science*. Quinley and Revalyn were much needed in their creative writing and reading programs. She sighed. She understood why Queen Sealyn selected Quinley and Revalyn as the new members of her Vinurs of the Court. They were brilliant but very spirited.

Perhaps their mannerisms would captivate a classroom's attention?

"Naedon, please hand that necklace back to your professor. Remember, we are still learning about these tools. Once everyone knows more and students have logged a sufficient amount of practice time, you'll have them back full-time." She leaned back in her chair behind her desk, which was filled with papers and books. "Now, since the whole school witnessed this, you will have to face the consequences. One week of mucking out Nightlight and Gorm's barn."

"But their poops are huge!"

Quinley and the ladies laughed.

"The punishment fits the crime, and don't worry. You won't be alone; Coven and his little sidekicks will be joining you."

Once the children had left the room, Kailani pushed herself up from leaning on the wall and said, "Well, that was the crappiest punishment I've ever heard of."

Chapter 42

<u>Kazimir's Wisdom</u>

The darkness curled its welcoming fingers around the cracks and corners of the damp, cold, and unforgiving dungeon. The smell of human ammonia burned their eyes, and the sounds of vomiting stirred an unrelenting nausea. Despair was the only friend in these lonely, forgotten cells. Another tear slipped from Sealyn's cheek, landing on the musty, faded yellow straw beneath her head. She lay on her side, her bones feeling the hard, uneven stones beneath her. She pulled her knees to her chest, still with Max and Madilina's blood on them.

She rocked back and forth in sync with the rhythm of the dripping water, repeating the phrase, "It's all my fault. It's all my fault. It's all my fault."

Char pressed his head against the cold black iron bars of his cell near Sealyn, the chill stinging his cheek. "Hey, Sea. It's not your fault. We had no way of knowing how malicious that king really is."

"It's all my fault. It's all my fault. It's all my fault. It's all my fault. It's all my fault."

"Sealyn," Char said a little louder, not wanting to sound cruel. "They volunteered. We all knew the risks. There was nothing you could have done." Char felt the grief of losing Max as a good friend, but to take their deaths as their fault was a burden none of them could bear.

"It's all my fault. It's all my fault. It's all my fault. It's all my fault." Sealyn sobbed over and over.

"Sealyn …"

"Leave her alone," Jem interrupted. "Let her process."

Char scooted to the other side of his cage, damp straw and dirt sliding with him, sending offended mice scurrying. Char whispered, his voice still raw from screaming, "What are we supposed to do? I've never seen her in such a state."

Jem sat with his back against the icy stone wall, his arms resting on his bent knees. He regarded the decaying ceiling. "Your guess is as good as mine. We'll probably be sent to the slave mines."

"The what?"

Jem pulled his head forward from the wall. "You Elysians seriously didn't know about the underground cities of Glatania?"

"Underground cities? Slave mines … what are you saying, Jem?"

Jem grunted. "How do you think Glatania sparkles so much?" He stretched out the word "so," revealing his disdain for the Glatanians. "It's because of all the slaves working below. That steamy, rich, flowing chocolate river—yeah, um, that's heated by enslaved Fire Nichts."

Char grabbed the bars aggressively. He loathed slavery. "This can't be true. How do you know so much?"

"Havas and Glatania have enormous secrets, maybe even more than Stoltland if you can imagine."

"I doubt that," Char grumbled.

Jem sighed. "It's true. There's a barter trade for slaves between our two kingdoms."

"Barter?"

"Havas sends Nichts and anyone showing certain magical abilities to Glatania, and in return, Havas has free reign to capture anyone who steps on the Glatanian Sult Plains."

Char shivered at the sound of another inmate's moans. "You're telling me that Havas is allowed to kidnap Glatanians … on Glatanian soil … with no repercussions?"

"As long as we keep supplying them, yes."

"What are the Sult Plains?"

Jem looked around his cage, squinting his eyes, deep in thought. "It's like this. You know how you Elysians have your Reformation Rock for your cursed people?" Char nodded. "And Len Nove has the catacombs, and I'm guessing Golden Lake is Shunal's place for its cursed. Well, Sult Plains is the equivalent for Glatania's cursed. They mainly come from the cities. Guards round up those who can't handle the curse any longer and then dump them in the fields."

"That's terrible."

Jem laughed. "Listen to you—the high and mighty Elysian. Have you ever been to your Reformation Rock?"

"Well, no …"

"Then you have no idea what condition that island is in."

Char and Jem continued their conversations about Havasian and Glatanian history while Sealyn sank deeper into her guilt-riddled grief. She felt as if her limbs weren't her own, and the shackles burned against her wrists. She attempted to channel Dun, but there was silence from the great green phoenix; even King Nawrooshall's constant mammoth reminders had vanished. She expected to at least hear something from Mauor, yet his wisdom did not speak to her.

Her left palm began to itch and pulsate. She looked at the ebony spiderweb of veins, pumping its vile energy, eager to kill. Wait, did that mean she had access to Kazimir? Sealyn closed her eyes as more tears fell and tried to call to the dark serpent but was met with silence. She felt truly alone, which scared her. She reached out again, wanting nothing more than to feel the rejection once more—she almost welcomed the sting, but instead, she was met with a hiss.

"*What do you want, you incessant girl!?*" Kazimir snapped.

"Kazimir?"

"*Who else do you think this would be? Stupid child.*"

"How? How is this possible? The shackles. They …"

Another hiss. "*You don't live thousands of years without learning a few tricks around your pesky human race's tools.*"

"Wait, can you talk to Mauor for me?"

Silence.

"Kazimir?"

Silence.

"Kazimir!"

"*Yes,*" he replied reluctantly. "*No, Mauor, I'm not giving her all that sentimental encouragement. She shouldn't be so weak and feeble. What an embarrassment.*"

"Embarrassment? Kaz, I can still hear you, you stubborn gecko."

"*Gecko? How dare you insult me with one of the most...*" he chuckled his sinister laugh. "*Ah, this means my precious emerald queen is returning to her snappy self. Excellent, so who are we going to kill today?*"

"Well, I'm kind of chained up and in a cell, so the odds of that happening are slim to none."

"I'm bored. Goodbye."

"No, wait! Kaz, I need your help."

"Say that again."

"Kaz, I'm really in no mood for your games."

Silence.

"Kaz?"

Silence.

"Uh, Kaz. Fine. I need your help."

He chuckled. *"How may I assist?"*

"Well, first, how do I break these chains?"

Echoes of doors closing vibrated off the walls. Marching footsteps made their way to their cages. Sealyn, Char, and Jem walked to their cell doors and glared at the Glatanian commander.

"Use your wit, Sealyn. They are evil men but fools. Listen for gaps in their words," Kazimir said.

"Good evening," the Commander said. "I'm sorry things turned out this way, but you angered the king. There are consequences for that. However, we Glatanians believe in balance, so the king is prepared to offer a good deed in return."

Sealyn's ears rang. Good deed? What good deed could possibly compensate for Max and Madilina's deaths? She wanted to strangle this commander for even uttering those words. Her palm burned, begging to have the commander as its victim.

"The king will hold a ball in your honor in two days, and to further demonstrate his mercy, each of you will be taken to your private guest room filled with royal spoils."

A ball? The king thinks throwing a party is equal to their deaths. He had to be mad.

"Pay attention, bird! Did you catch that?" Kazimir sneered.

"Catch what?"

"He means to separate you from your comrades."

She glanced at Char and Jem. They could converse easily in these cells. Sealyn couldn't believe she had overlooked that. The phrase "honeyed tongues" accurately described these monsters. She would need to be very cautious.

"No," she shouted to the commander.

"No? Queen Sealyn, what are you doing?" Jem questioned.

Sealyn ignored Jem. "Yes, we'll attend your ball, but no to the private rooms. I request your largest suite for all three of us to stay in, and if you deny this request, then we will remain here, and your balance to slaughtering my people will remain unfulfilled."

The commander shifted his feet and pulled at his thick, bushy, unkempt beard. "Uh, I. Well, I will need to consult the king first. I will return momentarily." He didn't wait for a response. He turned on his heels and rushed into the dungeon's darkness, leaving the prisoners alone.

"What are you playing at, Sealyn?" Char asked.

"They're trying to split us up. I don't trust anything these murderers have to say."

"Wise, my queen," Jem smiled.

"Shut it, Jem," Char said. "You look better, Sealyn. How are you?"

Guilt still plagued her. She felt it pushing down on her shoulders and scraping its claws against her bones. She wanted vengeance. She wanted to slaughter that king's entire family in front of him, then hang him for the crows to eat. But right now, she needed to beat the old tyrant at his own game.

"I'm coping, but we need to stick together. We have to find the source of Glatania's power quickly. Jem, have you heard anything that might indicate what that could be?"

"Nothing that would lead me to think it would be the source."

"I promise you, it might not be what you think. Any small detail may reveal exactly what it is," Sealyn encouraged. Could she trust Jem? Adma had turned out to be a spy, so what was Jem? He came from one of the slyest kingdoms of all seven, but he was still here, risking his life. Why?

"All I know is that if we have to confront their mythical creature as you did in Len Nove and Shunal, then we're in big trouble."

Char chuckled. "What could possibly be worse than that Naehass serpent?"

Kazimir hissed. *"I'll eat him!"* Sealyn refrained from laughing.

Jem sighed. "A short-faced bear called the Galkon Bear."

"Bear?!" Char flinched, recalling how frightening that Arkootha bear had been, the kind of bear that had killed Lady Rivers and had charged at him, Sakul, and Sealyn—before Sealyn had split the ground with her magic in Len Nove.

"Yeah, it's unnaturally large. Larger than a grizzly, more the size of an elephant with giant muscles and massive claws. It's wicked fast, too."

"Oh great, I was hoping the elephant-sized, muscular bear was fast. I wouldn't want to face a snail-paced one," Char said sarcastically.

Jem rolled his cherry-red eyes. "I don't know of any story where someone has fought it and survived."

"Yet," Sealyn whispered. "Where does the legend say this creature lives?"

Jem shrugged. "Stories offer conflicting ideas about that. Some say it's in a cave to the north where no one goes.

Others claim it's on the tallest peak of the Frosting Ridge Mountains, but I tend to lean toward the more recent claims. There's a rumor that the Glatanians drugged the bear and kept it in a prison below as a threat to their slaves."

Sealyn rested her bloody head on the cold, iced-over bars. "That sounds more like them."

"*Use your brain, little phoenix*," Kazimir said. "*See the patterns.*"

She didn't know what Elysium's source was. That information remained a secret from the monarchy. Len Nove's source had been around Nawrooshall's neck, frozen in time. Shunal's source had been chained to the Naehass's neck, suggesting that a kingdom's source would likely be near its mythical creature. Would this also be around the bear's neck? Excellent—now all they had to do was escape from the king, find the hidden passage to the underground slave world, locate the cell of an angry bear, and take whatever object he was most likely guarding.

Sealyn pushed back from the bars and folded her arms. "Well, gents. Looks like we need to find ourselves that Galkon Bear. The source is most likely with it."

Char let out a long groan. "Why can't it be simple, like go into the flower meadow, and there a group of Peri Pixies will hand you the source of power, and afterward, unicorns will sing and dance for you?"

Sealyn giggled. "Oh, Char. If only it were that simple."

As if on cue, Sealyn felt her palm burn again; the guards were returning. She tried not to scratch it, fearing she might puncture one of the veins of venom. She shoved her hand into her pocket quickly.

Kazimir growled. *"Remember, child. With my power, you can kill anyone you choose with just a few drops of my venom. The question is—who do you trust the least? And as for those chains,"* he hissed. *"You already know the answer. All you have to do is believe in its power and say it."*

Chapter 43

<u>Three Royals</u>

Morning sunbeams threaded through the plum trees, casting a shimmering glow across the resistance's mauve treetops. The forest was filled with the scent of fresh dew and evergreen, carrying the promise of a new beginning. Jace took a deep breath, his knuckles white against the deck's railing. He needed to forget his nightmare. The dream of Sealyn, bloodied and begging for help, made his chest ache. He couldn't wait any longer; he had to rescue her now.

His mind trailed to the words, *"Master the monster before the monster becomes our master."* He whispered them again out loud.

"Good morning, King Jace," a sweet voice said.

Jace jerked his head to find AeLeer approaching with two wooden mugs. He hoped she hadn't overheard him. "Good morning, AeLeer. That smells suspiciously like coffee."

She smiled. "You're smart to be suspicious. This is coffee's impostor and much healthier for you. It's dandelion root tea. I find it delicious. Here, give it a try."

She handed him the mug, their fingertips grazing. Jace thought he saw something twinkle in her periwinkle eyes. He brought the cup to his nose and sniffed. She laughed. He tipped the steamy, dark liquid to his lips, and to his surprise, it did taste like coffee—earthy and without a sour aftertaste.

"Well?"

"Not bad. Not bad. I could handle this."

AeLeer beamed and placed her mug on the banister. She gripped the railing with both hands and stared out over the plum-hued, ethereal radiance of her forest. She twirled around, crossed her arms over her chest, and leaned against the handrail, watching Jace.

"You look pained, King Jace. May I ask what troubles you?"

Jace sipped the tea, still not knowing who to trust. "Just missing my wife."

"Ah, yes. The famous Queen Sealyn. I'm curious. Why were you two on different ships?"

Jace furrowed his brow, slightly shaking his head. "Say again."

"You crashed on different ships, right? So, I'm asking, why weren't you two on the same ship?"

It was an innocent question, but it led to an embarrassing answer. He didn't want to share private details, yet he hated playing the game of deception. "I'm ashamed to admit it, and I'd prefer not to discuss it if that's okay?"

"Oh, certainly. I didn't mean to pry. My curiosity often gets me into trouble, so you'll most likely have to forgive me several more times."

Jace nodded. "It's quite all right."

"King Jace …"

Jace raised his hand. "Please, you can call me Jace while we're standing here."

She blushed, and her lips curled. "Very well, Jace. Do you really think Elysium can break our curse? I mean, isn't a Glatanian supposed to do that?"

"Sure, if that Glatanian was a third-generation bloodline resisting the curse." Jace tilted his head. "Has there ever been one of those or anyone close?"

AeLeer lowered her head and moved closer to Jace. He could smell pine and herbs surrounding her. "The closest we had was our former leader, Permont. He had royal blood in his lineage, and he was the second generation to resist, but nine months ago, we faced our largest battle against the cursed, and …" She sniffled, wiping a tear from her ivory cheek. "He was killed in that battle. We felt lost—like our chance was gone. But my brother stepped up and has been putting the pieces back together ever since. Then you showed up, offering us hope again."

Jace held up his free hand. "Whoa, easy. I'm not the hope here. Only Sealyn is. Her blood is the key."

"Sure," she giggled. She turned and picked up her tea, then faced Jace. She folded one arm across her chest while sipping it, swirls of steam spun in the air. She stepped closer. "Let's talk about how you all are keeping one big secret from us."

Jace swallowed, uncomfortable with how close she was. "Secret?"

She smiled. "Yes. How is it that you Elysians have among your numbers a princess of Glatania … and failed to mention her."

"Uh, um. Well." Jace leaned back as AeLeer stepped even closer.

"What's the meaning of this?" Laekian forced loudly.

AeLeer jumped back, spilling her tea. "Laekian! Why'd you do that?"

"I'll call out any man who stands that close to you, especially a silver-eyed married one."

"Watch it, Laekian," Jace growled. "Nothing was happening."

"Exactly, brother. Now, would you go away? We were discussing something … something private."

Laekian's eyebrows almost touched the treetops. He could hardly believe what his sister was saying.

Jace stepped away from AeLeer. "No. No. Look, uh, this should have been brought to your attention once they arrived, but everything felt insanely overwhelming yesterday."

"Discussed what?" Laekian glared, tightening his fists.

Jace set his mug down on the small table and folded his arms. "So once Queen Sealyn was crowned queen, she created a Council of Lands. This council included a representative from each kingdom who met a long list of qualifications. To make a long story short, the representative for Glatania turned out to be a spy and none other than Princess Adma, the youngest princess of Glatania's throne."

"What?!" Laekian hissed.

"Yup. Yup. Yup. But it gets worse."

"Worse? Jace, how can it be worse?" Laekian asked.

"Well, because she's here … with us. As in, staying in your homes, eating your food…with us."

Laekian walked in circles with his hands on his hips. "You mean to tell me your people brought a royal into our camp, so now she knows our exact coordinates, and Creator only knows how many other secrets she's been taking notes on?"

AeLeer grabbed her brother's tattooed, muscular arm. "Easy, brother. This is a gift."

"A gift," Laekian said incredulously.

"Yes, one we can use to our benefit. Now, we have blackmail."

"I first want verification. AeLeer, you go with King Jace and bring the princess to the meeting hall."

Queen Graelynd, King Jace, Princess Adma, the Pirate Captain, and Commander Tilmond entered the grand, mystical meeting hall led by AeLeer. The building stretched between two trees, creating a long aisle lined with deep cauldrons on either side. The walls looked like stone but were crafted from wood; several sections featured carvings of ancient battle scenes, with tables at each adorned with lit candles in their honor. High glass archways spanned the ceiling and second-floor balcony, illuminating the enchanted symbols painted on the floor and walls. The balcony extended around the room's perimeter for those who wished to observe the meetings from above.

At the end of the aisle, steps led to the heart of the meeting hall, where the twisted tree throne stood proudly, and in it sat Laekian. Standing on the steps to his left was Corvus, who looked as smug as the day they met him. More wooden chairs lined either side of the walkway, occupied by other high-ranking resistance members, each as eager as the next to see the princess.

Jace looked at Adma, who was sweating. She appeared pale, and her hands trembled. He almost felt pity for her. He could understand how someone might get lost and become entangled with the wrong side without realizing it. Perhaps he just needed to talk to her and explain how much better life would be once the curses were lifted.

AeLeer kept walking up the steps, stood on Laekian's right side, and nodded to Corvus. He smiled rakishly back at her.

"Welcome, Elysians and pirate." Laekian bit. He wasn't a supporter of the pirate lifestyle. "We've gathered to discuss your captive, Princess Adma. Princess, give me one reason why I shouldn't gut you like a fish right here, right now."

The room split between gasps and cheers.

Adma opened her mouth but choked on sobs and tears. Her breathing quickened as she placed a hand on her chest, trying to steady herself. Queen Graelynd stepped in front of her, eyes narrowed. "She's no prisoner."

"Well, King Jace. Do you need another monarch to speak for you?" Corvus sneered.

Jace pointed at the hooded rebel. "Stuff it, Corvus. Queen Mother Graelynd is one of the greatest queens to ever exist, so yeah, she's perfectly fine to speak for Elysium."

Graelynd cracked a smile, her cheeks flushed with a rosy tint. "Laekian, Princess Adma has been a valued member of our council for many years. We only recently uncovered the true purpose behind her joining our team, which, to be candid, mirrors the rationale for which Queen Sealyn established the council. She sought to glean every detail she could concerning each kingdom, but it is no simple task to betray one's royal nation. She provided us with limited information, yet what she did share proved instrumental in saving our lives."

Adma dropped her head. She didn't know whether to be grateful to Graelynd or feel ashamed.

Laekian lifted his hand. "Thank you, Queen Mother Graelynd. You speak beautifully, but it doesn't change what her father has done to our people."

"And the sins of a father shall be attributed to the child?" Graelynd asked.

Laekian titled his head. "No, but she stood by him this entire time. Those who you choose to surround yourself with are those you will be judged against. If we abide by Glatanian law, the punishment for a spy, traitor, or murderer is death."

Adma began to whimper. She knew the laws—probably better than anyone here. Tears streamed down her cheeks as she wiped them, disturbing her round spectacles. The second half of that law terrified her.

"That's no different than Elysian law, and we're not letting you just kill her," Jace added.

Laekian grinned. "Ah, but King Jace, there's another piece to the puzzle that even you can't stop." He pushed himself up and walked slowly down the steps. "The law states that only a decree signed by three monarchs can allow a convicted criminal's charge be overthrown, and her father ..." He pointed behind Graelynd, who stepped sideways to peer down at Adma.

She was shaking and crying, gasping for breath. She understood her fate. She was aware of how her father kept order.

"Well, her father makes sure only two monarchs are ever alive at one time. He even killed his parents and his wife to make this true!"

Adma cried louder, feeling the pain of her mother's death all over again. Her father kept her mother alive until her eldest brother was of age to be considered a monarch, and then she was beheaded—all for this law.

"So, because three monarchs aren't present to sign for her, I am choosing to hang her body in the middle of the Sult Plains. That should send a clear message to the king."

Graelynd's face paled. Adma begged for mercy. Soldiers stepped forward and grabbed Adma's arms.

"No! This must stop," Jace said.

"It's the law," Laekian replied, with no mercy in his voice.

Graelynd turned to Jace, gripping his arm tightly as panic surged through the air. Adma's anguished screams echoed hauntingly in the chamber while frenzied chants and raucous cheers pulsated off the walls, creating a cacophony of excitement and dread. Negative shouts erupted from the Elysians in the balcony, heightening the tension. Just as chaos threatened to explode, the Pirate Captain thrust his way through the crowd, confronting Laekian with fierce determination, face-to-face.

"I will sign the decree along with King Jace and Queen Mother Graelynd, the monarchs of Elysium."

"You are just a pirate," Laekian laughed.

"No. I am Tyrdon Steig, the true heir and king of Korpam's throne, and yes, even the king of the pirates, too."

Jace's mouth dropped open. Tyrdon Steig—that name. The Steigs. Blood; so much blood. Spots clouded his vision. He stammered back. Was this true? Could it be real? The

Stoltlanders had killed his father's family. He had touched their blood. Jace could barely breathe; his chest felt tight. He needed Sealyn. Oh, Creator, where was Sealyn when he needed her most? The room spun, and then the greatest revelation of all hit him.

If this were true, with his mother as the queen of Stoltland, his father the rightful king of Korpam, and himself as king of Elysium, Jace would be the most powerful monarch in history. He could rule three kingdoms—an unprecedented feat, as no one previously dared to marry a silver-eyed person, let alone place one on the throne. This also rendered him the most perilous individual to all other kingdoms. His reign would span all the southern kingdoms; he had now become the most significant target.

Chapter 44

<u>22 Years Ago…</u>

Black snowflakes floated in the icy air, settling on heaps of shimmering, inky snow that covered the streets and rooftops of Stoltland. The fire crackled and popped in the multiple black stone fireplaces of the Stoltland Palace Library. Most of the books, especially those on the third floor, were covered in dust and cobwebs. Deep blue and midnight threaded rugs adorned the stone floors, while clusters of ancient couches and cushioned chairs were scattered throughout the octagonal room. Dark iron chandeliers hung from the starry night painted ceiling, casting eerie shadows around the room, and nestled in one corner was Jace, reading a book.

Reading another pirate adventure book, Jace was amazed that other kingdoms had white snow, unlike theirs. He hoped that it was real and not just a made-up story. He heard a door close and echo through the palace. He counted the seconds. No one entered the library. After the pyre-burning horror, Corentine made Jace attend morning sword-fighting lessons with Larson and evening card games with her. This was her way of keeping tabs on him. As long as Jace arrived on time for each task, he was allowed to move about freely at all other times.

Jace chose to spend his free time in the library. It was warm and cozy; he loved the stories, and his stepbrother never entered this room. Jace had also been collecting information. He wanted to research more about the story of the powerful silver-eyed man, but he didn't want to be caught, so he noted each of the comings and goings of people.

It was day eleven, and still, no one had come to the library; only an older man had entered on day three to clean, but he couldn't manage the stairs, so he only cleaned the bottom floor. Jace was shocked by the absence of people, which explained the thick layer of dust on the second and third floors. He found the emptiness peaceful and more enjoyable. He decided to take it upon himself to clean the second and third floors; this way, no one could trace his steps and see which books he had read.

Three days. Three days it took him to clean the entire second floor. He felt like he was swallowing dust and dirt, but he finished it. However, the third floor proved to be a much tougher challenge. The shelves were higher, the dust was thicker, and the spiders … well, the spiders were huge and numbered in the hundreds. But honestly, Jace didn't mind. This work kept him occupied, keeping his mind engaged. He didn't want to think about what his mother had told him—about all the deaths on his shoulders.

After five days of cleaning and the eleventh day of investigating, Jace was ready to start searching for books about silver eyes. Thankfully, each floor was organized alphabetically, so he began with "S." On the first floor, he found nothing. He continued searching on the second floor but ran out of time. He hurried to his card game appointment.

On day twelve, he finished searching the second floor and a quarter of the third, but with no luck. This continued into day thirteen. On day fourteen, he searched under "G" for gray eyes, but by day seventeen, he still hadn't found anything. He sat, hopeless and frustrated, wondering if the woman had told him the story just to make him feel better rather than it being real. He wiped his nose, feeling defeated.

Like a silent prayer answered, something silver flickered in the fading sunlight. He scanned the area and squinted at the bookshelves. Jace hoisted himself up and walked to the gleaming book. The "M" section. Jace's heart sank. He pulled the book from the shelf and read aloud, "*The Monsters That Live Among Us: Silver Eyes.*" He huffed. "I should have known," he said to no one. At least he knew where to look now.

The next morning, Jace's sword fighting was lackluster. His mind was in the library, not on his footwork. Larson tripped him again.

"Jace, seriously, what's wrong with you today?"

Jace grunted and peeled himself up from the dark snow; wet patches covered his trousers. "I'm sorry, Larson. My head's a little fuzzy this morning."

"Well, get it together. Don't waste my time like this." He tapped Jace's wooden sword twice. "Let's go. Attack me."

Jace advanced, but Larson easily deflected him. Larson never let Jace win. Jace appreciated that Larson didn't cater to his youth. He believed this would help him improve his skills faster. Jace charged again, but Larson spun around and struck Jace's back, sending him crashing face-first into the snow, a rush of icy cold slapping his face.

Larson let out a loud laugh. He grabbed Jace's coat and pulled him up; black snow crystals melted down Jace's tan face.

"Do you not remember how to cover that spin …" Larson froze, glancing over Jace's shoulder to see Corentine running towards him. She typically observed from a distance and never revealed herself during training. Something was definitely off.

Jace turned and saw what had frozen Larson like an icicle. "Mother!" he sang out. "Mother, come watch. I'll show you a spin move Larson taught me." Jace began his twirling footwork.

"Not now, Jace," Corentine said, breathing heavily. "Larson, I need to talk to you. Let's go in the barn where it's warmer." She looked down at Jace. "Stay here, son."

Jace watched them rush into the barn, leaving footprints in the dark snow. He tilted his head, realizing he could match their footsteps, and they would never know he had approached the barn to listen. He scurried across their snowy prints and peered through the cracked boards.

"Oh, Larson, it's bad. It's really, really bad."

Larson clasped Corentine's hands in his. "What, darling? What is? Just tell me."

"I'm pregnant," she whispered.

Larson dropped her hands and shrugged. "Why is that bad? Pregnancy is a good thing. It's what you wanted, right?"

"It's yours."

"You can't know that."

She laid her head on his chest. "The timing only fits you."

"But he won't know that."

She sniffed. "What if the child looks like you?"

"It won't matter. He and I have the same hair color, so if the child has dark hair, then it's from the father—him. And say the face is yours."

"And if the hair is red and the face doesn't look like me?"

Larson dropped his head and folded his arms. "I don't know what else you want me to say. You can do this. You can make our child his. This is what you needed."

She wiped her nose and contemplated every emotion on Larson's face. "You're right. You're absolutely right. This child is my way to securing the throne. We must stick to the plan. Once the child is of age, you will take him away and teach him how to be a warrior. I will ensure he receives the best education a prince can have until then." She kissed him. "And when Queen Phyre is old and frail, which doesn't look like that will take long, I will have secured enough soldiers for my own army to stage a coup." She kissed him again, tasting him, enjoying his lips and tongue. "And when I'm queen, I will orchestrate the best poisoning of a king anyone has ever seen. He will die, and I will call you home, and we'll finally be together—in public, forever."

He held her tightly. "So, what's the timeline for you and me finally being together?"

"I'm sorry, my love. It will take years. We can't afford to rush anything. People must forget they ever saw you. They must grow tired and angry with Queen Phyre. My husband must learn to follow my every command."

Larson kissed her nose. "Promise me a sign. Promise me a true Queen Corentine sign that it's almost time for me to come home to you."

Corentine leaned back in his arms. "Hmm. Let's see. Well, what if I claimed a certain kingdom for you? Elysium?"

"Ha! No, that claim would take entirely too many lives. I don't want to risk my fellow comrades for my happiness."

"Fair enough. What about Len Nove?"

"Given the amount of ice covering that land, it's hardly worth your time. However, if the dragon training starts, you'll definitely need those barrels of ice, as the water supply will evaporate quickly."

She kissed him again. "You're so smart." She kissed him again. "I know. Havas."

"Havas?" he questioned.

"Yes. Havas." A wicked grin slithered across her face. "When I fully claim Havas, I promise the king will die in a matter of weeks. I will leak reports everywhere so that news reaches your ears as fast as lightning."

"Then, Your Majesty, may your invasion of Havas be ever successful." He kissed her hand.

She whispered back, "If you catch even a hint of a rumor that anyone suspects you of being the father, you run. You know where to go. You know where Stoltlanders dare not tread."

"Understood. Now, no more talking." He carried her to the hay and laid her down.

Jace jerked his head away. He didn't want to see or hear anything like before. He carefully made his way back to where they had been training, twirling his sword around and leaving fresh footprints in the fallen snow. He replayed their conversation over and over in his mind. Her child was not her husband's child, which meant that if it was found out, the child would have no claim to the throne and would, by law, be put to death. Corentine would be beheaded, and then he would surely be tortured and killed. He vowed to protect his mother's secret for the sake of the unborn child, his mother's life, and his own—forever duty-bound to Corentine, his mother.

Chapter 45

<u>Abyss Breath</u>

The fresh, crisp autumn winds swept across the school's lake, creating ripples over the crystal blue waters. Fire Nichts sat by the water's edge, ready to heat the water to the right temperature for the children. Several tables decked with herbs, vials, and cauldrons were also arranged near the lake. Today, Princess Kailani and Professor Draemamoor were teaching a class together. Kailani agreed to teach a class focused on the history of Mer-people and the biology of aquatic plants, which Siany was shocked that Kailani accepted.

"All right, class, settle down. I know we're outside, and everyone is excited not to be in our classroom, but we still need to maintain order. Today's lesson will be a group project. You will need to form groups of three," Professor Novaly Draemamoor remarked. Novaly wore a flower crown made of orange and pink coral, complemented by a seafoam day dress. She always dressed with the day's theme in mind.

Wullen and Naedon immediately grabbed Skarpin and pulled him to them. "He's with us," Naedon said, eyeing Elladelle.

Novaly clapped her hands. "Hush, please. I need everyone to stay focused. Here are your tasks: one of you will dive into the lake and retrieve the water plant needed for this special potion. Another will create the potion, and finally, the third partner will test the potion in the lake." The students looked at one another, confused. Novaly laughed. "Would you all like to know what potion we're making today?"

Students yelled, "Yes!"

"Excellent. Today, we will create Abyss Breath. Before I proceed, please divide into your groups and select a table to work at. Be sure to take notes, as this will be on the final examination."

Moans resounded.

Saedeen leaned into Elladelle. "Why don't we ask Paezel to join us? She's a good swimmer."

Elladelle shrugged and turned to Paezel, who was pretending to search through her satchel. Paezel was new to Avondelle, having moved from the southern Hill Chimes territory two weeks ago, and she was struggling to make friends. She had curly, frizzy red hair, freckles on her nose and cheeks, bright pink lips, and was very skilled at growing strawberries.

Elladelle tapped Paezel on the shoulder. Her head snapped up, curls bouncing. "Uh, hi, Paezel. I'm Elladelle, and this is Saedeen. Would you like to work with us?"

Paezel blushed and smiled, trying not to look so eager. Skarpin blushed, seeing Paezel smile. "Really? Me? You mean it?"

"Of course. I hear you're a good swimmer. Is that correct?"

Paezel nodded her head rapidly. "Oh, yes. I love swimming. Our old house was near a lake, and I used to swim almost every day."

"Perfect," Saedeen said. "You should be the one to swim out first. Sounds like you can hold your breath a lot longer than us."

The girls took the table next to Skarpin, Wullen, and Naedon. With a healing busted lip from the previous day's game of Feydom, Naedon snickered as he watched Skarpin stare at Paezel. Naedon nudged Skarpin's arm. "Stop drooling."

"I'm not drooling!"

"Yeah, you are. You're in love."

"Shut up, Naedon. Am not."

Wullen laughed. "Skarpin's in love with the new girl."

"Am not! Cut it out!"

"Boys. Boys, settle down. Quiet, everyone," Professor Draemamoor said. She looked around, wondering where Kailani was. "Okay, so here are your notes to learn and remember. Abyss Breath is a potion that will help you breathe underwater for twelve hours, and legend has it that those who can brew a proper potion can even talk to the aquatic creatures."

Students gasped and whispered to one another, a wonderous moment it would be to talk to water animals.

"You need to assign each teammate a task, and whether you've guessed it or not, I want to be absolutely clear: the person who drinks the potion will test breathing underwater, so you all must follow the instructions very carefully. You can find the directions and ingredients on page seventy-two. Oh, and one more thing before you begin: the top three teams to finish first will receive a special tour of the castle by invitation from the Grand Queen Mother Karis.

Squeals and cheers erupted.

"And you may begin." Novaly skimmed around the grounds once more for Kailani. Of course, she would leave her hanging on her first day of class. Never trust a mermaid. *Never* trust a mermaid!

"Saedeen, since you're top of our class, I think you should make the potion. I wouldn't trust any potion I created,"

Elladelle said, her shoulders slumping in embarrassment about her lack of potion skills.

"Hey, Ells, you brave enough to drink the potion?" Wullen jeered.

Elladelle flicked her long, chocolate hair. "You bet I am."

"Cool, looks like it'll be me and you competing. I'm guessing Saedeen is making your team's potion, then?"

"Of course," Saedeen said. "I hope for your sake that Skarpin is making your team's." The girls giggled.

Professor Draemamoor cleared her throat. "Less chatting and more focusing. Pay attention to your instructions and diagrams. If you pick the wrong plant, things could go very wrong."

Paezel swallowed. "Oh no. What if I pick the wrong plant?"

"You won't," Elladelle encouraged. "Just memorize this drawing. Look." Elladelle pointed to the plant's drawing in the textbook. "The Dew Drop blossom."

Paezel focused on every detail. It was a plant unlike any she had seen before. Dark, leaf-like stems bore transparent pods filled with a sparkling, magical, bluish-green fluid. Each pod had what appeared to be a short antenna attached to the top, though Paezel didn't know its purpose. "Um, am I just supposed to take the pod or the whole thing?"

Saedeen shook her head. "I don't know." Her panicked, green eyes followed her finger as she scanned the instructions over and over. "They don't specify."

Splash. Splash. Splash. Students were already jumping in the water.

"Oh, no. We're the last ones!" Elladelle whined. "Hurry, Paezel. Just grab a pod and see what happens."

Paezel nodded. "Right." She removed her jacket. They had all been instructed to wear swimwear for the day, which initially excited everyone, but now the pressure was mounting. She dove into the lake wearing her green and gold swimsuit. She feared the water would be cold, but it felt just like bath water, thanks to the Fire Nichts. She would thank the red-haired creatures after class. She blew bubbles out of her nose the further down she went, descending deeper into her watery adventure.

She almost choked when she saw Princess Kailani swimming with the students. Kailani was stunning in her mermaid form, just as the rumors had claimed. She noticed that the blue-skinned Kailani kept shaking her head at the students. They were apparently searching in the wrong place—perfect.

Paezel surfaced for air, then dove back down in the opposite direction of her classmates. Searching through the blurry vision and underwater fields of kelp, she finally caught a glimpse of a glow deep within the thick water grass. She kicked her legs hard, feeling the water glide over her freckled, ivory skin. She parted the grass like a curtain and saw the glowing Dew Drop blossom. The glow illuminated her face, and Kailani's lips curled, a presence that Paezel didn't realize was near her. The princess winked and swam away, her tail swooshing gracefully through the water.

Paezel grinned, bubbles floating from her lips. She grabbed a pod, but the moment she pulled it from its stem, the pod burst, sending thousands of sparkles swirling through the water, accompanied by what sounded like voices. Paezel started to panic as her lungs began to burn. She needed air, and she saw Naedon swimming toward her. She dug her fingers around the base of the plant and yanked. The entire plant came up, two more pods still intact.

Relieved, she flipped and pushed up from the grassy, squishy bottom and launched upward, fluttering her legs as fast as they could go. Paezel gasped for air as she surfaced; her lungs thanked her efforts with every breath. She heard Elladelle and Saedeen cheering for her. At that moment, she felt a sense of belonging for the first time since her arrival. She swam awkwardly to shore with the plant in one hand and ran to her table, legs wobbling.

She cautiously handed the Dew Drop plant to Saedeen, not wanting another pod to bust.

"Careful, Saedeen. I already busted one in the water."

Saedeen nodded and gently set the plant on their table, studying the glowing and sparkling pods. "When did it bust?"

"What?" Paezel asked, not understanding why.

"I need to know the exact moment it busted; otherwise, I could lose all the contents before I even make it to the cauldron."

"Ah, yes. Okay, that makes sense. Wow, Saedeen, you're really smart." Paezel placed a finger on her chin, thinking. "Once I pulled it from the stem, that's when it exploded." A shadow crossed Paezel's face. She recalled the voices. She didn't want her new friends to think she was crazy, so she kept her mouth shut about them.

Saedeen ran her ebony finger down the ingredients list. "We need one Dew Drop pod."

"Check!" Elladelle sang and giggled.

A smile tugged at Saedeen's lips. She loved her friend's positive spirit. It was one of the reasons she and Elladelle had bonded so quickly. "Also, one crushed mermaid scale."

Elladelle held up a round bluish-green piece of glass. "This must be the scale. Check!"

"Wait, let me finish. Three teaspoons of sea kelp powder and two sprigs of Gingko Biloba." Saedeen nodded to Elladelle.

Elladelle picked up a vial of purple powder and two herb sprigs. "Check and check."

Paezel and Saedeen giggled.

Elladelle looked confused. "What's so funny?"

Saedeen grabbed the vial of purple powder from Elladelle's hand. "Because you picked up a bottle of acai powder, not sea kelp." She set down the wrong vial and picked up a pear-shaped bottle containing a palm leaf green powder. She shook the bottle slightly. "See? This is the powdered sea kelp."

Elladelle let her head drop back dramatically and let out a grunt of frustration. "I'm hopeless. It's a good thing you're making this potion."

Saedeen chuckled softly. "Let's make it as a team. The pod is the last addition, so since the water is boiling, Elladelle, you measure out the three teaspoons of sea kelp, and Paezel, you can add the Gingko Biloba sprigs while I crush the mermaid scale."

"Noooooooo!" a student shouted. The class glimpsed over and saw that all their pods had exploded, and the Dew Drop collector was rushing back to the lake. Tension rose. That would cost them time.

"We can't allow the pods to burst before they are over the cauldron," whispered Saedeen.

Splash. Another student was back in the water, diving again for the plant.

Elladelle glanced over at Wullen, Naedon, and Skarpin. They were performing well. Skarpin was providing clear instructions, just like Saedeen. She watched as Wullen dropped the last of the teaspoons into the cauldron. Her team needed to hurry, but she didn't want to win unless her other friends could come to the palace with her.

"Hey, so should we tell the boys how to handle the pods?" Elladelle asked quietly.

"Skarpin probably knows," Saedeen said.

"Why would you say that?" Elladelle asked.

Saedeen wiped her hands together over the cauldron after dropping the crushed pieces of mermaid scale into the steaming iron pot. "Because he's smarter than all of us, probably smarter than all of us combined."

Elladelle stumbled backward. "What? No, he's not. You're top in the class."

Saedeen huffed and leaned her hands on the table. "I've seen his test papers. He gets all the questions right, but every professor marks at least one right answer wrong—every time."

"But why? That doesn't make sense. Should we report the professors? Are they discriminating against him?" Paezel asked. She was worried for him. No one should discriminate against another because of their eye color.

Saedeen shrugged off Paezel's accusations and rolled her shoulders back, getting ready for the final ingredient. "I don't know, but I don't think they're discriminating against him. They love Skarpin. My theory is that the palace wants to keep it a secret. If everyone knew how intelligent he was, how many people would treat him differently? They probably just want to help him fit in."

"But that's not fair. Just because someone's smart doesn't mean they should be treated any differently," Elladelle folded her arms, ready to protest.

"I agree with you, but he's already different. He's the adopted son of Queen Sealyn and King Jace, and he's from Shunal. Those golden eyes are hard to miss."

Elladelle dropped her arms and grunted. "I know. I know. So, what do we do with this secret?"

Saedeen sighed, weary of the distraction. "I don't know. Just keep it. Let him be himself. Now, could you please let me concentrate?"

Saedeen cradled the plant in one hand and held it over the cauldron. With a slight tremor in her other hand, she plucked it from the stem. A blast of gooey, shimmering liquid splattered onto the girls' clothes and the table, but barely a drop fell into the cauldron. The boys burst out laughing.

Saedeen slowly turned, covered in clear, glistening slime, and looked at the boys. She saw Skarpin shaking his head. He still had one pod left on his table. He held the plant in his hand and pointed to the small antenna at the top of the pod. He made a gesture as if he were pulling it off, then pouring the pod into the cauldron. As Saedeen had suspected—of course, he knew.

Saedeen wiped her eyes and grabbed the plant. She had only one more chance. The other students were already out of the lake and back at their stations. She narrowed her eyes at the glowing pod and slowly pulled the antenna, which popped off like a cork. She gently poured the sparkling liquid into the cauldron just as Skarpin finished filling their potion bottle with the shimmering aqua fluid. Green and blue bubbles boiled to the top and gurgled, then settled. Saedeen stirred the contents quickly and marveled as the liquid changed from dark green to lime green to aqua blue. It sparkled and smelled like a fresh sea breeze. She had done it!

Excitedly, she took a ladle, scooped the enchanting swirling liquid, and emptied it into another pear-shaped bottle. The girls gushed over how magical the potion looked.

"Okay, Elladelle. You're up." Saedeen handed her friend the bottle of spinning glistening aqua potion.

"Elladelle!" Wullen called. He waved her over. "Come join me. We'll go together."

Elladelle snatched the potion and dashed to Wullen. She felt nervous yet excited. She clinked bottles with Wullen, turning them upside down as they swallowed quickly. They sprinted toward the water and dove in. Once they touched the water, their cheeks morphed into gills, allowing them to breathe, and their ears transformed into hand-sized otoliths with tiny nerve hairs, resembling the ear stones found inside a fish's head, positioned behind its eyes.

Kailani swam up to the students in her greenish-blue mermaid form, pink hair floating in the water. "Well done, children. You are the first to complete this task, so let's see how powerful your potion is." She looked around and spotted a family of lake trout. She rolled her eyes. Trouts were overly little gossips and melodramatic, so she loathed to hear what the irritating fishes had to say. She pointed to them. "Try to speak with them."

Wullen and Elladelle looked at one another, then shrugged. They swam toward the trout fish.

Wullen bobbed in the water, not wanting to scare them. "Uh, hey fishes. What's going on?"

The fish turned sharply, and twenty pairs of eyes stared in shock at Wullen, mouths opened. Then, the stories of the lake began pouring out.

"You need to tell that bubble dragon to leave us alone!"

"Yeah, those dragons don't even eat fish; they just like to irritate and chase us."

"I didn't care for those Fire Nichts either, and did you know Clyde—he's the turtles' governor—is organizing a band concert every Friday?"

"It's awful! They're terrible singers. When can we get extra fish food?"

"Is Professor Hueweyn coming today? I have suggestions for his classes."

"Is Queen Sealyn back?"

"Who are you?"

Bubbles floated out of Wullen's and Elladelle's mouths and gills. They could hear fish talking. Elladelle snorted, more bubbles burst into the water.

"How rude!" The lake trout yelled and swam away.

Kailani laughed. "Ignore them. They're probably the most annoying fish in all seven kingdoms."

"This is amazing," Elladelle said. "I can't believe we can hear and talk to fish!"

"Yeah, what else can we talk to?"

"All aquatic life. It appears your teams crafted the potion perfectly. You should hurry back. The gills and fish ears will vanish once you surface—in theory." She winked and swam away.

Chapter 46

A Pair of Glowing Eyes

After the trial of Princess Adma, the resistance confirmed sparing her life but requested a private debriefing. Jace isolated himself from everyone and returned to his guest lodge. He wanted out. He wanted to rescue Sealyn alone. He needed her. Anger and guilt surged through him. How much longer would his past continue to tear him apart? Would peace ever be possible for him and Sealyn's futures? He would leave today; enough was enough. Grabbing another pair of socks, he stuffed them into his pack, grumbling to himself.

A knock sounded, making Jace jump. "Who is it?"

"It's your brothers," Laisren said.

Jace sighed. "Come in."

Taeg and Laisren entered with fresh ales. Laisren handed one to Jace and tapped his wooden cup to Jace's.

"Sorry, Jace," Taeg started. "We thought you knew who, as you call him, the Pirate Captain was."

Laisren swallowed his swig. "Exactly, or else we would have told you. Honestly, we don't really know what you know and don't know, and we probably don't know everything, ya know?"

Taeg rolled his eyes. "That statement had entirely too many 'know's' in it to make sense. Regardless, Jace, we're sorry, and we want to help—just tell us how."

Jace cleared his throat, but before he could get any words out, Laisren cut him off. "Wait! You're packing. That's a packed pack, right? Why are you packing?"

Again, annoyed by his brother's overuse of one word, Taeg stepped to Jace and grabbed his shoulder, "What's going on, brother?"

Tears threatened to spill from Jace's eyes. He had always wanted brothers like this, a family who cared. He even dreamed of having a team just like Taeg and Laisren to go on adventures with, to fight bullies with, and to play games with, but he always woke up alone. "I need to leave. I can't stay here any longer and do nothing. Sealyn is out there …"

"Okay, we hear you. We can be packed in five minutes," Laisren said matter-of-factly.

"I can't ask that of you."

Taeg and Laisren snickered. Taeg patted Jace's back. "We forget you're still learning. It's never an ask for brothers. This is what we do. If you're going on a quest, so are we."

Laisren downed his ale. "Exactly. Besides, Queen Sealyn is technically our sister-in-law, so our sister's in trouble. Let's go get her."

Jace felt his chest tighten. Family. He finally understood what it meant to have a family of his own. This was it. You fought *for* one another, not against them. You sacrificed *for* one another, not against them. You loved unconditionally until your last breath. These were his brothers, and they stood firm with him.

The doorframe creaked. They jerked their heads to see Nyx leaning against the frame, twirling her dagger. She gave a coy smile. "Well, sneaking off, are we?"

"The king doesn't sneak. King Jace leaves when he wants and how he wants because he's a freaking king," Laisren snapped.

She raised her hands. "Easy, boys. I merely want in."

Jace folded his arms and scoffed. "In? Seriously? Why would you, of all people, want to come with us?"

"Because my currency is in secrets and favors, and having Queen Sealyn, *of all people*, owe me a favor sounds like the biggest pile of treasure a girl could ask for." She walked forward and slid her hand down Laisren's arm, then positioned herself in front of Jace and raised her eyebrows.

Jace shook his head. "No, absolutely not. I don't trust you."

"How about I give you a secret for payment? Then it's not about trust."

Taeg raised his hand in disbelief. "That's probably the dumbest thing a human has ever said. It makes no pragmatic sense at all."

"Hush, Taeg," Laisren said, clearly starting to fall for Nyx's flirtations. "Let's make a different deal. If your secret has any value to us, then we'll consider you joining us."

Nyx smiled wide. "Oh, it's not my secret. It's Jace's."

"What?" Jace dropped his arms. What could she possibly know about him?

"Care to know the status of your Stoltland king?"

Jace's stomach dropped. A chill ran down his spine. His mouth went dry. He took a big gulp of the ale and swallowed, welcoming the burn. He replayed his vows to his mother—sworn to forever serve her. With narrowed eyes, he forced himself to ask, "What do you know?"

"Our spies tell us he took ill several days ago, but have no fear; some reports are saying he will recover."

Jace grabbed her arm. "What is the status of Havas?"

Nyx's brow furrowed. "What? Havas? Why do you ask?"

"I need to know."

She stepped back and ripped her arm from Jace's grasp. "Stoltland has officially claimed them. That news about your king came weeks later."

Jace flopped onto his bed. She couldn't have. She couldn't have. But, of course, she would. He hated himself for not revealing more of what he knew to Sealyn. Murder was no stranger to Corentine, but this news also meant something else. Something much, much worse. Jace stood up quickly, too quickly. His head spun.

"Look. The Stoltland king will die in a matter of days, and …"

Nyx folded her arms. "How do you know that? Our scouts are saying he'll live."

"You scouts are wrong! They're being fed what she wants you to hear."

"She?"

"Corentine. I don't have time to explain how I know all this, but I'm telling you what's coming is about to be much worse."

"What's coming, Jace?" Taeg asked.

"Who will take the throne next with her is what's coming."

"Okay, almighty prophet, who might that be?" Nyx shook her head, still in disbelief.

Like a painful punch in the gut, Jace remembered his face. He finally allowed himself to remember his enemy's hands on his mother. He remembered the threat he had buried deep inside. Jace composed his nerves and readied himself to betray his allegiance to his mother. "Larson, the one my mother truly loves. The actual father of the king's youngest son."

"Your story just keeps getting better and better," Nyx said.

Jace grabbed Laisren's shoulder. "Listen, Larson is aggressive and power-hungry. He will stop at nothing to rule all seven kingdoms. They've been planning this for years."

Master the monster before the monster becomes our master.

Jace grabbed his pack and slung it over his shoulder. "We're leaving now."

Nyx pressed her hands against Jace's chest. "You won't get far. We need the cover of darkness if we're going to get past our guards."

Jace looked at Taeg and Laisren. They both shrugged. "She's our best shot at getting out of here," Taeg said.

After spending so long in the treetops, the ground felt unfamiliar to them. They carefully navigated over violet, mossy roots and leaped across streams that meandered through the forest, twisting like snakes. A twig snapped. Nyx raised her hand, peering through the darkness of the trees. Jace, Laisren, and Taeg froze, their hearts pounding and breaths swirling in the frosty air. She motioned for them to continue. They rounded a massive tree trunk that resembled a giant face with closed eyes and a beard. Jace ran his hand across the nose, feeling the coarse, jagged bark.

The forest was eerily quiet—too quiet. Something wasn't right. Jace heard scuffling sounds approaching. He drew his sword; Taeg and Laisren did the same, only to be met with laughter. Jace knew that laugh.

From behind an odd rock formation, Laekian stepped into view with Corvus and AeLeer beside him. "Well, isn't this a fun little reunion?"

"Laekian, what are you doing here?" Jace asked.

"I could ask you the same question, but I don't need to. Nyx filled me in."

The brothers looked at Nyx. She smiled and skipped toward Corvus, who wrapped his arm around her shoulders. "Excellently done, Nyx," Corvus said.

"So, you're okay with lying?" Jace snapped.

"Technically, I didn't lie. I shared a secret with you. I got you out of our headquarters, which was my favor, so now you owe me."

Laisren charged forward. "You did us no favor!"

Corvus shoved Nyx aside. "Back off, pirate. You three wouldn't have lasted a day without us. She saved your lives, and Laekian saved your reputation, young king."

"Explain," Jace said through gritted teeth.

"Once Nyx told us your plan, I knew there was no stopping you, so my council and I sat down like civilized leaders and devised a strategy," Laekian smirked. "Your people think you three volunteered to scout the first few miles with our dear, sweet Nyx for our quest to rescue the Elysian queen. We bid your farewell for you like a king should when leaving on a mission—you're welcome for that."

"Enough with the snide remarks," Jace said. "I'm sick and tired of people treating me like I'm bound by some set of rules. I'm not, and none of you are trustworthy, so I'm going nowhere with you all."

"What about with us, King Jace?" a voice said from behind Laekian.

Ashur, Finn, Dinyelle, JaeDorn, and Tyrdon Steig walked into the moonlight.

"Where is Queen Mother Graelynd?" Jace panicked.

"The answer to your question is why I should be trusted," Laekian responded. "You see, I do recognize our blessing in having *the* Queen Mother Graelynd in our lives, so I appointed her in charge of our entire resistance. She will govern and lead in my absence with the support of my cousin Vinzil. Your Commander Tilmond won't leave her side, and the rest of your soldiers and comrades remain behind, so put your worries to bed; she's well protected."

Jace loathed himself for leaving Graelynd the way he did. She had been like a real mother to him, accepting him without question. She didn't deserve that. He hung his head, weighed down by guilt. A hand came into his view. He looked up to see Laekian standing nearby with his arm extended, waiting for Jace's. Jace clasped Laekian's forearm, and Laekian reciprocated. From that moment on, they would be allies.

"Something's coming!" Nyx whispered loudly. "Draw your weapons."

Every member of the crew brandished their weapons, poised for combat against the unknown. The ominous crunch of twigs and rustling leaves reached their ears, signaling an unwelcome presence that seemed indifferent to stealth. Soon, a pair of glowing eyes pierced the darkness, emerging from the depths of the forest. The crew instinctively altered their stances, gripped with uncertainty about the creature lurking beyond. A bone-chilling growl reverberated through the shadows, sending icy shivers down their spines.

"What is that?" AeLeer whimpered.

Jace lowered his sword. "Wait. Those eyes. I recognize those eyes. Lower your weapons." Jace stepped toward the reflecting eyes. "Shep?"

A low growl rumbled, and then Shep pounced from his position, landing in front of Jace. They all jumped at the sight of the tiger. Shep sat pleased with himself, watching how scared each person looked.

"Not cool, Shep. Not cool," Ashur exhaled, hand pressed to his breathing-heavy chest.

"Wow. I've never seen a tiger with green and gold stripes before," AeLeer exclaimed.

Jace's heart pounded. Shep would never leave Char. Something must have happened. "Shep, we're going to ask you questions, and you need to nod or shake your head in response."

Shep eyed Corvus and softly growled.

"Shep! I'm serious," Jace snapped.

Shep glared and bowed his head.

"Is Sealyn alive?"

He nodded.

Jace let out a breath; tears threatened his eyes. "Are the rest okay?"

Shep shook his head. The group gasped.

"Char?" Nod. "Max?" Shake. Gasps. "Madilina?" Shake. Cries. "Jem." Nod.

Dinyelle wiped the tears from her cinnamon skin. She truly admired Madilina, who was legendary for winning Feydom at Len Nove under Commander Malum's cruel rules. Madilina was also the first to channel the Caelidon, receiving feathered wings from the winged horse that allowed her to soar through the clouds. Dinyelle knew the kingdom would greatly miss them both.

Ashur patted Finn's shoulder. Finn and Max were best friends, both renowned archers in the Elysian military, but Max was the leader. Finn dropped to his knees, shaking his head. "This can't be right," he choked out. "Max can't be dead."

Jace hated seeing his friends in pain. He couldn't believe Elysium had just lost one of the best couples he knew. He would ensure their sacrifice was honored when they returned, but for now, he had to keep his group focused. Jace cleared his throat. "Shep, can you lead us to where they are?"

Shep nodded.

"Wait," Laekian said. "You can't be seriously thinking about following a tiger?"

"This is no ordinary tiger. He's linked to Char, Queen Sealyn's cousin, who's with her."

Nyx stepped into the moonlight. "Linked? What do you mean?"

Realization dawned on the curse-breaking crew that these Glatanians couldn't access the ancient magic. But why?

Dinyelle raised her hand slightly. "Are you saying that none of you are Luxens?"

AeLeer scrunched her face. "A what?"

The Elysians looked at one another in disbelief. Jace shook his head. "Well, this explains a lot. I guess we better show you. Team, necklaces on."

The crew reached into their pockets and satchels, revealing their enchanting necklaces. They draped them around their necks, preparing themselves. Jace nodded at Dinyelle, who smiled through tears and clasped her necklace. She knelt, touching the ground with her other hand. Bursts of bright red, orange, and yellow poppy flowers sprang from the dirt, followed by blooming light pink and dark red dahlias. She surrounded everyone with joyful blossoms, then straightened back up, pleased with her masterpiece.

AeLeer's mouth fell open in astonishment. She knelt down, the flowers softening her descent. Gently, she caressed the petals, tears welling in her eyes. "Look," she said, her voice breaking. "Look at these colors. Have you ever seen anything so beautiful?"

Laekian tried to mask his shock. His brow furrowed as he looked at Dinyelle. She turned to her husband, JaeDorn, indicating it was his turn. JaeDorn pricked his finger with a knife, allowing drops of blood to fall onto his necklace. Instantly, his shoulders rounded further, and the palms of his hands transformed into the pads of gorilla hands. He turned and pounded his fist against a large boulder, cracking it, then scurried up a tree, swinging from branch to branch.

Laekian's jaw dropped. Laisren and Tyrdon did the same, with their blood and necklaces ready to feel the connections to their creatures. Their eyes transformed into feline-like orbs. Laisren exhibited the speed and agility of a cheetah, while Tyrdon showcased the strength and night vision of a tiger. Finn and Taeg nodded at one another, both already performing their blood sacrifice to their necklaces. Finn reached out to the nearest tree, and vines began to grow, twisting and adapting to his needs. He fashioned steps and bridges, easily walking above the group.

Taeg decided to be a bit more mischievous. He touched the ground, and heaps of briars surrounded the Glatanians. AeLeer screamed. Feeling guilty, Taeg released the command, and the briars scurried back into the earth.

Finn slid back down from one of his vines, landing beside Ashur. He nudged Ashur. "C'mon Ashur. Don't be shy."

Ashur shook his head. "It's not funny."

"What's not funny?" Nyx asked.

Ashur rolled his bright green eyes. "My Transference powers. They're a little embarrassing."

"They're not. I think it's awesome what you can do," Finn encouraged, but also trying not to laugh.

Jace folded his arms. "Come on, Ashur. We need a little cheering up. Tell us your powers, and have fun demonstrating."

Ashur moaned and sighed. "A mouse, okay? I can channel a mouse." The group snickered. "He is a really cool mouse, to my defense, and he did give me the most unusual gift."

"Show them," Jace said, smiling.

Ashur pricked his finger and dropped his blood on the necklace, then poof! He was gone.

"Where'd he go?" Nyx questioned, looking around the flower-covered forest.

"Look down," Finn said, pointing to the tiny figure standing in Ashur's boot print.

"Oh, my purple sky!" Nyx said. "The mouse gave you its size?"

"Yes," Ashur squeaked. The boys burst into laughter. "Shut up! I can't help how I sound," he said in a very mousy, high-pitched voice. None of them could stop laughing.

Ashur released the channeling, returned to his normal size, and smacked Finn's arm. Laekian stepped forward, arms crossed, and nodded his head. "Impressive, King Jace. It seems all your people have tapped into the ancient magic we've been warned against. What about you?" Jace tensed. "What powers does a silver-eyed king possess?"

Jace's eyes twitched. He realized that the reason the resistance didn't have access to the magic was due to their misguided information. If they believed the magic was dangerous, they would never have the chance to be open to Luxen magic. He wished he could ignore Laekian's question, but he didn't have the answer and didn't want to appear weak. "The love for my kingdom—that is all the power I will ever need. Now, we're wasting time. I hope we've shown you why you should trust us when we say to follow the green and gold tiger."

Laekian stared at Jace. "Fine, but my gut tells me you're hiding something."

"Then maybe your gut should eat something," Dinyelle snapped.

Corvus entered the center of the group. "Sorry, Laekian. I stepped away to relieve myself. What'd I miss?"

Shep growled.

Laekian looked at Jace. "Nothing … absolutely nothing."

Chapter 47

<u>The Curse of Glatania</u>

Toffee-wrapped doors opened to the spellbinding palace suite, where gusts of wind carried the sweet, intoxicating scents of freshly baked blueberry cream cheese puff pastries through the village, and the smell of hot apple cider blew past the Elysians, melting their worries and tempting them to take a taste. They entered an intricate display of royal hospitality: dazzling white and purple fireflowers hung from the ceiling, a fully stocked bar featured all the famous Glatanian wines and ales, and plush indigo pillows adorned the large, moon-shaped velvet couch.

The expansive floor-to-ceiling window unveiled breathtaking views of the fluffy cotton candy gardens and vibrant candied apple orchards. Luxurious plum and royal purple rugs elegantly draped over the cool stone floors, while lush grapevines spiraled around each column, adorned with clusters of glistening, sugared red grapes. Char stood, mesmerized by the enchanting opulence surrounding him.

Although he wasn't initially a fan of purple, he found himself increasingly drawn to its rich allure.

Servants knelt in front of their feet, untying their boots. Char stepped back, almost crushing the girl's fingers. "Hey! What are you doing?" he asked.

Another servant, resembling a servant leader, stepped around the bar with a full tray of pastries and ciders. "Forgive us, my lord; we desire to offer you the royal treatment. Our rugs are thick and will help relax your feet. Please allow them to remove your shoes, and then come enjoy refreshments on the couch."

Sealyn observed the tray of delicious treats. Her mouth felt dry, like it was filled with cotton. She craved the food and drink. Quickly, she slipped off her boots and handed them to a servant, moving swiftly toward the couch. Char's eyes widened at Sealyn's eagerness; something was off.

"I am Yarvon, your suite butler. If you need anything, just pull this ribbon beside the window, and I will come right away." Char and Jem joined Sealyn on the couch, still mesmerized by the glamorous room. "Queen Sealyn, your room is through those doors to my left, and the other two rooms …" He pointed to doors on both sides of the bar. "Well, you gentlemen can decide which room you'd like. They're made up the same, but each of you gets your own private room—as requested." He bowed his head at Sealyn, who was already on her second puff pastry. The butler smiled. "I will bring you dinner in one hour. Feel free to bathe and change." He bowed and exited gracefully with the other servants.

"Okay, so what's the plan?" Char asked once he felt it was safe to speak.

Sealyn licked her fingertips, drowning in stupendous joy. "Plan? What do you mean?"

Char leaned forward, jutting out his chin with a confused expression. "Uh, what? Sealyn, this was your idea to keep us all together. Remember the whole 'they're trying to split us up' bit? Surely, that was all because you have some kind of plan, right?"

Sealyn swallowed her last sip of cider and stared blankly at Char. "I think you should learn to relax more, dear cousin." Char and Jem exchanged glances. "Seriously, look at you two. You're both so tense. Here, have a pastry. They're absolutely scrumptious. The cream cheese just melts in your mouth."

Jem gawked over Sealyn while licking her fingers. He swallowed hard, his jaw tightening. Staying in the same suite as her would be much more complicated than he anticipated.

Char smacked away the silver tray. "I don't want treats. I want to know our escape plan."

Sealyn stood up. "With that attitude, I'm going to take a bath and change. Yarvon will be back in an hour. We don't want to look like all we did was sit around and yap about how we're going to escape. We all smell and look awful." She noticed her hands still stained with her friends' blood. She swallowed a lump in her throat. "See you in an hour." She turned abruptly and walked quickly through the double chocolate doors leading into her room.

Char's mouth was still open as he turned to Jem. "Can you believe that?"

Jem, who had started to sweat, shook his head. "She doesn't seem like herself."

Char really didn't want to talk about the countless ways Sealyn was no longer herself with Jem. The curses were gradually taking over, and soon, she wouldn't be the cousin he once knew. She would be something foreign. Would she even recognize him? Would she simply turn to dust? How could she survive this? Char wasn't sure he could trust Jem, but he was the only ally he had. He cursed the king for killing Max and Madilina.

"Okay, listen, red eyes. I want to trust you; I really do. Honestly, I struggle to trust anyone, but if we're going to have any chance of making it out of here alive, then I have no choice."

Jem scoffed. "Thanks, Char."

"You know the curse of Glatania …"

"Yeah, gluttony."

"Right, so on each quest, Sealyn has been affected by that kingdom's curse."

"What? How? She's Elysian. She has green eyes—beautiful, emerald green eyes." Jem's gaze drifted to the crack in Sealyn's doors. His heart skipped a beat. Sealyn was bathing on the other side of those doors.

Char snapped his fingers. "Jem! Listen! She's the third-generation bloodline and broke Elysium's curse, which means the curses want to stop her from breaking them. They turn on her when she declares her intentions. Half the time, she wanted to sleep or give up when we were in Len Nove, and Shunal … her lungs filled with gold when she was on that Golden Lake. She almost died."

Jem's red eyes flared. He was scared for Sealyn. "What do you think is happening now?"

"Well, I was hoping you could shed some light on that. How does Glatania's curse work?"

Jem shrugged. "It's basically a coping mechanism. When someone hurts you, you indulge in sugary treats. When you feel grief, you gorge on all sorts of food, especially sugar. If you feel lonely, scared, anxious, bitter, or angry—food becomes your comforter. But for Glatanians, they literally can't stop themselves. They will eat and eat and eat until they can't move, become sick, or die. The royals ship those on the verge of death to the Sult Plains. Each person receives a box of sugar cubes laced with enough magic potion to keep them alive until the Havasians arrive."

"That must be happening to Sealyn. She's grieving Max and Madilina, feeling the weight of breaking curses, lonely, and scared. I'm sure those puff pastries gave her a boost of comfort. You saw how her entire attitude changed. We must watch her and keep her from gorging."

Jem nodded. "I agree." Jem stood and walked toward his door, then turned back to Char. "Hey, Char?"

"Yeah?"

"If Sealyn's life is on the line and I can find a way to save her, I'll do it. I'll risk everything to protect her. You have my word." Without waiting for Char's response, he turned and walked into his room.

Char felt a nervous twitch in his gut. Jem's exact words sent a wave of paranoia through him, wrapping him in an unsettling mystery that he couldn't shake off.

Jem bathed and changed quickly. Not wanting the butler to snoop around their rooms, he made sure to be in the living room quarters before the butler arrived. He felt refreshed after washing the stench of the dungeons off, and the velvet mulberry tunics were soothing. He rummaged through the bar's wines and found a nice red bottle made from sugared grapes and plums. He poured the dark liquid into a silver goblet and took a long sip, savoring the tartness and fruity flavors.

He heard movement from Sealyn's bedroom, and his cherry-red eyes glued themselves to the small opening in her doors. He took another sip of wine, and his body began to move toward the door against his will. It was as if she was a magnet to him. He wanted to resist; he needed to resist, but every bone in his body urged him to touch her, to caress her, to kiss her, to possess her.

A knock sounded at the main door. "Who is it?" Jem called out, thankful the spell was broken.

"Yarvon, my lord. I have your dinner."

"Yes, of course. Enter."

Jem noticed Yarvon's surprised expression and realized how close he was to Sealyn's doors. Not wanting the butler to suspect anything, he blurted out the first thought that came to mind, "I like to keep a close eye."

Yarvon nodded and placed a large silver tray with a silver cover on the mahogany table in front of the half-moon couch. The other servants did the same with smaller trays.

"My lord, would you like me to pour you another and perhaps pour two more?"

Jem looked at the nearly empty contents of his goblet. "Yes, and yes. Thank you."

Yarvon poured the deep plum liquid into the shiny silver goblets. "My lord might be interested to learn that there are several Havasians staying here."

Jem's head snapped up to meet Yarvon's violet eyes. "Why do you say this?"

"Merely to inform you that they will attend the ball. I am confident it will provide an excellent opportunity to engage in conversation with fellow individuals possessing crimson eyes." Yarvon's gaze lingered slightly longer than necessary, suggesting that his statement held a more profound significance.

Sealyn entered the living room wearing an indigo velvet robe with white fur around the collar and trim, with a train dragging several feet behind her. Jem sucked in a breath. How he would dream of nothing else tonight. He smiled and handed Sealyn a goblet.

Sealyn smiled. "Why thank you, Lord Jem. What do we have here?" She waved her hand across the covered silver trays.

Yarvon and the servants unveiled the trays, showcasing a vast spread of steaming food. "Allow me, Queen Sealyn. Sliced honey-orange chicken, caramelized potatoes and mushrooms, and strawberries dipped in rich milk chocolate. And for dessert …"

Jem scrunched his face. "The chocolate strawberries aren't dessert?"

Yarvon chuckled. "No, dear friend." He pulled open another tray. "We have a double chocolate layered cake, blackberry tartlets, and peach pie with vanilla creamed ice."

Sealyn's mouth fell open. "This is how the palace eats every night?"

Yarvon smiled. "Yes, Queen Sealyn. They have a very rich diet. If there's nothing else …" Sealyn shook her head, and Yarvon bowed. He left but made sure to give Jem a sidelong glance with a raised eyebrow before exiting.

Sealyn reached for a blackberry tartlet. Jem's stomach dropped. She must be struggling against the curse. "Uh, Queen Sealyn, we should start with the chicken so it doesn't get cold."

Sealyn paused, her fingers dangling over the tantalizing dessert. Her mouth watered as her mind spiraled through feelings of guilt, regret, and loneliness. She felt lightheaded, yet the phrase that echoed in her head was simply, "One bite, and it will all feel better. Just one." Her fingers crept closer to the tartlet.

Jem saw he was losing her. He scooted closer, grabbed a potato, and held it close to her mouth in his fingers. Sealyn's eyes grew wide. He shook it playfully, like a parent would to a child. Her eyes twitched.

"What is going on?!" Char yelled. He had a towel draped around his shoulders, hair still dripping wet.

"Uh, just a game, Char. Nothing more." Jem slid further away, tossing the potato in his mouth, and sipped more wine.

Char grumbled and sat between Sealyn and Jem. He closed the lids on the desserts, resting his hand on the last one with a sigh. He needed to reason with Sealyn. "Sealyn, the Glatania curse is affecting you. You can't eat any more sugary foods."

"How dare you give me orders!" She stood up and started pacing. "I am your queen. If I want a small tartlet, then I'll have one."

"Can you hear yourself? Usually, I couldn't care less if you eat cake or a freaking pillow, but now? Now I care, Sealyn. *Now*, I have to care. Can you not see what's happening?"

Jem tried to avert his gaze from how captivating Sealyn looked, draped in the purple velvet robes, so he concentrated on the floor and hoped his words would make a difference. "Queen Sealyn, Char is right. This curse is not to be taken lightly. It destroys people's lives, deceives on every level—it can kill you."

With her long hair cascading around her, Sealyn sank onto the plush purple rug, fighting back tears. She gazed up at the glass ceiling garlanded with dangling fireflowers. The stars sparkled through the vines, reminding her of the time Jace gifted her the moon and stars. Her heart begged for Jace, and her insides felt as if they were ripping apart. "I don't know how to do this," slipped from her lips in a whisper.

Char knelt beside her. "You're not alone. We can fight this together."

Sealyn looked into her cousin's caring jade eyes, the only ones she knew she could trust. "How? We're literally in a castle made of chocolate. With every breath I take, I hear a whisper from that curse."

"Order only healthy food from the butler. If he brings sugar, then throw it out the door. We can stay busy," Jem said, looking to Char for ideas.

Char nodded. "That's right. We'll play games. I might even read a book with you."

Sealyn giggled. "You would read a book with me?"

"I just might," Char paused, contemplating the pain in Sealyn's eyes. This woman was prepared to sacrifice everything for her people and for those she would never meet. He had to help bear the burden. He cleared the lump forming in his throat. "This curse seems similar to Len Nove's. In that case, you broke their curse because you had already planned how to help them through accountability. Perhaps breaking this curse is the same?"

Jem snorted derisively. "You don't believe that, do you? How does only accountability break Glatania's curse?"

"Well, not only that, but it's a start," Char snapped. The room fell silent, filled with vacant thoughts and unvoiced apprehensions. One by one, they turned their attention to their goblets of wine and healthier food choices.

After eating the chicken and potatoes, the three played a few card games, which Sealyn or Char won, never Jem. Char performed a one-man reenactment of his favorite play, and while Jem read aloud from *The Tales of Bovine, the Hunter of Bears*, Sealyn and Char fell asleep. Jem closed the book and set it gently on the table. He stood and quietly walked over to where Sealyn slept on the couch. He wanted to brush the wisps of hair from her face and stroke her cheek. His body urged him to scoop her into his arms and never let go. He flexed his hand and clenched it into a fist.

He needed a way for Sealyn to be his. Yarvon mentioned that other Havasians were present in the palace, hinting that they wished to speak with him. If Havas was still at war with Stoltland and Glatania needed to maintain good relations with Havas, then Glatania would have to negotiate a deal with Stoltland, as it was only a matter of time before Havas would be overrun. He despised the thought of Stoltland taking over his kingdom. What could he offer Stoltland in exchange for leaving Havas? His lust-filled, crimson eyes lingered on Sealyn, taking in her breathing. Suddenly, a brilliant idea struck him: a way for him to possess Sealyn while Havas could reclaim their kingdom. His heart pounded loudly. He grinned and clenched his jaw. Those lips would belong to him for all eternity; he just had to be patient.

Chapter 48

<u>22 Years Ago…</u>

Months passed in reading, yet Jace remained steadfast in his quest. Arms stretching for another book about the silver-eyed monsters, Jace grunted when the book finally slipped into his grasp. He traced the outline of the glimmering silver letters that read, *Why Filthy Monsters*. He hoped this book would finally answer the question that had been plaguing him his entire life. The book was larger than most he had read, which made him feel optimistic. He curled up in his usual chair and pulled the ebony fur blanket over his small frame.

He began to read, but then he heard a loud, crippling scream—it was his mother. It was a cry of pain, not anger. He dropped the book and ran down the stairs toward the commotion. He saw female servants rushing down the black marble corridor with towels, sheets, and buckets of water. More screams followed. She was in labor. She had to be in labor, which also meant her lover would have to leave. Jace smiled to himself, glad to be free of him.

He felt a large hand on his shoulder, then was spun around by that same man: Larson. His dark eyes resembled the endless night sky, devoid of any emotion except hate.

"You do anything to ruin our plans, and I'll chop your hands off."

Jace's eyes widened, and tears formed. "But I ..."

"You can never leave your mother's side. She will be queen one day—this new child ensures that, but to secure her reign, we need the monster that resides within you. If you're not with your mother once I return, I'll gut anyone you love, anyone you care about, and I'll make you watch; then I'll burn your peace to the ground." Larson shoved Jace aside as his boots clicked against the inky floors, his snarl reflecting against the marble.

Jace silently prayed that Larson would catch the sickness and die, but he wasn't sure if that was the kind of prayer Creator answered—but just in case, he said it one more time. He surveyed all the people gathered near his mother's chambers and decided his presence would only get in the way, so he wandered through other less crowded hallways until he came across the least expected person hiding.

"Haedon?" Jace asked the shadows.

"Go away, Jace," Haedon sniffed.

He was crying. Jace was stunned. He had never seen his stepbrother cry. He thought the only emotion he had was using his fist.

Curiosity got the best of him. "What's wrong?"

"I said, go away! Don't you get it?"

"Get what?"

"We're nothing now. Well, you were always nothing, but now … uh, now, everything changes. That stupid baby just stole my crown."

"Oh …" Jace said.

"Yeah … oh. I heard some woman say that she knows it's a boy."

"How can she know that?"

"I don't know, but if it is, then I'm done for."

"You're still the eldest in line for the prince, so why wouldn't you receive the crown?"

"I forget how dumb you are," Haedon sighed. He sat up from lying on the floor and crossed his legs. "My father married your mother. They banished my mother, so my claim was weakened by that. Stoltland only wants pure bloodlines with reigning monarchies, which puts that baby at the top of the list."

"What if it's a girl?"

Haedon leaned his head against the coarse, dark grey stone wall. "Not sure. It might be a toss-up. Or I could just kill it, and then there's no problem."

Jace gasped. "You'd kill your own blood?"

"For me being passed over, yes. Yes, I would. That's a slap in the face, Jace. You wouldn't understand because you'll never be accepted as a royal."

Jace wanted to lash out, but this was the longest conversation he and Haedon had ever had. He didn't want to ruin the moment. He wanted to savor it, to hold on to this feeling as if he had a true brother—someone with whom he could share ideas and frustrations, someone who made him feel less alone. Jace slid down to the cold floor and wrapped his arms around his knees. What was he supposed to say? He couldn't agree to killing the baby.

"I know my opinion doesn't count, but I think you'd make a great king."

Haedon rolled his eyes. "You … think I would make a great king? And why's that?"

Jace shrugged. He didn't want to be caught in a lie. "Because you've been trained to be, right? Isn't that how you spend your time? In like king school or something?"

Haedon laughed. "King school," he snickered again. "That's funny. Maybe I'll make you the court jester when I'm king." Jace sighed. Haedon flicked a fat beetle that was crawling across the floor. "First thing I'd do is bring my mother back. She never should have been banished."

"Why was she?" Jace honestly didn't know. No one ever talked about the former princess.

Haedon hesitated and cleared his throat, feeling uncomfortable. "Because she cheated on my father. He wanted to kill her but found out she was pregnant, so he felt bad. From what I've heard, she married the other man and has, I don't know, maybe three or four kids with him. I've never met them."

"Oh, uh, I didn't know. At least she's still alive."

Haedon stood so abruptly that Jace fell to the side in surprise. "One." Haedon held out his finger. "My father should have killed her. He's weak—that's why he didn't. Two." He held out two fingers close to Jace's face. "Keeping her alive and banished is torture for me, and he doesn't care. He only cares about himself. And three." He leaned back, holding up three fingers before crossing his arms. "When I'm king, I'll do what he didn't have the guts to do; I'll kill you and your scheming mother." Haedon stomped away, but not before giving Jace a solid kick in the stomach before leaving.

Jace groaned and curled into a ball, praying the pain away. Just when he thought he was making progress with a brother, it vanished as quickly as a snowflake falling over fire. Was it so wrong to hope for companionship? For family? For love? Would anyone ever fight for him? Would anyone ever truly love him?

Chapter 49

<u>Everyone Has Secrets</u>

With silk ribbons of shimmering marigold, deep plum, rusty orange, and maroon, the Avondelle palace overflowed with Perdonair decorations for Elysium's autumn festival. Every column and banister was draped in lush evergreen garlands adorned with autumn leaves, juicy red apples, and tiny bright pumpkins. The delicious aromas of toasted cinnamon and baked apple pies mingled with the rhythms of traditional Perdonair music throughout the palace hallways and royal sitting rooms, leaving everyone eager for the festival just days away.

Skarpin took another large bite of his pecan pie as he sat beside King Father Ryker. He smiled at his friends gathered around the grand table, relishing their winnings. They had already explored the gardens and other permitted palace rooms, including Skarpin's bedroom, and were now enjoying their meal. Skarpin tried to focus on what his friends were discussing, but he couldn't help but overhear the hushed voices among the royals.

"So still no word?" Headmistress Siany asked her father.

Ryker shook his head. His crown sparkled in the sunlight streaming through the windows. "It's possible they had to go dark. There's still so much about Glatania we don't know. I wish she had waited—always so impulsive," he said through gritted teeth.

Siany placed her hand on her father's. "We need to have faith, Father. She can do this—you know that. You've taught her well."

Ryker nodded. "Still, something seemed off about her. She hasn't been herself since Shunal. Did she speak to you about the powers she inherited from the Naehass?"

Siany huffed. "The two-headed snake? No. Nobody wants to discuss that creature. She said that Mauor offers her good advice, but she's pretty closed off when it comes to the Naehass."

"Seems simple to me," Grand Queen Karis said with a dainty voice.

"Does it?" Ryker questioned. "And what exactly are we talking about?"

She wiped her mouth with an emerald cloth napkin, savoring her sweet pie. "Well, she received her *unique* Luxen powers because she broke our curse, but it's a bit unclear what power she received from Dun. I'll get to that later, but from the mammoth king, Nawrooshall, he gave her his strength. So, if creatures give the best of themselves, then what would the Naehass give?"

Ryker smiled. "You're brilliant."

"Did you know you're my favorite son-in-law?"

"I'm your only son-in-law."

Karis chuckled. "Semantics. Does anyone know what the Naehass possesses?"

Skarpin leaned forward. "I do."

Siany sucked her teeth. "Skarpin. What have we told you about eavesdropping?"

"I can't help it," he whined. "But I know the powers of the Naehass."

Lady Ebbalee, King Father Ryker's mother, swallowed her vanilla cake and cleared her throat. "Then say it, and for the record, I see nothing wrong with this child's eavesdropping. It sounds to me like he keeps proving himself to be quite the hero time and time again." She winked at Skarpin, delighted to have an adopted grandchild.

Skarpin blushed. He loved having grandparents. "So Mauor, that's the golden head. He has a potion that can heal you, even if you're about to die, but the potion can't bring you back to life if you're already dead. On the other hand,

Kazimir—that's the black head—he, um … he has venom, which can kill quickly."

The royals stilled. Tension filled the table. They looked at each other with deep fear and worry in their eyes.

Karis pressed two fingers to her lips before speaking. "Could it be that the Naehass gave Sealyn the power of life and death?"

Ryker took a sip of his lemonade and shook his head. He hated what these curses were doing to his daughter. Bearing the weight of life and death on her shoulders was surely too much. He wished he could bear that weight instead of her—not his baby girl. "It's entirely possible, and it makes the most sense why she wouldn't act like her usual self. Carrying such a substantial …" he choked on his words.

Ebbalee placed her hand on her son's shoulder. "We all face that choice, my son. We can choose to either take life or enhance someone's life every day. Sealyn will figure this out."

Siany tilted her head. "Wait, Grand Karis, you said we weren't certain about what power Dun granted to Sealyn." She scanned her family. "What is his gift to her?"

Ryker gazed out the window, seeing the large green phoenix in the distance, guarding his kingdom. "The mythical creatures give the best of themselves, so what would Dun give of himself to Sealyn?" This is the question that remains unanswered.

Skarpin and his friends were thrilled to have the rest of the day to explore the grounds before returning to school. They ran up hills, climbed trees, rolled down the hills, and dangled their feet off a giant rock ledge. This was the perfect day, and what could make it better? Why a secret stash of Puffin Pies, of course.

As he dug into his satchel, Skarpin asked, "Anyone want a Puffin Pie?"

Wullen's hand shot up. "Me!"

Saedeen sifted through her bag as well. "I have something secretive, too." She pulled out small bottles of the Abyss Breath potion and smiled.

Elladelle gasped. "Where did you get those?"

"I made a few extras from the unused Dew Drop plants while you all were swimming. There were several on the other tables."

Naedon looked confused. "What do you expect to do with them?"

Saedeen shrugged. "Maybe go test them in a lake?"

Elladelle folded her arms and scowled. "Um, it's cold. We don't have the proper swimming attire." Elladelle looked to Paezel for support, but Paezel glanced down, unsure how to gauge the dynamics of this friend group.

Skarpin leaned further over the ledge, eager to glimpse what lay below. He shuddered at the thought of falling, yet his curiosity craved an adventure. He spotted the sun glistening off something—was that water?

"Hey, I think there's water down there."

They all looked at each other, unsure of how to respond. Saedeen flipped over onto her stomach and inched forward to get a better look. Her friends followed suit. They all saw the sparkling electric blue water swirling with invites. Saedeen stood up. She wanted to be brave. She wanted to take risks like Lady Sorcha. If she hoped to join one of the big Elysian adventures someday, she needed to start with something small—something completely out of her comfort zone. Plunging into the unknown, freezing waters was definitely out of her comfort.

She took off her coat and readied herself to drink the potion. Elladelle flipped over and shrieked. "What do you think you're doing, Saedeen?"

The boys flipped over and stood quickly, wondering if they needed to prevent their friend from jumping.

"I want an adventure. Don't you? What if the potion helps you stay warm in the water? Did you notice any temperature change?"

Wullen, Paezel, Naedon, and Elladelle exchanged glances. "Well, no, but the Fire Nichts were providing the heat," Wullen replied.

Saedeen lifted her hands. "But they were meant for swimmers to dive for the plant. I bet the potion even aids in temperature control. Come on. Let's see what's down there. Who's with me?"

Elladelle sat cross-legged with her arms folded. "A. We could hit rocks and die. B. We could be swept away by a current and die. C. There might be a dangerous creature down there, and we could die!"

Naedon glanced at Wullen, then at Skarpin. Grins spread wide across their faces. "Count me in," Naedon said.

"Me too," Wullen and Skarpin said.

They high-fived Saedeen and stood next to her, peering down at Elladelle and Paezel. Saedeen felt guilty. She didn't want her friends to feel pressured into doing something they didn't want to do.

"You don't have to come. Why don't you two be the lookouts?"

Naedon snorted, knowing his cousin better than anyone else. He folded his arms and, with a smirk, said, "Then we'll hear Elladelle's complaints for weeks about missing out. Remember how much she complained about those secret tunnels? Where's that sense of adventure now?"

Elladelle hated how well her cousin understood her. She wanted to go, so why was she so scared? Something told her that whatever they uncovered down there would change everything moving forward, but what did that mean? Would they get into trouble? Would they disturb an unknown creature that would seek vengeance upon the land because of them? She always imagined the worst possible scenario first, but what about a positive outcome? What if they found something that could help their kingdom?

Elladelle grabbed one of the vials from Saedeen's hands. "Fine." She turned it upright in her mouth and swallowed. "Let's go!" The boys cheered as Saedeen handed out the potions. Paezel even took one, more to fit in than to be ready to jump off a cliff. But fears aside, she had to admit—a magical adventure with the most famous kids in Elysium was too good a quest to pass up.

They clinked their small glass bottles filled with sparkling blue liquid together and drank. Standing several feet from the cliff's edge, they held hands and nodded. Then, sprinting toward the drop-off, they jumped with nothing but hope and prayers. The drop wasn't as long as they had thought, and with a big splash, they landed in the cool cave waters. The potion immediately took effect, giving each of them the ability to breathe and talk underwater. They all giggled and pointed at how different they looked, sending bubbles to the surface.

Skarpin turned his head, seeing an odd light. He pointed. "Hey, look at that."

Naedon took off at his athletic speed. He loved adventure and couldn't wait for his first real military quest. He secretly hoped to be commander one day, an ambitious dream. He felt a gentle current pulling him forward through a dimly lit tunnel. He was glad for the current's assistance. He looked back, happy to see everyone effortlessly following along with the current, too.

He popped his head up as soon as they entered a shallow pool area. With water cascading down his ivory skin, he brushed his wet chestnut hair back and surveyed his surroundings. All their mouths dropped in awe at the most beautiful scene they had ever witnessed.

They breathed in the sweet, fresh air as they climbed out of the cool, blue water, leaving wet footprints in their wake. Saedeen pointed at the haven's small waterfall, which fed a sparkling blue pool filled with lily pads—each one adorned with white and silver flowers. She giggled, took hold of Elladelle and Paezel's hands, and spun around beneath the stone walls draped in lush green vines. They leaped onto the sparkling stepping stones while Wullen opted for the soft, velvety grass instead.

Skarpin froze in front of the table and chair under the stone archway. He felt confused. Why would a table and chair be here? He glanced around, searching for answers, but all he saw were the enchanting flowers drooping around the table. The one thing that stood out even more than the table and chairs was the golden chest sitting atop the table. The group huddled together, looking at one another, hoping someone might have an answer.

"Should we open it?" Wullen asked.

Saedeen folded her arms; water dripped from her elbows. "I don't know. It could be a trick."

Naedon picked up a smashed piece of the lock. "Looks like someone already opened it, so it might be empty." He held up the piece as if examining it could reveal something to them.

Elladelle leaned on her hands, palms flat against the table. "Well, we came down here for an adventure, so what could be more adventurous than finding a treasure chest? I say we open it." Her friends' eyes sparkled, but that familiar feeling returned deep within her. Elladelle knew whatever was inside would alter their history. She placed her hand on top of the chest, marveling at the gleam hidden beneath years of grime. "Before we open the chest, I have this feeling …"

Paezel's eyes widened, full of fear. "What kind of feeling?"

Elladelle sighed, not wanting to frighten them. "It might be a warning, or it could be nothing. I just feel like whatever is in there is going to change our lives— not just ours, but the entire realm."

Naedon snickered. "You're always so dramatic. C'mon, do you really think the six of us are going to discover something that huge?"

Saedeen locked her elbow with Elladelle's. "We did create those necklaces, and now the entire kingdom is making them. We're a more powerful kingdom because of our invention."

Naedon nodded. "Alright," he chuckled. "You got me there. So, let's make a pact. No matter what's in here, we stick together on how to handle it." He wanted to think like a commander, but he wasn't entirely sure what a commander would do in this situation.

They all nodded, and with a deep breath, Elladelle opened the chest, its hinges resisting with loud squeaks. Like a puppeteer was controlling them, all six mouths dropped in unison. Skarpin pulled out the largest emerald he had ever seen; his eyes glowed, feeling the tug of his kingdom's curse.

Elladelle snatched the gem from Skarpin, noticing the glow in his eyes. "Careful, Skarpin. I know your kingdom's curse has a lesser effect on you here, but those eyes of yours were glowing."

Skarpin's cheeks flushed as he looked at Paezel. He felt ashamed and dropped his head. Wullen put his hand on Skarpin's shoulder. "Hey, it's okay. We all struggle with the curses."

Skarpin met Wullen's jade eyes. "Really?"

"Yeah," Wullen said with a laugh. "But we've been told that talking about our jealousies helps combat them. It's not easy and feels a bit embarrassing, but for some strange reason, it almost makes the jealousy vanish."

"No way," Skarpin remarked.

Wullen nodded. "I'm not joking. Back when Naedon first discovered his fire magic, I was super jealous. It was all I could think about, so I told my father, and he said I must talk to Naedon about it. I thought that was strange, but I did. It was awkward, but once I got it out, I wasn't jealous anymore." Wullen elbowed Naedon, who smiled. "Naedon's been a great friend, helping me through it. I'm grateful for my powers and understand that ol' Naedon has a huge responsibility with his magic."

"Wow. I didn't know Elysians still struggled with the curse," Skarpin said, tugging at a thread on his shirt.

Elladelle placed the large gem back in the chest. "Yes, that's why it's so important to have close friends and family to talk to. My parents always tell me to help carry each other's burdens because life is too heavy to handle alone."

Saedeen smiled as she dug into the chest, moving aside the golden chains and pulling out a worn scroll. "Wow. This looks incredibly ancient." Ignoring the musty smell of the chest, she turned her head and breathed in the sweet scent of jasmine, which relaxed the butterflies in her stomach, and then unrolled the parchment on the table. The group crowded around her and the ancient scroll. The ink was faded, but they could still make out the drawings and texts of each kingdom.

Naedon pointed to an empty space. "Hey, wait. Pax Island is supposed to be here." He knew this because his Uncle Char was notorious for his rogue winnings there.

"That's right," said Elladelle. "Gosh, how old is this scroll for Pax Island not to be on it? Hold on." She leaned in, eyes squinting. "There are several islands not drawn."

Saedeen tapped the top. "But look at that. What word is this?"

"Ek-kka-lae-zee-a," Wullen sounded out slowly, not pronouncing it perfectly. His brow furrowed. "What does that mean?"

Skarpin's heart pounded. He recognized that word. But it came from the old language. He had discovered several books and scrolls in Sealyn's room and remembered seeing that word etched in the center of a page. It was accompanied by a warning. Not everyone would appreciate that word. If Eklaezia was written on this parchment, then it signified that it was from before the Second Chance.

Skarpin let out a breath. "It means assembly or to assemble."

Paezel snapped her head toward Skarpin, her wet red curls bouncing. "How do you know that?"

He dropped his head. "I was snooping, and I saw it written."

Saedeen's dark green eyes narrowed. "And you just happened to remember that particular word? How's that possible?"

Elladelle observed Skarpin struggling. She could see how deeply he wanted to keep his secret. At that moment, she recognized how long he had been living in solitude, even after all these months with them. It was time to grant him the freedom he so desperately needed.

She cleared her throat. "Because Skarpin's a genius."

Wullen snorted. "Ha! No, he's not."

Elladelle tilted her head and raised her eyebrow. "Yes, he is! Tell them, Skarpin. No one will think less of you. If anything, we'll accept you more for you finally being you."

Skarpin wanted to cry. He wanted Sealyn. He wanted Jace. He wanted to be anywhere but here. He swallowed the large lump in his throat, feeling the sudden dryness in his mouth. "She's right."

"You've been lying to us?" Wullen asked with a loud voice.

"Not lying …"

"Don't, Skarpin!" Wullen raised his hand. "Don't try to justify yourself. You've been dumbing yourself down to make us feel better—haven't you?"

Skarpin sniffed, trying hard to hold back the tears that urgently wanted to fall. "I … I …"

Wullen threw up his hands. "I can't believe this. The entire time, you've been pretending not to do well in class so we wouldn't realize how smart you are. It's like I don't even know you. I would never do that to you!"

Warm tears streamed down Skarpin's olive-toned cheeks. His lips trembled. He had never experienced the pain of disappointing a friend because he had never had any friends. He felt lightheaded, and shame washed over him, leaving him feeling nauseous. "I didn't mean to …" Skarpin stammered through thick tears. "I just wanted friends. I never meant to hurt …"

"Stop that!" Elladelle snapped. "You don't owe anyone an apology, Skarpin." She whirled around and smacked Wullen on the arm. "How dare you! Skarpin's been through enough. He kept this from us because he didn't want us to feel inferior to him. Look how jealousy is already ruining a friendship. It's our job to welcome his gifts and not shame him."

Paezel intertwined her fingers with Skarpin's, and they both blushed. Saedeen crossed her arms and stepped beside Elladelle. "That's right. Skarpin is our friend. It was his secret to keep and his secret to share when he felt it was appropriate, which makes it none of your business, Wullen."

Wullen looked to Naedon for help, but Naedon wasn't one for drama. He rolled his eyes. "Oh, come on, Wullen. Skarpin's secret is kind of like your secret crush on Elladelle."

"Naedon!" Wullen yelled. Elladelle gasped. Saedeen giggled.

Naedon smiled a goofy grin, very pleased with himself. "See, everyone has secrets," Naedon shrugged. "So, before any more awkward moments happen, let's look at this map again."

Relieved that none of her secrets were spilling out, Saedeen gently placed her ebony finger at the bottom of the map and let it follow the words as she read aloud: "Assemble the seven. Unite as one. All hail Eklaezia."

As soon as she said the name "Eklaezia," the leaves in the haven shook, and the water rippled. They peered around the hidden tranquil jungle, hearing the plants sing. What kind of magic was this? Could there be power in the name Eklaezia?

Chapter 50

The Honeyed Tongue Deceived

Thick periwinkle blades of grass blanketed the rolling hills before Jace. It was still hard to believe how different each kingdom was. He stole a glance to his left, spotting the tall mountain range in the distance, where sugar hung in the air over their lofty peaks. Jace longed for home. He wished to return to the Garden Library and be with his family in front of the fireplace alongside Sealyn and Skarpin. He envisioned Sealyn sitting on the floor pillows, with Skarpin nestled in her lap, reading his favorite book. Tears threatened to spill from his silver eyes.

The emerald and gold tiger walked beside Jace, sniffing the sweet-tasting air. He let out a low grumble toward Corvus. Jace peered from Shep to Corvus, wondering why the old, wise tiger appeared so displeased with him. Footsteps behind him snapped twigs, pulling Jace from his thoughts.

"The purple rolling hills of Glatania. They really are something," Laisren said. Jace nodded, unsure of what to say. Laisren cleared his throat. "So, brother. I know our plans have been delayed, to say the least, but have you thought more about … you know."

Of course, Jace knew. It was all he ever thought about, but finding a way to execute their plans now felt like a fool's dream. He couldn't risk injuring himself, not when he needed every ounce of his strength to save Sealyn. "I'm not sure if this is the right time, Laisren. I would be wounded myself—for my own sake—when our kingdom is at stake. I can't be that selfish."

"I hear you, but what if unleashing your powers could help us?"

Jace looked up into the light purple haze, watching strange creatures fly above. "I can't take that risk. I'm not saying no; I'm saying not yet."

Laisren nodded. "Understood. Just know if you change your mind, I'm here for it."

"Here for what?" AeLeer interrupted.

"Nothing," the brothers said.

AeLeer eyed them suspiciously. "Look, I know my brother can be a bit much, but he means well."

Laisren scoffed. "No offense, but your brother's a jerk. I've never seen such a good guy be so hot and cold."

AeLeer folded her arms, not liking the insults thrown at her family. "Well, maybe that's because we're finding out another secret you people have been hiding, which happens almost every five seconds. I mean, we should have known since pirate runs in the bloodline."

"Easy, princess."

Jace placed his hand on Laisren's shoulder. "No need for that."

"And just a moment ago, both of you were scheming more secrets. How can we ever trust you? It's no surprise my brother can't tell if you're full of honeyed tongues or just plain paranoid."

"Are those our only two options?" Laisren jeered.

"To put it lightly, yes," she said.

"Then I'd like to choose crazy paranoid, please."

Jace chuckled. "Truly, AeLeer, there's no need to worry. Some parts of my life are meant to remain private, which doesn't imply being secretive—it simply means that the details of those aspects will stay mine and only mine. If I choose to share them, then that's my business."

She dropped her arms. "I can live with that."

"Good. Now, refresh my mind here." Jace pointed at the horizon past the rolling periwinkle knolls. "Once we cross the hills, we enter the Sult Plains?"

"That's right. We had to take this route because of the military base on the other side of our kingdom. There are hardly any soldiers out here. We'll stay close to the mountain base. You really don't want to see what happens in the plains."

Laisren and Jace looked at one another. Laisren smiled at AeLeer. "Now, who's being cryptic?"

AeLeer grunted. "It's just sad is all. It's painful to see. People aren't in their right minds out there. You should have seen Corvus when he was brought to us. I wasn't sure I could bring him back."

"Corvus?" Jace asked, noticing Shep's ears perk up.

"Oh, yes. He was one of the ones rescued from the plains. There's an elderly group that dedicates themselves to saving banished Glatanians. They call themselves The Aged Ploemas." She began laughing.

"Why is that so funny?" Laisren asked.

"It's more cute than funny. They're the most wonderful humans you'll ever meet. They wear freshly sprouted Ploema Mushroom caps on their heads to entice the banished. Just in case they're caught, they barely eat to look the part, too—very dedicated to their cause."

"I'm guessing the banished end up starving themselves to death in the plains?" Jace asked.

"Some do, but most end up as slaves in Havas. We can't afford to get caught interfering with tradelines, so we stick to saving people in the Ploema Mushroom Forest. We accept anyone the elderly bring to us, even though not all survive. For a person to be sent to the Sult Plains, the mind must be completely infected with the curse. You have the sugar craze; food is all you can think about, and nothing satisfies."

Jace crossed his arms; an odd feeling tugged at the back of his mind. "Yet, Corvus did."

AeLeer's big purple eyes twitched. "Yes. As I said, it was a miracle he did."

Jace looked at Shep, who grumbled. Something felt off. Corvus appeared deeply committed to the rebellion's cause, yet they had overlooked mentioning that he came from the Sult Plains. Perhaps his dedication stemmed from being eternally grateful for their rescue, but his story carried an undertone of darkness. Jace turned back to the group, wrapping up their water and refreshment break, and observed Corvus. He seemed normal, joking with Laekian and helping to carry supplies—so what was it about him that troubled Jace and Shep so much?

The group continued hiking over the lush hills, but these were no ordinary landscapes. Their footsteps vibrated the mauve candied lupin flowers, causing them to pop up every five steps. These were no ordinary lupins; where there should have been petals, there were grape-flavored hardened candies instead. Dinyelle watched the Glatanians wince at the tantalizing blooms. This was likely another reason the rebels avoided coming to these hills. She couldn't imagine putting herself through such torture every day. Did these same flowers share the same fate as the Ploema Mushrooms? She didn't want to test to find out.

Jace slowed his walking, allowing Corvus to be in front of him. Ashur and Finn took to Jace's sides.

"Everything okay, my king?" Ashur asked. He didn't like the change in Jace's demeanor.

Jace nodded toward Corvus. "I want to keep an eye on Corvus," Jace whispered.

"Why? What do you suspect?" Finn whispered back.

"I honestly don't know, but something's off about him. Shep senses it, too."

Ashur chuckled. "Shep doesn't like anyone, only Char."

"I'm serious, Ashur. I need all eyes on him. See if he does anything different than the other rebels. Anything."

They walked silently, which was cut short when Dinyelle approached from behind. "My king?"

"Yes?"

"I really feel bad for the Glatanians walking through these grasses. Is there no other path for us to follow?"

Jace scrunched his face. "What do you mean?"

"Have you not seen their pain when the candied flowers spring up?"

Jace, Ashur, and Finn whipped their heads back toward the Glatanians and watched. Sure enough, a shiny mauve lupin popped up in front of AeLeer, Nyx, and Laekian, making them tense. Laekian clenched his fists while AeLeer squeezed Nyx's hand.

Jace grabbed Ashur's forearm. "Wait. Did you see that?"

"See what?" Ashur asked.

"Watch Corvus when that plant shows up. Wait for it. Just a few more steps. Here it comes."

Another sparkling mauve lupin burst forth before the purple-eyed rebels. Three avoided it as if it carried a contagious disease, but one … One picked a small, candied petal and slipped it into his mouth.

Jace froze in place. Ashur, Finn, and Dinyelle stopped, too. JaeDorn jogged over to the group.

"What's going on?" JaeDorn asked.

Jace motioned for the rest of their group to join. The pirates hurried over, trying not to draw attention from the rebels. Jace leaned in, still watching the Glatanians. "Listen quickly. Corvus. Something's wrong with him. We just saw him eat the candied flower."

"So?" Laisren said.

"So, the others are flinching. They're resisting sugary foods and only eating what's good for the body. They never gorge themselves nor purge their tables for comfort. That man is not resisting the curse." Jace's heart pounded. "There's more. They found him in the Sult Plains. He was apparently banished, then rescued." Jace looked into everyone's eyes, but they weren't connecting with him—except for a certain pair of fiery orange eyes.

Tyrdon grabbed Jace's arm. "He left. He left during the magic demonstration."

"Yeah, Father—to pee. The man had to pee. Gah," Taeg said, exhausted.

Tyrdon looked at Jace intensely. "No. He was gone long enough to send a message. He's a spy."

Jace's eyes widened. Everything clicked. Corvus was a traitor. The king had sent him to infiltrate Laekian's forces. He needed to think quickly, but he couldn't gather his thoughts. He heard the Glatanians calling out to them.

"What message would he send? And what would a cursed king do with that message?" Jace asked his father.

"Exactly what any deplorable would do. Cut down a monarchy."

Jace looked at the Glatanians approaching, then back to his father. "Graelynd. He told them where to find Queen Mother Graelynd. Oh, Creator, no."

"Yes. Son, we must return to the camp. We must protect her."

Jace felt as if his heart were shattering. He had to choose between his bride and her mother. Either way, he was killing Corvus. The Glatanians finally joined their group, looking confused.

Laekian lifted his muscular, tattooed arms. "Uh, what seems to be the problem?"

Jace swiftly unsheathed his sword and pressed it against Corvus's throat. AeLeer screamed. Nyx and Laekian followed suit, drawing their swords and prompting the others to do the same. Shep let out a roar and took a fighting stance beside Jace.

"Jace, what's the meaning of this?" AeLeer squeaked.

"He's a spy!"

"Nonsense. He's one of us," Laekian deflected.

Jace pressed his sword into Corvus's neck; blood slid down his pale skin. "Tell them. Tell them now!" he yelled.

Corvus swallowed, feeling the sharp blade, and then a coy smile molded across his face. He laughed. "It's too late. You're all too late."

Laekian dropped his sword. "Too late for what?" He grabbed Corvus's shoulder, shaking him. "Too late for what?"

An evil cackle resounded from Corvus. "The king's army should already be there. Your Queen Mother will die before nightfall."

Jace pressed the blade hard and sliced his sword across the traitor's neck. Corvus coughed; a torrent of blood poured from the wound. Jace let the body drop with a loud thud. The Glatanians stared at Corvus' lifeless form, unsure of what to say. Corvus and Laekian had been so close. It was difficult to accept that every word he had spoken was a lie, but a honeyed tongue will always deceive.

"Get back to the camp!" Jace shouted. The group turned and raced back to the rebel hideout, praying they weren't too late, but all Jace could feel with every stride was dread. He knew he would encounter death. Unfortunately, it came down to who … who would he lose today?

Chapter 51

<u>A Game Within a Game</u>

After the last seamstress left her chamber, Sealyn threw herself onto her bed, pulling the deep plum blankets over her body. She let the tears flow. She missed Jace and Skarpin. She needed her family. She felt drained from her lack of power. Max and Madilina's deaths still loomed over her. They needed a proper burial, but those wretched murderers wouldn't tell her what had happened to them. Being stuck in their suite was driving her mad, and the curses didn't help either. She needed to plan her next moves.

Tonight was the king's ball, and she feared every second that ticked closer to it. She didn't understand this king's game. He was ruthless yet intelligent, which made him incredibly dangerous. She did not want to underestimate him. She groaned, knowing the seamstresses would return in the next couple of hours with the lavish dress they had been working on for days. She was sick of purple: purple rugs, purple pillows, purple walls, purple eyes, purple freaking food. She never wanted to see this color again.

She heard Char and Jem talking outside. She wiped her tears, tugged at the cuffs—still enslaved—and peeled herself off the bed. She grabbed the velvet indigo robe from the stupid, purple chaise and wrapped herself in it. She greeted Char and Jem as she entered, then froze at the sight of them in their fancy outfits.

"Wow. I almost didn't recognize you two."

Jem smiled, puffing out his chest even more. His thick blonde hair was neatly combed back with freshly shaved sides. He wore a purple coat, a cherry-red vest adorned with gold buttons, and a white shirt underneath. His light tan pants were tight, accentuating his muscular definition. Light from the fireflowers reflected off his polished dark brown boots as he stepped in front of Sealyn. He took her hand and kissed the top of it gently. "I hope you save me a dance tonight."

Sealyn jerked her hand back. "This isn't for fun, Jem. Tonight, we must find a way to escape."

"Sorry, Sealyn. I mean, Queen Sealyn. I only meant to joke—lessen the tension. These confined days have been hard on all of us."

"Understood." She turned her gaze to her cousin. "And you... Your face is naked. I guess dirt and grime weren't in their wardrobe selection?"

Char laughed, pleased to hear Sealyn's personality returning, rubbing his freshly shaved jawline. "Not this time. I need to break a few hearts tonight." He winked. Char's hair was half pulled up, while the rest curled down to his shoulders. He wore an emerald tunic trimmed in gold and a gold belt with brown leather pants and shiny boots. He felt nervous about the ball. The king was full of tricks and clearly lashed out in anger, so what awaited them?

Char scratched his chocolate-brown beard. "Let's make sure we remember our roles tonight. Jem, stay close to Sealyn and listen for any gossip that might reveal what they're planning. Sealyn, avoid all sugary treats."

As soon as Char mentioned sugar, the grief over Max and Madilina's deaths, the fear for her mother, the longing for Jace, and the worry for Skarpin flooded her body. Her chest felt as if a horse were standing on it, and her arms suddenly felt heavy. She looked at the fresh plate of mini lavender blackberry cheesecakes, each topped with a plump blackberry and a sprig of lavender. Her mouth watered. Just one bite— only one wouldn't hurt. She just needed the serenity of sugar on her tongue.

A voice hissed in her mind. It sounded familiar, one she hadn't heard since arriving at the royal chambers. She stepped closer to the tempting treats. Char moved in between them, placed his hands on his hips, and then handed her a cluster of red grapes.

"If you're looking for a snack, have these. I just plucked them from the vines on the column."

Sealyn scowled as she snatched the grapes, dropping a few onto the floor. She watched them roll across the stone surface. Her memory flashed back to when she first met Jace in the Garden Library. He had been so startled by her presence that he dropped grapes from his plate. Jace. How she needed him. Tonight, she would escape and find her lighthouse, her Just Jace. She popped a grape into her mouth, crushing the sweet fruit as she focused on their plan.

"And you, Lord Char—do you remember your part?"

Char grinned and took a dramatic bow. "Of course! I'm going to party like there's no tomorrow." He raised a finger. "At least that's what those poor souls will think." He tapped his nose and pointed at Sealyn, a silly childhood gesture they had grown fond of.

After the seamstresses finally returned with a gown adorned with feathers and sparkles, Sealyn was dressed and ready for the Glatania ball. Her heart raced as she peered into the silver-trimmed, full-length mirror and cringed at the amount of purple she was wearing.

The ballgown had royal purple long sleeves stopping in small green feathers at the shoulders. Its sweetheart neckline was decorated with tiny green and violet feathers, framing her décolletage. The large, hoop-shaped, sparkling, deep violet skirt was embellished with long fronds of emerald and fern feathers. The stylist had curled her long, dark brown hair, allowing it to fall naturally to her waistline. They gathered part of her hair, securing it with a crown of tiny forest green feathers and large emeralds, each surrounded by small amethyst stones. Sealyn traced the outline of the deep purple jewels engulfing her neck and winced. Although she saw beauty before her, she was disgusted. This wasn't her. She had had enough; she had a mission.

"Finally, welcome back to the entire point of your existence," Kazimir hissed.

"Where have you been?" Sealyn snapped at the snake voice in her head.

"Waiting on you to figure out that food won't solve your problems."

Sealyn rolled her eyes, eager and motivated despite her frustration at his accuracy. She had lost sight of everything, but now she was determined to make amends. Tonight, she would fight for everything she believed in. Tonight, they all needed to find a way out and break the curse.

The doors to Sealyn's bedchambers swung open, and Jem felt his knees weaken at the astonishing sight before him. He admired Sealyn's beauty; her presence almost commanded submission. His heart raced in his ears, and nothing else seemed to matter except her. Everything would change after the events of the evening; he couldn't show fear. All his dreams could come true if he played his cards right.

He watched Char escort Sealyn out the door and then remembered how to move. How could someone make you forget the simplest things, like breathing or talking? He rolled his shoulders back; this was it—no turning back. He would claim Sealyn as his, one way or another.

All three descended the mauve stairs, inhaling the intoxicating aromas of chocolate, sugar, and baked fruits. Sealyn squeezed Char's arm tighter. He would be her distraction; family would help her get through this.

"We can do this, Sea," Char said, patting her hand.

Sealyn attempted to smile, yet something felt amiss—a sensation she hadn't experienced in ages had returned. Every nerve ending stood on high alert. Her left palm burned, the palm of death. What was happening? Her emerald eyes darted around the glittering ballroom with wild intensity. The palace ballroom showcased sparkling shades of purple ballgowns twirling gracefully on the silver dance floor while several small chocolate fountains adorned the walls.

Char felt Sealyn's tension. "What's going on, Sealyn?"

Sealyn opened and closed her mouth. She didn't know what to say, as she also didn't understand what was happening. It was just a feeling. "Something isn't right," she whispered.

"Do we change plans?" Char asked, scanning the room with narrowed purple eyes fixed on them. He was accustomed to attention, but these looks were filled with pure hatred.

"I don't know," she gasped. She sucked in a breath as the monarchs approached her. Was the dark mist following them? She could just poison his wine and be done with this, or was that considered murder? She found it increasingly difficult to tell. If they were at war, she could justify it, right?

"Ah, Queen Sealyn, glad you decided to join us."

Char watched the king. He felt the king's buttons might pop off their threads. Char glanced at Sealyn, uncertain about what to do. If he abandoned her, would she fall apart? He leaned his head back further, signaling Jem to be extra careful.

Char disliked trusting a Havasian—the people of the cunning fox.

Char cleared his throat. "Maybe I should get us some drinks." He nodded, and before Sealyn could drop her hand, Jem caught it with his arm.

"Queen Sealyn, it would be an honor to have the first dance of the night with you." His scarlet eyes sparkled with hope and passion.

Sealyn gave a slight nod and glared at the king. She walked out onto the dance floor, wishing she had reassurance that the unsettling feeling came from the king, but she didn't sense the dark mist's presence nearby. Was that even what she was feeling? She inhaled the warm, velvety fragrance of the chocolate fountain, and her eyes dilated, shifting into shades of purple.

"My queen, tell me something I don't know about you."

Sealyn's brow furrowed. "What?" Her eyes returned to their emerald green.

"Surely, there must be something I don't know. Tell me."

Jem spun her around, catching her waist, and then stepped in time with the rhythm of the melodies. "I, um ..." She glanced at Char. Family. Family would help her through this. "I'm not allowed to sit beside Char when we play cards."

Jem chuckled, surprised by her response. "I'm scared to ask, but why?"

"We cheat," she let out a laugh. "At this point, it's almost a sport to see if anyone can catch us. I think that's become part of the game we're playing."

"A game within a game."

"Very good. Yes, a game within a game."

"Wait … was that why I couldn't win against you and Char these past days?"

"Yes, it was way too easy." Sealyn found herself relaxing and enjoying the moment. Her memories of family triumphed over her fears.

Jem smiled and spun her around again. "I knew I wasn't that bad."

A cold shiver ran down Jem's spine as he spotted several pairs of blood-red eyes through the crowd. His people were here, just as the butler had mentioned. He needed to speak with them to confirm the plans. Char approached with drinks in each hand. Jem was determined to seize this opportunity.

"This has been a wonderful start to the evening. Everything will be fine, Queen Sealyn. Why don't you have a drink with Char while I check the room for any suspicious activity?"

After hours of dancing, drinking, mingling, and eavesdropping, Sealyn felt completely drained. She sensed her guard slipping. She needed to locate their escape plan, but this palace was heavily guarded. She heard the king clap his hands for everyone's attention. This must be the final speech of the night. Time was slipping away. She desperately scanned the room for Jem. He was nowhere to be found. She noticed Char chatting with two blondes with massive chests; ugh, Char.

"Ladies and gentlemen, my esteemed guests, it is time for our final goodbyes. But as always, I will end with a special surprise, and tonight will prove to be the biggest surprise in our history."

Sealyn didn't like where this was going. Butterflies raged in her stomach.

The king raised his chubby arm. "Queen Sealyn, will you join me?"

Sealyn understood that it wasn't a question; it was an order. She tilted her head at Char. With her heels clicking against the silver floor, she walked cautiously toward the king in the center of the ballroom.

"Wonderful," the king said. Guards flanked on either side.

Sealyn glanced back at Char, but she couldn't see him. Her heart raced. Had he abandoned her? Breathing became difficult. The scents of chocolate and sugar filled her nose, darkening her eyes a shade of dark purple. She was losing the battle. She couldn't concentrate. She needed help.

"Peace is the ultimate job for a king, and I have secured us that peace. You see, we pure and holy Glatanians don't recognize the marriage of silver eyes as legal nor lawful."

Sealyn snapped her head and scowled at the king, her eyes flashing back to green. Now, he had her full attention. She felt her wrists burning against the cuffs. "Careful what you say," she growled.

"Oh, no, no, no. You don't speak now," he held his large finger close to her face. "Due to our beliefs, we view Queen Sealyn as unmarried and in need of a proper husband."

"What?" Sealyn yelled. She took several steps back, but guards crowded her position.

The king glared and leaned in closer, just for Sealyn to hear. "One more word out of your mouth, and my guards will gut your cousin." Sealyn's stomach dropped. No wonder she couldn't find Char. They had taken him. Of course, he wouldn't abandon her. The guards must have Jem, too. She had to be very careful—play the king's game until it wasn't his any longer.

The king looked back at the crowd and smiled broadly. "As you can hear, she's quite excited to finally have an appropriate match." He clapped his hands. "Guards, bring in Queen Sealyn's betrothed."

Betrothed? Had this evil man lost his mind? She wasn't betrothed, nor was she about to marry anyone. She glanced toward the far end of the ballroom, where Lord Jem, flanked by a group of Havasians, was leading the fox pack. A game within a game, indeed. He was a traitor. Her mouth fell slightly open.

"Wonderful. Queen Sealyn Araelien of Elysium will marry Lord Jem Anwir of Havas."

Sealyn frantically searched the room for Char. She needed to know if he was safe, but all she found were the faces of strangers. Tears welled in her eyes. She would not betray her oath to Jace; she would die before crossing that line. Jem stepped closer to Sealyn. She glared.

"Sealyn, please, it was the only way to keep you safe."

"Sure, it was," she snarled.

The king grabbed Jem's hand and slid a blade over it, drawing blood. "Let us bind these two together, for with their bond, this unites three kingdoms."

Sealyn scrunched her face. Three? Who was the third? Then she felt it. Darkness crowded around her feet. The dark mist was here. She looked up, searching. That woman had to be here. The crowd parted, and Sealyn watched the red-headed witch slowly stomp toward her: Queen Corentine of Stoltland. Every fiber in Sealyn wanted to scream and lash out, but she remained still.

Time froze. Sealyn heard the click of Corentine's boots. Faint whispers. The sound of her heart thudded in her ears. She watched a droplet of Jem's blood drip and splatter on the floor, then glanced at her own palm, pulsing with onyx blood. She looked into Corentine's inky eyes, and her stomach churned. She had to think fast; she would do what was necessary—she would not betray Jace. A game within a game.

"Queen Corentine of Stoltland has graciously entered into an accord with us, provided that Lord Jem marries Queen Sealyn, thus annulling the marriage between Queen Sealyn and the silver-eyed Jace. She agreed to allow the couple to spend their days in Havas." He extended his hand to Sealyn. "Now, your hand to bond with his: blood for blood."

She hesitated for only half a second. Thrusting her left palm across the blade, she grabbed Jem's bleeding hand before he realized what had happened. Jem felt the sting and burn of the ebony venom entering his bloodstream.

Sealyn leaned in, her nose almost touching Jem's. "A game within a game. Now, die a traitor's death." She let go of his hand, and Jem collapsed to the floor, foaming at the mouth and convulsing.

"What is the meaning of this?" the king shouted. "I thought she had no powers!"

Corentine sent black mist ropes around Sealyn. Sealyn squirmed, but shackled as she was, she was no match for the dark magic. Corentine walked closer, stepping over Jem's twitching body.

"I must admit, I didn't think you had it in you, little bird."

"For Jace, I'd do anything."

Corentine scoffed. "Same, child. Same. You have no idea. You might want to know that your mother and the rest of your Elysians are most likely dead by now." Sealyn's chest tightened. "Ah, yes. Did we forget to mention that the king had a spy in the rebel camp? Long story short, the Glatanians and part of my army will crush your little rebellion." She spun to face the king. "Well, this puts a damper on our agreement. I will refuse peace and declare war on Glatania unless you do one thing for me."

Sealyn's mind spun in confusion. She felt her will to resist the grip of the dark mist slipping away. Her mother. Her mother couldn't be dead, could she? Her friends? Jace? Corentine wouldn't kill Jace, would she?

The king bowed. "Name it, Your Majesty."

"Enslave this unfit queen. I want her beaten and worked until she's broken. I want the name Sealyn Araelien to hold no meaning, no significance, no hope in its sound. I want her to be entirely unaware of who she is. Do I make myself clear?"

The king nodded. "It shall be done. Guards! Seize her." The dark mist released Sealyn, and the soldiers surrounded her. She kicked and struggled, trying to break free, but they were too strong and too great in number.

With a bloodied face and bloodied sword, Char reentered the ballroom from the opposite end. He shouted, "Sealyn!"

The guards and Sealyn glanced back. Sealyn's spirits soared at the sight of her cousin alive. She had to protect him, but there was nothing she could do. "Run, Char!" Panic surged as he took two steps forward. "Run!!" Her final command.

Chapter 52

<u>Four Years Ago…</u>

Fifteen years had passed since … After all the torture, secret training, and stealing food, Jace had grown into a striking young man. He stood tall, taller than Haedon, with defined muscles and a jawline that made women turn their heads, even though he had illegitimate gray eyes. Most had developed an acquired taste for Jace as long as he acted in a servile manner. He navigated the villages through his hidden trails and stayed in the shadows; it was essentially second nature for him. He understood how to be invisible.

His position at court evolved into that of an errand runner, and he found himself enjoying it. He created challenges for himself by timing his speeds from place to place. He knew all the shortcuts, so sometimes he would opt for the longer routes to make the task more difficult. Jace discovered that being an errand runner came with perks—one perk in particular was reading the discarded reports. His favorites were about the other mysterious kingdoms.

He still dreamed of one day embarking on an outrageous pirate adventure or rescuing a fair maiden from a hungry dragon, but he had accepted his fate as the lonely outcast. Sure, a few slave girls had caught his attention, but in the end, they viewed him as beneath them too, so he focused on his job and collecting all the reports he could.

On this day, he was returning to the palace with the livestock reports for Queen Phyre when he froze on the palace steps. It was his half-brother's carriage, Lord Tahbert. Why would he be back from his training with Larson? Jace's gut twisted, remembering Larson's words. "If you're not with your mother when I return, I'll gut anyone you love, anyone you care about, and I'll burn your peace to the ground."

Jace dashed past the abandoned onyx carriage, racing up the stairs two at a time, panic gripping him. He couldn't let Larson think he had deserted his mother. As he turned a corner too sharply, he lost his footing and nearly fell, his heart racing. Regaining his balance, he sprinted onward, skidding to an abrupt halt before the family drawing room. His hands were slick with sweat as he reluctantly raised them to knock, feeling the weight of uncertainty pressing down on him.

The butler opened the door and nodded to him. Jace stepped inside anxiously, wiping his sweaty palms on his worn tunic. He hadn't seen Larson since he left so many years ago.

How would Larson react to his presence? Jace was also curious about how his half-brother would behave.

"Ah, Jace. Do you have the livestock reports?" Jace nodded. "Good. Bring them to me," Queen Phyre said, extending her hand.

Jace hurried to the queen, who sat on the black leather couch near the obsidian fireplace that seemed to hiss and snicker at him. He handed the scrolls to Queen Phyre and bowed. Then he glanced at the other couch across from the queen, where, between his mother and stepfather, sat his half-brother, Tahbert. Jace froze, searching his mind for any reason his brother would be here. There were no holidays, no festivals, no significant events that would justify such a visit, so why was he back?

He cringed as his mother gushed over Tahbert. He hated himself for the jealousy coursing through his veins, and even as a grown man, he still yearned for his mother's approval and love. Jace observed Tahbert's shaggy, midnight hair, darker than his presumed father's. His eyes were cold and unfeeling, devoid of emotion. His frame was small, clearly inherited from Corentine. Jace knew the Stoltland kingdom wouldn't take kindly to a frail-looking king. Aware that his welcome would soon wear out, he bowed his head and started to leave, but Queen Phyre called him back.

"Jace, stay a moment. We have some interesting news that will even include you."

Jace froze. News? What kind of news? Was he being accused of something? Did they know about his stash of discarded reports? The room began to spin, and objects started to blur.

Queen Phyre summoned the rest of the family scattered around the drawing room to gather close. Jace stole a glance at Haedon, who looked as if he had just eaten something sour. Jace was puzzled about why his mother's twin sisters were present, along with his step-uncles. What was happening? He never attended family meetings. Perhaps they would finally accept him, and this would become a new normal routine.

Phyre cleared her throat. "As you know, the rumors about Elysium are increasing, and our spies have confirmed them. The green haze from their curse has almost dissipated."

Haedon shrugged. "Okay? So, what does that mean? How is that even possible?" Jace watched Haedon squint around the room at Stoltland's inky haze.

"Well, young prince, it's as we feared. Elysium is developing a method to break their curse. It started with their King Saevon, and we thought Queen Graelynd would eventually fail, but she has proven to be more resilient than we anticipated."

"Is there a formula for breaking the curses, Grandmother?" Tahbert asked.

Phyre's obsidian eyes narrowed, wrinkles deepening on her face. "You address me as Queen. I don't want the grandmother connotation attached to my name."

Corentine patted Tahbert's hand. Jace couldn't believe Tahbert was so naïve about Stoltland's curse of pride—he should have known better. Jace was completely intrigued by Phyre's news. He had read several reports about Elysium— one of his favorite kingdoms because of the rumors he had heard. He often daydreamed about sneaking away there.

Phyre continued, "According to our scholars, who have studied all the ancient texts they could find, a pattern of three emerges. Their theory suggests that if three bloodlines resist the curse, they will be able to break it."

"Can we really be certain about this?" Corentine questioned.

Phyre raised her eyebrow. "Unless you have a better idea?" She watched Corentine cower and shake her head. "I didn't think so."

Jace shifted his stance. He felt the tension in the room. None of the information so far would explain why Tahbert returned. He already knew most of it from different reports, so why now? What had changed?

Phyre looked at Haedon. "My dear Haedon, it's time for a strategic match for you."

Haedon dropped his folded arms. "What? You must be joking."

"I assure you—I'm not." Phyre stood and handed a gold and green royal invitation to Haedon.

He snatched it. "What's this?" He opened it and started reading. "An invitation to a coronation. From Elysium?"

Gasping filled the air around the group. Stoltland and Elysium never participate in anything except battles between the kingdoms—not parties and certainly not coronations. This would astonish every kingdom.

"Is someone playing a prank?" asked an uncle.

Phyre's lip curled. "No. I received word from Korpam and Havas that they received invitations too. It seems the Elysians have invited all kingdoms to join this specific coronation."

Haedon looked up from the alluring, sparkling parchment. "Wait. This sounds like they might accept a match for their new queen with someone from another kingdom."

Phyre's head tilted. "It does, doesn't it?"

"But why? Why would they do that? A match from different kingdoms would result in silver-eyed heirs. No one wants that," Haedon said. He tried not to look at Jace.

Jace wasn't offended; he was curious. He had the same questions. Was Elysium playing a game? Surely, the monarchy wouldn't choose a suitor from another kingdom because the heirs wouldn't have pure blood. If this was a game, then what kind of game was it? What would Elysium gain from it?

Pointing at the bottom of the invitation, Haedon asked, "What about this last portion? What does it mean?"

Queen Phyre spun around to face the fire, its glow illuminating her weary expression and silvering hair. "Why don't you read it for everyone to hear? In fact, read the entire invitation."

Haedon sighed. He didn't like reading out loud. With another groan, he began,

"King Ryker and Queen Graelynd Araelien of Elysium invite you to attend the royal crowning of their daughter, Princess Sealyn Araelien."

Corentine's head snapped up. "Wait? You didn't tell us they chose their youngest daughter? I thought the eldest was being groomed for the crown. What's her name? Sandy or … Cindy?"

Phyre turned back and faced her curious family. "Indeed. We all thought Princess *Siany* would be next, but apparently, she turned down the offer."

A wide, devious smile spread across Corentine's face. "So, they're putting an untrained little girl on the throne?"

"Information about Princess Sealyn is limited, particularly concerning her training for the monarchy; there are many details about her beauty, but even more about her unpredictability," Phyre said.

"Then, she should be easy to overpower and maybe even fall victim to their curse?" another uncle asked.

Jace smirked. Hadn't the uncle just heard that the princess was unpredictable? This literally meant they wouldn't have a clue how Elysium would be ruled or how the queen would respond to Stoltland. He found himself liking more and more of what he heard about Princess Sealyn. He had read numerous reports, but most spies only commented on her looks. He wanted to know what her character was like. King Ryker was notably one of the wisest kings in history, so for him to believe that crowning Sealyn as queen would benefit his kingdom, there had to be more to Sealyn than just her appearance.

Phyre waved her hand dismissively. "Not necessarily. She could end up being an easy monarchy to control, or she could be something entirely different." She clapped her hands. "Now, Haedon, keep reading."

"We encourage you to bring all male heirs to this festive occasion; princesses are welcome, too."

"Stop," one of the twins said. "They do mean to marry off their daughter to another kingdom. This is absurd—a scandal on the highest level."

Bickering and theorizing erupted among the royal Stoltlanders, but Jace remained silent. He still didn't understand why he was there. He wondered if all the other kingdoms were as confused as they were. Was this Elysium's intent? He enjoyed witnessing his family's panic, but when this family panicked, people usually died. Goosebumps prickled his skin as he recalled the slaughter of the Korpam royals.

"Stop this noise at once!" Queen Phyre raised her voice, straining her throat. She coughed and snapped her fingers for a goblet. The butler scurried over, handing her a silver goblet filled with black cherry wine. She sipped it, soothing her throat. "What you fools can't seem to grasp is that Elysians are notorious for riddles and games. You can't trust anything they say. The truth is usually buried deep behind their words."

Or perhaps in plain sight, Jace considered. The Elysians invited male heirs but also the princesses, so maybe it meant nothing. It was just a tease with wordplay; still, none of this explained why he was at the meeting.

"Because I know they're tricksters, we will bring the male heirs: Haedon and Tahbert." Tahbert lifted his head, ebony strands of hair falling over his curious onyx eyes. "If the Elysians are foolish enough to marry their new queen to a foreigner, then Haedon, you will be that lamb to the slaughter."

"What!? No!"

"You dare defy me?"

"No—I just. I." He dropped his head and folded his arms. "If I marry her, that means I lose another portion of my claim to the Stoltland throne. You're going to give the crown to Tahbert, aren't you?" He looked at his father, then at Corentine. "Well, say something."

His father cleared his throat. "Nothing in this life is certain. We must all make sacrifices."

Haedon raised his arms and dropped them, slapping his legs. "That's it? That's your big advice? Riveting, Father, just riveting." He started pacing the floor.

"Haedon," Phyre began. "I don't believe the Elysians will pair their daughter with a foreigner." He paused and looked at his grandmother. "I suspect they want this to serve as a distraction, and if that's the case, then we need to put on our best performance, convincing them that we've fallen for it." She pointed to the parchment, now crumpled in Haedon's hand. "Skip over the dates and times and read the last part."

Haedon relaxed his fist and unfolded the crumpled invitation. "Please also bring a candidate to represent your kingdom for a potential new position on the future Queen Sealyn's Council of Lands, with the aim of fostering unity and prosperity across all seven kingdoms."

Silence filled the room, broken only by the crackling of the fire, a door closing near the drawing room, and the coughing of an outside grounds worker. Jace could hear his heart beating. What could that mean? Was this new queen really going to attempt to bring peace to the kingdom? She sounded ambitious. A smile curled over his lips; he liked this princess.

Phyre extended her arm toward Jace. "Jace, will you come stand beside me?"

Jace's insides twisted in knots. He hated attention, and being in the spotlight always led to some kind of punishment. He moved carefully, noticing his mother narrowing her eyes at him. He swallowed hard, feeling as if he had consumed a mouthful of sand.

Phyre patted Jace's arm, eyeing him as if he had a contagious disease that she didn't want to catch. "Jace will be our candidate."

The room lashed out with swearing, gasps, and laughter. Jace couldn't believe what she said. His mind started running. He felt dizzy. This couldn't be happening—not to him.

"Silence! Such fools," Phyre groaned. "As I mentioned earlier, we have to play their game better than they do. I don't think they will mix blood on their throne, so when she inevitably turns down Haedon, she will select a candidate for her absurd Council of Lands. This is where our decoy, Jace, comes in."

"Me?"

Phyre smiled. "Yes, you. The reality is that no monarchy will choose someone with silver eyes for any significant role, so the new little queen will see our candidate, turn her nose up at him, and then choose Haedon instead."

And there it was—he was a deterrent. A means to an end. He was supposed to disgust the queen enough that she would choose his brother instead. How could he have ever thought, even for a moment, that his family would choose him to be part of something greater than a scheme? He dropped his head, not wanting to make eye contact. He hated feeling embarrassed; he should be used to this by now, but it still stung.

The rest of the family meeting was a blur of motions and sounds. Jace didn't care. He knew his role and would fulfill it effortlessly—he just needed to be present and show his eyes, his rotten silver eyes. But one good thing came from that meeting—he would be going to Elysium.

Days turned to weeks, and before Jace knew it, it was time for them to set sail for the emerald kingdom. The large wooden ship creaked as the raven sails whipped powerfully in the wind. Jace nodded at the sailors as he passed and walked to the vessel's bow. He dropped his pack with a thud and leaned against the worn wooden railing. He felt at home on a ship. Why? He didn't know, but something felt natural when he was at sea. His stomach fluttered with a thousand butterflies, but he was ready to see the kingdom of green eyes. He had devoured every book and report he could find about Elysium. He felt a rush of excitement because he had read about the delicious foods, vibrant music, and endless days of entertainment. As he gazed out over the open horizon of the vast, deep blue sea, he couldn't help but feel a strange tug. This must be what it feels like to be a traitor.

He had been deceiving himself, unwilling to admit that he, too, wanted to see the beautiful princess. Everything about her captivated him, prompting him to seek out any information about her. However, he never anticipated what he would do with that privileged information. In recent weeks, scouts and spies submitted numerous reports detailing Sealyn's royal education, her military training and skills, and even her favorite companions. Yet instead of handing those documents to Queen Phyre, he destroyed them. He didn't even understand why. He simply did it.

He needed to find a way to stay in Elysium. He had heard it was a more accepting kingdom, so perhaps they would show him grace and permit him to remain. If not, he had already resolved to disappear into the lush lands of the mysterious curse-fighting kingdom. He would not be returning to Stoltland. The sea breeze lightly kissed his tanned cheeks, easing his tension. He drank in the salty air, ready for his adventure. No matter his past, a new future awaited him—he could feel it. His whole life was about to change ... forever.

Chapter 53

<u>The Perdonair Dinner</u>

Enjoying the Perdonair celebration, King Father Ryker sipped his lemon-lime juice as he listened to his family's conversation around the palace dinner table. He was happy to finally have a conclusion to his exhausting day, yet his mind plagued him. An overwhelming sense of doom and gloom kept weighing on him. His heart ached as he regarded the empty chairs that would usually be filled by his wife, daughter, son-in-law, and nephew, Char. He took another bite of roasted chicken and pondered when to send reinforcements to Sealyn.

"You're just mad because you lost, so pay up," Lady Ebbalee told her son, Lord Menry.

Menry swallowed his potatoes. "I'm not paying you anything. We didn't officially bet."

Ebbalee raised her hand at him and looked at her husband, Lord Marin. "You see. You see what kind of dishonest man you've raised."

"Me? Woman, somewhere around this giant castle, probably in the darkest of corners, are all your lost marbles."

The table chuckled, trying not to shoot liquid out of their noses. Ryker laughed at his parents' banter and skewered a potato while thinking about how lucky he was to have such a close family. He was glad to have Prince Toven and his wife back since the loss of their son, Ezen. They all still felt the pain of his death at the hands of those Stoltlanders.

"I think I won the most," Lord Jdru said. "I went big on the Red Phoenixes, not just because my son plays for them, but because I heard the Yellow Phoenixes were struggling with camaraderie." Jdru looked down the long table where the children were seated and winked at Naedon. Naedon winked back, beaming.

"Ah, so you have insider information. I suppose that means you cheated," Ebbalee remarked, smiling as she anticipated her grandson's argument.

"No, Grandma. It's more about taking in the surrounding gossip, making my own decisions, and placing full confidence in my genetics." Jdru raised his sparkling gold goblet and stood. "Let us raise our goblets to Naedon and toast the Red Phoenixes for their victory in Feydom."

The family raised their goblets toward Naedon, who blushed. They praised him in unison. Elladelle giggled at

Naedon's pink cheeks. Naedon felt relieved when the family returned to their adult conversations.

He looked side to side to Elladelle and Skarpin. "I can't take this secret any longer. We've got to tell them."

Elladelle shooshed him. "No, we agreed that we would get in so much trouble if we said anything. We must keep this to ourselves."

Naedon looked at Skarpin with pleading green eyes. "C'mon, Skarpin. I know you must be feeling the same. Don't you think King Father Ryker deserves to know?"

Maekel fluttered nearby with a note for Princess Siany but overheard the children's whispers. Should she say something? Surely, it was harmless childhood chatter, so it wouldn't carry much weight, but those children, in particular always seemed to find themselves in big drama. She handed the note to Siany and hesitated.

"Maekel? Is something the matter?" Siany asked.

Maekel's pink wings fluttered, and her large brown eyes darted from the children back to Siany. "I'm sure it's nothing."

"Then let's hear it," Siany pressed.

"I overheard the children speaking. I'm sure it's innocent fun, but it sounded like whatever they were hiding might be for King Father Ryker's ears."

Siany looked at her father, who sat to her right at the head of the table. "My father? Well, I think we need to find out what's going on. Thank you, Maekel. We'll handle it from here."

Maekel bowed and flew out of her Nicht door. Siany turned her attention to the whispering children. She clinked her spoon against her goblet, capturing the table's attention.

"Now that I have your attention, I believe Elladelle, Naedon, and Skarpin have some news for our king."

Nausea bubbled up from the children's stomachs. Skarpin started to panic. His golden eyes filled with tears, but he blinked them away. He thought about how brave Sealyn and Jace were; he wanted to be brave like them. He would take the blame. There was no need for his adopted family to be in trouble. Skarpin pushed his chair back and walked slowly to King Father Ryker, ignoring his friends' questions.

"Uh, well, you see—I discovered a hidden lagoon of some sort, and there was a treasure chest. It had the biggest emerald I had ever seen, too, but um ..." He fidgeted with the gold hem of his emerald tunic. "There was this old map—like, a really old map; more like ancient—before the Second Chance ancient."

Ryker's posture stiffened at the mention of the map. Any map that existed before the Second Chance was almost unheard of. If Skarpin truly had one of those maps in his possession, it would be vital to their mission.

"We, I mean me—just me. I saw an unusual word on the map, and when I read it out loud, the leaves and water moved. It was like that word commanded them."

The room was so quiet that Siany thought people could hear her heartbeat. Elladelle and Naedon looked at each other. Elladelle leaned in and whispered, "This isn't right. We can't let him take the fall for this." Naedon nodded in agreement. They both stood and joined Skarpin.

"What's this?" Ryker asked.

"Skarpin didn't discover this alone. It was all of us, including Saedeen, Paezel, and Wullen." Naedon smacked Elladelle's arm. While rubbing her arm, she scolded him. "What? They were going to find out anyway. Parents always do." She rolled her eyes.

"Let's get back to the map. What was the word?" Ryker's eyes sparkled with curiosity.

Grand Queen Karis leaned in close, eager to hear if the child would speak of what is only whispered in people's dreams.

Skarpin rubbed the golden hem again; the gesture calmed his anxiety. "Eklaezia."

The plants in the corners shook, and the water inside the table's pitcher spun.

Prince Adomin stood amazed, knocking his chair back. "What is this magic, Ryker?" he asked, pushing up his spectacles.

Grand Queen Karis slightly raised her wrinkled hand. "If I may?" Ryker nodded. "This is the purest form of Cognition magic from before the Second Chance."

Prince Royce took a long sip of his wine. "You're going to have to explain that one, Mother."

She smiled softly. "We haven't spoken openly about this, but it might be time. What is shared in this room, stays in this room." All heads nodded. "Good. I'm sure you've observed by now that our Queen Sealyn is a Cognition." Eyes darted from one family to the next. Skarpin's anxiety grew. "We know the stories of Cognitions' fates, but Sealyn is strong. If you've noticed her abilities, then you've also seen how her power works. She's tethered to nothing and needs no creature's permission to wield her powers. Everything resides in her mind. True Cognitions can speak the old language and wield magic like we've never seen." She looked at Lord Rielen, who had seen these powers for himself.

Rielen, nephew of King Ryker, had accompanied Sealyn on the Len Novian quest and watched from the trenches of Commander Malum's dreadful amphitheater as Sealyn conjured magic with nothing but her voice. At that time, he had no understanding of its significance. Everything was new and sometimes still felt that way. The scars from that quest continue to haunt him.

Karis continued, "The most powerful Cognitions were legendary. It was said that one Cognition grew so powerful that he received his power directly from Creator, granting him the ability to write words infused with magic." She paused, noticing that everyone was captivated by her words. She nodded at Skarpin. "I believe Skarpin has found a map that must have belonged to that Cognition."

"What are we to do with this information?" Siany asked.

Ryker smiled and pulled Skarpin in for a hug. "That word means to assemble. This is our mission. We will unite all seven kingdoms, and from now on, we will call them by their old title: Eklaezia."

Chapter 54

A Warrior's Last Breath

Legs and lungs burning, Jace leaped over another boulder, following the Elysian tiger. Screams and clanging swords echoed through the forest; death hung in the air. They were so close—despite their bodies begging for rest, they pressed on. The metallic stench of blood filled their nostrils, but whose? Jace saw the tiger pounce on the first Glatanian soldier, who bled out immediately from the tiger's teeth ripping through his neck.

Jace tackled another soldier but stumbled back when he noticed that this soldier had black eyes. The Stoltlander laughed and lunged at Jace. Jace rolled and scrambled back to his feet. He swung his sword, missing the soldier's stomach by inches, but it didn't matter; Nyx had already driven her weapon through the Stoltlander's belly, and blood gushed from the wound. Jace nodded to her, then looked up, trying to spot any of his people in the treetops. He could see fighting, but that was all.

Laekian sprinted up the winding staircases since they couldn't use the pulley system. He threw Glatanian soldiers off the stairs as he passed, with AeLeer and Nyx on his heels. Jace signaled to the rest of his crew to follow the rebels. Their legs burned, but they persevered, fueled by the cries and screams of their people.

When they finally reached the top, they froze, breathing heavily. Obsidian-armored Stoltlanders and deep purple-leathered Glatanians were everywhere, battling Elysians and rebels. Laekian and Jace exchanged glances and nodded. They sprinted forward, shouting their battle cries, hoping to distract their enemy.

Dinyelle slid under a Stoltlander's blade and spun around on her knees, slicing into his calves. Down the Stoltlander went, but his head soared over the railing after JaeDorn's killing swing. They were a fierce couple to duel against. JaeDorn stabbed another Stoltlander from behind and pushed him over the railing; the body fell into darkness. Dinyelle juked around a Glatanian soldier, then leaped high on one foot, pushing off a wooden wall, and descended onto the enemy. Her sword plunged through the female soldier's trap, penetrating deeply into her body. Dinyelle wrenched her bloodied sword from the corpse, enraged by the betrayal.

Finn cut his finger and grabbed his necklace, creating vines from the railing and forming a nest out of reach of the enemy. He fired arrow after arrow, taking out as many Stoltlanders and Glatanians as he could. A Stoltlander cornered AeLeer, disarming her of her weapon. Blood splattered on her face. She blinked her periwinkle eyes, and her mouth gaped at the arrow protruding from the soldier's left eye. The body fell, and she nodded to Finn. She picked up her sword and chased after her brother.

Laisren blocked another attack from a Glatanian soldier and thrust him backward, but he collided with someone else. He whirled around, expecting another enemy, only to be met by a pair of green eyes belonging to Jashun.

"Jashun," Laisren exhaled.

Jashun's eyes widened. "Duck!"

Laisren dropped to his knees. Jashun sank his sword into a Glatanian soldier's stomach; hot blood poured onto the back of Laisren's head and neck. Jashun extended his hand to Laisren and pulled him up.

"Thanks, J. Where's Queen Graelynd?"

"She's in the meeting hall. Commander Tilmond and Doebromir are guarding her. That's also where most of our soldiers are, but we're greatly outnumbered."

They both jumped back, barely dodging attacks from two Stoltlanders. The clanging of metal swords, shrieks of pain, grunts of exhaustion, whistling of arrows, and the crashing of broken furniture and bones echoed through the treetop city. Too much innocent blood dripped from the cracks in the floorboards. They were losing. The resistance was failing. Even with their magical powers, their numbers couldn't compete against two large armies.

Jace finally arrived at the meeting hall, but his heart sank when he saw the smashed doors. He heard swords clashing from inside. Graelynd. He had to reach Graelynd. He heard coughing and peered around several overturned barrels. Princess Adma was drenched in blood, and a wound at her side was oozing her crimson lifeline. She coughed up blood once more; it dripped down her lips and chin.

"Jace," she coughed.

"What happened?" Jace asked, not wanting to waste time.

"I-I … had to …"

"Had to what?" Jace yelled, not liking where this was going.

"Prove to my father, but … but …" she coughed more. "Stoltlanders. They betrayed …"

From the shadows, Nyx thrust her knife into Adma's other side. "No, you betrayed your own people. You betrayed our only hope. You will die like a traitor." She jerked her weapon out and watched with mixed emotions as the life in the princess's eyes drifted away.

Nyx stood nose to nose with Jace, expecting him to scold her. "For my people." Tears formed in her grieving, plum eyes.

"And for mine," Jace said, giving her the approval she needed to confront the upcoming battles.

"We must kill their commanders. Without leadership, these soldiers will stop," Nyx said.

"If only it were that simple. We need more help."

A loud roar, louder than any sound Jace had ever heard from Shep, exploded. He looked up at the top of the meeting hall's roof and saw the mighty tiger. What was he doing? Then they heard wind. Wind? That couldn't be right—it sounded different, like wings, but of what? On their bat-like wings, an army of Felistilios soared with fury in their glowing eyes, teeth bared and claws ready, slicing through the necks of Stoltlanders and Glatanians with the sharp blades of their tails.

Now, it was a fair fight. Jace looked back, confident in the Elysian soldiers still battling on the rope bridges. He observed Ashur, Dinyelle, JaeDorn, Jashun, and Finn working together like a perfect unit. He couldn't help but feel impressed by his brothers, too. Taeg wielded a whip of briars while Laisren leaped over soldiers' heads, dragging his blade across their faces. However, Queen Graelynd needed his attention.

His father patted him on the shoulder. "Let the flying cats do their part. We must protect Queen Graelynd."

"I'm with you," said Nyx.

"So are we," AeLeer said, catching up to the group with her brother. "I think our cousin is in there, too."

Jace was honestly scared to see what destruction lay ahead. He spun and took off, running to the meeting hall, navigating over the rubble, and jumping past the bodies at the door of both Elysium and Stoltland. He knew death was waiting. He just needed more time.

Inside the grand meeting hall, Doebromir blocked another swing from a Stoltland soldier. His muscles were growing weaker. Cuts and bruises covered his body. His vision began to blur, but he fought—he fought for his kingdom, for his queen. He would not give up.

Tilmond, Ajorn, Sune, Brehan, and Sakul formed a barrier around Queen Graelynd. She loathed feeling helpless. If only she understood her Transference powers better, she might devise a plan, but everything still felt so new to them. Watching her people die for her and rebels perish for their cause certainly distracted her from forming a strategy.

Frantically, she scanned the room from the top of the stairs, desperately trying to forget the blood pooling on the floor. As she stepped back, she bumped into the throne. She touched the armrest, and a warm sensation washed over her.

"Arrows!" Sune yelled.

Fortunately, the meeting hall had shields displayed on the walls, which they grabbed first for their protection. "Shields up!" Tilmond commanded.

Arrows landed in their shields and whizzed past their heads.

"Graelynd, stay behind me!" Tilmond ordered.

An arrow penetrated Sakul's upper thigh. He cried out in agony as he fell, tumbling down the stairs and dropping his shield. Blood oozed from the wound and from scrapes on his head. Time seemed to slow. Sune noticed the archer drawing his bow, aiming at the vulnerable Sakul. Love triangle aside, Sune was resolute in his determination to save his comrade. He sprinted down the stairs. The arrow released, gliding ominously through the air.

Sune threw himself over Sakul and held the shield to his back, hoping it would be enough. The arrow smashed into the shield. Sakul's sage eyes filled with tears. Both men stared at one another with a profound understanding and appreciation they had never shared before. Sweat and blood dripped from Sune's nose, landing on Sakul's sweaty tunic. His arms shook from the weight of the shield and the exhaustion of his muscles. Another arrow embedded itself in the shield, causing them to flinch. Their lips quivered; the end could be near. They both gave their silent permission for whoever survived to take care of Lady Sorcha.

An arrow struck Sune's hamstring. He cried out but kept the shield firmly over his back, protecting Sakul. Tears streamed down Sakul's bloodied ebony cheeks. He didn't want Sune to die, not like this—not for him.

Brehan let out a loud, "Noooo!!" He was not about to let his comrade sacrifice himself. Panic surged through him, looking for options, but there were none. He felt a resolving presence fall over him—Brehan knew what he needed to do.

Another arrow sunk into Sune's injured leg. He faltered, dropping the shield, which flipped down the stairs with a series of loud clashes. Tears and sweat streamed down Sune's face. He stretched his body over Sakul and whispered into his ear, "Take care of her." Sakul's heart pounded. Neither wanted this to be their final moment.

The archer pulled the bow back and fired his dark arrow. It sliced through the air like a hot knife cutting through butter, striking Brehan in the chest. Sune heard his comrade choking above him. Sune turned his head, arching his back, feeling the pain of the arrows, and broke at the sight of Brehan, holding the arrow lodged in his body. Sakul blinked in shock. Why had he done that? Guilt filled Sakul's heart.

Brehan had sacrificed himself. His final thoughts were of Sune being captive. He believed Sune deserved a life of abundance. He was resolute in giving his life for his comrade.

Ajorn cried out over the loss of his best friend. Brehan was like a brother to him, sometimes even a father figure. Queen Graelynd grabbed her knife and sliced her hand. She let her blood flow over the necklace, then seized the throne chair. Enormous green phoenix wings burst out on either side of the throne, spanning a full twelve feet for each wing. Stoltlanders and Glatanians froze in awe at the grand sight. Ajorn didn't hesitate. He sprinted down the steps and lifted Sune over his shoulders. Doebromir raced behind Ajorn and helped Sakul to his feet. He draped his arm over Sakul's shoulder and began running up the stairs. Ajorn hated leaving Brehan's body behind, but he was already dead; a lifetime of memories— gone.

Graelynd commanded the wings to curve around them. She recalled how Dun's wings had shielded Sealyn from the dark magic, so she hoped these could do the same. "Hurry! Get inside the wings!" she shouted to her soldiers.

The weight of Sune on his shoulders felt heavy as he sprinted up the stairs, but Ajorn wasn't about to let Brehan's sacrifice go in vain. They heard commotion from the far end and thought they recognized familiar voices. Ajorn laid Sune on his stomach beside the throne and turned back, bracing for the worst. With several arrows lodged in his shield, Tilmond stood firm in front of Graelynd. Doebromir was almost to the phoenix wings when he heard the familiar voice of his king: "Graelynd!"

He turned back and saw Jace covered in blood with the rebel leaders. Several Elysian soldiers and rebels were still battling with their swords below, including Vinzil, cousin to Laekian. Doebromir's heart stopped when he saw the archer turn his focus on King Jace. He removed Sakul's arm and pushed him forward. "Go, my friend."

Doebromir charged toward the archer, feeling the ache of his old injury, but he didn't care. No one was going to harm his king. The archer fired an arrow at Jace, slicing the Elysian king's cheek. Jace saw Doebromir running behind the Stoltland archer. He hoped to keep the archer's attention, but Doebromir stepped on broken glass, drawing the archer's focus, who turned and released his arrow, sinking it straight into Doebromir's stomach.

Doebromir paused and placed his hand on the arrow; blood dripped from his mouth. He knew his time was up, yet he was determined to take one more with him. With fury in his eyes and his last battle cry, he raced forward. Before the archer could fire his arrow, Doebromir's sword plunged through the archer's throat, sending them both crashing to the floor.

Jace dropped his sword and slid underneath Doebromir, cupping his head in his lap. "No, Doebromir. Hang on. Please hang on."

Doebromir tried to speak, but he choked on his blood.

"You're going to be okay. It's going to be okay. We can fix this."

Doebromir's eyes closed. Overcome with grief and panic, Jace smacked his cheeks frantically. His bloodshot eyes opened, and a smile crept across his bloodied lips. He raised his hand to Jace, who grasped it tightly. Jace pressed his forehead against Doebromir's, tears falling from his silver eyes. He felt Doebromir's body relax and go still. Pulling back, he examined his comrade and screamed at Doebromir's lifeless body.

He heard another yell, jerked his head to the right, and saw a Glatanian sink his sword into Vinzil's chest. Laekian caught his cousin before he fell to the ground. The Glatanian ran and grabbed the archer's quiver and bow. As he reached top speed with AeLeer trailing behind him, he readied his bow and shot arrows at the green phoenix wings, but they deflected off like pebbles against a wall.

AeLeer leaped, slamming her enemy to the ground. She scrambled on top of him and stabbed him in the neck over and over, blood spattering her face with each stab. Then, an eerie and mournful silence enveloped the great hall. They had triumphed, but the loss of life felt more like a defeat.

Chapter 55

<u>Imprisoned</u>

Dripping water woke Sealyn. She could only open one eye and felt the pain in the other. She was hanging by her wrists in the middle of a damp, cold dungeon cell. She tried to lift her head, but everything was excruciating. Her mind flashed back to being dragged down to the dungeons.

She had fought back fiercely. With her hands tied, she threw her body against one of the soldiers and head-butted another. She spun around and kicked a soldier in the gut, but two other guards swarmed her with blades at her neck. Her lip quivered, aware of what she would face next. One guard struck her forcefully in the stomach. They pulled back their blades, and she dropped to her knees, coughing. She recalled being punched in the face, but it was her head striking the stone wall that knocked her out.

"Look who's waking up," a sinister voice said.

"Time for some fun before the transfer," a different man said.

Sealyn tugged at her chains as blood dripped down her dirty, bruised face. She hated that she was still wearing the stupid frilly gown. She needed her warrior clothes to fight these men. They unlocked the cage and stepped inside with smug expressions. One of them waved a knife in the air while the other licked his chapped lips. Sealyn felt nauseous. Torture awaited her.

"A slave can't work in something so fine," the dirty blonde said, through cracked lips. He began ripping the feathers from her skirt. At least it was just the feathers. Sealyn's heart pounded along with her head.

The other dark-skinned man grabbed the middle of her skirt and began cutting away yards and yards of fabric. Once he was done, Sealyn took advantage of his proximity. She wrapped her legs around his head and jerked, snapping his neck. His body fell dead to the stone floor. She felt a blow to her head, and then everything went dark.

Sealyn awoke to a bucket of freezing cold water being thrown on her. Her body shivered. She looked around with her one good eye and saw the blonde man smiling.

"You did me a favor, really. Now, I have you all to myself." He slowly stepped closer.

Sealyn realized that her sleeves had been cut away and that she no longer had an underskirt. Only the jagged, royal purple strips from the outer skirt remained. She could see the expression in this man's eyes. He was a monster, and she was his prey. Blood dripped from her nose and the gashes on her head. Her shoulders ached, and her joints pleaded for relief, but no one was coming. No one would hear her cries or witness the shame this man was so determined to impose on her body.

She attempted to pull her legs back to kick him away, but he had shackled them to the floor. She could do nothing. She was nothing. She was merely a failure, a lost thought in the wind. He stepped nose-to-nose with her, displaying his yellowed teeth. He dragged the edge of his blade across her bloodied lips and down her bosom. Tears welled in her emerald eyes. Think of Jace, she told herself.

A loud bang echoed through the dark chamber, and she heard boots pounding. Guards led by the commander appeared in the lantern light.

"Drefan, away with you. I have business with our new slave." Drefan shuffled to the side, glaring. The commander lifted Sealyn's head with his index finger. "You look relieved." He sucked his teeth. "You should be anything but." He removed his finger from her chin; her head dropped rapidly, rattling the chains. "We are moving you to your permanent home, Your Highness." He stepped back, examining her from head to toe and shaking his head. "My, how false your legend was."

Why did she feel embarrassed? Why did his words sting so much? She slumped as a guard released one wrist and then tipped forward as he undid the other. She caught herself on the cold stone floor, scraping her hands. The guards tied her wrists together and then unclasped her ankles. She gazed at her palm, still plump with ebony venom, but the wound had dried, leaving behind crusted black remnants.

Once the guards finished securing shackles around her feet, they began their procession through the Glatanian streets. The commander ridiculed her as the crowd hurled moldy bread and rotten fruit at her.

"All hail the mighty Queen Sealyn Araelien—the breaker of curses, the great Phoenix rider, the powerful mammoth whisperer, the esteemed tamer of the Naehass. She pales in comparison to the great kingdom of Glatania!"

The pain of shame struck her every time bread crumbled on her skin or the foul stench of rotten juice splashed across her face. She didn't know how far they had walked, but it was enough to give her feet blisters. They stopped in front of a building made of chocolate and candy. She hated feeling the pull of the curse, and her stomach growled. They opened the door, and Sealyn was hit with a wave of body odor and mold. What was this place?

The building served merely as a cover for a staircase that led down a dark pathway. Sealyn attempted to swallow, but her mouth and throat were dry. She had never experienced such profound homesickness. She wanted to break down, but when she stepped off the last dark stair and turned the corner, she was stunned. Slaves of all kinds were everywhere.

Fire Nichts in shackles heated the chocolate river, while Ice Nichts tirelessly created cream of milk for Glatania. She saw every type of Nicht enslaved, as well as Glatanians and Havasians. As she walked past the dirt-covered people, she gasped. Silver eyes. Hundreds of silver-eyed individuals were bound by the same magical cuffs and shackles as she was. Where could Glatania have gotten so many silver eyes? Of course—Havas; the sly, red-eyed devils. She wanted them to pay.

They turned a corner down a dark cavern. Sealyn could smell the strong scent of decaying bodies. At last, she saw the rough, rusty bars. She began shaking her head and pulling against the guards. They swung their fists and beat her until she stopped fighting. The doors of the large cage opened, and they threw her on the dirt floor.

The commander entered the room as Sealyn looked up at him. "This is your home now. I won't lie; you will experience the worst forms of torture mankind has ever seen, and we will break you. Hunger and thirst will be your only companions. You might believe you can endure, but you won't."

He snapped his fingers, and a large, muscular guard brought over a giant bucket of water and set it down in front of Sealyn. Sealyn considered the water and scrambled to her feet. She attempted to run, but the shackles tripped her. The commander seized her long, tangled hair, and before she could catch her breath, he thrust her face into the bucket.

Sealyn jerked and tried to stand, but the commander positioned himself over her, his foot pressing against her bent knee. She attempted to push up with her trapped hands, but her bound wrists prevented her from generating any force. Her lungs burned as she choked on water. She needed air.

She felt the surge of life return to her lungs as he lifted her head out of the bucket. She spat and coughed, all the while just trying to catch her breath. She gasped repeatedly, blinking as water flowed over her eyes. He grabbed her wet hair and slammed her face into the water again. She screamed underwater, forgetting she needed that air. Her feet struggled to break free, worsening her blisters as she clawed at the hard dirt for traction.

He repeated this three more times, then threw her down on the wet dirt. She vomited, wheezing and gagging on water and dirt. He kicked the bucket over, creating a muddy surface.

He grabbed her dripping face. "You will suffer, and you will beg me to end your life."

Out of the corner of her eye, she saw a small silver-eyed child who looked scared, starved, and alone. She could *not* give up. She was fighting for a better world. One in which children just like the silver-eyed child could live freely and safely. One where curses no longer existed. One where her family was safe.

She looked into the commander's deep purple eyes and said, "Never."

He grinned. "We'll see about that." He spat on her. "Fellas …"

The soldiers scooped up handfuls of mud and hurled them at the emerald queen. She shielded her face with her tied hands.

"Let's go."

One by one, the guards filed out, but Drefan leaned in and whispered in her ear, "I will have my way with you. One of these nights and many more to come, every time you start to close your eyes, remember I'll be coming when you least expect it." He chuckled and slid his muddy finger along her bare legs, leaving a trail through the dirt and grime.

She didn't move until she heard the lock click. Oddly, that was when she felt safe. She propped herself up and slid until her back met the jagged cave wall. She leaned her head back and glared at the commander. From the darkness of the cave came a low growl. Sealyn snapped her head toward the other end of the cave. She couldn't see anything but darkness. She looked back to the commander.

He chuckled. "Oh, yes. One more thing. Careful not to venture too far. You might disturb the bear."

Sealyn mouthed the word "bear." Her throat hurt too much to speak. She watched the guards leave. They grabbed the silver-eyed child and shoved him back to work. Never had she loathed a group of people more. She took a moment for herself and slowly breathed. Everything hurt.

She heard the low grumble again and froze. She was trapped, not just in a cage, but sealed in with a bear. How had everything gone so wrong? She felt she had failed everyone. She prayed that Char had escaped and was far away from this place. She couldn't give up; too much depended on her. She wished she knew the fates of her mother, Jace, and the rest of her people. Her mind drifted back to her secret refuge, recalling the scents of jasmine and the sounds of the waterfall. Her eyes felt heavy; her mind and body were so tired. She closed her eyes, pushing away the threats posed by the soldier, and let her dreams wander among the fireflowers and the stone walkway of her haven.

She envisioned herself reclining on the lush grass with her feet dangling in the cool, refreshing water. Sealyn slipped into a deep sleep, dreaming of the day she would be reunited with Jace, and so the imprisoned queen didn't realize the word that escaped her lips: "Eklaezia." Her cuffs quivered slightly, and even the dirt trembled.

Chapter 56

<u>Hope ...</u>

Sealyn's hand fell to the muddy ground, still chained and bound to a fate worse than death. But outside, high above in the treetops, a pair of vengeful, glowing green eyes kept vigilant watch, poised and ready to seize the opportune moment to rescue his family, his cousin, his queen.

My dearest cousin, Queen Sealyn,

I do hope the quest is progressing successfully. As you know, documenting all my discoveries can be quite perilous at times, so I eagerly await our upcoming meeting.

I'm communicating with you discreetly. You may not appreciate what I am about to say, but I initiated the use of spies over a year ago. I can anticipate your thoughts, yet I urge you to listen. What I have discovered regarding Abyss magic is not aligned with your expectations. The Mer Clans will not provide the solution. It is imperative that you revoke their powers for land usage immediately, as their abilities pose a significant threat, potentially resulting in numerous fatalities.

I found your answer. I've pieced it together. Sealyn, the solution is Jace. It's always been him. I will only ask this once, and I'll believe you: did you know? Please tell me that wasn't the reason you married him.

Regardless, I'm sailing back to Elysium and will return to Avondelle once I'm on dry land.

Until we see each other again,

Yours always,

Lord Prince William (Will) Dovinus

THE EMERALD QUEEN SERIES WILL CONTINUE WITH BOOK 5...

Library of Creatures

- <u>YUPPATHITE:</u> Yuppathites glide gracefully through the air. Their white wings resemble round stingrays swimming. Yuppathites have silky wings, four legs, a neck like a swan, a shorter nose like an elephant, and a tail like a phoenix. The males are larger in size and usually have blue eyes, while the females are smaller with golden eyes. These creatures are among Elysium's favorite beings because they can learn songs and often soar overhead singing Elysium's famous tunes.

- <u>NICHT:</u> Nichts are classified as non-human winged creatures. Nichts originate from the old magic and continue to thrive in population even after the attempt to annihilate their species. Earth Nichts are the largest, growing to the size of a human toddler. Others are as small as a human's hand. They all have brown eyes but different hair colors that sometimes correlate to their wing color. Their heads and eyes are much larger than normal sizes, and they have pointed ears. Nichts' wings are crystallized and similar to a butterfly's wings. There are nine different types of Nichts, each with their own special powers. Nichts are known to make words plural when not necessary— yet some are now learning a new way to speak.

•　CAELIDON: A Caelidon is a winged horse with its mane and tail composed of feathers. Fastest of the winged horses, very dangerous to ride. They are usually solid white with green eyes.

- <u>MIRRON</u>: First mentioned in Chapter 20. Mirrons have coarse hairs that have reflective properties like a mirror. They resemble a horse but are larger and faster, yet very rough to ride. Due to their reflective hairs, Mirrons are often hard to see and can seem invisible.

- <u>FELISTILIO</u>: First mentioned in Chapter 23. Felistilios are native to the Glatania kingdom. Felistilios have bat-like, shimmering, blush-colored wings. They have the body of a scaled cat and a long, dragon-like tail. Its hues range from pink to purple, with hints of blue near its belly. Felistilios are recognized for their dismissive attitudes, yet they can sense danger for those to whom they feel loyal. They become protective and will even fight to the death for those they consider worthy.

• LENETTE: Lenettes are creatures from the old magic with black eyes that look too big for their tiny head. Smaller than butterflies—they have bodies of golden caterpillars with two sets of wings: pink outer wings and orange inner wings. During the day, they soak in the sun's rays and then illuminate the darkness at night.

• NAEHASS:. Naehass is a legendary creature from the old magic. It is a giant two-headed serpent. One head is black with black eyes. The other head is gold with golden eyes. The rest of the body is a dull yellow color. The fangs of the golden head have a healing potion, but the fangs of the black head are full of deadly venom. The serpent reaches as tall as pine trees and as thick as an oak tree.

• FENNEC FOX: Fennec Foxes are native to Havas. They can withstand harsh, blistering heat and roam for days without water. Book five will expose more about these creatures.

- <u>GULLINN MONGOOSE:</u> Gullinn mongooses are shimmering gold with almost scale-like fur that protects them from snake bites. Gullinn mongooses are docile, so most Shunalians have them as pets. They also have child-like personalities, making them a favorite creature among the Shunalian people.

- <u>BERSERKER BADGER:</u> Berserker Badgers are the size of mountain lions. They're grey with a deep burnt orange stripe down their back and face with long, razor-sharp claws and teeth. After two years, their brains snap and turn rabid. They lose all sense of life and kill for sport. They are considered extremely dangerous and deadly. If you see one, run. Don't invite them into your home.

• <u>BUBBLE DRAGON OR BELLUS DRAGON</u>: Bubble dragons are born from Noxhorn dragons. They remain small in size, growing to the size of a small dog. They are white with yellow eyes and have green tongues. Bubble dragons spit innocent bubbles instead of fire. Their saliva and bubbles have special magical properties.

• <u>NOXHORN DRAGON</u>: Noxhorns breathe blue flames, the hottest of flames, for the longest period of time. They're also the smallest of the fire-breathing dragons. Their electric blue scales aren't as hard as other dragon scales, but they fight like nothing can kill them. They are blue with white bellies and blue eyes. These dragons are highly intelligent.

• <u>SQUIFFLEWIG</u>: Squifflewigs are glowing, sparkly, plump creatures that bounce instead of walk. They have wings too small for their purple furry bodies. They only have round heads and chubby torsos, along with tiny legs that are completely useless. They constantly swear, are always rude, and only like to be around other rude humans. Squifflewigs communicate via sign language with their leafy antennas. Don't poke them; they're easily offended.

• <u>PERI PIXIE</u>: Peri Pixies started as deformations of the original Nichts. Most died, but enough survived to create a new species. They have tiny bald heads with silver skin, and their total height is that of a person's pinky finger. They have green-tinted wings, and their ears look like another set of wings. Male Peri Pixies have legs with greenish-brown scales and small, webbed feet, while the females have pink-scaled legs. They have slightly wider-than-normal noses and have child-like faces with their eyes spaced farther apart than human eyes. They can't perform strong magic like the Nichts, but they can make themselves look like anything. Peri Pixies only appear when they sense no danger, and they love sour foods.

• <u>QUAM-QUAM BEARS</u>: Quam-Quam bears are small, fuzzy, grape-colored bears with shiny white horns protruding from their heads. They enjoy eating honeycomb, trout, chocolate bars, and cupcakes. Most Glatanians have them as pets. They often grab their feet and roll from place to place, causing chaos by colliding into people and shops.

- <u>ARKOOTHA BEAR</u>: These bears are larger than most bears and solid white with blue underbellies and blazing blue eyes. The outside of their front paws have long, sharp hooks that are curved like a mammoth's tusk. Arkootha bears have a high-pitched growl. They're also very fast, even in snow. They resemble polar bears but have heads more shaped like grizzly bears.

- <u>RANA FROG</u>: Rana frogs usually grow to the size of a large dog. They have jagged mouths and red eyes. Some have smooth skin, and others have warts covering their backs. Rana frogs love foul foods and, well, anything that smells horrible. Their colors range from midnight black to chocolate brown.

- <u>MER-MARA</u>: Mer-Maras have the same tail as mermaids, but their torsos and heads look like a seahorse with a snout shaped like a horn. Their snouts play enchanting music while they hunt with mermaids. They usually eat krill, but they like the occasional crab or lobster, too.

- <u>ARCHETYDON</u>: Archetydons are extra-large squid-like creatures. They have multiple thick tentacles and massive heads with bulging yellow eyes. Their mouths have rows and rows of razor-sharp teeth. The mouth is large enough to bite a whale in half. Archetydons are usually a dusty red color, but some less hostile ones are light blue.

- <u>NEEDLEBOB</u>: Needlebobs are in the spiny rodent classification. Most Needlebobs are shimmering gold, but those found in Stoltland have black tips. Needlebobs love thick forests and spend their days under ferns' shade, hunting beetles. Needlebobs may look cute, but beware—their needles contain powerful hallucinogenic poison. Once a needle pierces its victim's skin, the poison takes thirty seconds to release its effect. Hallucinations can last for hours and, in some worst cases, days. Needlebobs prefer to roll from one place to the next instead of walking. Their needles tuck and form around its body, allowing it to form a shell for easy rolling.

- <u>MAGNA CONSTRICTOR</u>: Magna constrictors are yellow and orange snakes that are as thick as a grown pig yet short in length. They have a very friendly disposition. Most Shunalians have them as pets. They are vegetarians with dull teeth and like to lay in the sunshine during the day and swim in the lake at night.

• <u>JORMUNGON</u>: Jormungons have ginormous heads the size of an elephant's body with long tails. They are green with yellow stripes and mouths with dull teeth like humans. The bottom of the mouth has an extra row of teeth on the inside. Jormungons can swim fast, reaching speeds of sixty miles an hour, making them the fastest snake in Shunal.

• <u>SURZEE</u>: Surzees are like mice. They have giant ears, small round heads, and big blue eyes that glow. They have light blue tails that are skinny with fuzzy white tips. Their bones are light, making them almost weightless. They bounce from place to place like tiny mice. They have razor-sharp teeth that are strong like metal.

• <u>ROPE SNAKE</u>: Rope snakes are extremely long snakes, sometimes stretching for hundreds of feet. They are found only in the Echo Forest of Shunal in the treetops. Their bodies are the diameter of the thick rope found on ships and are usually gold with yellow eyes and have mouths full of sharp teeth.

• <u>SLITCHES</u>: Slitches are flying snakes, very small. Bodies like short, skinny snakes. Wings like bats. Mouth like a snapping turtle yet can speak like a parrot. The military uses them as scouts. They have excellent eyesight and hearing.

• <u>HYDRUS SNAKE:</u> Hydrus snakes are a mixed breed of snake and dragon, native to Stoltland. It has the body of a thick snake, two legs with sharp claws, wings like a dragon, but a head like a snake with horns. The Hydrus snake spits water, not fire.

• <u>EXIGUUMS</u>: Exiguums have a genetic code that prevents them from growing beyond the size of a newborn elephant. They still mature just like normal elephants but remain small for their whole lives. Exiguums have special colors. Mainly purple and blue, but sometimes grey. Exiguums are fuzzy instead of rough. Their eye colors vary from green to blue.

• <u>METUS DRAGON</u>: Metus dragons are large orange dragons with two sets of horns on their heads. Metus dragons breathe lightning and have a roar that sounds like thunder. The tails have sharp spikes and red claws.

• <u>SNAPPLE SEEF DRAGON</u>: Snapple Seef dragons are small dragons with no ability to breathe fire or anything harmful. These tiny dragons are usually purple with yellow bellies and have incredible strength. They're able to lift and carry objects ten times their size.

• <u>NOVIEN ICE BACK DRAGON</u>: Novien Ice Back dragons are native to Len Nove. These are white dragons with blue eyes, claws, and teeth. They are slow in flight but spit ice instead of flames.

Recipes

<u>Puffin Pies</u>

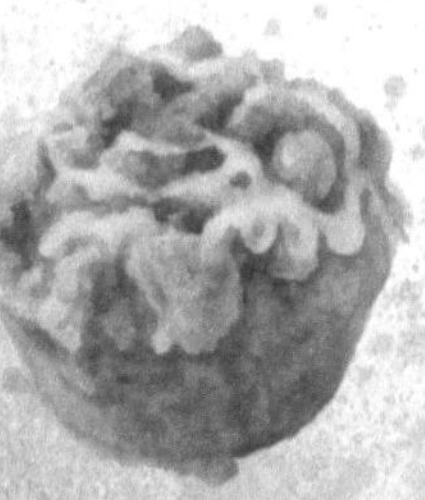

<u>Jam Pies</u>

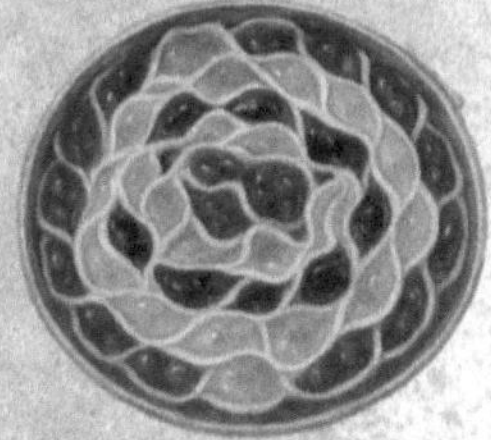

<u>Blackberry Mini Tarts</u>

Puffin Pies

Ingredients

<u>Crumb Topping</u>

1/3 cup (67g) packed light or dark brown sugar
1 Tablespoon (15g) granulated sugar
1 teaspoon ground cinnamon
1/4 cup (4 Tbsp; 56g) unsalted butter, melted
2/3 cup (84g) all-purpose flour

<u>Muffins</u>

1 and 3/4 cups (219g) all-purpose flour
1 teaspoon baking soda
1 teaspoon baking powder
1 teaspoon ground cinnamon
1/2 teaspoon salt
1/2 cup (8 Tbsp; 113g) unsalted butter, softened to
room temperature
1/2 cup (100g) packed light or dark brown sugar
1/4 cup (50g) granulated sugar
2 large eggs, at room temperature
1/2 cup (120g) yogurt or sour cream, at room
temperature
2 teaspoons pure vanilla extract
1/4 cup (60ml) milk (any kind), at room temperature
1 and 1/2 cups (180g) peeled & chopped apples (1/2-
inch chunks; you need about 2 medium apples)

<u>Vanilla Icing (Optional)</u>

1 cup (120g) confectioners' sugar
3 Tablespoons (45ml) heavy cream (or milk for a
thinner consistency)
1/2 teaspoon pure vanilla extract

Puffin Pies continued…

Instructions

1. Prep Oven & Pan: Preheat oven to 425°F (218°C). Grease or line a 12-count muffin pan (recipe yields ~14 muffins).
2. Crumb Topping: In a bowl, mix brown sugar, granulated sugar, and cinnamon. Stir in melted butter, then gently fold in flour with a fork to form crumbles. Don't over-mix.
3. Dry Ingredients: Whisk flour, baking soda, baking powder, cinnamon, and salt in a large bowl.
4. Wet Ingredients: Beat butter and sugars until creamy. Add eggs, yogurt, and vanilla; beat until mostly smooth. Slowly mix in dry ingredients and milk until combined. Fold in apples.
5. Assemble: Fill muffin cups to the top with batter. Add crumb topping, pressing it down lightly.
6. Bake: Bake at 425°F for 5 minutes, then reduce to 350°F (177°C) and bake for 15–18 more minutes. Cool for 5 minutes in pan, then transfer to a wire rack.
7. Icing: Whisk icing ingredients and drizzle over muffins warm or cooled.
8. Storage: Keep covered at room temp for a few days or refrigerate up to 1 week.

Jam Pies

Start with unrolling your pie crusts onto cutting
board. Choose your favorite pie crust recipe. Cut out
circles in your crust with a 4"cutter, then place on
parchment paper.
In small bowl whisk together egg and water.
Brush each hand pie with
egg wash until completely coated.

~~

Top with about 1 Tablespoon of your
favorite pie fillings.
Fold the circle like a taco then pinch the ends
together. Leave the filling as open faced.
*Sealyn's favorite fillings are strawberry, blackberry,
and peach.

~~

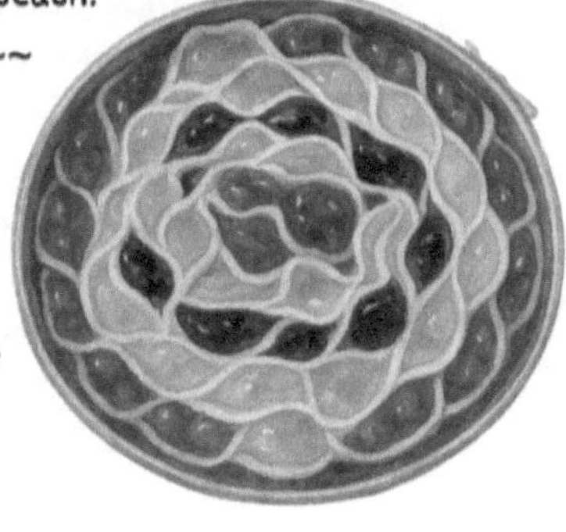

Place in a cast iron pan or
other circle pan in an upright
position and continue placing
each hand pie in concentric
circles. Bake at 425 degrees F
for 15 minutes until golden
brown.

Blackberry Mini Tart

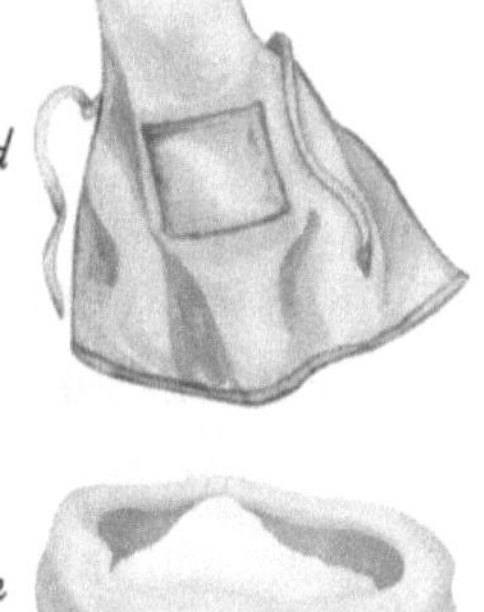

Ingredients:

Blackberry Topping:
6 oz blackberries, pureed and strained
5 tbsp sugar
2 1/2 tsp cornstarch
Crust:
3/4 cup graham cracker crumbs
2 tbsp sugar
3 tbsp butter, melted
Lavender Cheesecake Filling:
12 oz cream cheese, room temperature
1/2 cup sugar
1 1/2 tbsp flour
1/4 cup sour cream
2 tsp lavender extract
1/2 tsp vanilla extract
2 large eggs, room temperature
Violet gel icing color (optional)
Whipped Cream Topping:
1/2 cup heavy whipping cream, cold
4 tbsp powdered sugar
1/2 tsp vanilla extract
Violet gel icing color (optional)
12-14 blackberries for garnish

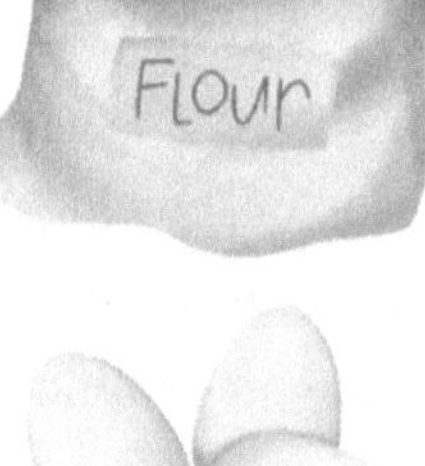

Instructions:

Blackberry Topping: Cook pureed blackberries with sugar and cornstarch until thickened; cool.
Crust: Combine graham crumbs, sugar, and butter; press into cupcake liners. Bake at 325°F for 5 minutes.
Cheesecake Filling: Blend cream cheese, sugar, flour, sour cream, extracts, and eggs. Add color if desired. Fill crusts and bake at 300°F for 18-20 minutes.
Cool: Turn off oven, keep door closed for 10 minutes, then open slightly for 15-20 minutes. Chill in fridge.
Assemble: Top with blackberry sauce, whipped cream, and a blackberry.
Prep Time: 1 hr 30 mins, Cook Time: 55 mins, Total Time: 2 hrs 25 mins
Servings: 12-14

Acknowledgments

This fourth book was almost my undoing. I think I quit writing five times and cried countless hours, but through it all, I did it, and I hope you enjoyed it! But I truly couldn't have accomplished this goal without an amazing support team.

My incredible husband, Kyle Massie: I needed all the pushing and grace you gave. I know it's not easy being married to an author, but just know, I appreciate your support so much. I love you as much as Sealyn loves Jace.

My supportive parents, Rhett and Gwen Salley: Thank you for showing up. Just being there for long phone calls, book signings, events, and lunches is more than most can dream of, yet you continue to be there. Thank you for demonstrating dedication.

Mindy Salley, my sister: The Dress Maker! Thank you for making Sealyn's dress—it's truly been the most beneficial to my marketing yet! You're the best sister the Lord could have blessed me with.

Jess Tully Menges, author of *The Birch Cabins, Our Mother Nora, Ionne Chaffin and the Christmas Reaper*, and *Stag's Manor* and C.A. Meadows, author of *Lost in a Nightmare, The Secret Inheritance, Giovanna, and Ashlynn:* Thank you for connecting. Authors need other authors to hold each other accountable and have *those* conversations that only authors understand. I'm glad I'm not alone in my writing.

To my friends: Thank you for understanding my declines. It is not easy to say "no" to events or hangouts, but I needed to decline many times to finish writing. Thank you so much for the feedback, especially for the cover—greatly appreciated. I'm very grateful for your understanding, patience, and participation.

To my Beta Readers: Michelle Blair, Cecilia Meadows, Gwen Williams, Kayla Falcone, Theresa Tacopino-Shaw, Nicole Berry, Alissa Ronnie, Jessica Linville, Cory Ann Freeman, Lydia Rose Hancock, Holly, and Bella Trefny. Thank you for taking the time to read each chapter in its raw state. Your feedback truly made a huge difference in editing and content for the book. I really appreciate you all so much.

My editor, Kristyn Winch: Without your editing, I'm sure the book would be painful to read. Thank you for not only being a great friend but for being brave enough to give me proper feedback. Thank you again.

Miblart: Thank you for another excellent book cover. I also appreciate your patience in working with me and all the edits. I'm grateful to be working with your company with promos, as well.

YukKami Art, digital artist: Thank you for the beautiful character and creature art you've done. Each piece is always loved and adored. I appreciate your talent and time.

Ruth (@forestcabinreads): Thank you for the excellent sketches found throughout the pages of this fourth book. You're not only an incredible artist, but an even better friend.

Above all, the entire credit and glory goes to the good Lord above. Thank you for giving me a creative mind and the many blessings you have given me. All praise to you.

About the Author

MAEGWEN SALLEY-MASSIE is the author of *The Emerald Queen Rises, The Mammoth Awakens, and The Serpent Emerges*. She will be writing four other books to complete this series. She grew up in the Pee Dee Low Country of South Carolina with her loving parents and sister. Her childhood was spent mainly outdoors: building forts, riding horses, playing capture the flag, riding ATVs, and playing volleyball. She began writing *The Emerald Queen Rises* during the pandemic as therapy and since then fell in love with writing her high fantasy series. She is a woven polypropylene specialist by day, COO of 963 Film Group, and a fantasy fiction author by night. Her favorite food is sushi, and she loves to travel the world. Maegwen currently lives in Myrtle Beach, S.C., with her husband, Kyle, their cat, Khaleesi, and their new Australian Shepherd, Pogue.

Books 1, 2, & 3
in
The Emerald Queen series

For more information about Maegwen and her
books, please visit:

www.greenfernspublishinghouse.com
www.theemeraldqueenrisesbook.com
www.maegwensalleymassie.com

Or follow her on Instagram @MaegwenAuthor

**Please consider leaving a review on
Amazon, Barnes & Noble, and GoodReads.**